THE EVERLASTING ROSE

DHONIELLE CLAYTON

 **FREEFORM** BOOKS

Los Angeles   New York

First Edition, March 2019
10 9 8 7 6 5 4 3 2 1
FAC-020093-19018
Printed in the United States of America

This book is set in 10-pt. Palatino and Gill Sans/Monotype
Designed by Marci Senders

Library of Congress Cataloging-in-Publication Data
Names: Clayton, Dhonielle, author.
Title: The everlasting rose / by Dhonielle Clayton.
Description: First edition. • Los Angeles ; New York : Freeform Books,
2019. • Series: [The Belles ; 2] • Summary: Camille, Edel, and Rémy, aided
by the Iron Ladies and backed by alternative newspaper the *Spider's Web*,
race to outwit Sophia, find Princess Charlotte, and return her to Orléans.
Identifiers: LCCN 2018034809 • ISBN 9781484728482 (hardcover)
Subjects: • CYAC: Beauty, Personal—Fiction. •
Sisters—Fiction. • Dating (Social customs)—Fiction. •
Counterculture—Fiction. • Newspapers—Fiction. • Fantasy.
Classification: LCC PZ7.1.C4925 Ev 2019 • DDC [Fic]—dc23
LC record available at https://lccn.loc.gov/2018034809

Reinforced binding

Visit www.freeform.com/books

SUSTAINABLE Certified Sourcing
FORESTRY
INITIATIVE www.sfiprogram.org
SFI-00993

THIS LABEL APPLIES TO TEXT STOCK

For all the angry girls.
There's nothing wrong with you.

"Beauty is blood and bone and sovereignty;
a perfect smile is its greatest weapon."

—Orléansian proverb

The Goddess of Beauty chose the first queen of Orléans. Beauty searched for the one who would treasure her most sacred gift—the Belles. She knew she wouldn't be able to journey back and forth between the sky and the ground for much longer. The tension among the gods required her to pick a realm. She enacted a series of tests—the Beauty Trials—to draw out the woman who had the right qualities. The one who could nourish their precious talents. The one who would never be jealous. The one who would, above all, keep them safe. When Queen Marjorie of House Orléans emerged the victor of the Trials, she pledged that she and her descendants would forever revere the Belles as extensions of Beauty herself; to be treated as if they were as delicate and precious as the petals on an everlasting rose.

from The History of Orléans

Maman never told me what to do when the world falls apart like a dress ripped at its seams, the beads scattering into faraway corners, the fabric a storm of shredded pieces left destroyed and unrecognizable. She never told me how to battle the nightmares that creep in like icy shadows, lingering behind closed eyes. She never told me what to do when all the color leaks out of the world like blood oozing from a mortal wound.

She gave me a mirror to see truth. I clutch it, the glass warming inside my palm.

But what happens when the reflection peering back is ugly, and when all I want to do is set everything ablaze, and she's not here to help me?

The past three days are a chaotic blur, a télétrope in perpetual motion—the palace, Sophia's dungeons, Charlotte waking up, and Arabella helping us get here with false papers.

"Are you listening to me?" Edel snaps. "You've been gazing out that window for almost a full hourglass."

I don't pivot around to face her or the small boardinghouse room we've been stuffed into. I fixate on the sun as it sinks behind the row of shops across the street and watch how it turns the sky the color of a peacock's tail. Sunsets are much more beautiful this far south. It feels like the Spice Isles are at the very edge of the world and poised to float right off.

I press my nose against the frigid glass; the cold-season wind attempts to push its way through. I wish it would wrap its icy fingers around me and cool my insides. In the distance, the cluster of islands almost kisses at the Bay of Croix, and the capital city of Metairie overlooks them like a huge house-lantern out at sea, drawing ships safely near. Golden bridges connect the four isles and radiate like fireworks as evening arch-lanterns are lit. Decadent river coaches skate over the waters beneath, the light glinting off their gilded trim. Grand spice plantations stretch out in all directions with large white mansions overseeing fields of mint, lemon balm, lavender, and sage. Plant-lanterns crest over the crops, paper-thin bees carrying sunshine and nutrients.

This place feels even stranger than the palace did, so different than our home. I used to want to see every far-flung corner of this world, but now, all I think about is what it would be like to watch Orléans burn, each island turning to ash, clouds of thick smoke clogging the skies and stamping out the sun, the seas blackening from the leftover debris. Would the gods intervene?

I gaze back down at the maps littering the desk. My charts of the trade winds. My theories about how far Princess Charlotte could have gotten if she sailed west toward the Glass Isles or maybe east around the base of the imperial island.

Overcome with frustration, I throw the compass rose Rémy gave me, and it lands on the floor with an unsatisfying thud.

Edel picks it up. "Camille, I need to show you something!" She looks over my shoulder at my maps. "Come now. You don't even know if Charlotte made it out that night."

"Rémy said the queen's private schooner was spotted. Who else could it be?"

"A thief? Pirates? Some drunken courtiers who got on the wrong boat?"

I scoff. "He said no one knows who was on it, and now you're putting all your hopes into a girl who was unconscious for four years."

She touches my bare shoulder. I jump.

"Your skin's hotter than a cookstove," she says. "Are you ill?"

I want to tell her a never-ending fire burns in the pit of my stomach now, the flames fed by my rage.

"And your fingers are like ice," I reply.

I grab the compass from her and trace another potential route Charlotte might have taken, putting her north of the imperial island. "She was coughing and waking up when Amber and I rushed out."

"Let's forget Charlotte and storm the palace. We could take down Sophia ourselves."

"Then what? Rule Orléans?"

Edel nibbles her bottom lip. "Maybe."

"If Charlotte is queen, then she can return Orléans to what it used to be. The way Queen Celeste wanted."

"I don't want to go back. I won't be in another teahouse again. I won't be forced to—"

I take her hand, and she swallows the rest of the sentence. "We need to hope. If we can find Charlotte and bring her back to the palace, she can confront her sister. She can put an end to all of this." I hold her close. "Then we will find a different way forward, a different life for us. I promise."

"Fine, fine," Edel mutters under her breath and pulls away. "But I have something more important to show you . . . something that will help us when we leave this place." She's shaky and casts nervous glances at the door. "I've been waiting until we were alone."

"What is it?" I turn away from the maps.

"Watch." Edel closes her eyes, concentrating so hard she looks minutes from laying a golden egg. Veins swell beneath her white skin and a red blush sets into her cheeks. The pale blond hair at her temples soaks with sweat, which beads across her forehead like a strand of pearls. Her hair lengthens down to her waist inch by inch, then turns the color of midnight.

I scramble backward, smacking into the tiny cage of sleeping teacup dragons. They squeak with alarm.

"We're not supposed to be able to do that." I put my hand over my mouth.

"I'm calling it our fourth arcana—glamour." She takes my trembling fingers and pushes them into her hair. It still maintains the same fine texture it's always had, but the color is utterly unfamiliar.

"Our gifts are for others. . . ." My heart flips in my chest. My arcana hums just beneath my skin, eager to learn, eager to experiment with this dangerous trick; my mind fills with a thousand possibilities.

"No. *This* gift . . . this is for us. This is how—" Edel starts.

"We will outsmart Sophia and her guards," I interject. "And find Charlotte."

The possibility of success wedges itself down to my bones and mingles with the anger living there. I'd always built my life on doing the unexpected and wanting it all—to be the favorite, to be the most talented Belle, to shape what it meant to be beautiful in Orléans—and now I'm presented with doing the biggest thing I've ever had to do and with the risk of danger far greater than I could ever imagine. All of it breathes life into my ambition.

A full grin spreads across Edel's face. She takes a deep breath, and the dark shade of midnight in her hair lightens as if morning sun pushes through each strand.

"How did you learn to do this?"

She glances at the door. "It was an accident. Madam Alieas was yelling at me, laying out all the things I'd done wrong. She barked about how I needed to be nicer, and how she'd wished she'd gotten Valerie instead. I was twirling my hair around my finger." She lifts one of the strands. "Growing angrier and angrier, thinking of our sister, and then it darkened to Valerie's brown shade."

"What does it feel like?" I stroke Edel's hair again, and it shrivels back to its previous shoulder length.

"Remember when we'd sneak up on the roof at home before the first snow? Our fingernails would be purple and blue. Our nightgowns would catch the wind, the fibers almost freezing."

I nod as the memory flickers through me. All of us on the roof after Du Barry and our mothers had fallen asleep, waiting for the clouds to release their crystals, waiting to catch a snowflake on our tongues, waiting to see the white mounds frost the tops of the dark forest behind our house.

"It feels cold like that. I panicked at first. I didn't think it was real. Thought my arcana was low, my eyes playing tricks on me.

So I experimented with sections of my hair." She walks in circles. "Adding a wave or a highlight, and testing how long I could hold it."

My stomach flutters. Trusting untested aspects of the arcana feels like trying to harness a windstorm. "Did it make you sick?"

"Nosebleeds, headaches, the chills."

"Then maybe—"

She puts a hand up, sweeping away my worries. "That lessened as I got stronger. It just takes practice. I moved from my hair to aspects of my face."

"Does it weaken you like after we've done beauty treatments?"

"Yes. I use the sangsues and chocolate to help me hold a glamour and to feel better after using one." Edel takes my hand. "Quick. Let me show you."

I stretch across the thin mattress Edel, Amber, and I share. The springs dig into my back. Maman's mirror sits just under my breastbone on its chain. I press my hand to it, wanting its truth and wisdom to push down inside me, fill me up, and make me feel like Maman is still here, ready to fight alongside me. What would she think of all this? The things I've done. The things I'm about to do.

"Close your eyes," Edel directs.

A tremor pulses in my stomach.

Edel pushes my curls away from my sweaty forehead. Is this how our clients feel on our treatment tables? Tiny, exposed, vulnerable?

She takes my trembling hand. "Are you afraid?"

"I'm angry."

"Good. That will make you strong." Her soft fingers graze over my eyelids, forcing them closed. "Now, think back to when we were little girls first learning our second arcana, and Du Barry

made us do all those lessons on visualizing our clients like paintings or sculptures. Remember?"

"Yes."

"Instead, try to see yourself."

Du Barry's childhood warnings are sharp echoes inside my
head: *"Belles must never be vain, for the Goddess of Beauty shall punish
those who hoard their gifts. The arcana are favors from the Goddess of
Beauty to be used in service."*

I push her words away, bury them deep down with the rest
of the lies.

Edel squeezes my shoulder. "Go back to Maison Rouge. You'll
see."

I take a deep breath, let my muscles relax. Edel describes the
home where we spent our entire lives until we turned sixteen last
year. The pale white trees growing out of the bayou like bones, the
rose-shaped bars on the house windows, the crimson-and-gold-
papered walls leading into the lesson rooms, the Age chambers
with their terrariums of dying flowers and bowls of rotten fruit,
the Aura rooms with their treatment tables and Belle-products, the
nursery full of crying babies, the black forest—a shadow behind
our house.

"You're tensing your muscles," Edel says, stroking my cheek.
"Let the arcana wake up. Focus on that."

At the mention of the word *arcana*, their power throbs inside
me, rising quickly to meet my request. All three skills—Manner,
Aura, Age—are threads ready, able, and eager to be tugged and
bent to my will.

The veins in my hands swell beneath my skin. My nerves
prickle with thick energy.

"Think of your own face," Edel whispers. "Your curly hair and your high forehead. Your full lips. The shade of your skin is the brown of the almond luna pastries Rémy brought us this morning for breakfast."

When I would see clients for beauty work, a familiar warmth would race through me like someone had let a candle flame graze across my skin. But now, a deep chill settles in, replacing that feeling. My teeth chatter, and a shiver makes me jerk.

"You're all right. Keep going," Edel says. "Change your hair to match one of the crimson Belle-roses from our home solarium with petals as large as plates."

The flower sprouts beside the image of my own face in my mind. Its color bleeds into the strands of my hair, twisting around the coils like ribbons of blood. A headache erupts in my temples. My lungs tighten like I've just raced up a winding staircase.

"It's working," she says.

I sit straight up.

"Don't break your concentration."

"Why does it feel this way?" I ask, out of breath.

"I don't know. But you're doing it." Edel rustles through the beauty caisse Arabella sent with us, retrieving a small mirror and thrusting it into my hands. "Look!"

I gaze into it. The frizzy curls at the crown of my head are a deep fiery red like Amber's, like Maman's. I play with one curl and twist it around my finger to examine it more closely.

"How long does it last?" I grimace through the cold. It grips my bones, a radiating ache splintering my insides.

"As long as you can hold it in your mind and your levels stay strong. I've been able to maintain it for almost five hourglasses when I'm rested and focused," Edel boasts. "But I know if I push myself or drink Belle-rose tea or elixir, I could go longer."

"I can't concentrate any longer."

The red fades away and the brown appears once more. I crumple on the bed.

The door snaps open. Amber marches in, her presence a landquake. A nest of red hair peeks out from under her hood.

Edel stands. "You're back early."

"There were too many guards, and I lost the mask you gave me," Amber reports, then surveys the room. "What's going on?"

"Edel was just teaching me how to—" I start to say.

"Quickly refresh your arcana." Edel's eyes burn into mine.

I purse my lips and flash her a puzzled look.

"Where's Rémy?" Edel asks, taking a porcelain bowl from a nearby table and fishing out two wiggling sangsues. She wraps one leech around my wrist like a cuff, and in a whisper says, "Don't say anything."

"He's doing one of his rounds before coming upstairs." Amber rushes to the dragons' cage and lifts the blanket. They're tangled together in a pile and remind me of jeweled bracelets made of pearls, emeralds, sapphires, rubies, and gold. "I brought them some pig meat and found these sweet necklaces." She dangles the collars from her fingers and sets them in front of the cage.

"Why'd you spend our money on those?" Edel snaps. "You were supposed to get hair dye for all of us."

"I did." She yanks two pot-bellied jars from her pocket and throws one at Edel.

Edel catches it.

"All she had left was evergreen."

"That's going to help us blend in," Edel replies sarcastically.

"The whole city is at a shortage of Belle-products with the teahouses shut down. And she gave me those collars at a discount.

The dragons need leashes for their training." She hands me a crumpled page. "Found this on the lobby table."

Four cameo portraits stretch across the page: Amber, Edel, Rémy, and lastly, me.

My own eyes stare out, looking haunted. The animated portrait shifts through a series of my most notable looks: one with my hair in a signature Belle-bun full of camellia flowers; another with it down and around my face in a big, curly cloud; and the last with the strands all ironed straight and resting on my shoulders. The text calls us dangerous, cunning, and traitors to the crown. Sophia has promised 850,000 leas and 275,000 spintria for our capture. That would make a person instantly one of the wealthiest individuals in all Orléans, ready to join the circle of the kingdom's finest.

WANTED: ALIVE AND IN GOOD CONDITION.

SUITABLE FOR USE.

What does that mean? Are we cattle headed to the slaughterhouses on the Isle of Quin?

Amber places fresh food in the teacup dragons' cage, then plops down in one of the wooden chairs. "I hate this place."

Edel starts to cough. "I need water," she says.

"Are you sick?" Amber asks.

"Thirsty," Edel replies. "Can you grab some?"

"Why can't you?" Amber's eyebrows lift with suspicion.

"You always get the water. You know how to work the house pumps." They lock eyes. "Plus, I'm not dressed, and you are."

"Amber, please. The teacup dragons need some as well," I add.

She shrugs, then leaves the room.

As soon as the door closes, Edel stops coughing and turns to me. "Don't tell her about the glamours."

"Why?" I ask, feeling Edel's distrust of Amber like a flash of heat.

"She's too weak to try it right now. We should wait until we know exactly how it works. We both have always been stronger and more willing to experiment than she is."

"But we'll need to show her soon." I study Edel's face.

"Of course," Edel says, avoiding my eyes. "When the time is right."

2

The sun hasn't risen when I sneak out of bed and dress to go out. Rémy is off on one of his night-watch rounds. I don't bother using the cold water in our basin for fear of waking Amber and Edel. I'm getting used to the dirt. The memories of onsens full of claw-foot tubs and rose-shaped soaps and sweet oils and honey scrubs, perfume blimps leaving behind their scents, and beauty-lanterns dusting us with perfect beams of light are clouds drifting out to sea never to be caught again.

I put in the eye-films that Arabella gave us, then blink until they settle, and I can see the small room again. We've fallen into a synchronized rhythm like the dancing koi fish that used to live in our fountain at Maison Rouge: Amber fetches fresh water from the house pumps every morning and even scrounges up small pieces of lime soap so we can make an attempt at bathing; Edel keeps the room tidy by stealing the house mistress's broom each afternoon; Rémy watches every movement in and out of the boardinghouse;

and I nurse our teacup dragons, teach them how to fly, and secure our nightly meals.

At times it feels like we could go on living this way if we wanted. Move from boardinghouse to boardinghouse to evade the imperial guards. Take care of one another. Fold into the regular population of Orléans and live in secret. But my desire to see Sophia fall has become a whispered refrain making my body restless, as if my limbs and heart know that this isn't the place for us. That I must face her. That I must make her pay for what she's done. That I must do what Queen Celeste would have wanted.

Amber and Edel are still a mess of legs and arms and quilts in the bed we share. I have only a few moments to get out the front door of the boardinghouse before Rémy returns. I ease down the staircase, careful not to hit any of the squeaky wood planks. This is the second time I've sneaked out since we arrived.

In the main salon, a few night-lanterns putter low along the ground. Three teacup cats wander across the long tables in search of crumbs. One meows at me.

"Shh," I whisper. "Don't ruin my plan."

I tie the ribbons of the mask Edel gave me. It's made of rich black velvet and lace, and hugs the contours of my face and neck like a soft glove. *Guaranteed to protect one's makeup from the cold-season weather.* Or shield one's identity. The southerly winds make these popular here, creating the perfect locale for staying hidden.

I unlatch the hook on the front door and close it gently behind me.

An early-morning mist covers the city, choking the buildings with fog. The day after Maman died, the world outside the windows of Maison Rouge looked the same. Through the rose-shaped bars, I watched the dark forest catch rain clouds, trapping them down from the sky. I always imagined them as the Goddess of Beauty's tears, shed over the death of another one of her gifts to our world. I wanted to race out the back doors and venture deeper into the forest than we'd ever been allowed to go before, scream for Maman to be brought back, and wait for the Goddess of Beauty to answer me.

I gaze up at a wakening sky. The plum darkness cracks open like an egg, releasing ribbons of orange and yellow and tangerine.

"Are you up there, Beauty?" I wait to hear her voice boom down from the sky. "Were you ever there? Or are you a lie, too?"

Nothing.

A milk vendor and her cart plod along, leaving the noisy trail of clinking glasses. "Fresh pints to go with your morning pastries. Get them here!"

Her calls hasten me forward. Last time I sneaked out, the streets were empty.

Black mourning-lanterns drift about, casting their shadowy light over the cobblestones. Portraits of the departed Queen Celeste hang from banners and populate nearby avenue boards. The sight of her beautiful face wrenches my heart. How upset she'd be about what has happened, her warnings about Sophia now prophetic. Blimps snake through tall towers and post-balloons zip around their large frames. Their bulbous underbellies leave behind swaths of darkness and shadows.

A woman exits a shop.

My heart beats against my rib cage.

A warning. A sign to turn back.

I duck into a nearby alley, waiting for her to pass. She slows down and stops to look in my direction. She wears a peculiar mask that curves around all the edges of her face, neck, and chest, reminding me of a gilded mold for a bust or statue. The moonlight exposes its delicate iron edges and intricate etchings.

I press myself farther into the shadows.

The noise of the milk vendor pulls her attention. She abandons her curiosity about me and runs off.

I should go back to the boardinghouse, but I count to twenty, then leave my hiding spot, and press on. I turn onto the Imperial Mile that stretches from Metairie's royal mansions and empties out at one of the island clusters' many bridges. Gauzy arch-lanterns scatter strips of light like bars of gold. I've memorized each street and avenue and alley near the boardinghouse under Rémy's guidance and his expert maps. *"You must know how to get out of here without me,"* he'd said right after we'd first arrived. *"If anything should happen, I need to know that you'll be able to navigate."*

The avenue boards don't even shimmer at this time of the morning, my lonely presence not strong enough to animate them. Orléans's most famous singer stares back at me with bright eyes and a frozen grin and rich light brown skin like hazelnut butter. The shops wear CLOSED signs and burned-out night-lanterns float over their doors like stormy, ominous clouds. In a few hours, these avenues will bloat with bodies.

I hook a right down the street that ends with a perfume shop. A trio of eccentric-pink flowers glows in the front windows. Almost there.

"Lost, dearie?" a voice hisses.

I whip around. Red eyes flash at me from beneath a hood. The Gris woman bares her teeth, yellowed and crooked and meant to be a smile, but it looks more like a threat.

"No," I say, steadying my voice.

The woman's shriveled gray skin catches the moonlight. "Any leas to spare?"

"Sorry, I don't have anything."

"You look like you have spintria. I'll take that, too."

I wish I did have something for her. I used to have a pocket full of beauty tokens and possess enough bags of spintria to easily fill a thousand safes. But her words are a surprise. We were told many of the Gris choose to remain that way, the madness pushing them to the edge, erasing any desires to pull themselves up and earn enough spintria to join regular society.

"I have nothing," I say, rushing ahead, but she follows, muttering nonsense. Fear crawls over my skin. I remember the first Gris woman I ever saw. My sisters and I had just turned thirteen, and the older girls were practicing using their arcana in the lesson rooms. Hana and I sneaked into the Aura chambers and hid beneath the treatment tables when women as gray as a thunderstruck sky were marched in. We pressed our faces against lace tableskirts as the women were laid over us, their screams quelled with mouth bandages. The tussling melody of their fighting bodies was stamped out with thick leather straps pinning them down as vial after vial of Belle elixir was administered in an attempt to calm them.

"Only spiders come out this early," she says.

"Leave me alone," I whisper hard.

"Out past curfew," she screeches and wags a crooked finger at me.

"Go away." I try to dodge past her. Panic races through my veins like it's replaced the arcana.

She slaps me and knocks my mask askew.

I scramble to fix it and swallow the cry of shock and pain clawing its way up my throat.

"I know you. I've seen you before."

The heavy stomp of soldiers' boots echoes in the morning quiet.

She grabs my wrist, digging hooked fingernails into my skin. "You're the one they're looking for."

"I don't know what you're talking about." My heart speeds up.

Her throaty chuckle becomes a wheeze. "Who are you fooling?" She points her other finger at me as I jerk away. "Not me, that's who." Her eyes narrow. "Guards! Guards!" she shouts. "I shall be rewarded. The newsies told us we could change our stars if we made sure to pay attention for the fugitives. I didn't believe them. They tell so many lies. But now, it's true."

Sweat pours down my back despite the chilly air. I shove her, but her grip tightens. We crash into a window box of cold-season flowers. The arcana almost hiss beneath my skin. An instinctual reminder. I tug at the fibers of the holly plant, forcing them to grow like hair. The roots burst through the wooden sides of the box and tumble along the cobblestoned street. They coil around the woman's arms and legs, yanking her away from me. Her red glare burns into me and she screams.

I force the leaves to grow and cover her mouth, silencing her protests. She thrashes until she clobbers her head against the wall and loses consciousness.

My heart plummets. What have I done?

I touch her face. Cold. Clammy.

The noise of the soldiers grows louder. They run in our direction.

She wouldn't stop, I tell myself.

I had to.

Is she dead?

The sound of my pulse thrums in my ears. I dart left off the Imperial Mile and run the rest of the way down the avenue. Only a single shop boasts a morning-lantern over its glass windows—a signal that it is open for business. Glittering rose-colored lanterns bear apothecary symbols—a snake curled around a mortar and pestle. The wind bats them like balloons.

Nerves flutter like tiny wings inside my chest. Maybe it's from being recognized. Maybe it's from using the arcana. Maybe it's from interacting with a Gris person up close for the first time. Maybe it's from hurting someone.

I gaze through a gold-trimmed window. Three apothecary bulbs sway and glow in shades of ocean blue and emerald green. Spiderwebs climb over them and glisten in the light. Day-lanterns cruise about the store. The walls are alive with color and hold endless shelves of glass containers that twinkle like bottled stars. A beautiful sign hangs above the doorway, and in cursive lettering announces: CLAIBORNE'S APOTHECARY.

I glance behind me at the now empty street before ducking inside. The scent of a crackling fire and medicinal pastilles meets my nose. The large room has three stories of mahogany cabinets separated by curled iron balconies and sets of spiraled staircases. Bottles wear handwritten labels and lea prices. I recognize many by sight—foxglove, belladonna, poppy, bay laurel. Others contain blue-glass poison bottles, bei powder, wafers, metal instruments—saws, scissors, knives, lancets—and patent medicines boasting cures for fever, lumps, and other illnesses.

Mr. Claiborne, portly and close to losing his eyesight, pops out from behind a curtain. His light brown skin is covered with freck-les and moles, and I wonder why he chose to have so many. "Is that you, little flower?" he says. The sound of his voice puts me at ease.

"What if I said no?" I reply.

"I would say that someone was walking around in your skin. There's a natural perfume you have. Different than ours. You might want to mask it with pomander beads. Le Nez should be releas-ing their new year's scents soon. If you don't, you could be eas-ily caught by a soldier with a keen nose." His mouth lifts with a smile. "But not to worry, I have several new formulas if you care to take a look."

"You could've turned me in days ago," I say.

"Why would I do that?"

"The reward," I counter, taking off the mask.

"I'm in no need of leas. My father left me a boon and this shop. What I needed was a challenge—and you've provided it. This is a once-in-a-lifetime type of exploration. Furthermore, my wife—if awake—would have none of it. She's longed to spend more time with Belles. Always been fascinated by your kind. I think every person in this world believes at one point or another that they'd love to switch places with you all."

"Only because they don't know the truth."

"What is the truth anymore? With the papers profiting from lies and people scrambling to outdo one another. The truth is what-ever you say it is." He turns and whistles. His teacup peacock struts along the counter and places gold lea coins on a set of scales. "Good work, Sona. Well done," Claiborne praises.

I roll up my sleeve before he asks me to. "You need to dust off your window bulbs. They're full of cobwebs."

"Spiders are always welcome here," he says. "Now ... on to the reason for your visit." He rummages through cabinets beneath the counter, retrieving a small wooden case. He opens it and exposes a set of gleaming needles. "I have some not-great news for you, little flower. I'm loving this puzzle but finding it difficult to crack."

I sigh with disappointment.

"Well, rather . . . a challenge to get precise, and I require precision above all else. The items in my apothecary contain promises, and I want this tonic to fulfill your wishes. I've mixed nightshade and hemlock, even a bit of strychnine extract, with your blood, and found our elixir continues to be unstable. Too little of my tonic and it does nothing to the arcana proteins in your blood. Too much and it kills them and any other healthy ones around it."

"What should we do?" I try to keep the desperation out of my voice as part of my plan becomes a post-balloon set off in the wrong direction, unable to be caught and re-sent.

"Let me show you the conundrum first." He fixes a monocle to his left eye, then takes an optic-scope from a nearby shelf. The apparatus resembles a large beauty-scope—a slender end to gaze through and its opposite stretching out like a horn plugged with glass. "Ready?"

I nod.

He pushes a needle into the crook of my arm and draws a vial of blood, adds a few drops of it to a sliver of glass, and slips it into the base of the optic-scope.

"Look into the oculus," he directs.

I press my eye to the slender tip. My blood. The blood Arabella said had the strength to grow the next generation of Belles. "It looks like a glittering net holding rose petals."

"Quite the poet you are," he replies. "Those oblong-shaped objects—the petals, you call them—are what make up your blood.

The net is your arcana. If you were to look at mine, the threads wouldn't glow. That is your gift from the Goddess."

"A curse."

He chortles. "I suppose now it is one." He uncorks a small bottle and uses a metal dropper to draw out its contents. "Now pay careful attention. One pearl-size bead or so..." He squeezes the top, and a fat drop slides onto the glass, mixing with the blood. The net of arcana threads hardens like bone, then shatters into pieces.

I gasp.

"Keep watching. A little more..." He adds a half drop, and the red circles shrivel and darken like raisins. "Too much of this and someone could die." He looks up and taps the oculus to get my attention. "You have to be very, very careful, my flower."

His warning wraps around me and squeezes tight.

He pats my hand. "I will package it with specific instructions while you go and visit my wife."

"Has she woken?" I ask while glancing into the oculus one more time. Now, the red circles resemble black pebbles.

"Only briefly. But I'm certain she will regain her wakefulness soon. She falls into those deep fits of sleep from time to time. I have to get her balanced and my patent medicines do that. Me and my trusty assistant Sona here." He ruffles the peacock's tiny feathers. "We'll work it out. When she does wake for a longer spell of time, she'll be happy to see her beauty maintained. I only have you do this for her benefit, you see. I don't care how she looks, as long as she gets well."

"I understand."

"But it'll keep her invigorated to recover fully and maybe avoid the things that put her in these sleeping spells to begin with."

I nod at him.

"Sona, will you lead our guest like a good host?" He sets the peacock on the floor and lifts the curtain separating the front of the shop from the back. "Don't mind the mess, little flower. I've been busier than usual."

The little bird trots forward down the long hallway. Night-lanterns bathe her in soft light, catching the rich blues of her tail. I follow, stepping into a world of cupboards lined with bottles of every shape and size, liquids the color of honey, amber, and licorice; bulb-shaped vials and vases of curious construction; and shelves featuring flasks of pickled items, delicate glass instruments, and piles of drying herbs.

We climb a winding staircase up to the second floor. Healing-lanterns bob and weave through the room, scattering balls of cerulean-tinted light. Madam Claiborne's long frame swallows a too-small bed. Her arms and legs hang off of it like dead branches discarded by trees as the windy season comes to an end, and her skin struggles to hold on to the alabaster color I gave her two days ago. The gray pushes through, and her veins resemble threadbare yarn ready to unravel. Stick-straight hair cascades over her chest like spools of midnight, and she has the beautiful curves of an hourglass. Thick, sinewy, and full.

I made her look like a blend of Hana and Valerie. My heart squeezes at the thought of what they both might be going through; what all my other sisters must be experiencing. The newsreels report that those from my generation are being held hostage. Hana in the Glass Isles and Valerie at Maison Rouge and Padma in the Bay of Silk. An angry knot coils tight in my chest, the desire to rescue them competing with the need to find Princess Charlotte.

The handmade beauty caisse Mr. Claiborne made for me rests on the nightstand beside mourning tablets for Queen Celeste.

Belle-products sit on tiered trays—miniature skin-paste pots and rouge-sticks and bei powder. Shiny rods lie on a velveteen cushion like cylinders of silver and gold.

I run my fingers over them, then hover above her bed.

"Madam Claiborne," I say. "It's Camille. Can you hear me?"

Her chest moves up and down in a soft rhythm. It makes me think of Charlotte—the memory of her body jerking and the sounds of her cough. I try to hold it in my heart like a precious jewel that I never want to lose. She's out there somewhere.

I sprinkle the bei powder over Madam Claiborne's arms. I close my eyes. The arcana meet my command. I touch her again and think of Queen Celeste. I deepen her coloring to match the departed queen's luscious black skin and add a rich gloss to her dark hair.

Mr. Claiborne enters the room. "She'll love this look you've given her." He gazes down at her. "Thank you."

"You are helping me, remember? This is the least I could do," I reply.

He holds up a velvet pouch. "It's ready. As much as it will be." My heart lifts with relief.

"Now, little flower, this tonic is essentially a poison." He places it in my hand. "Are you sure you still want this? You weren't completely honest about why you wanted it in the first place."

"I need to know that if I'm ever captured, I can't be used. That I can kill the arcana in my blood."

His jaw clenches, but he nods. "In the Matrand Dynasty during periods of unrest, powerful houses had small armies to guard their land, and many were given tiny poison pellets to ingest if taken prisoner. Information required protection at all costs." He closes my hand around the pouch. "But please only use it if you must.

I'd love to see you again when all of this is over, and I know my wife would like to properly meet you under other circumstances."

I look down, staring at the swollen veins beneath my skin, pulsing like green serpents as the arcana proteins rush through my bloodstream. I think about all the things that they can do: make others beautiful, grow Belles, and now, change me.

If all goes well, I'll never be taken or used, never have to ingest his poison, never have to take this risk, but I somehow feel comforted as I slip the vial into my pocket.

The weight of it contains the promise of freedom.

3

I make my way back to the boardinghouse through a wakening city. The aurous glow of Metairie's gilt-lanterns freckle the salt-white buildings with golden leaves as they're lit for the morning. The port bells ring, and the first ships move into the harbor.

Carriages start to fill the avenues and lanes. Many empty themselves of well-dressed passengers. Women parade about in billowing gowns made of fur and wool, wearing headdresses and holding all manner of objects for sale. Men wear frock coats with tails that drag along the snow-dusted streets. Heat-lanterns are miniature suns following behind people. Some disappear into glamorous shops and others stop at sweets pavilions offering cold-season treats: spiced teacakes, chrysanthemum-shaped marzipan, snowmelon meringues, hot beignets piled high with sugar, and bourbon tarts. Tiny wisps of steam trail hot mugs of molten caramel and chocolate.

Passersby wear grim expressions, their lips pursed, brows furrowed, as imperial soldiers swarm the crowds, stopping to interrogate people at random. They rustle up merchants and shoo away Gris beggars. Their heavy footsteps create a terrifying melody, and their black armor glistens beneath the cold blue market-lantern light, severe as a murder of crows. Sophia has deployed her entire arsenal to find us.

I lingered too long at the apothecary. I hurry past vendors shouting slogans through slender brass trumpets.

"The Spice Isles grieve. Get the best mourning cameos of Her Majesty Queen Celeste."

"Vivant scarves that change color—silk, cotton, wool, even velvet. Only sold here!"

"Get your very own replica of Queen Celeste's mortuary tablets for your family altar."

"Invisible post-balloons—undetectable for the utmost privacy. Leas-back insurance guarantee. We have the best price."

I adjust the mask on my face. Sweat soaks through the lace and velvet.

A trio of guards steps into my path.

I avoid them, making a sharp left into the seedier areas of the market—the part Rémy warned us to avoid. Gris women and men hold signs begging for food, leas coins, and spintria. Others with skin nearing gray and hair poking like straw out of their hats skulk about toting tattered baskets and peddling shoddy wares. Shopkeepers and stall owners chase them away to make the passageways clear for customers.

"Make way for the Orléans Press Corps," someone yells. "The morning reports are in!"

Newsies swarm the market like the rush of snow flurries that have started to fall. They thrust their papers about, the animated ink scrambling to hold on to their headlines, and their screams assault my ears.

"From the *Orléansian Times*," one shouts. "Must be indoors at three hours after sunset! Imperial curfew moved up until dangerous fugitives caught!"

"The *Daily Spice Sentinel* states if the poor can be beautiful, what's the point?! Beauty lobbyists petition new queen for spintria increase," another hollers.

I press my hands to the sides of my head as I rush through the throng of bodies but can't block out their voice-trumpets.

"The *Trianon Tribune* first to report. New imperial law decree straight from the Minister of Law and Her Majesty. Any person caught with beauty work that mirrors the looks of the criminals will be fined and jailed."

"The *Imperial Inquirer* is holding the most lucrative kingdom-wide lottery," one boasts. "Place your bets! Guess the date when the fugitive Belles will be caught. Pot is up to twenty thousand spintria for the most accurate prediction. A bonus of five thousand for location of capture."

"The *Chrysanthemum Chronicle* has the exclusive—Queen Sophia's wedding to Minister of the Seas' youngest son, Auguste Fabry, will take place on the first warm day of the new year!"

The sound of his name is a punch to the chest.

I stop. Bodies shove into me.

"Move out of the way," one complains.

"Keep going!" another says.

"No standing here," a third barks.

Memories of Auguste—the clever smile in his eyes, the way his too-long hair always escaped the knot he put it in, the taste of his lips—flood through my arms and legs and stomach, creating a circle around my heart where the warmth of it all hardens like glass ready to shatter.

I remember his touch. I hear him whisper my name. I can almost see him standing there before me in the masses: shoulders arrogant and pulled back, the pitch of his voice full of confidence, and everyone turning to listen to every word he has to say.

The thoughts fill me with rage.

"Get away from my stall," a cardamom merchant shrieks, startling me. "You're blocking customers." She thumps a porcelain spice scoop on my shoulder, and her sharp voice stamps out Auguste's image like a candle extinguished.

I step back into the crowd. A second wave of newsies gluts the market.

"We've got Her Majesty's favorite paper, the *Herald of Orléans.* In eight days on the first day of our new year, the queen is to present the body of her beloved sister, Princess Charlotte, before the court and the people of Orléans. It will signal the start of her Coronation and Ascension celebration. The deceased princess will lie in honor and remembrance."

My heart all but stops. But Charlotte isn't dead. What body will she present? A look-alike? How will she forge the identification ink on Charlotte's neck? Or did Sophia find her before I could, and kill her?

No. I refuse to believe that. This is just one of Sophia's games. Still, dread rattles me. We have to leave right now and find Charlotte before this lie becomes truth.

I hurry down the street where Pruzan's Boardinghouse sits. This news bubbles in my chest, ready to spill out. A blimp skates over my head with fluttering silkscreen banners that hold portraits of my sisters' faces as well as my own and Rémy's. They sparkle and flash like lightning trapped on parchment, the sky candles creating bright pictures even in the daylight.

Soldiers choke all the alleys. "Out of the way!" they shout.

"There's been a sighting of the fugitives!" someone hollers.

My stomach plummets. I push through the bodies and sprint up the creaking staircase into the boardinghouse. Other boarders dart to their rooms as the noise of the soldiers grows louder. I leap up the stairs two at a time to the second floor and rush into our room.

"They're everywhere," I whisper, yanking off my mask. "They know we're here!"

Rémy pulls me inside and presses a finger to his mouth, signaling me to be silent. He goes to the window, glancing out at the street below.

Heavy footsteps reverberate through the house.

"We have to get out of here." Edel scrambles to pack our things into satchels.

"How did they find us?" Amber asks.

"I don't know. Maybe the housemistress reported us," Rémy says. "Hurry."

I tie my waist-sash around me and tuck the sleepy teacup dragons into it. Shouts echo through the walls.

"Eye-films in and mask on, Amber," Edel directs.

I fumble to put mine back on, my fingers shaky with nerves.

Rémy touches my shoulder and nods, his quiet confidence a temporary balm.

Amber jams in her eye-films. "I can't see anything."

"Blink and they'll settle," Edel replies.

Amber struggles to tie on her mask, her eyes watery, her

fingers fumbling. The ribbons rip as she pulls them too tight, but there's no time for me to help her before we're slipping into the hall behind Rémy.

"All boarders are summoned to the common room," a voice commands.

"We'll leave through the kitchens," Rémy whispers. "Pull your hoods tight."

The boarders swarm the space with confusion and chaos, allowing us cover to sneak down a back set of stairs. My heart thumps with each step I take. Soldiers rummage through rooms, flipping up beds and snatching open closet doors.

"Any of you found to be harboring fugitives will face the maximum punishment allowed by the Courts of Justice," a soldier barks. "That's fifteen days in a starvation box. The Minister of Justice will not be lenient."

We ease into the kitchen.

A soldier steps out of the pantry. "And just where do you think you're going?"

Rémy shoves straight through, knocking him to the ground. Another soldier appears in the doorway behind us. I grab the nearest cast-iron skillet and hit him on the head. He crashes into the table.

"Run!" Rémy yells.

Edel pushes through the back door first.

I stumble out with Rémy at my side. We duck behind a carriage just as a scream cuts through the air.

Amber.

Instinctively, I turn back toward her, toward my sister, toward my best friend. She thrashes about in the arms of two soldiers, writhing in their grip.

"We've got one of them!" a soldier hollers. "The others must be nearby!"

The world slows around me.

Amber's wails pierce the air; each one hits me like the stab of a knife.

I start to go to her. Rémy grabs me by the waist. "We have to leave. We've already been seen. The longer we linger, the more of them there will be."

"No." I wrestle with his tight grip. "We can't."

"Camille, he's right. We'll all be captured. And they want you the most." Edel squeezes my chin, forcing me to look at her. "We can't help her right now. If we're taken, too, it's over. We can't find Charlotte. We can't fix all of this. We can't do anything."

Tears storm down my cheeks.

"We'll find a way to get her back."

Edel tugs me forward, toward the dark shadows of the alley, as the guards drag Amber away and she disappears, like a post-balloon snatched by its ribbons.

4

We weave through Metairie's network of markets, moving as far away from the boardinghouse as possible. My heart swells with heaviness. What will Sophia do to Amber? Will she torture her? How bad will it be?

"We need to go back for her," I whisper to Edel. "We should follow them and see where they take her."

"She lingered behind us," she replies. "I don't understand why she'd do that."

"What do you mean?" I ask. "She was struggling to get her mask on."

Rémy shushes us. "Not out in the open. Too risky. Whatever happened, we'll discuss it later."

I turn to him. "Where are we going?"

"To a place where people rarely ask questions." He pulls his hood tighter, reassembles his mask around his face, and leads the way forward through the crowd. We venture deep inside, headed for its edges, where the city lanterns darken from blues to plums. The cobblestones trail off. Stalls and shops are pitched at strange and rather worrying angles, each having sunk a little too far into the muddied ground. Signs advertise beauty-scopes featuring nude men and women, products claiming to steal another's beauty, and tonics with the promise of love, money, and fame.

"Prisms for good fortune when the rainy season returns. Trap a rainbow, get good luck from the God of Luck," a vendor says.

"Wish dolls sold here. Best in the marketplace!" another shouts through a voice-trumpet. "Best in all of the Spice Isles. Exact your revenge. Or make your dreams come true. My pins will unlock it all. I've collected the metal myself from the Goddess of Death's caves!"

"Care to know your future?" A masked woman cuts off my stride.

I almost slam into her. Glass beads dot the veil she wears, and her mask is etched with a curious pink flower. She lifts it and whispers, "A new year and a new moon is coming. The threads of danger slowly thickening. You should draw from my cards." She fans them out, exposing their hand-drawn faces.

I flinch. Spiderwebs stretch across them. Why does it seem like spiders are following me everywhere this morning?

"No, thank you," I say, sidestepping her to keep up with Rémy and Edel.

"There is anger around you. I can lift it," she calls out behind us. "Come back."

No one can get rid of this fiery cloud.

Rémy heads for a salon that can't make up its mind if it's a teahouse, a shop, or a limestone mansion. A tiny door holds a porthole-shaped window and red sill-lanterns sit behind two pairs of windows like glowing eyes. The lip-shaped sign RED VELVET SALON flaps from a gust of wind.

"Is this..." I start to say.

Rémy clears his throat and doesn't meet my eyes. "A place where no one will search for us. And if they did, the soldiers would be easily distracted."

"Smart," Edel says, patting him on the shoulder. "I knew you were good for something."

He stiffens. "Wait here." He pulls his mask tight and vanishes up the stairs.

A nervous tremor pulses through me. I look around, alert with adrenaline. Women push a variety of pavilion carts advertising the strongest bourbon pies and the savoriest meat skewers and the perfect ale to warm one's belly. Men and women stumble in and out of the buildings along the street—some holding bloated purses ready to gamble in the card salons, and others looking for love and companionship. Many readjust their masks to cover garish makeup and hold on to their face embellishments, the trend of jewel-embedded skin very popular here. Gris beggars rush to every available person asking for spare leas and spintria.

"We need to go look for her," I repeat.

"No," Edel spits back. "I'm not risking my life for Amber."

"She's your sister!"

"She's *your* sister." Edel crosses her arms over her chest. "As far as I'm concerned, she's changed."

A few newsies parade through with their voice-trumpets. Their shouts hit us in heavy waves.

"Buy the *Daily Orléansian* for exclusive first pictures of construction on Queen Sophia's new prison being built in the middle of the Royal Harbor," one cries out.

"Power of Belle blood discovered."

Edel and I freeze and lock eyes.

"Royal scientists give first interviews about the breakthrough to the queen's favorite newspaper, the *National*." The newsie waves around a reel. "Watch it now."

"Disgraced Guardian of the Belles, Madam Ana Maria Lange Du Barry missing. Report just released via the *Orléansian Times*."

The sound of Du Barry's name sends a shudder through me. I step forward to buy the paper, but Edel grabs my arm and shakes her head. I stand frozen beside her as the newsies' headlines hit us one after the other. "Did you hear that? About Du Barry?"

"She could be found at the bottom of the Rose Bayou for all I care." Edel points up. Blimps skate overhead with silkscreen banners holding our pictures. No longer Amber's portrait. The leas reward has doubled.

The sight of it makes my heart somersault.

It happened so fast.

"We should buy the papers, then go back for Amber. I know you and she have never been the closest, but she—"

"I saw what she did," Edel says.

"What?"

"A leaked newsreel circulated after Sophia's lady-of-honor Claudine died. I watched that arcana challenge Sophia made the two of you participate in at her dinner party. The tattlers had it until Sophia threatened to shut down the press and made them come before the Minister of News."

The memory of that night hits me in waves:

Claudine's vacant eyes.

Claudine's slack mouth.

Claudine's dead body.

"I saw how she acted. She wouldn't stop. She was the same old Amber. Always needing to win. You tried to stop her. I saw the pain on your face."

My heartbeat quickens with each accusation Edel lobs at Amber. I'm unable to defend her.

A vendor stops to stare at us. "Care for a bourbon pie?"

Edel runs her off.

We step a little away from the Red Velvet Salon staircase.

"We were both at fault. I should have refused," I whisper to her.

"She should've helped you both get out of that game. But Amber has always, *always* had to win above all else." Edel balls her hands into fists. "The one with the best marks from Du Barry. The one who got the first pick of dresses and desserts. The one who had to go first with every group lesson given to us. I thought it was just a bad habit from when we were little. Her maman spoiled her. I thought she'd grow out of it—"

"She—"

"No excuses. The rest of our sisters don't behave like that. You don't do that."

"Sophia tortured her during her time as favorite. You can't—"

"I don't trust her anymore."

Another blimp crests overhead, bathing us in a dark shadow.

Rémy reappears at the top of the entrance stairs. Edel rushes up toward him, leaving me and our conversation behind.

I climb the stairs and step through the door. The space reminds me of the candy houses we'd built as little girls to celebrate the new year and call sweetness from the God of the Ground. Red-and-gold-papered walls hug us inside a decadent living room that looks up to five wraparound floors. Blush-pink lanterns putter about, bathing each level in pale shades of light. Perfume blimps squirt rose water. Velvet chaises and tufted chairs hold glamorous powdered and primped women and men.

We follow Rémy to a hall that smells like dried flowers and clove smoke, then up a flight of stairs and down another hall. My body is tense, my nerves coiled up like a spring. My argument with Edel replays over and over again in my head. Her words—"*I don't trust her anymore*"—drumming through me like discordant music on a stringed misen.

He opens a door and ushers us inside. Night-lanterns float through a pleasant bedroom. Two beds are pushed against opposite walls. A gold-striped couch and matching armchair sit beside the solitary window. Mirrors hang above a modest vanity.

"I'm going to go buy the most recent papers and get a sense of where the guards are," Rémy says as he leaves the room.

I let the teacup dragons out of my pouch. They stretch their tiny wings, then hiss and tiptoe through the room, sniffing every object in their path. I call out the names Amber gave them—Feuille for the green, Poivre for the red, Or for the gold, Eau for the blue, and Fantôme for the white.

Edel flits them away as they circle her, begging for attention. "We were tracked. Had to have been," she mumbles angrily.

"I think it's my fault," I say with a shrug. "I've been sneaking out."

"What? Where have you been going?" Edel demands.

I drop my hand in my dress pocket, the raised glass grooves of the poison bottle finding my fingers. I almost show it to her, but a twinge in my stomach makes me bury the secret.

"I couldn't take being stuck in that tiny room all the time. I needed air—some space to think," I lie. "Maybe I was followed?"

"That's too easy." Edel brushes her hand along one of the bed frames, then sits. "They would've just arrested you on the spot. Why follow you to the boardinghouse? Why interrogate all the boarders and do a search?"

The green teacup dragon, Feuille, climbs into my lap and curls into a tiny ball. "Maybe one of us was spotted while running errands, but they didn't know which boardinghouse we'd returned to."

"Someone like Amber?" Edel asks, arching an eyebrow.

I take a deep breath. "What do you think she did, exactly?"

Edel snaps upright. "Look! I know you've always loved her more than you love the rest of us."

"I have not. You're all my sisters." I set Feuille on the floor and rush to sit at Edel's side. I touch her, and she yanks away.

"We all felt it. Hana, Valerie, Padma, and me. It was always the two of you. . . ." She purses her lips. "You can't see it. Or maybe you don't want to see it. But she's hiding something . . . I know it."

The door snaps open. Rémy returns with an armful of newspapers and the latest newsreel.

Edel stands and turns to Rémy. "What are the papers saying?"

"Find the room's télétrope," Rémy says.

Edel riffles through the nearest bureau and retrieves a dusty télétrope. She opens the machine's bottom compartment, fishes out a wobbly matchstick, and lights the tea candle in its base.

I take one of the papers from Rémy's stack. Poivre tries to nibble its edges, but I wrestle it from the teacup's tiny fangs, his mouth warm with the promise of fire.

I think of Amber. Edel's words linger, sinking into my skin. A whisper echoes inside me: *What does my and Amber's closeness have to do with her not trusting Amber?*

A knot squeezes in my throat, thickening with regret and threatening to choke me.

Edel takes the film from Rémy and inserts it into the télétrope. "Close the curtains, and blow out the night-lanterns."

Rémy extinguishes them. I bunch the curtains closed. The tea-cup dragons squeak and flutter about, protesting the dark until the newsreel projects on the wall. An image of Sophia appears. She's seated on her throne surrounded by her teacup animals—her monkey, Singe, at her shoulder, her elephant, Zo, in her lap, and a small bunny on her scepter. Her grating voice drifts through the télétrope's tiny voice-box. "The time of the Belles is over. Orléans has been at the mercy of their powers for too long. They've been able to lord it over us. But never again, now that I am queen."

Edel paces.

My cheeks warm as if the arcana are waking up. "We've lorded it over them? No! They beg for our help. They work us until we're sick. Du Barry was the one who profited—not us!"

Sophia continues: "We will take back control. I will regulate the entire beauty system—it will cater to all our needs when we're at the very heart of it. Those who don't cooperate will meet a deadly fate. The Fugitive Belle Act has just passed without a single protest vote in my new cabinet. I'm going to round up all the runaway Belles. They will live in my prison, the Everlasting Rose. They will be raised and trained there, and prepared for their duties to our great country. They're dangerous and aggressive, and need to be watched and controlled for their own benefit. My loyal subjects, the reward for bringing me Edel Beauregard has risen from eight hundred fifty thousand leas to one million leas."

Edel gasps.

"And anyone who brings me Camille Beauregard, my disgraced favorite, the Belle who killed two of my most beloveds: Lady Claudine, Duchesse de Bissay, and"—her voice breaks in mock-upset—"and my best friend, my sister, Princess Charlotte..."

"What?" I cry.

Tears fall down her cheeks as the people in the crowd before her shout in agreement. My pulse is a throbbing drum, counting down the moments of this newsreel like racing sand in an hourglass.

"Yes, it has been confirmed that she experimented on my sister's weak body and stopped her heart," Sophia says. "And she *will* be punished. Two million leas for anyone who brings her to me. And if she is delivered by the time of Princess Charlotte's viewing and the coronation, I'll give you your own small palace. My mother's favorite summer one on the Isle of Minnate. You have seven days. An auspicious number revered by the Goddess of Love." She smiles, showing the perfect sliver of teeth. "My dearly beloved mother was a passive queen. I will not be."

The newsreel ends. The sound of its tail flapping cuts through the silent room. I hear my own heartbeat thrumming and each of the deep breaths Edel and Rémy take. I let out a guttural scream. Rémy rushes to me, clamping his hand over my mouth.

I snatch away from him. "Don't."

"People can hear—"

"I know...I know..."

"There's more." Rémy reads from one of the papers. "After the Coronation and Ascension ceremony, no sitting queen can be deposed or challenged according to imperial law."

A tense bubble engulfs us, its edges charged, ready to smother all three of us.

He opens another paper, the *Orléansian Times*. A two-page spread showcases a massive structure floating in the middle of the Royal Harbor.

The headline reads: QUEEN SOPHIA'S NEWEST ENDEAVOR—THE EVERLASTING ROSE—HALF-COMPLETE.

The animated portrait of a circular building flickers like a chandelier-lantern the size of Trianon's Coliseum. The picture flashes and takes onlookers on a tour. Outer window bars twist in the shape of Belle-roses. Our older sister, Ivy, stands on an enclosed lattice balcony spanning the structure's entire circumference. Half her face is masked; the other battered. Pale pink sill-lanterns bathe her cheeks in soft light. Her falling tears glow; she looks trapped in the gilded filigree of a jewelry box. The portrait pans out, showing a thorny garden growing around a great tower in the center where Sophia waves and blows kisses.

"A cage for us. Like rabid animals," Edel says.

My eyes scan the article:

The construction of the Everlasting Rose, affectionately named after the eternal "everlasting" roses that bloomed in the Goddess of Beauty's garden, has been under way day and night, with labor teams toiling without pause. Located on the edge of the Isle of Chalmette, its glow can be spotted from the rooftops of Trianon's limestone mansions. Newsboats sit in the Royal Harbor reporting on every moment of construction and every coming and going of visitors to the site. The newly titled Minister of Belles, Georgiana Fabry, said, "We'll be opening the building soon. The citizens of Orléans will be able to enter the world of the Belles. No more secrecy. We're starting new traditions."

The Rose, as it's been nicknamed, will replace Maison Rouge as the locale where all Belles will be trained to serve Orléans. Tours of the building are slated to begin after the Coronation and Ascension of Queen

Sophia. Tickets will go on sale during the auspicious festivities. Citizens will be able to reach the structure via special rose-coaches and lavish wire carriages currently being built.

I shove the paper away. "This is where they're going to take Amber. She's going to be tortured. We have to help her."

"And risk all of us getting locked in that prison?" Edel snaps. "No, I won't do it."

"Edel—"

"Stop arguing," Rémy says. "And look at this last paper."

It's one I've never seen before. The pages are black as night and the ink white as clouds. The articles and headlines appear and disappear depending on where I touch it. The border contains webs holding beautiful seedlings, unfurling and blossoming into tiny teardrop leaves, curls of stems, and oval petals in soft lavenders and magentas and pinks. I remember these from the solarium at Maison Rouge.

Cleome flowers. Maman's favorite.

I thumb the top.

"What is it?" Edel peers down over my shoulder.

"The *Spider's Web*. An underground paper," Rémy replies. "The publication the Minister of News doesn't regulate because he doesn't know it exists."

"How'd you get it?" Edel's eyes grow big.

"They circulate in this part of the city. I admit, I've never seen or read an issue before. I've only heard about it. I didn't think they were real. The Minister of War taught us that people don't resist." Rémy removes the tea candle from the télétrope and waves it over the paper. "The newsie said to hold the light over it and the ink will settle and sharpen."

The letters rise on the black parchment like drizzles of cream in steaming hot coffee. The headlines sparkle and snap like whips.

QUEEN SOPHIA IN TALKS TO START RANKING BEAUTY
WORK KINGDOMWIDE, USING THE MEASURE TO ALLOCATE
LAND, JOBS, TITLES, AND FAVOR WITH THE MONARCH

DON'T BELIEVE THE MORBID DEATH LIES!
PRINCESS CHARLOTTE IN HIDING DESPITE
FALSE REPORTS FROM PALACE OFFICIALS

DECEASED QUEEN'S PARTNER, LADY PELLETIER,
SPOTTED IN VARIOUS APOTHECARIES. PERHAPS
LOOKING FOR PRINCESS CHARLOTTE'S CURE?

AFTER UNFORTUNATE CAPTURE OF FIRST FAVORITE
AMBROSIA BEAUREGARD, QUEEN'S GUARD CONFOUNDED
ABOUT LOCATION OF OTHER FUGITIVE BELLES

IRON LADIES GATHER MORE NUMBERS AS THEY PLOT
TO END QUEEN SOPHIA'S TYRANNICAL RULE

"Who are the Iron Ladies?" I demand, anticipation rising inside my chest.

"The Resistance," Rémy replies.

5

Each time I close my eyes and try to sleep, Sophia lures me into a nightmare. She's always in a long white nightgown like a spirit that's escaped the Goddess of Death's caves, and she leads me down a twisting corridor with no end in sight. She glances back with a sly smile that reveals a hint of teeth; her pupils dilate so big her eyes are two gigantic black pools.

The dream darkness fills with smoke and ash, the world burning around me like a rose set aflame, each petal shriveling and whitening, furious at being stripped of its color and perfume. The cameos of her courtiers appear along the walls, shifting and morphing within the angry fire. The frantic pulse that lives inside her ripples out like waves, crashing into me, while the screech of her laughter pierces the silence like a thunderclap.

I wake up soaked every time.

"Can't sleep?" Rémy asks, his heavy whisper bouncing off the walls like a skipping stone across the bayou waters at home. He shifts in a high-backed chair beside the door and lights a small night-lantern, setting it adrift in the room. His rich brown skin glows when beads of light find him.

"How can you?" I sit up and pull my sweat-soaked curls into a low bun before they start to frizz. Beside me, Edel turns over and sighs in her sleep.

"I barely sleep. You know that," he replies.

I sigh. "Right."

I gaze out the window. The sky looks like it's in mourning—the dark streaks of blue mirror tears and the gashes of purple bruises. Maybe the heavens are troubled by what's happening below. "What time is it?"

"The evening star rose about two hourglasses ago. Only a few more until dawn," he says. "Want some tea? Maybe it'll help."

"Yes," I reply.

I slide out of bed.

Rémy quickly stands and turns his back to me. "Tell me you're changing next time." His shoulders tense.

The cotton sleeping-gown hugs my edges. "Yes, all right," I whisper, blushing. We're still finding the rhythm of being in small spaces together.

I slip on my traveling cloak. "I'm ready."

He inches open our door, so it doesn't groan.

We tiptoe into the hall. Shabby night-lanterns pockmarked with holes and covered in nets of dust struggle to reach the ceiling or to provide us with light.

"The kitchens are empty right now," he reports, leading me down a back set of stairs. Deep snores escape from behind nearby doors and mask the noise of our footsteps. The red sill-lanterns have been extinguished, and the ladies of the house have all gone to bed. We've only been here a few hours, but Rémy has started a detailed ledger of their movements.

Thin walls allow the wind to find its way inside. Its icy, sharp fingers send a shiver through me.

"Are you cold?" he says.

"I'm fine."

"Your teeth are chattering."

"Do you hear everything?"

"I guess you could say that. My maman used to say I could even hear the smallest mouse pee."

"That's ridiculous!" I laugh, then try to swallow it.

His face lights up like the time I saw him talking to his sisters. He lets out a deep chuckle, full-throated and from the very bottom of his stomach. It vibrates across my skin. It's the sort of laugh that makes you sit up and pay attention and wish you were always the one to laugh with him.

I think about how long I spent hating him, and blush with regret.

We arrive at the kitchen. He motions for me to wait, then ducks inside, stalks around in the dark, and reappears tugging the strings of a night-lantern.

"No creatures waiting to eat me?" I ask with a smile.

"Looks fine," he says. "And I'm shocked you stayed put."

"I guess I've learned to listen."

"Or to trust me." He leads the way and sets the night-lantern afloat. A fire burns low in the hearth. A monstrous stone stove hulks in the corner like the fire-breathing bayou bird Maman used to tell me stories about as a child. Jars of bits and bobbles and thingamabobs clutter the shelves. Shoddy cabinets hold cracked glass panes. Dishes are stacked in perilous towers in a sink. Remnants of the cook's stew sit in a pot on the long worktable, calling out to any critters looking for a meal. A stack of night-edition newspapers blinks their headlines.

"You walk like you own the land beneath your feet." His laughter fades, but he doesn't stop smiling. "Like my sisters. I could always tell when one of them would enter the house. I knew them by the sound of their footsteps. Mirabelle, quick and light, always a little too excited. Adaliz, heavy and demanding, ready to order someone around. Odette, jumpy and timid, looking for something coming around every corner." He sighs.

"You miss them?"

"Desperately," he replies. "I'm used to being away on assignment or for training. But this feels—"

"Different," I say.

He nods.

"What do you think they're doing?"

"Getting prepared to celebrate the new year despite being worried about me," he says. "They're also anxiously checking the newspapers and watching the reels every day."

"I should've never dragged you into this," I say. "I'm sorry."

"If I recall, I got myself into it by helping you escape." He smiles.

"You could be doing so many other things right now."

"Like what?" he says as I lean back against the kitchen counter.

"Taking your sisters for a cold-season holiday in the mountains of the Gold Isles."

"Fine."

"Or off training somewhere."

"I could be doing that."

"Maybe getting married," I say, and as soon as it pops out, I want to press it back in. I don't know why I thought of it. Or I do know but push it down inside, tucking it away like the poison bottle heavy in my pocket. Always with me, but never taken out into the light. A heavy warmth blooms in my cheeks.

He scoffs. "I've never had much luck with courting. My sisters say I'm not charming enough."

"I wonder why," I tease, thinking for the smallest moment what he might be like in a relationship. Would he always be so protective? Has he ever loved someone romantically? Or been kissed? "Tell me about the Iron Ladies," I say to brush away those feelings.

"I don't know much." He shrugs. "When I was training on the Isle of Quin, there were rumors about one of the generals who'd been passed over by Queen Celeste to be the Minister of War. She disappeared—like a spider, hence the title of the paper—and wasn't seen again. She's thought to be the leader of the Iron Ladies."

Could they help us? Would they want to help us?

"Most of it always sounded like fairy tales. A whole civilization of people living away from the cities, learning to survive with the grayness, plotting and planning to change things."

"What if it is true?"

"Then, maybe they'll help. But I trust nothing that I read in the papers." He motions in the direction of the stack. "It's too easy to make things up, use parchment and ink and words to distort opinions."

"Do you trust anyone? Do you trust me?" I ask.

The question crackles between us like the fire in the hearth. Each letter of that small and complicated word an ember.

"Why do you want to know?"

"Well, you did stab me." I touch my side where his dagger pierced me only a week ago.

"For good reason. It was part of the plan."

"You could've told me about it."

"And have you ruin it?" Rémy says. "No. You didn't have confidence in me at that point. Barely even liked me. You hadn't had a chance to test me with that mirror of yours."

I press a hand to my chest. "How do you know about that?"

"I'm supposed to know about everything when it comes to you."

"I...don't even know what to say to that."

Rémy leans closer. "I'm not him. You don't have to hide things from me. I'm not watching you or trying to find things out only to hurt you with them."

The word *him* lands hard.

Auguste.

I bristle at the mere thought of his face.

"My mother left the mirror for me, but it was Arabella's," I whisper.

"Does it always show you the truth?"

"Yes." I fish it out from under my nightgown and show it to him.

He runs the pad of his thumb across the grooves, his hand so close to my chest that maybe he can feel my heartbeat. The perfume of his skin is different than Auguste's—almost like warm-season rain and fresh Belle-rose leaves. "It's beautiful. Will you show me how it works?"

"Soon." I take it from his grasp and tuck it back under my nightgown, the metal now warm from his touch.

He stares at me, but I don't meet his eyes. His long arm reaches over my head to rescue a plump white teapot from a hook.

"Are you skilled in the art of making tea?" I ask.

"Add leaves to boiling water." He lifts an eyebrow.

I sigh at him and roll my eyes.

His brow furrows, crinkling like the brown ridges in a molasses cookie.

"Step aside." I swat at his shoulder.

He smirks. I wash out the pot, fill it, and set it on the stovetop. He hands me a fire-stick from the hearth, and I light a flame beneath the pot's round body, then open a cabinet of tea tins. Worn labels advertise their contents—mint, chamomile, almond, lemongrass, and Belle-rose. I run my finger over the last label, remembering how many pots I'd made at the Chrysanthemum Teahouse and the palace until Bree took the process over.

I close my eyes, seeing Bree's delicate hands at work: her small frame hunched above the tiny hearth on the treatment carts, her scooping out dried leaves and making tiny mounds in tea nets before dropping them into the porcelain pots, or rolling up Belle-rose petals plucked from the solarium garden to steep in piping-hot water. The memory of her tugs at the walls I've built inside, and bring tears to my eyes.

"What's wrong?" Rémy asks.

"Just something in my eye." I turn my back to him and wipe away a tear before it falls. "It's nothing."

"All your thoughts show up on your face, Camille. You can't hide anything." He approaches the stove, his shadow looming over me.

"Everything is fine."

"Something is bothering you. I can tell." His eyes study me, pricking my skin, sharper than needles. "You keep biting your bottom lip and your left eyebrow is all twitchy. And you're scowling."

A wave of embarrassment hits me like he's seen me without my clothes on. The presence of his body feels like Auguste's did once—inviting and a little dangerous. A lump of thick, hot betrayal simmers in the pit of my stomach.

I fuss with the teapot. He puts a hand on mine to still it.

Rémy fishes for my gaze, his eyes big and brown with the tiniest bit of red pushing through. His words sink into my skin like warm water, the heat going right through muscles and tissue down to my bones.

"I must've done something. What is it? I didn't even yell at you for disappearing this morning while I was on my perimeter check. I didn't even ask you what you were doing out at that hour."

"Lucky me." I pull my hand out of his grip. It drifts into my nightgown pocket where the tiny poison bottle sits. I can't tell him about this yet. Though I desperately want to.

"I had every right to. Had a whole speech planned out."

"I need to refresh your irises," I say. "And remove that stripe from your hair. It makes you too recognizable."

His hand finds his soft, tight curls and the silver streak down the middle marking him as a soldier in the House of War. "You've been telling me this, but—"

"You're stubborn."

"I'm just not ready to let it go yet. The hair powders you gave me have been covering it for now."

"We will run out soon. I should change your skin color, too."

"Only when you tell me what's wrong."

"You'd risk becoming a Gris again?"

The teapot screeches. I remove it from the flame.

Rémy places two chipped teacups on the table. "I'm not afraid of the grayness."

"What's it like?" I ask, and remember one of Du Barry's lessons about the Gris: *The madness overtakes every part of you, itching to be free.*

"I haven't experienced it since I was a child. People say it's painful. Like a long-lasting sickness. The sweats, a headache, vomiting, and rabid, racing thoughts..."

"We would see little Gris babies, shriveled, angry, and hot from escaping their mothers' wombs. But they only stayed that way for an hourglass's worth before we'd mix Belle-rose tea into their milk and they'd endure their first transformations." I stir a spoonful of honey into each of our cups. "I've seen more Gris people in the Spice Isles than ever before."

"The House of Orléans continually expels them from the imperial island. Rounding them up to disperse, to the irritation of other powerful houses. You must be on high alert."

I think about the Gris woman who attacked me while I was on the way to see Claiborne.

"They aren't any worse than Sophia," I say. "Nothing can be."

"You will get rid of her," he says. "It'll show the world how to resist tyranny."

The image of the *Spider's Web* newspaper drifts into my head. "Du Barry only taught us how to obey."

"And it seems you've learned that lesson well," he chides, pulling a reluctant smile out of me.

"There are so many things I don't know."

"You'll learn them."

"We spent our entire lives being lied to."

"And now, you're waking up. You're lucky. Some people never do."

I turn away from him to avoid his gaze. I stare at the night edition of the *Orléansian Times*. A familiar face winks at me. The Fashion Minister. He's beneath a headline: GUSTAVE DU POLIGNAC, BELOVED FASHION MINISTER, IN THE SILK ISLES PREPARING TO PRESENT DRESSES FAVORED BY QUEEN FOR HER CORONATION AND ASCENSION.

I tear out the article, fold it, and slip it into my pocket with the poison bottle.

"What is it?" he asks.

"Nothing."

He spins me around by the waist and takes my hands. "I know when you're lying."

Our fingers are wrapped together like sweetcanes of chocolate and caramel. He doesn't look up at me, his gaze fixed on them. The firelight dances across his beautiful dark skin like the glow from the red bayou flies at home.

He leans down so our foreheads kiss. "Tell me."

"I'm formulating a plan."

"All right," he whispers.

"We will find Charlotte. We will take down Sophia," I whisper to him.

"Sophia won't go away easily, and the damage she's done will linger—"

"I will kill Sophia if I have to."

"Taking lives is hard."

"She's ruined so many."

"That may be true, but the act of it . . ."

"What do you think we should do?" I pull back.

"What do you want to do?" he asks.

"I want to find Charlotte. I want my sisters to be all right. I want Sophia to not be able to hurt anyone again."

He squeezes my hand.

"You don't have to kill anyone to accomplish this," he says. "It's not as easy as you think."

"I don't think any of this is *easy*. And if you believe what I want to do isn't right, then what should we do? You usually have so many opinions. So many directions for me."

"Not this time. You've got to figure it out," he says.

"I will do what I must," I say. "Whatever it takes."

6

A knock pounds the door in the morning. It startles Edel and me awake. Rémy signals for us to go into the closet.

We squeeze in. A quiver starts in my feet, traveling up my legs to my stomach and chest. I can't still myself. A landquake is erupting inside me. My heart might never find the right beat again.

Edel leans against the wall, her jaw clenched, and fists balled. "They've found us again," she mutters. "I can feel it."

"You don't know that," I reply.

But her words suffocate the small space. If there are guards at the door, how will we get away from them now? What if Rémy were taken—or hurt? How would we be able to help him from in here?

I press my ear to the door and catch three words: *morning paper delivery.*

"You can come back out," Rémy says. "It's all right."

My whole body deflates, my knees buckling, the worries sputtering out like wind. We ease out of the closet. The teacup dragons squawk and push their faces against the bars of their cage. Rémy holds the tail ribbons of a pearl-white post-balloon dragged by a plum-colored teacup dragon.

"I thought it was the papers," I say.

"So did I," he replies.

"Who's it from?" Edel asks. "No one knows we're here."

I take a piece of dried pork from our food pack and whistle. The teacup dragon dives toward me and lands on my shoulder. Rémy grabs the ribbons, breaks open the post-balloon's back, and retrieves an empty perfume bottle and a miniature porcelain jar with several sangsues in it.

A cold stone drops into my stomach. "There's no note."

"The lid is engraved." Edel crouches over my shoulder.

I squint at the tiny script, and read the word *Listen.*

I uncap the perfume atomizer. The sound of a woman's voice echoes through the room. "You only get a single chance to hear this. Pay attention."

"What's that?" Edel asks.

"Shh." I lift the bottle to my ear.

Edel and Rémy huddle closer. My heart trembles. The identity of the speaker crystallizes in my head.

Arabella.

"Camellia and Edelweiss, meet Ryra, my teacup dragon. Please take care of her well. Listen closely. Track the headlines, though we all know they don't tell even a fraction of the story. With Sophia as queen, we cannot trust them to publish the truth unvarnished, but they furnish clues to the storm she's trying to create. There are newsies doing her bidding, spreading the things she wants everyone to believe.

"Sophia has taken all the generations of Belles—Ivy and her sisters, plus yours, Valerie, Padma, Hana, Amber, and the new little ones.

They're in the most complete wing of her new prison, the Everlasting Rose. She's growing new Belles here at the palace. I must feed my blood to two hundred fifty pods, with more to come. Sophia intends to start selling Belles to the highest bidder as soon as these new ones are big enough to do beauty work.

"You must stay as far away as possible until I can figure out the rest of what she's up to. Here's what I need you to do: feed a teacup dragon— *Ryra, if she's rested, or any of yours—one of the sangsues I've sent, which hold my blood. Doing this will tether the dragon to me, so it can find me wherever I am, and we can send messages back and forth. Send word that you're safe. Be careful.*"

The memory of Sophia's threat about building a golden auction block in Trianon or the Royal Square coils around me like the silver chains and jeweled collars she'd use. The ones Madam Claire looped around the throats and wrists of the other Belles at the Chrysanthemum Teahouse.

"Who was that?" Edel asks.

"Arabella," I tell her. "She's an elder Belle. She lives at the palace and helped Rémy, Amber, and me escape."

"What does she mean *growing*? She said something about pods." Edel must have a million questions about how this was possible. "What is she talking about?"

The image of the clear vats in Sophia's palace nursery, the Belle babies floating in gilded cradles, being fed Arabella's blood, takes horrifying shape in my mind. "Belles are different from Gris," I tell her. "We're grown . . . in vessels."

"I don't understand." Edel shakes with rage. "Babies develop in their mothers' wombs."

"Not us. Belle babies are more like flowers in bulbs." The words coming out of my mouth feel thick and laden with lies.

Unbelievable, even though they are the truth. This is not what Du Barry told us about our births. She said that the Goddess of Beauty sent us here in a rain of stars to be her vessels. But I've seen it with my own eyes.

I shake the bottle, waiting and wishing there was more.

"We have to go to the palace," Edel says.

"Arabella told us not to."

"So? Who put her in charge?" Edel presses. "We need to break our sisters out of prison and end this."

It's not lost on me that she had no interest in this line of thought when it was only Amber who'd been captured.

"Let's send her a message saying we're safe, as she asks, and tell her of our plan to find Charlotte. Based on my maps, I believe her to be—"

"We can't *only* chase Charlotte. She could be a spirit for all we know. Sophia's setting up a grand reveal of her body. What if she's actually dead? What if this plan of yours is doomed?"

"What if she isn't? Arabella would know if this was one of Sophia's lies. We can ask her."

"And how long will that take? Waiting around for another three days for a reply?" Edel says. "Sending messages and charting winds isn't getting us anywhere." She throws her hands in the air. "It's taking more time that we don't have. The closer we get to the Coronation and Ascension, the less opportunity to challenge Sophia. She's rushing a ceremony that should take months of planning. Tradition and rules will allow her to—"

"We can't just storm into the palace, Edel. We have to have a precise plan. Every move of it certain and calculated. I want to take Sophia down as much as you do. Maybe even more so. I want to get our sisters. But we can't afford to make any mistakes." I pull out the night-edition newspaper clipping to show Edel the head-line about the Fashion Minister. I feel the heat of Rémy's gaze, but don't look at him. "I have an idea. I want to go—"

"No!" Edel strides angrily between us. Her dress, now tattered at the bottom, catches the splinters in the wooden planks. Her anger is loose like the snap of a newsreel spinning out of control. "While you two are playing with compasses and writing letters, I'm going to do something about it."

Rémy clears his throat. "Edel, if you would simply—"

"Don't tell me what to do. Go back to staring at Camille and watching for guards!" she barks.

He flinches.

"That's unfair and rude," I say, reaching for her.

She snatches away and stalks to the door.

"Wait! Edel!" I shout. "What are you going to do?"

"Not sit around and wait for a pretty post-balloon."

She stomps out and doesn't look back.

7

Rémy and I walk through the crowded stalls near the salon in search of a vendor who sells invisible post-balloons. Two of the teacup dragons—Fantôme and Poivre—squirm in my waist-sash, attempting to peek their heads out and sniff the air; the scent of roasting meat and mulled cider mingle in this section of the Market Quartier.

"Are they still restless?" Rémy asks.

I lift my mask a little to answer him. "Yes. It's probably because I fed Fantôme the leech Arabella sent. She and Poivre seem close. Connected. They affect each other."

"Like you and Amber?"

I shrug, thinking of what might be happening to her right now. If she's all right. If she's surviving Sophia's torture. If she will ever forgive me for not coming to her rescue.

"Your mask is loose," he says, reaching around the back of my head to tighten the top ribbons. "I saw a headline about how they're going to ban these soon, force people to take them off, and check identification marks."

His fingers flick my hair, and it sends a rush along my scalp.

"Then I should change your skin color and facial features."

He scowls as he ties the bottom ribbon. "Maybe. Soon. I am getting tired of the mask. Too hot."

"But you need to protect your makeup and make sure you don't get caught in the scandal sheets without maintaining your beauty."

A small chuckle escapes his mouth.

"Also, I'm sorry about what Edel said."

"It's not your fault."

"But it is. She's taking out her frustrations with me on you. She's just..."

"A lot."

"Always has been."

He finishes knotting the ribbon and shifts back to my side. "You know that I don't stare at you. I'm not—"

"I know." My cheeks heat up beneath my mask. I want to tell him that I look at him, too. That I love it when he looks at me, his eyes carrying an energy I don't fully comprehend, one I'm not sure I want to, one I enjoy. "Let's get these post-balloons and hurry back so I can deal with her."

He turns into a narrow alley. "What's your concern with Arabella?"

"It's complicated."

"So, tell me what you're thinking. It might help you work through it."

I shoot him a skeptical look.

"Truly. It's something I used to do with my closest friend at the academy. We'd discuss our plans when the Minister of War would give us challenges. Sometimes, it helped me see ways forward that I hadn't before."

Snow begins to fall. Delicate white flakes crest the market lanterns with tiny coats and collect on windowsills and inside garden boxes full of cold-season flowers.

"That was definitely Arabella's voice, but I need to know if she sent it on her own or if it's one of Sophia's sick games. Arabella could've been threatened—forced to say what she said."

Rémy nods. "Smart."

"Indeed, I am," I spit back.

"No one is questioning that. Least of all me."

"Edel is. She doesn't agree with my plans."

"I get the sense that she wouldn't agree with anyone's plans." I let out a laugh.

"Where do you think she went?" Rémy asks.

"Wherever it is, I hope she doesn't get herself caught." The worry of losing another sister sits like a limestone brick in my stomach.

"It doesn't matter what she thinks. Or even what I think. I always trust my instincts. Soldiers are trained that way. And if you need to have the information verified, then we'll do it. But invisible post-balloons aren't perfect and can often be intercepted." He points at a shop called Ombre and a window sign boasting the best invisible post-balloons for sale.

"But it's all we have. Hopefully, Fantôme will deliver it safely and bring back a reply."

The shop looks nearly desolate—only a worktable littered with post-balloon wire nets, ribbons, parchment, a series of empty shelves, and a single dusk-lantern whizzing around a beautiful woman.

"There's nothing here," I say to Rémy.

"Ah, don't be so hasty," the woman replies, popping up from a high-backed chair. Half her head is shaved close to her scalp, but on the other side, her hair falls over her shoulder like a river of fire. Her smile is crooked in the best way possible, intentional and making her look clever, and her skin is a soft shade of beige—like honey and caramel swirled together in steaming milk.

"Wait here," Rémy whispers, leaving me at the shop door.

I turn my back to the shop, pretending to watch skittish people who don't want to be spotted in this part of the city move through the narrow market alleys.

"Come in. Don't be afraid," she says to Rémy, almost purring. "Our post-balloons are the best. We truly have the highest success rate."

I steal glances over my shoulder at the woman. Her eyes are filled with light and excitement as she takes Rémy in, a smile curving across her lips.

Rémy steps inside the shop and jumps as if he's been touched.

The proprietor chuckles. "Be careful, the post-balloons are everywhere. I should've warned you, handsome," she says. "So, how can I help you? What exactly are you looking for? With some blessing from the God of Luck himself, it'll be a wife."

Rémy's shoulders stiffen and he clears his throat. "I don't see any post-balloons for sale."

"I can't hear you very well. Mind removing your mask? Or does your makeup need protecting at this hour?"

My panicked thoughts trip over one another.

He flips up the bottom of it. "I'm ill and contagious."

She leans back. "Oh."

A smile tugs at the corner of my mouth.

"Where are your post-balloons for sale? Since you say you have the best," he says.

"You felt them when you first walked in. Let me show you." She unhooks the tail ribbons of her dusk-lantern, drags it forward, and closes the shop's drapes.

I yank the curtains back open.

She eyes me. "Can I help you?"

"She's with me," Rémy blurts out.

"Well, then, come in. You're messing up my show." Her eyes flicker over me, assessing every inch of my body, tallying and deciding if I might be beautiful under my layered winter dress and cloak and mask. I've watched the women do this at court.

Seemingly unimpressed, she turns back to Remy. "Watch."

As the dusk-lantern circles the woman, it reveals the outlines of dozens of post-balloons.

I gasp.

Rémy tries to catch one, but it disappears again.

"Impressed?" she says.

He huffs. "How much?"

"By the looks of you, I'd say you have leas to spend. But maybe if you let me see your face or throw in a kiss, I'll give you a discount." She sidles closer to him.

An unfamiliar feeling crops up inside me. My fists ball and my feet itch to wedge myself between them. *Does he think she's beautiful? Does he like the look she's chosen for herself? Is this how people interact with each other outside of court?*

Those questions grate across my skin. She winks at him, and he smiles.

"Are you all done?" I ask, and Rémy's mouth resumes its usual frown.

The woman's eyes are fixed on Rémy. "We've just started negotiations. And he looks like he's a wealthy guy."

"Looks can be deceiving," he replies.

"Oh yes, in this world." She clucks her tongue. "Forty-two leas for one."

"I'll give you seventy-five for two," he replies.

Her eyebrows lift with surprise, and she licks her lips. "You're very clever." She runs a painted fingernail over his jacket lapel.

He steps back. "Flattery will get you nowhere with me. Seventy-seven," he replies. "Final offer."

"Offers are never final unless you're dead," she quips.

He fusses with the leas in his pocket, then glances over at me, catching my grimace. Our eyes meet. I turn away, pretending to stare out at the bustling crowd.

"Seventy-eight," I hear Rémy say.

"If you buy five, I'll give them to you for one ninety."

"I'll give you three hundred fifty leas for ten."

"Done. And only because I feel like you might be handsome under that mask, and I'm a sucker for pretty men," she replies. "Have you ever bought one of these before?"

"No," he replies.

"Let me show you how it works. If you don't follow directions, you are at risk of your messages being intercepted, so pay attention."

He takes a tentative step forward. She bats her big green eyes at him. "The secret to an invisible post-balloon is the reactive parchment. Light a candle and wait for the parchment to awaken. You'll be able to see its edges for thirty beats. Enough to run your fingers along its curves." She runs her hand across his. He doesn't move. "You already look like you're good with your hands, so this shouldn't be a problem."

I make a noise, and he flinches.

"To put your note into the back, open this flap. See here?" She leans closer to him, and I swear she sniffs him.

My stomach flips, a riot of new emotions battling within it. "We know how to light post-balloons," I grumble loud enough to be heard.

She pauses, and her heavy gaze lingers on me.

"Then, handsome, light this charcoal candle. The special oil allows it to smolder slowly and give the post-balloon enough air and energy to reach its destination, but without the brightness of a regular post-balloon candle. Add two if it's going beyond the imperial island." She hands him the parcel, but doesn't let go when he takes it. "You were such a delight to talk to, despite your guard over there." She nods in my direction. "I rarely get such interesting customers."

"Thank you," he says, tugging it out of her hands.

"No, thank *you*." She laughs. "I don't mean to be so forward, but are you married? I'm in need of a husband."

"Yes," I blurt out. A sharp warmth crawls up my chest, and my heart pounds against my rib cage. "Why else do you think I'm here?"

He glances at me, surprised. Not that I blame him. I'm shocked by what I've just said. But then Rémy jauntily opens the door for me. "Let's go, Mrs. Chevalier."

"Mrs. Chevalier?" I stammer out, my words in a tangle.

"It's tradition for one of us to take the other's last name. I guess I could be Mr. Beauregard. But everyone is looking for you. So, my name would probably be best."

I chuckle. "They're looking for you, too."

We both laugh, then get quiet.

"Were you upset?" he asks, and I can feel the smile behind his mask.

"Uh, no . . . that's not the right word. I was—"

"Jealous?"

I laugh. "No," I lie. "She was strange."

"She was flirting."

I ease this question out: "Did you like her?"

"What do you mean? Her personality was—"

"No, did you think she was beautiful? Would you have taken her up on her offer? She said she needed a husband."

"Soldiers don't marry. We take one vow—to protect the kingdom."

"And nothing else?"

"Above all else queen and country."

I don't know what I'm really asking. I don't know how to form the question or pluck it from the depths of my heart and give it breath. The silence between us feels loud in contrast to the noise of the Market Quartier.

"I'm still a soldier even though I'm here with you," he adds.

Night-lanterns are lit as the sun sets behind us. News blimps start to fill the sky, their silkscreens and sky candles scattering the first of the evening headlines around.

We turn right and Rémy stops. I crash into him.

He pulls me close to the side of a nearby building. I take a deep breath. My heart trembles. His bottom lip brushes my forehead. He looks down at me. An energy tethers us in place.

Is he going to kiss me? What would that be like?

Those questions simmer in my stomach. His eyes drop to my

lips. I lean forward a little to close the gap. I let the desire and curiosity loose from the place I'd hidden it inside. I admit to myself—*I want him to kiss me.*

"Don't move." His words graze my skin.

The sound of heavy boots clomp behind us. I glance over my shoulder. Guards march up the stairs of the Red Velvet Salon.

Panic and worry weaken my legs. I almost fall forward. His hands grip tight around my waist.

"Edel," I say.

8

We stand in the alley and watch the Red Velvet Salon until our fingernails turn blue and the teacup dragons in my waist-sash can't keep me warm any longer. Rémy's body is stiff behind me.

"What if we go into the card salon across the street? We can keep an eye out for Edel," I say.

"We should go to another part of the city to be safe." His eyes scan every person walking by.

"We can't. What if Edel was taken?"

"We'd know. I've seen no movement in and out of the salon yet."

I feel like I've fallen down several sets of stairs—the air in my chest too thin, my head spinning like a télétrope, and my legs shaking beneath me, threatening to buckle under my weight. "I can't lose another sister."

"You won't." He reaches for my hand, cupping it with his, and tries to warm it. "You're freezing." His brown eyes drift over my face. "Your nose is red as a cherry."

"How are you not cold?" I push my other hand into his grasp. He lifts them to his mouth and blows warm air over them. It streams through my knit gloves, the sensation sending a rush of tingles into my limbs. The energy from before is back, the desire welling up once again.

"The Minister of War trains us in the harshest places, conditioning our bodies to adapt to any circumstance." He turns back to the street. "I guess we could wait inside for a little. They do have private game rooms. But we'd have to spend money we don't really have."

"We must." I shove the leas purse into his hand.

He bunches his scarf around his neck, pulls down his mask, and adjusts mine to cover more of my face.

"Everyone is subject to a check," a guard yells as she harasses as many people as she can. But Rémy and I quickly duck into the Queen of Spades. Maroon house-lanterns drift over plush tabletops ringed by high-backed chairs. Men and women slam down porcelain chips or clutch cards or place bets. Laughter and excitement ripple through the room. Parlor workers push treat carts through the labyrinth of game tables.

"Wait here," Rémy says, then he goes to a speak to a man at a nearby desk. He returns with a skeleton key. "A room for a few hours, and with a view of the street."

"How'd you pull that off?" I ask.

"Told him we were just married," he says. I fight the smile erupting across my lips. "Well, you put the thought in my head!" he adds.

We scurry up a set of stairs and into a long hallway. It forms a balcony that overlooks the main room. There are a few potted plants sitting along the railing, and I crouch down and peek between them, to ensure no one followed us. Slanting shafts of lantern light dance across the ground.

Rémy opens the door. Large square windows look out onto the street. A four-poster bed swallows most of the room. At its foot sits a pair of matching armchairs and a card table with a plush red top.

He watches the movement along the street, then draws the curtain and ties a night-lantern to a nearby hook. "We have to leave the Spice Isles tonight. I'm adept at hiding, but they seem to anticipate my every move."

"We're going to the Silk Isles," I declare.

Rémy turns to look at me. "Is that where you think Charlotte is?"

"No." I reach into my pocket, giving the poison bottle a comforting squeeze, and I retrieve a crumpled newspaper segment instead. "We need to see him." I unfold the scrap to reveal the face of the Fashion Minister. "In order to find Charlotte, we need money. Gustave will help."

"Can you trust him?"

"Yes." The comfort of that truth brings back memories of him helping me as favorite: the little jokes, the advice he'd given me, the secret warnings about Sophia. I have to believe he'll be on our side. He knows what the queen truly is. "First, I need to send a letter to Arabella. I'll make sure Sophia didn't force her to send that message, and once I'm satisfied of that, I'll tell her of our plan to locate Charlotte. She might know in which direction the princess sailed the night we escaped." I release Fantôme and Poivre from my waist-sash. They fly about the room, their scales twinkling like snow and fire in the dim light.

I scribble across the page:

Arabella,

Two things:

What do I carry of yours?

How did your teacup dragon find us? We're not in the place where you told me to go.

Love,

Camille

"Fantôme," I say.

The tiny dragon flies over to me.

"Good girl."

"The training has worked," Rémy comments. "She didn't even need an incentive to come. That's a good sign."

"She's ready."

She has to be.

"Do you have your knife?" I sweep Fantôme into my arms and sit on the edge of the bed.

"Always. Why?"

"I don't have our sangsues, so I need blood."

He furrows his brow. "Maybe we should wait until—"

"No." I roll up the parchment. "The night air-postmen will be leaving the sky to obey the curfew, so this is my chance to send her out without being detected. The skies will be empty."

"Maybe that's the biggest danger. Maybe we should wait to send, so that there's too many things to watch. In a sky full of birds, it's harder to find a certain one."

"We don't have a choice."

Rémy leaves his post at the window and eases down beside me on the bed. His body radiates like a star caught in a jar. The question eases back between us, that energy hissing and crackling like the fire in the room's hearth as each moment passes.

"Cut my thumb," I order.

He removes a knife from his pocket, the sheath white as porcelain. "Do you think—"

I cup my hand over his mouth. The softness of his lips sends a flutter through me. "Do it."

He nods.

I take my hand down and turn it palm up. Fantôme perches on my knee, watching.

His hands quiver.

I purse my lips, trying to mask a smile.

"You nervous?"

He grunts a response, then presses the blade into the pad of my thumb. I bite my bottom lip as the silver ridge pierces the flesh and the blood rises to meet it. The sting and throb of it rush in as a red stream trickles down my hand.

"I've cut too deep." Rémy cradles my wrist and frowns.

"It'll heal fast. I promise," I say through a grimace. "Come closer, Fantôme."

The white teacup dragon trundles across the folds of my dress, then leans down to sniff the wound with her hot nose.

"Go on," I urge her.

She licks the blood from my hand until the cut seals itself shut, my arcana proteins stitching me back together without hesitation.

"And you're *sure* she'll go to Arabella?" Rémy asks.

"They're instinctual. They'll find the person whose blood they've ingested first, then return to me once that's passed. I fed her one of Arabella's leeches earlier."

"And you trust it?" His eyes hold doubt.

"I have to. I have to trust her."

He runs his dark brown fingers across her scales, and she nuzzles and licks his hand.

"Can you prepare the invisible post-balloon since that woman gave you such *specific* instructions?" I look away from his penetrating gaze.

He stands and unpacks the parcel on the small side table. "She told us both," he says with his back turned.

"She only wanted to talk to you. She *liked* you."

His shoulders tense.

I bite my bottom lip, regretting saying that as the silence thickens around us.

"I didn't like her," he replies.

It makes me wonder if he could like me.

"You ready?" He turns back around.

I hand him the letter. He slides a charcoal candle inside the post-balloon. It flares briefly as it fills with air, floats up like a tiny cloud, then disappears.

I wave a hand and graze its invisible form, then run my fingers down its base to discover its translucent ribbons. Once I have a grip on the balloon, I grab the night-lantern from the wall hook and hand it to Rémy, who holds it over me and Fantôme, so I can see where to tie the ribbons along the teacup dragon's neck.

Rémy opens the window.

I set the dragon on the iron railing. "Little Fantôme, go straight to Arabella, then come to me in the Silk Isles." I kiss her nose and inch her off the perch. "Be careful."

My heart squeezes as I watch her disappear in the thick snowy clouds.

9

The street outside the Queen of Spades empties as the kingdom-wide curfew sets in. We have watched out the window for Edel all afternoon. Guards disperse in all directions, their coats shining beneath the night-lanterns like beetle shells. The laughter in the game rooms grows louder, pushing through the thin walls of our room.

Rémy closes the window drapes. "We can go back now, check on Edel and the dragons, and pack to leave for the Silk Isles. Then I'll go to the docks and see if they're still scheduling the midnight ships. Many people are already making their way to the imperial island for the Coronation and Ascension. They've allowed a certain number of ships to continue to sail despite the curfew."

I nod and tuck Poivre into my waist-sash despite his protests, and pack the remaining invisible post-balloons. We dash across the street and into the salon. The house is a chaos of flipped-over furniture, shattered teacups, and crushed lanterns. Mud stains crisscross the plush carpets. The women cry as they clean, attempting to put everything back together again.

Rémy and I try to remain calm as we walk upstairs.

I slowly open the door. My heart thuds. I hold my breath and clench my body, bracing for the worst possible outcome.

"Edel..." I say in a whisper.

She is on her knees lifting the bedskirts.

I dart over to her and hug her as tight as I can.

"All right...all right," she complains.

"What happened?" I ask.

"I'll tell you when you stop choking me. But first, help me get the four dragons from under the bed."

I crouch down and spot the rest of the teacup dragons curled up, shivering in fear. I release Poivre from my waist-sash.

"Come out from under there," I call out. "All is well now."

They bat their eyes, then shuffle forward, stretching out their wings. Edel sighs with exhaustion. She plops herself in the nearest chair.

"Tell me," I say.

"I used a glamour to throw the guards off," Edel says.

"A glamour?" Rémy replies with confusion.

Edel grins like a cat who's just caught a fish. Her hair changes from pale blond to cherry red, the straight strands twisting around each other in a storm as they turn into a mess of corkscrew curls.

Rémy stumbles backward, knocking into a chair. "How... what..." he stammers out.

Edel curtsies and her hair returns to its previous color and texture.

He turns to me. "Can you do that?"

"Barely," I answer.

"Is it dangerous?" Rémy asks.

"I haven't experienced any issues so far," Edel says.

"It doesn't mean there won't be," he says.

Edel levels him with a glare.

"Where did you go earlier?" I ask.

"I went to check on the Spice Teahouse."

"What? Why would you do that?" I almost yell, anger slipping into every syllable.

"All the teahouses are closed." Rémy strides to the table and holds up one of the afternoon papers. The headlines of the *National* and the *Orléans Globe* scramble as he shakes it.

SPICE ISLES TEAHOUSE CLOSED UNTIL FURTHER NOTICE

TRAVEL VOUCHERS TO THE IMPERIAL ISLAND
FOR BEAUTY MAINTENANCE—COLLECT YOURS;
ALL METAIRIE RESIDENTS ELIGIBLE

"Yes, Rémy, thank you for pointing out the obvious as always." She drapes her travel cloak around her shoulders.

"Edel, they will assume we'll try to go to the teahouses to find our sisters," I say, trying to keep my voice low. "That was the most dangerous thing you could have done!"

Edel's eyes flash. "You want to find Charlotte, right? And I want to get to the palace. Moving around requires money. Amber squandered much of ours. I thought if I scoped out the teahouse, we could break in and take some of the Belle-products to sell. People are desperate to hide their gray until the teahouses reopen. The items would fetch us leas."

I blink at Edel, surprised. It's actually not the worst plan. If we're to go see the Fashion Minister, we'll need to pay for tickets on the midnight ship to the Silk Isles, which will deplete what we have left, and I couldn't bear to sell one of the teacup dragons, not even Arabella's Ryra, who has folded into the pack.

"Plus, we need more sangsues to hold glamours. Ours have become weak from overuse."

"I actually—"

"I'm not going to argue about this with you," Edel interjects. "It's a good idea."

"If you'd let me finish, I was going to say that I agree with you. We need money for food, and also to buy tickets to the Bay of Silk."

"Why are we going there?"

I hand her the crumpled picture of the Fashion Minister. The headline is no longer animated, the ink trapped in the wrinkles. "We're going to go see him and ask for help."

"Oh no..."

"Yes. He will help us. I know he will. And he's one of the most well-connected men in Orléans. He must have some idea about where Charlotte might be. We can trust him."

"We can't trust anyone." She shoves the balled-up scrap of newsprint back into my hand.

"He was good to me while at the palace," I tell her. "He warned me about Sophia."

"No one in her cabinet is our friend."

"We have to try."

I start to pull off my scarf and coat.

"Don't," Edel says. "We're heading out now."

"We shouldn't risk it," Rémy adds. "There are more guards here than I anticipated. I never thought they'd be able to deploy so many and so quickly."

"In fact, you'd better get a second scarf, I can feel more snow coming," she tells me, ignoring his warning.

Rémy gazes at her, exasperated. "You think it won't be suspicious if the two of you march over there so close to curfew? You think you won't be seen? You think they're not monitoring the teahouses at all? It's possible someone spotted you earlier and they've sent a whole platoon there to lie in wait for you to come back. This is a reckless errand."

"Didn't you see my trick? We can appear how*ever* we want to," Edel says. "Are you coming? Or do you want to go fetch our tickets on one of the midnight boats while we go do this?"

He sighs and turns to the door.

"Ready?" she asks me.

"I need to practice the glamours more, Edel. I've only done it once," I say. "I'll just wear my mask."

"You're a fast learner, little fox. Always have been." She pats my shoulder and grins. "Masks on, hoods up, and scarves bunched around the base of our faces. Once we get close to the teahouse, we'll change. I don't want to waste a drop of energy on the walk over. I'm still recovering."

She leads the way out of the room. My mind is an unexpected whirlwind of worries with each step we take. What if I can't hold the transformation? What would we do if caught? The poison bottle taps my leg like a swinging pendulum as we hustle down the stairs. It may kill my arcana, it may kill me, but either way, I won't ever do Sophia's bidding again. The reality is a small, terrifying comfort.

The women share meals at long tables in the kitchen. Hunched over bowls of food and caught in heated conversations, no one notices us slink out the back door and into the falling snow. The street is empty aside from early-evening vendors selling warm ale and thick stews, before the curfew sets in.

"The new year is coming. Make it sweet, be sure to build your candy house."

"Best stew! Get it here."

Edel makes sharp turns through Metairie's Market Quartier. Plum market-lanterns fade to dark blue, then lighten to pale pinks as we cross into the aristocratic Rose Quartier of this city. It reminds me of Trianon. Du Barry taught us that every Orléansian city organizes itself similarly to receive blessings from the God of the Ground, who values order, symmetry, and the divine number four.

Ominous news blimps float overhead, their banners bathing us in pockets of gloom. Street-sweepers brush away the fresh snow with long brooms and polish cobblestones so they glisten like pearls under the light. Carriages drop passengers at beautiful mansions that hug a square edged by the Bay of Croix. Ornate river coaches sit at house piers. Newsboats bob in the shallow canals, newsies frantically organizing navy story-balloons and black gossip post-balloons to send out for the night editions or attempting to grab portraits of well-dressed courtiers heading home with their light-boxes.

The Spice Isles' teahouse perches like a glass egg over the quartier. The wind jostles brown-and-red house-lanterns above a door emblazoned with the Belle-symbol. Bronze sill-lanterns sit in dark windows. Royal buildings flank its sides like a jeweled nest made of pearl, marble, and gold. A funicular rail sends empty golden chariots to an entry platform.

"There's no way we're getting up there," I say. "The porter station is closed."

Edel points to a small alley. "We'll use the servant entrance—the stairs. I found them earlier."

Rémy gazes around. "The fewer people out on the street, the more likely we'll be seen."

"You might be spotted since you refuse to let us change your looks," Edel snaps at him. "So maybe *you* should stay down here and wait for us."

"Not happening," Rémy replies. "I'm trained to not be seen, but you two are not."

"We'll be fine," Edel says, then pivots to me. "It's time to change."

My hands quiver. The warnings we received all our lives about our gifts and the way they're supposed to be used pile into a mountain that sits upon my chest.

This is wrong.

This is dangerous.

This will have consequences.

"I don't know if I can," I reply.

"You have to. You have no choice." Edel closes her eyes and takes a deep breath. Her skin darkens from milk white to the color of sand, and her hair knits itself into a long braid—a shiny rope hanging over her shoulder.

"Hurry," Edel says. "I don't want to have to hold this for longer than necessary."

The arcana quiver just beneath my skin. My heart rattles in my chest.

I close my eyes. I try to picture myself, but only darkness greets me. The noises in the square grow louder—newsies dropping the evening papers through mail slots, the light honk of river coaches approaching house piers, a sweet-vendor pushing a cart along the cobblestones, men and women laughing as they return home, the sounds of teacup animals squeaking at their owners.

I tremble with doubt.

A hand slides into mine; a little rough and a little warm but nice.

Rémy's hand.

I take a deep breath. I think of Maman: her soft gaze, the rich red of her hair, and the curve of her cheekbones.

A headache drums in my temples. I feel myself change, my limbs frosting over, my hair straightening and landing on my shoulders, my veins flooding with cold, my skin prickling with gooseflesh, and my legs stretching and lengthening.

Edel jostles my shoulder. "You look just like Maman Linnea. And you're taller. I haven't tried changing my body size and height yet."

My eyes snap open. "I didn't mean to." I drop Rémy's hand and finger my now red hair. I look around for the nearest reflective surface and spot myself in the window of a télétrope shop. My breath catches in my throat.

I touch my face. I am almost her. The pain of wanting my mother back floods my heart, drowning it with sorrow, longing, and anger.

Rémy gawks, his eyes bulging with a mix of curiosity and horror.

"It's still me," I say.

He opens his mouth to comment.

"No time to admire your brilliance." Edel grabs my arm and yanks me forward.

We hustle into the alleyway and climb the winding staircases to the teahouse's side door. Rémy easily breaks the lock like it's nothing more than a clockwork toy, and we tiptoe inside.

The walls burst with violets and turquoises like an anxious sky tumbling into nightfall. The ceilings bloom in pinks and tangerines like a spice box of the gods. Doors inlaid with leaf-shaped jewels dot the long corridor that opens up into a grand foyer. Plush cold-season rugs stretch out beneath our feet, and bronze house-lanterns graze the floor like sunken rocks. It smells of burnt candlewicks and rancid honey and damp wood.

None of my sisters were placed here after our Beauté Carnaval. The Belle from the previous generation, Anise, remained. Dark chandelier-lanterns hold her cameo portrait. The silkscreen flutters and ripples from the draft we let in. I wonder where Anise is now and how many other Belles had been secretly kept here. Were they chained? Were they overworked?

"It looks so different from the Chrysanthemum Teahouse," I whisper.

"They're all unique to the specific islands," Edel says. "The Fire Teahouse always looked like it would burn down any minute with all the oranges and reds and yellows. If this teahouse is set up like the others, the storage rooms are in the back left corner nearest to the servant lifts." She grabs a house-lantern from the floor. Rémy hands her a matchbook before she asks, and she lights the lantern, setting it afloat. Once it gathers enough air, she tugs its tail ribbons forward.

We scramble up the stairs, tearing past treatment rooms, linen closets, and servants' quarters until we locate the glass-walled storage room. Belle-products sit on cushioned shelves and in colorful cabinets ready to be plucked for use: complexion crème-cakes, mineral powders, kohl-ink bottles with jeweled lids, perfume blocks, beads and ointments, rose water, hand pallets, beeswax resins, pomatum boxes, rouge crayons, pumice stones, false brows made from mouse fur, tooth sponges, tinted wool pads, hair powder, and more. The products bear the Belle-emblems. I thumb each one and suddenly feel a swell of homesickness.

"I wonder why no one has broken in here yet," Edel says.

"They will if the teahouses don't reopen. It's only been a few days since the queen died," I say, though it feels like a lifetime.

"Desperation will set in soon," Rémy adds.

"You get the bei-powder bundles and as many skin-paste pots and complexion-crèmes as you can carry for us to sell them, Rémy," Edel orders. "And, Camille, you get the Belle-rose leaves and some soap. I'll search for the sangsues and see if they also have Belle-rose elixir. That's all we really need."

Edel and I dig through drawers and cabinets, filling our dress pockets and satchels with the supplies. My mind unravels a series of memories—the glorious treatment rooms in the palace Belle-apartments, making women and men and children feel beautiful and their best, the clients I loved to work with the most, Queen Celeste trusting me to help Charlotte. Regret grips me. If only I'd healed Charlotte sooner, she might be on the throne right now. We might not be in this mess. Why did I resist for so long?

I hold a skin-paste pot in my hands and think of Bree. I glance out the window overlooking the Bay of Croix. Bodies are bent over like question marks in the fields. Their gray hands pluck leaves and carry baskets. Wide-brimmed fur hats crest their heads and heat-lanterns nip at their backs as they navigate the rows. I wonder how late into the night they are forced to work. I wonder how much their lives mirror ours.

"Camille, focus! Your glamour is wearing off," Edel warns. "Your hair is frizzing."

I move away from the window and try to grasp the image of Maman once more. The cold pain cuts through me as the glamour resettles itself.

A rush of footsteps echoes through the teahouse.

We freeze.

Rémy puts a hand up and motions for us to duck out of view. I press myself flat to the floor.

A lady stalks past the room, seemingly frustrated, her long dress swishing back and forth like a pavilion bell. She's hunched at the shoulders and ghastly white. Her black hair is swept into a bun similar to the one Du Barry always wore, and her mouth is painted so red you'd think her lips were coated with blood.

"The new queen wants this place up and running again," she yells at someone I can't see. "There will be more Belles than ever before. All rooms will be occupied like in the olden days, she said. As if she has any idea what the olden days were really like. As if any of us do. Complete incompetence."

Anxiety thrums through me.

I exchange tense glances with Edel and Rémy. My stomach becomes a storm of nausea. A thin trickle of blood escapes my nose. I grab a handkerchief and wipe it away.

"She's already trying to decide which of the newest generation of Belles will be favored and placed at the teahouses. They're still young girls. I went to have a look at them. They barely know how to do anything with Du Barry gone. But either way, I want top pick, so this place has to be in the best shape. I'm learning our new queen likes to be impressed, and I want to show her that *this* will be the premier teahouse in all of Orléans. Maybe she'll even let me open up a secondary one to complement it. Now is the time to expand the teahouses. It'll allow us to serve more people." The woman's voice trails off and she disappears from view.

"Your glamour is gone," Edel whispers. "You have to focus."

"I can't," I reply. "My nose keeps bleeding."

"Try again," she says.

"We don't have time," Rémy whispers. "We have to go."

"I'll lead the way out," Edel says.

"No, I will," Rémy replies. "I knew this was a bad idea."

Edel scoffs and jams the remaining vials of Belle-rose elixir into her already full dress pockets.

Rémy slips into the hall. I hold my breath until he returns. He waves for us to follow. Night-lanterns coast through the halls now, and the sounds of tinkling glass and running water reverberate within the house.

We navigate the corridors as quick and light as mice. The servant door is propped open and the moonlight is a beacon ahead.

We run.

A man steps out of a nearby room. He wears an imperial guard uniform like the one Rémy used to wear. "Hold it right there! No one is supposed to be in here," he shouts. "Just who are—"

Rémy slams right through him. The impact sends the man flying into a banister, and he passes out from the fall.

"Maybe Rémy's good to have around after all," Edel says.

"Keep going," Rémy shouts.

We tumble down the servant staircase and back outside.

Guards stand in the center of the square. They whip around and march in our direction.

"We have to split up to throw them off. Edel, go back to our room and get the teacup dragons and anything else you can't spare. Camille, go into a shop and wait until they start hollering about the curfew," Rémy says. "Once you see them harassing people about getting home, the chaos will afford you some cover. Then meet me at the docks. Pier seven. Ship doesn't leave until midnight, so we have time."

"But—" Edel argues.

"Listen to him," I snap.

Edel's mouth drops open to protest, but she nods.

Rémy squeezes my arm before ducking into the alley. Edel bolts in the opposite direction. I glance around. Many shopkeepers blow out their window-lanterns and close for the night. A chilling panic fills me as I search for somewhere to hide.

I turn to run for the Market Quartier, but guards swarm in as if from nowhere and block my path.

I'm trapped.

10

I mop the sweat from my brow and try to will my heart to slow down. I take a deep breath and pretend to be an aristocratic lady out shopping past curfew.

"Shops are closing. Start making your way home," a guard barks into a voice-trumpet. "Only those with curfew passes can remain out."

I've lost my glamour. I fumble with tying my mask. The guards call out behind me, but I don't stop or change my pace. The aristocratic women wave off their demands, seemingly unafraid. I try to mimic them and fill my motions with their confidence. I fold into a small crowd of people in line at a sweets pavilion. They complain as I push, accidentally knocking their bourbon pies to the ground.

Fardoux's Teacup Emporium sits in the center of the winding avenue. It's the only shop still alive with light. Gilt-lanterns dangle above the door like shooting stars caught by their tails.

Three WANTED posters stretch across the large glass window: one for Edel, one for Rémy, and one for me.

I turn the doorknob. A bell chimes as I step inside.

It's empty.

The room's crackling hearth sends its warmth through the space. Sunset-pink walls hold shelves full of teacup pets in golden cages. Tiny elephants sport painted chrysanthemums on their sides, little hippos wear red bow ties, small tigers and lions play with their pearl necklaces, miniature monkeys throw pastel balls to one another, and a zebra no bigger than my shoe prances through the shop. We learned that many of these animals used to be massive—oftentimes, the size of carriages or as tall as buildings—but the early queens of Orléans bargained with the God of the Ground for more palatable companions.

I find a mirror and adjust my mask, now battered from over-use, bunch my hair into my hood, and smooth the front of my crumpled dress. My outsides can't reflect the panic of my insides.

"Hoot!" a tiny teacup owl squeaks.

I jump.

The bird waddles across a nearby perch, and its eyes, big as leas coins, follow my every move.

A man pops out from behind a curtain. "Madam, may I take your coat and show you some of our newest pets? We don't have much time before the guards rush in here and remind me it's time to close to obey the nonsense curfew. I've lost so much business because of it, but I'm so happy you've found your way here despite the trouble. I have some excellent arrivals from the imperial island. And ones you can only get here. A sloth to fit in your palm. A panda for your pocket." The shopkeeper slides from behind a counter, grinning with a perfectly waxed mustache that curls into tiny spirals at the end. He's powdered and white like a fresh cream pastry hot from the oven. His waistcoat hugs his chest too tight, forcing his stomach to spill out of the bottom. "A honey bear for your boudoir."

I start to speak.

"Oh, wait. Let me guess. This is my favorite part. Matching teacup pets and owners. And by the looks of you, I think I have the perfect fit. Just in today. One moment."

He disappears into another room, and I'm grateful. Less time having to talk to him and more time to hide inside away from the guards.

I steal glances at the glass door, hoping the guards have cleared out so I can get to the docks, but they seem to be everywhere. In the windows, the backs of the WANTED posters also hold our images. There's no escaping our faces, not for any citizen of Orléans. It's a miracle we've yet to be caught. I squeeze my eyes shut and steady my breaths. I think about sneaking back out on the street before he returns. But the guards thicken in number as they shut down the sweets pavilion and step into nearby shops. In only a few moments, they'll be in here.

"It's a half hourglass past curfew. All must return home." The voice-trumpet warning echoes through the shop.

That's my cue, but there are so many guards on the street I won't be able to leave without being stopped.

The shopkeeper returns with a tiny Belle-rose-red flamingo.

"Thank you, sir, but I don't need a teacup pet."

He frowns. "Then why are you here?"

The stupidity of my statement slaps me in the face. I stutter, searching for a reason. "I need a supply of mice, or better yet, rats.

And alive, please. I have a teacup pet at home already that needs feeding."

"I can't hear you well due to your mask. Will you take it off? I don't suppose your makeup needs protection indoors, and I assure you there are no newsies hiding in here ready to snap a picture."

"I have a terrible and highly contagious illness," I say, remembering what Rémy told the post-balloon merchant.

He arches back and a deep flush colors his white cheeks.

"I just need mice or rats," I repeat. "And then I will leave you in peace."

"How many? I'll have to check my supplies. My little snakes have been eating so many lately."

"A week's supply for a newborn drag—I mean, lion. Yes, my sweet little lion." I cringe. I'm making a mess of Rémy's plan.

"Hmm, teacup lions often prefer pig meat. Mice are full of bones."

"Give me both then." I set leas coins on the counter. The purse is so light, I'm afraid if the Fashion Minister doesn't help us or we can't sell any of the stolen Belle-products, we won't have enough left to buy food.

He stares at me a beat too long, then fishes in his pocket to retrieve a quizzing glass. He scrunches his nose and puts it up to his eye to examine me. "Don't I know you from somewhere? Have you come in my shop before? I never forget a voice."

My stomach binds itself. "Impossible. My husband and I only just arrived today on the queen's tide." Sweat drips down my forehead. My pulse races. "And if you would please, sir, hurry. My pet is ravenous after the long journey."

He grumbles but shuffles into the back.

I glance at the street thinking I should just run out of here while he's gone, but the guards are hustling people in lines to check them.

I hold my breath until he returns with a small cage of sleeping mice and a paper-wrapped parcel.

"Thank you," I say, checking the guard count outside the window again.

"They'll be quiet for a while. I've given them a little lavender-infused cheese." He eyes me again. "You seem *so* familiar to me . . . but I can't place it. My wife would say it's the brandy. The weather has me indulging."

I grab the cage and parcel. I turn toward the door, but he cuts off the path.

"I think I know you." He scratches his beard. "You have the shape and voice of . . ."

"Geneviève Gareau. Yes, I know. The famous opera singer. The princess's—excuse me, I mean, now, the queen's—favorite artist." The word *favorite* almost burns my tongue. The arcana hiss beneath my skin, ready to protect me. My eyes dart all around. "I get that a lot since I, sadly, copy a lot of the most popular beauty looks. I should probably be more creative."

The door snaps open behind the shopkeeper, startling him.

"I've been looking for you all over," Rémy says. He wears a garish hat that covers most of his head and cups his cheeks. "Please excuse my wife, she has a penchant for teacup pets." He slides his arm around my waist. Heat ripples out from his touch. "I can't let you out of my sight, it seems. You'll get us both fined for being out late, and this poor man will get a business infraction for keeping the shop open to cater to your whims."

I scowl at him, and he winks.

The man steps to the side and eyes Rémy with curiosity and suspicion.

"Have you spent our entire fortune and gotten everything you need?"

"Yes." I nod.

"Thank you for taking such good care of her." Rémy does a little bow and opens the shop door.

"Wait!" the shopkeeper yells behind us.

"Hurry up, wife," Rémy says with a sheepish grin.

A smile bursts across my face. He can't see it behind my mask, but I wish he could.

Rémy and I dash out of the shop and into the nearest alley. I suck in a deep breath and hold Maman's image in my head again. The arcana in my veins turn cold and piercing, worse than the gathering wind around us.

He lifts his mask, his eyes comb over my face as if searching for me.

"It's still me."

He shrugs, then peeks out at the street, noting the number of guards.

"Ready?" I say, taking his hand.

He nods.

We lock arms, ease back into the crowd and right past the guards, headed to the pier.

11

The sea looks almost black from the ship's portholes. The dark stretches out like a blanket. We could sail to the end of the God of the Sea's ocean and be in the caves of the dead before we knew any better. Edel and I huddle in our steerage-class seats paid for by three complexion-crèmes we'd stolen from the teahouse. We are desperately trying to hide inside our thick hoods to keep warm. Rémy stands close by, jaw clenched, watching every person who passes.

Edel moans in her sleep, the sea's rough current making her sick. I pull her hair back and stroke her sweaty neck. The five teacup dragons curl in my dress skirts, the heat of them like tiny coals. I wonder how Fantôme is faring, and I miss her presence. Her being so far away kicks up a thousand worries.

I add another pair of leeches beneath Edel's jaw, hoping it'll rebalance her levels and battle the seasickness.

"How long's the trip to the Silk Isles? I should get her something," I whisper to Rémy.

"It's the second port stop. Carondelet is about two more hour-glasses," he says. "We'll arrive as the sun rises."

I stand up, steadying myself against the low slanted ceiling.

"I'm coming with you," he replies.

"We can't leave her alone."

Edel swats at me, only semi-awake. "Go. I'll...be...fine...."

Rémy and I walk slowly through the narrow aisles, trying to hold ourselves straight as the ship rocks like a cradle caught on a stormy current. Cold air blasts me as we reach the top deck. I lift my mask, welcoming the air beneath its lace and velvet threads. It has kept me safe up until now, but it's starting to suffocate me. The deck spreads out long and flat. Carriage-shaped cabins sit in rows like jeweled plums along a center promenade. Rich courtiers sleep in comfortable beds or peer out of windows through eye-scopes at the ocean expanse or the stars above.

A midnight sky looms over us, full of warning and promise.

"Fresh barley water for seasickness," a vendor calls out.

"Sailor cakes straight from the hearth. Red bean, pork, and saltfish," another offers.

I buy a cup of barley water for Edel. The purse of leas given to us by Arabella is about empty. Twenty coins left. We'll run out of money by tomorrow. The Fashion Minister has to help us. We need a cushion. We can't only rely on the hope of selling more Belle products.

Very few people walk along the ship's promenade. We find a corner to stand in.

"Look," Rémy points out. "You can see the lantern-houses along the coast."

The tiny pinpricks of light glow like trapped stars in the distance.

"It's beautiful," he says.

"Nothing is beautiful anymore."

"She wins if you let her take everything. Even momentary happiness."

"I don't think I'll ever be happy again. I don't know if I want to be now that I know all these things." I shiver as a gust of wind hits us.

He steps closer. Warmth radiates from him like a heat-lantern. "There are people in this kingdom who have had to live with worse."

I scoff.

He leans closer; his voice drops an octave. "I'm not trying to be an ass, but think about what you read in the *Spider's Web*. Many have dealt with the ugliness of this world for a long time."

"You don't understand." A flare of anger erupts inside me.

"I will probably never fully understand, but I'm seeing new things, too. Parts of this kingdom that I never knew existed. I didn't know what life was really like for you, for Belles. They taught us you were here to serve—like us—but always made it seem like you weren't real. You were poppets and dolls to be used—not people. That we weren't the same."

I squeeze the nearest railing. The cold presses through my gloves.

"There are so many lies," he says.

I don't want to talk to him about this anymore. The teacup dragons stir in my pouch. "Maybe we should go back down to Edel. They seem cold," I say, trying to still the movements, but they clamber out of the pouch.

Rémy helps me secure them; gently tucking their small heads back into the waist-sash. The feel of his strong hands makes me want to lean into him, want to kiss him, want to erase all the worries and responsibilities—only for a moment.

His eyes find mine, the connection a thread thickening between us.

The dragons squirm again. I break eye contact and glance down. "No flying right now," I whisper hard.

Rémy tries to block me from the view of others on the ship's promenade.

Poivre wrestles from my grip and bolts over my head.

"Oh no," I say, trying to wave him back.

Rémy points up. "But look who it is."

Fantôme circles one of the ship's bows like a tiny cloud lost from the sky. Poivre chases her, a burst of red flame.

I whistle. Fantôme soars down to me and licks my face with her hot tongue. "Good girl. I've missed you, petite." A silver ribbon is tied around her neck like it's a bow and she's the present.

Rémy catches Poivre and slips him back into my waist-sash. He squeaks, and a hiccup of fire escapes his mouth, catching Rémy's finger. Rémy curses at him.

I attempt—unsuccessfully—to hold in a laugh.

Rémy's scowl melts into a grin.

I undo the ribbon around Fantôme's neck, and she dives into my waist-sash, reuniting with the rest of the teacup dragons, and the new one, Ryra. They nuzzle each other with recognition and start to tussle playfully.

I use some of Edel's barley water and sprinkle the post-balloon, so it's easier to see.

I rip open the back of it and fish out a note, a pair of half-dead sangsues, and a book.

A Belle-book.

It's inscribed with arabella flowers.

I hand it to Rémy, then fumble with the scrolled note, struggling to open it.

He reads over my shoulder.

Camille and Edel,

I understand why you needed a confirmation.

The answer to your questions:

1. My miroir métaphysique.

2. I fed one of your old sangsues to Ryra.

Watch the headlines in the morning. The early bird newsies will break the story that Sophia has taken Padma, Valerie, Hana, and Amber to her prison. But they aren't there. She brought them to the Royal Infirmary at the palace for a medical examination, but they were only here for five hourglasses' worth of time before she had them scattered all over Orléans again, reopening the teahouses secretly. Valerie is in the Silk Isles, Padma is at Maison Rouge, Hana in the Fire Isles, and Amber is in the Glass Isles. I don't know how long they'll stay there. Or if she'll continue to move them around like chess pieces.

She's creating a cat-and-mouse game to lead you into the trap. The longer you run, the more she believes the kingdom will turn in her favor. She envisions you arriving at the palace, trying to break into the Everlasting Rose, only to find your sisters are not there. She plans to record the incident and distribute the newsreels kingdom-wide, thinking this embarrassment will break you and the momentum you've gathered.

She's moving at a fevered pace—using my blood to create new Belles more quickly. But there's only so much that she can use on a daily basis without nearly killing me, and that will never be an option for her. I am the aether. One Belle in every generation has the strongest blood—additional

proteins that allow for her to help grow the next generation. Du Barry
called us the everlasting roses.

Camille, this is what I tried to tell you when I last saw you, but there
wasn't enough time. You are your generation's aether. This is why Sophia
has put a higher price on your head. She wants to use you, the way she's
using me. She even intends to combine our blood, to see what that yields
her. She thinks the strongest Belle ever made. The guards will not kill
you if they capture you. She needs us to populate her garden because
ultimately she wants to find a way to sell many of the Belles in Trianon
Square and will bleed us dry to do so. I keep hearing her say, "One for
every household."

I've sent along my Belle-book with more details on the matter. Com-
mit it all to memory, then burn the book. No one other than Belles must
ever know all the inner workings. This information cannot fall into the
wrong hands.

You need to bring your sisters together, but be careful, Sophia has
spies everywhere. More when I can.

—A.

I press the paper to my chest, the weight of her words holding
my breath inside.

"What do you want to do?" Rémy asks.

The ship jerks. A baby pram being pushed by a woman crashes
onto its side. Rémy races over to help her turn it upright and rescue
the baby from the ground. The baby cries, the pitch of it searing
through me, then blossoming an idea.

I tuck my hand into my pocket where the poison bottle always
sits like a dangerous treasure. What if Belle babies could be born
without their arcana? What if they could be healthy—and Sophia
unable to use them?

I think of Valerie. She worked in the Belle-nursery, raising the new Belles with the nurses. She knows how we're born, how we develop. If those Belle babies are born without their arcana, maybe they can be healthy and like everyone else, and will be unable to be used and sold.

Valerie might know exactly how to stop that part of Sophia's plan. We could work together to determine how to use the precise amount of this poison in the right way to kill arcana—how to save those Belle babies from this fate.

I read the letter again. It doesn't feel real. Hate simmers inside me, sharp, hot, and prickling. Arabella's words are tinder for the fire inside me.

12

"Last port ahead." A bell rings and a man stalks through the ship's underbelly. "Half an hourglass until docking."

Edel yawns and stretches out her arms. The teacup dragons hiccup and startle with annoyance.

"Get up," I whisper to her. "We need to talk."

She's sluggish.

"How do you feel?" I ask.

"I'll be better when we get on land," she mutters.

"Arabella sent a message."

"Why didn't you wake me?"

"No time to argue." I hand her Arabella's letter.

She unfurls the paper. Her eyes grow bigger and bigger as she reads, the words soaking in. She whispers the words *aether* and *sold* and *everlasting rose*. "How can any of this be true?"

"It's all in her Belle-book." I show her the cover. "She's put in clippings from old Belle-manuals and detailed everything."

She runs her fingers over the book, their white tips purpled with cold.

"While we're here, I want to get Valerie, too. I need her help," I say.

"I don't understand *any* of this," she says.

"I don't know all the details, but Valerie must. Once we find her, she can explain."

"Carondelet! Prepare to disembark."

Outside the circular windows, the sun spills buttery-orange rays across the water, lightening the dark waves to blue.

I refasten the ribbon leashes around the teacup dragons' necks and feed them tiny squares of salted pork. Ryra sits atop my hood. Happy and full, the others climb onto my shoulders, hooking their talons into my traveling cloak. I adjust the royal emblem Arabella gave me back at the palace—a dragon with a chrysanthemum hooked around its tail—that announces me as a favored reptilian merchant to the queen.

"Ready?" Rémy asks, taking a deep breath and putting on his mask.

"I have to be." I gaze around, wondering if others will put on masks, if that's the fashion here. "Should we wear these? Or will they attract more attention?"

"I don't have a choice," he says.

"If you would let me change you—"

"We don't have time to argue," he replies as the crowd moves forward.

I look at Edel. Her cheeks are clammy with the sheen of seasickness. "Can you hold a glamour until we find out if masks are popular here?"

"I think so," she grumbles.

We hold hands, close our eyes, and call our arcana. My skin goes cold, the frost-laced wind now inside us as well as outside. Edel makes herself look like Du Barry—dark hair and a round face and beautiful full figure. I think of Maman again, assuming her outer appearance, but with deep black skin.

Rémy gawks like he did the first time I used a glamour.

"It's still me," I whisper.

"I know," he claims, though his eyes say otherwise. "I'm just getting used to it is all."

We walk onto the deck. Rich courtiers crowd the front with their servants at their sides toting children and boxes stacked like pastel patisserie treats.

"I wonder if there'll be more guards in Carondelet than Metairie," a wealthy woman says while adjusting her large hair-tower. A sleeping teacup koala shifts higher into her strands, snuggling in to avoid the growing wind.

"The whole world is under arrest right now," her companion responds.

"It's time for things to return to order. I can't last much longer without my beauty treatments. They're going to be opening more asylums than teahouses if our new queen doesn't get this all sorted soon," another adds.

"She's made a lot of promises."

"That's what children do."

"You shouldn't talk about Her Majesty like that," someone barks.

"One must figure out the Belle situation," a voice calls out.

I stiffen. Rémy's hand finds my waist. I hear Edel take a deep breath.

"I'm tired of all the Belles fuss. I'm ready for things to go back to the way they've always been."

A nearby woman shouts, "The Belles cater to one class. What about the rest of us who can't afford weekly or even monthly treatments?"

The woman with the hair-tower gasps, then cranes, looking for the speaker in the small crowd.

"They'll have to bring in more to meet the demand. It'll solve all this mess," a man in a top hat replies, triumphantly. "Like télétrope sales. When they're up, make more."

"Oh, hush up," a woman beside him says.

"Or we could get rid of all of them."

"Yeah, what about finding another way?"

"All of this talk is upsetting my teacup sloth," someone shouts.

A loud bell rings, stamping out the conversation.

A charged energy ripples over all of us. Rémy, Edel, and I make eye contact.

"Line up to disembark. Keep the queue tidy," a man directs. "No pushing."

The islands appear in the distance as the ship enters the Bay of Silk. Buildings boast sea-blue domes trimmed with a rose gold that glitters as the sunrise hits it. Swaths of land are covered in huge spiraled silkworm cocoons and orchards of mulberry trees. Men and women climb ladders to reach the stacked towers, armed with silk collection baskets.

Edel whispers, "Wow."

City-lanterns drift about like fallen stars, illuminating all of Carondelet's wonders—deep canals cut through the quartiers grasping ornate watercoaches that sit on the blue like glittering jewels expelled by the God of the Sea. Advertising banners flutter behind vendor boats as they stop at piers and hustle their ornate wares to customers. A kaleidoscope of shops stretch as far as I can see.

It's one thing to be in the lesson rooms at Maison Rouge standing before Du Barry's massive tapestry map of Orléans and another to actually see it for yourself. The world is vaster and more beautiful than she ever described. Each corner of it feels different and unique, part of a puzzle with disparate pieces that somehow fit together.

The ship docks. Newsies swarm the pier with the morning papers. Others hold poles displaying silkscreen banners of the Fashion Minister, Gustave du Polignac. We disembark.

"Early papers available!"

"Get the *Silk Post* here!"

"*Daily Orléansian* over this way!"

"*Sucré* and the *Beauty Tribune* fresh off the presses."

The sight of the Fashion Minister's face sends a temporary surge of relief into my bones. The silkscreens shift through images—his full lips break into a smile that lifts his freckled brown cheeks into a stoic and regal grimace. I almost lose hold of my glamour.

"Queen Sophia's new vivant dress line debuts today in preparation for the Coronation and Ascension. Come for a preview this afternoon with the Fashion Minister himself at the Silk Hall in Carondelet's square," a newsie hollers. "Look your best for our new queen."

"I've seen samples of the dresses. They'll sell out quickly. Place your orders early," another newsie shouts. "You don't want to be left behind."

"Doors open at noon on the dot," a third reminds. "Lines already forming along the mile."

"Let's go get Valerie," Edel says, marching ahead.

"Wait! Didn't you hear? People are already lining up to get in to see the Fashion Minister," I say. "We should see him first."

"We have two hours. That's too long to hold a glamour, especially after being sick. And we can't go in there with these tattered masks. We'll look out of place."

"But what if we don't get in, and they close the doors?" I protest.

"They want money. That won't happen," she replies, turning to Rémy. "What do you think?"

"You care?" he asks.

"No, but she does, so break the tie."

He sighs. "I think we should go assess the teahouse, see how many guards are stationed there and how we might get in."

I cross my arms over my chest. "Fine."

Edel pats Rémy's shoulder and he tenses. "We agree on something," she says and leads us to the line to board a small city boat.

"The teahouse will be near the square," Rémy whispers as we wait to board. "Nearest to the aristocratic Rose Quartier and the city's Imperial Mile." He points at the narrow canal to another prominent island. "All the cities are set up the same way."

"Silk Teahouse, please," Edel tells the watercoach driver.

"But it's closed, miss," he replies with a crooked grin.

"Doesn't matter. We have business there."

He shuffles away as we find tufted seats.

The watercoach driver takes us to a nearby island where the Silk Teahouse sits. We climb out onto the pier. Rémy tells him to wait for us.

Marble spirals cover the exterior of the teahouse, mimicking the pattern of the silkworm's cocoons. A sloped roof is crusted over with snow, and its pier is red like a tongue that's tasted too many strawberries. White sill-lanterns sit in the windows, dull and vacant.

Guards stand at attention in front of the doorway and along the pier. Dozens of them.

My heart beats too fast. How will we get past them?

There is a Receiving House just ahead that's a tiny replica of the teahouse and has a woman sitting inside it. A sign above her head reads SILK TEAHOUSE RECEPTION.

"I'll stand here to not draw as much attention," Rémy says. "But I'll keep watch."

"Ready?" I ask Edel.

I take a deep breath and make sure the glamour is strong. I grimace as the cold pain radiates inside me and my bones feel like they might just splinter into shards.

Edel nods. Rémy reaches out and gives my hand a squeeze before we go.

We approach the woman behind a glass pane. She thumbs through a gossip tattler and wears a simple lavender dress with a royal emblem around her neck. It bears a silkworm coiled around a chrysanthemum, identifying her as an important courtier from the merchant House of Silk. A fire-lantern bathes her white skin in reds and oranges. The circuit-phones swallow the walls behind her.

She doesn't look up. Edel huffs, then taps the glass. The woman flinches in shock and the tattler drops from her lap, the fall shifting the portraits and animated ink across the parchment. Her eyes flutter over us and she is, apparently, unimpressed. She pins a CLOSED sign to the glass, rescues her tattler, and resumes flipping the pages.

"Excuse me?" I say.

"Don't you see the sign?" she barks.

Edel punches the glass, which causes the soldiers nearest us to look up.

I cringe. "Edel."

The woman yanks open the window. "You could've broken it, you know that? The fine would be at least three hundred leas."

"You should've been courteous enough to open it," Edel replies.

"We're closed," she snaps. "Who are you?"

"Courtiers from the House of Rare Reptilians, and in need of emergency beauty work," I reply.

"Let me see your emblems." She stretches out her hand, waiting for me to untie the ribbon and place the heavy crest made of coral and ivory and gold in her palm.

"What for?" Edel asks.

"Not that I need to explain myself, but there have been forgeries floating around. I need to inspect them."

I gulp and remove the emblem. I hand it to her, hoping Arabella gave me a real one from the palace.

"Hmm..." She turns it around in her hand, gazes up at the dragon sitting on my shoulder, then takes out a set of scales and a monocle. She weighs it, then lifts the glass eyepiece. "This one passes inspection, but what about hers?" Her discerning gaze turns to Edel.

I almost sigh with relief, then say, "She's my assistant. Now, when will the teahouse be taking clients again?"

"When Madam Kristina Renault reopens—"

The circuit-phone closest to her rings. The cone-shaped receiver shakes left and right on top of its slender base. She lifts it to her ear and says, "Silk Teahouse reception, Mira speaking, we are closed until further notice. May I please take your message or appointment request?"

A loud voice shouts: "Additional vats needed to the palace port before sunrise by order of the queen."

The voice sends a jolt of lightning through me.

Elisabeth Du Barry.

Edel and I don't dare look at each other. Elisabeth survived the palace dungeons and is still working for Sophia. That truth swirls around inside me. I want to strangle her through the phone lines.

"Ensure Valerie is prepped for transport afterward," Elisabeth barks.

I squeeze Edel's arm and look up at the teahouse's windows. The sill-lanterns are unlit. No movement in or out. A space seemingly vacant. But my sister's in there. Only twenty paces away.

We have to get into that teahouse.

"Will do," the girl replies before cupping a hand over the receiver. "No one is at the teahouse. We've been sending people to Miel's Makeup Galleria on the Imperial Mile because they have a limited supply of Belle-products. Best to try there. Good day to you both." She slides the glass window shut again and points at the CLOSED sign.

The plan to get to Valerie bursts like a popped bubble.

We have to find another way in.

13

We settle into another shabby room in another boardinghouse to rest after using our glamours. We still have three hourglasses' worth of time before the doors open for the Fashion Minister's exhibition. Anxious flutters irritate my stomach, all the unknowns growing into a ball of nausea.

"How do we get to Valerie now?" I ask Edel.

She doesn't answer, her face buried in Arabella's letter, mumbling to herself about the aether and Sophia, trying to put the pieces together. Rémy stares out the window, his eyes surveying every passing body. The teacup dragons dance and play, chasing one another and the dusk-lanterns. Their scales glitter like beautiful gemstones. I watch them, thinking how nice it must be to be them, clueless, and without a worry. Their joyful movements remind me of how my sisters and I used to be as little girls.

I comb through Arabella's Belle-book to pass the anxious time.

Date: Day 3,428 at court

Sophia's Belle-growing apparatus was unveiled today. The clear vats will hold future Belles like wombs. Sophia called them cradles. She thought it made what she'd created sound better. Sweeter and softer.

I sneaked into the birthing chamber. The walls are filled with them now, stacked like eggs in a carton. I traced my fingers along gilded tubes that connected to massive arcana meters and tanks to be filled with my blood. Nurses used rolling ladders to tend to them.

The sight of the room was maddening. Du Barry hid the truth. She said we'd fallen from the sky like seeds to be planted. She said she rescued us from the dark forest and put us into the hands of our mothers. She said the Goddess of Beauty made each one of us in her image. The beautiful lie burned a pit in my heart.

I flip forward.

Date: Day 3,432 at court

The ministers have been holed up in the Royal Law Room of the Imperial Library for two days straight. Beds were brought in, and they were forced to work through the night on the new set of beauty laws to be passed after Sophia's Coronation and Ascension to the throne. I sneaked onto the balcony to listen to them argue. I caught some of the rules on the docket:

Citizens will be required to register their beauty work with the cabinet, including but not limited to installation of imperial cameos in every household for monitoring.

Beauty capital (an individual's ability to present themself) shall be measured with a rating rubric (scores given monthly from the Beauty Minister). High marks will be rewarded by the monarchy, for Orléans will be full of only beautiful things.

No woman shall be more beautiful than the sitting queen.

The debates over a new beauty price list was next on their agenda.

The new Minister of Belles, Georgiana Fabry, insisted the prices go up. Beauty lobbyists backed her desires, but other ministers disagreed, claiming it will create disenfranchisement.

The price list was now segmented by arcana.

MANNER:

    ALL PERSONALITY ADJUSTMENTS   1,750

    TALENT:

        TIER ONE   PHYSICAL PROWESS   3,750

        TIER TWO   ARTISTIC   4,270

        TIER THREE   SKILL   5,980

AURA:

    SURFACE MODIFICATIONS:

        HAIR COLOR   105

        HAIR TEXTURE   126

        EYE COLOR RESTORATION   50

        EYE SHAPE ADJUSTMENT   60

        SKIN COLOR RESTORATION   90

    DEEP MODIFICATIONS:

        FACE:

            CHEEKBONE SCULPTING   4,000

            MOUTH PLACEMENT AND SHAPE   3,000

            EAR PLACEMENT AND SHAPE   3,000

        BODY:

            LEG AND ARM SCULPTING   4,500

            STOMACH, BREASTS, TORSO SCULPTING   6,100

            HIPS AND REAR SHAPING   7,000

            NECK AND SHOULDER SMOOTHING   3,000

            HAND AND FEET ADJUSTMENT   2,000

AGE:

   SKIN TIGHTENING   125

   WRINKLE REMOVAL   200

I turn back to the beginning of the book.

Date: Day 2,198 at court

I feel terrible about what I did today. The nurses started taking more of my blood now, too much for it to just be to check my arcana levels. They wouldn't tell me why. Claimed it was to keep me healthy. When one of the nurses, Zaire, came into my bedroom with her cart of needles and vials, I restrained her and made her tell me what they were using my blood for.

She called me the aether, one of the everlasting roses. I thought back to when I was a little girl curled up in my maman's lap with one of the storybooks from the library at Maison Rouge. I can still see the cover—a rose with petals of every color and a gilded stem. Its pages told the tale of the Goddess of Beauty's gardens, and the rare everlasting roses, grown from aether seeds in order to birth the other roses.

I don't know what this means.

The late-morning headlines pour through the window and interrupt my reading.

"The *National*, second paper off the presses. Countess Madeleine Rembrant of House Glaston jailed by the queen for stealing Belle-products from Trianon's premier shop, Sugar Rose."

"Beauty pamphlets *Dulce* and *Sucré* both report that plum buns will most certainly sweep the Glass Isles—maybe the entire kingdom—after famed opera singer Geneviève Gareau sported a full derriere at her last concert. If only the teahouses were open."

"We should go line up," I say, wanting to get away from the headlines and this room. I tuck the teacup dragons in my pouch and add Arabella's Belle-book to my satchel. "We have an hour left."

Edel shrugs but pulls herself off the bed.

More headlines drift inside, like incessant waves threatening to swallow us.

"Just in from the *Orléansian Times*, Belles officially labeled property of the kingdom of Orléans, entrusted to its monarch. Hiding them is now considered treason against the crown with the penalty death by starvation box."

I flinch.

"Property?" Edel says, gritting her teeth.

"We've always been that," I reply, the truth hardening me from the inside out.

"The *Silk Post* learns that the queen is labeling any and all rumors of her sister's recovery as false press. She is still planning the funeral and memorial for her beloved sister. Her body is to be presented on the first day of the new year as planned."

Rémy pulls on his cloak.

"Papers," a voice hollers from the hall. The thud of the bundle hits the floor outside our door.

We can't escape the news.

Edel peeks into the hall and swipes them. Her eyes scan over the headlines. "Arabella was right. Here's the report about our sisters—'Favored Belles Padma, Hana, Valerie, and Amber locked in the Rose.'" She shows me the pictures. Amber grips the rose-shaped bars, shouting through them, her hair a wild storm around her head. We turn the page, quickly, sending the animated ink scurrying to settle. "But, Rémy..."

Rémy turns from the window. "What is it?"

"Your family," she stammers out.

He takes the paper from her and scans the pages. His eyes fill with anguish. "I have to go."

DHONIELLE CLAYTON

"What is it?" I rush to his side.

Animated pictures of Rémy's family fill the front page under the headlines:

THE FAMILY OF THE TRAITOROUS IMPERIAL

GUARD—ACCOMPLICE TO FUGITIVE BELLES—

IDENTIFIED AND TAKEN INTO CUSTODY

His three sisters, Adaliz, Mirabelle, and Odette, are chained and being carted off. His veiled mother follows behind with her head bowed. His father tussles with the imperial guards. The three girls sob, a storm of tears flooding their dark brown cheeks.

I remember the depth of their smiles and the sound of their voices and how they gazed at Rémy like he would be their hero forever.

Rémy immediately starts packing the few things he's amassed since being on the run.

"You can't leave without me changing you," I say.

"I don't like being changed and there's no time," he says.

"You have to. The guards will capture you the second you get to Trianon, if not sooner." I quickly prepare the bed for beauty work, pulling back the sheets and fluffing the pillows.

"And you need food," Edel adds. "I'll go buy some bread, nuts, and hard cheese. Things that should last you."

My heart is warmed by her willingness to put aside their rivalry and help him.

"No. I'll be fine," he replies. "All your money will be gone...."

Edel is already out the door.

"Your image will be plastered all over, and more prominent than the old Wanted posters, now," I say.

"I know," he says. "I'm leaving you and Edel my maps. I have them all committed to memory. They'll help you navigate every inch of Orléans. The ink updates as the master maps in Trianon are updated." He heads for the door.

I grab his arm. "You're not leaving here unless I change you."

Rémy stares me down, but I don't budge and finally, he sighs. "You know all of this is unnecessary, right? I know how to stay undercover. I have that hair powder to cover the stripe."

"I need to do this," I tell him. "I need to do what I can to keep you safe."

I light a fire in our tiny cookstove and fill a small, chipped teapot with water from our room basin. The noise of the hissing flames and the gurgle of bubbles smothers his protests. I take out the caisse Arabella packed for us and retrieve dried Belle-rose leaves to steep into the pot. My hands work fast setting out all the beauty instruments we have—a set of miniature skin-paste pots, metal rods, and charcoal pencils. I combine them with the items we pilfered from the Spice Teahouse. The small collection isn't even a fraction of the supplies we once had.

My eyes close and I remember the shelves upon shelves of beauty products at Maison Rouge and the Belle-apartments. The scent of pastilles and wax and candles fills my nose, and I'm almost back there.

But when I open my eyes again it's just this small room.

"Take off your clothes and lie down on the bed."

He grumbles but complies. The heavy thud of his boots hitting the floor sends a nervous shiver through me. We've been cooped up in small spaces together for all these days, and I've never seen his feet. Or any of him for that matter. He's only allowed me to use the hair powder to cover his silver stripe.

I turn around to give him privacy as he undresses but can still feel his each and every move. A tiny fire sparks in my stomach.

The bed squeaks as he climbs into it.

"Are you ready?" I bring over a cup of Belle-rose tea and set it on the nightstand.

"As much as I will be." He's tucked himself under the quilts, and his long dark arms lie on top of them.

I laugh.

His brow furrows. "What is it?"

"You're too far under the blankets. How am I supposed to work on you?"

"Oh."

"Just lie across the bed and drape the cover over...you know..."

"I know," he says quickly.

I wait.

"Are you going to turn around?"

"Shy, are we?" My cheeks flame.

He sighs.

I pivot my back to him. My heart flutters like the tiny candle inside the night-lantern between us.

"Done," he replies.

His long legs dangle over the edge of the bed like great brown trunks of muscle threaded with streaks of gray. But he's beautiful without his clothes on, even marbled with the sad color.

"What will you do?" he asks.

"What do you want me to do?"

"Nothing if I could help it, but I'm guessing you don't take no for an answer."

I touch the scar that hooks under his right eye. His skin is warm and soft.

"I'd like to keep that," he says.

I pull back quickly. "It's pretty distinguishable."

"It's been with me since I was born. Well, according to my mother. It was part of my natural template. It reminds me of her."

"All right."

"I like my skin color. The darker the better."

"Anything else?"

"Longer hair, maybe?" he says.

"I'll give you little girl ringlets."

The edges of his mouth curve into a reluctant smile.

I wink at him and coat him with bei powder. The white flakes cover him like sugar dust on a molasses tart. I smooth them across his limbs with a brush. He watches my every move, his stare intense and like he's trying to listen to my thoughts. My hands shake with nerves.

I close my eyes. The arcana awaken easily, rising to meet my call. A rush of heat lifts from my stomach, and it feels like it's both my gifts and something else. My blood races through me. Beads of sweat dot my forehead. The veins in my body pulse, and my heart picks up its rhythm. I pretend that I'm home in the safety of one of the Aura lesson rooms. I pretend that all that's happened never came to pass. I pretend that Rémy is a regular customer here to see me for a routine session. His form appears in the darkness of my mind.

I darken his hair to the color of midnight. I lengthen the tight curls into long coils, then knit them together like soft yarn until they fall over his shoulder in a thousand tiny ropes. I deepen the brown of his skin color.

I stare down at him and a smile erupts through me. I can still see him inside this new outer form. I didn't want to lose all the things I loved about the way he'd chosen to look.

He bites his bottom lip.

"I'm finished. Need tea for the pain?"

"It doesn't hurt," he replies.

"But you're scowling."

"That's not the reason." He sits up. The heavy sound of his breathing extends between us. My heart flutters like a trapped bird. He smells like ink, leather, and me. His breath hits my shoulder, sending a tickle down my spine. Thoughts of him jump around in my head like bubbles in a champagne glass: his hands around my waist, his nose buried in my hair, the feel of his lips, the taste of his mouth.

I shudder.

"What's wrong?" His gaze pins me in place, then slides around me, hugging all my edges. His eyes almost swallow me whole, moving from my face, down the lines of my neck, and slope of my chest where the mirror sits, awaiting all his questions.

"Nothing," I mutter.

"Use the mirror," he says.

I press a hand to my chest. "I already trust you."

"Just do it, so you'll never ever question it." He runs a finger along the path of the chain on my neck, his finger pressing into my skin, leaving behind a trail of heat.

I pull the mirror from beneath my dress, then prick my finger with a pushpin from my beauty caisse. He watches as I rub the blood in the mirror's handle. The grooves soak with it. The liquid climbs to the top, bathes the roses, and the glass fills with an image of his face—kind eyes, a perpetual half-smile, and a creased and serious brow. I can feel him—his strength and loyalty, his selfless-ness and protective instinct, his affection for me. The overwhelm-ing power of it surges through me.

"What do you see?" he asks, searching my face.

"I don't want you to go." My voice breaks. Silent and unruly tears breach the fragile wall holding them in.

I wipe them away.

He looks at me, then reaches his fingers to my face, his hands heavy yet gentle. I don't flinch. I don't move away from his touch. His thumb catches a tear beside my mouth. He doesn't stop wiping until they stop falling. The warmth of his hand seeps into my skin.

"You make me feel safe," I say.

He leans forward. "And you make me feel the same." His whis-per gets tangled in my hair. "But safety is never permanent. I sup-pose like beauty, it's unpredictable."

More tears well in my eyes. Different ones this time. I don't know what this wild feeling is. I want him to touch me again. I want him to kiss me. I want to know what that feels like. A seam inside me starts to rip, taunting me with all that could happen if I let him in.

"I have to go," he whispers. "You will be fine without—"

I touch his face, then press my mouth to his, shoving those words back in, and knowing that we can't be together, knowing he has to leave, knowing that our joke about being married was just that—a joke. Still, a blush blooms in my cheeks.

He freezes.

I pull back. My heart does a nervous tumble. His eyes gaze into mine.

A pocket of silence encapsulates us, the edges of it expanding and stretching throughout the room.

Neither of us moves.

I search his eyes for the answer to the kiss. Would he ever want me in that way? Have I crossed a line with him? Did I misinterpret what I saw in the mirror? Am I allowed to have these feelings?

I open my mouth to try to say something. The words *I'm sorry* tumble out.

He runs his hand along the curve of my neck and cups my face in his hands. I sink into him. He kisses me gentle and soft. All the worries about whether he wants me drift off like post-balloons.

We kiss until our lips tingle.

"I don't want you to go." My voice drowns with fear.

"I don't want to go either." His mouth softens and his eyes crinkle at the corners. "But I have to."

"What if it's a trap?" I ask.

"Then I'll work my way out of it."

"What if something happens to you?"

"I know the palace inside and out." He pushes back one of my frizzy curls. "You should find Charlotte, get your sisters, and meet me there. We can end this together."

I bite my bottom lip to keep it from quivering.

"You'll always know I'm safe." He fishes three leeches from the perforated jar and puts them along his forearm. "Send the gold dragon for me. She's my favorite." With his other arm, he removes a small sheathed dagger from his pocket, the handle white as bone and encrusted with pearls. "Keep this on you always. Even when asleep. Use it without hesitation." He puts the belt around my waist and buckles it. "And lastly, these." He takes his leather-bound maps from his pocket. "Carry these. They will reveal the details of each city you go to. They were developed by the Minister of War himself."

"Won't you need them?" I ask, removing the leeches as they tug and gorge on the blood in his thick veins.

I open the caisse of sangsues and remove a small empty jar. I use a tiny quill to label it with his name, put the leeches inside, then tuck it back into the compartment beside the leeches Arabella sent.

"I'm going to the palace. I know that place. Trust me."

I lean forward and rest my forehead against his.

We look at each other as if there's a rope suspended between us throbbing and pulsing, pulled tight by our shared circumstance. He flashes a smile so devastating and heartbreaking, one that tells me that this might be the last time we see each other.

I kiss him until we run out of breath.

14

Through the bedroom window, I watch Rémy disappear into the midday crowds. People shift around his broad shoulders and tall frame in an almost synchronized rhythm as if they know he's important. He strides forward through the world unafraid that there might be someone hunting him around every corner. He doesn't glance back even though I wish he would.

I need to see his face one more time. In case it's my last.

My worries congeal into a lump in my throat. I try to follow him with my eyes for as long as I can. The memory of his mouth buzzes along my lips until it's replaced by a terrible feeling like a too-tight hug. The desire for him to stay tugs at me. A tiny voice whispers: *Rémy leaving is a bad idea. This is what Sophia wants.*

But I know he can't stay. His duty is to his family. Without them, there'd be no him.

Edel bursts back in the room with a small parcel. "He left? And without his food?"

I burst. Tears stream down my cheeks. She sweeps me into her arms.

"He's going to be all right," she says, stroking my back until I calm down.

"How do you know?"

"He's Rémy."

I chuckle a little and pull away. I wipe at my face, trying to erase the emotion. Of course he'll be fine. He's smart and strong and calculating.

"Do you love him?" Her blond eyebrow lifts.

I try to form a lie, but I can't. "Yes." The word tumbles out, feeling too little to encompass all of these emotions.

"When this is all over, will you be together?"

"Is it going to be over?" I pull on my coat. "And what would that look like?"

"I don't know."

A bell rings outside. Vendors start shouting, trying to lure customers to their lunch carts.

"We've got to get to the exhibition. We're late," I say.

We pack all of our things and adopt glamours. I deepen the brown of my skin so it matches the chocolate pies being sold right outside our window. I pull my hood tight around my face and tuck my tiny beauty caisse, the teacup dragons, and the maps into my fur waist-sash.

Edel resembles our maman Iris—Amber's maman—with her hair thick, each strand a soft coil, and plaited in two fat twists that hit her waist like ropes of onyx. She packs our remaining Belle supplies into her pockets.

I use Rémy's maps to navigate us back to the aristocratic Rose Quartier. The crowd stretches out as far as I can see, loud and excited, reminding me of the night of our Beauté Carnaval. They swell like a tide on the massive staircase leading into the Silk Hall. My stomach flutters, the energy of it all finding its way inside me as we fold into the rest of the bodies and make our way out of the cold.

The building is a gift box made of glass panels trimmed with ribbons of gold. Silkscreens of the Fashion Minister's freckled face hang from the high ceiling interspersed with portraits of gowns displaying their various wonders. The room's windowed walls give a full view of Carondelet from every vantage point. The blue domed buildings glimmer like cream tarts frosted with blueberry glaze. Day-lanterns zip overhead carrying voice-boxes, and heat-lanterns glow like newborn stars.

"Gather around, everyone. The presentation will start in a quarter of an hourglass," a woman announces through the voice-boxes.

The crowd takes out ear-trumpets and eyescopes, anticipating the start of the show. Sweet-vendors slither through the masses wearing garments that display their treats. A woman dons a por-celain teapot-shaped hat and pours the steaming liquid through her spout into cups; another wears a dress that glows like an oven complete with spiced pies and bourbon tarts. A little boy pushes macarons from his top hat to be caught and consumed. A tall man has a billowing waistcoat from which he extracts peppermint bark, chocolate buttons, and caramel sticks. Peach post-balloons deliver glasses of champagne to eager, awaiting hands.

The teacup dragons squirm as the scents tickle their noses. I tighten my waist-sash, pulling them closer, hoping the warmth and heat of my body lulls them to sleep despite the chattering noises in the cavernous room.

The Fashion Minister's well-dressed team of dandies march

through side doors and yank thick red curtains along the walls and ceilings. The view of the city and the sky above disappears. Night-lanterns are extinguished, replaced by sparklers. Attendants ease the spectators away from the center of the room and form the crowd into a perfect circle.

"Gentleladies, gentlemen, and gentlefolk of the great Spice Isles, this is the first stop of this glorious world tour. Prepare yourself for the greatest Fashion Minister to ever serve the glorious kingdom of Orléans—the one and only Royal Minister Gustave du Polignac."

The room bursts into cheers. At the center of the circle the floor opens, and a platform soars, carrying with it Gustave. He waves at the onlookers, his false hand now gold and studded with emeralds as plump as ripe grapes. His hair sits in a spectacular cone above his head, full of diamonds. I'm flooded with memories of him, of his kindess toward me. My heart lifts with a flutter like it's taken off. He will help us. I know he will.

Beauty-lanterns rush throughout the room as cloaked bell jars descend from the ceiling.

He lifts a voice-trumpet to his smiling lips. "Are you ready?" he teases.

The crowd erupts.

"But are you?"

They clap and jump and whistle.

I gaze around wondering how they can all be so deliriously happy and unaffected by what's happening in the world outside this room.

The velvet cloaks drop away from the bell jars, and the dresses are revealed.

The crowd gasps.

"Behold, little darlings of the Silk Isles, my latest creations," Gustave announces.

The jars swivel and move like post-balloons without a precise destination.

"I'll tell you a little about my favorites. Well, I love them all, but there are a few that hold a deep place in my heart." One of the dresses shifts right over him. The bell jar pivots left and right to show off all angles of the gown. "This one is called the Phoenix. Didn't the story go that the God of Fortune's phoenix changed his feathers when the Goddess of Death lured him away every month?"

The crowd hollers in agreement.

"Pay close attention."

The feathered gown shimmers in oranges and reds, then the feathers change to molten gold, then midnight plums and blues.

Everyone cheers.

"Save some excitement," he replies, "for the Jeweled Worm."

Another dress moves overhead, cylindrical and writhing like a silkworm. Layers unfurl, first exposing a tier of white diamonds and glass pearls, then shifting to shades of crimson studded with rubies.

The crowd drums their feet.

"The Striped Sensation is next." The Fashion Minister bows as a three-piece suit appears in the nearest bell jar. The black and white stripes change to gold and silver, then plum and turquoise, while its matching top hat mirrors the colors.

"Bravo!" someone yells.

"Chic!" another hollers.

The Fashion Minister accepts the praise with a slight smile. "In collaboration with our new queen, Her Majesty Sophia Celeste the

Second, by the Grace of the Gods of the Kingdom of Orléans and Her Other Realms and Territories, Defender of Beauty and Borders, wants all citizens of this great world to feel deeply connected to her. By wearing these original dresses, you will indeed be closer to the queen and her brilliance."

His forced smile is unrecognizable to onlookers, but I've seen it before. He doesn't believe a word he's saying.

"My beautiful dandies will take care of you. Place your orders. Dress with purpose. Show the world who you are. May you always find beauty!" He flourishes his cape, then the platform lowers him back down and he disappears beneath the floor.

His dandies saunter through the eager masses with pen and parchment, noting orders and requests. One approaches us. "Care to put in an early order?"

"A very large order," Edel replies.

"How many?" he asks.

I clear my throat. His eyes flit over me. "One hundred of the the Phoenix, and fifty of the Jeweled Worm."

His delicately drawn eyebrows lift with curiosity. "Do you oversee a harem?"

I don't laugh. Sweat inches down my back as I try to hold on to the glamour, appear confident, and keep the teacup dragons still in my waist-sash.

"We run a very prestigious school," I say. "We want to meet with the Fashion Minister himself to tell him more of our needs."

"Many want to meet with him. He's quite a busy man," the dandy replies.

Panic wraps its fingers around my heart like a fist, squeezing so hard, it might burst. I take out our leas pouch, fish out the remaining coins, and press them into his hand. It's the last of our stash. It's not much. But hopefully garish enough to make him think there's more. "We know him very well."

Edel's eyes burn into my cheek, but I don't dare look at her for fear I'll lose my nerve. "Tell him his little doll has many leas to spend." I try to keep the desperation out of my voice.

He pockets the coins and motions for us to follow him. We zigzag between groups of excited courtiers bidding on the displayed dresses and placing orders for additional ones.

"Why did you do that?" Edel whispers. "Now we have nothing." Her anger makes her glamour waver.

"He'll give it back to me, and more. I promise."

"But if he doesn't, we can't pay to stay at the boardinghouse tonight."

The gamble burns in my stomach.

"Then it's good we packed our things and brought them with us." I try to sound more confident than I feel. I try to maintain a haughty smile. I try to be the old me, who wasn't afraid to take any risk no matter the cost.

The Fashion Minister won't let me down.

The man taps his cane on the ground as he strides forward, the crowd parting for him, and he turns down one of the endless ornate hallways. Portraits dot the walls—depictions of royal families and famed courtiers enjoying all the Silk Isles have to offer. They sit in plantation carriages overseeing Gris workers or strolling through silk farms with lily-white parasols drifting over their heads like warm-season clouds.

He escorts us into a tea room. The walls soar in stripes of the Silk Isles' signature colors—ocean blue, cream, and gold.

Day-lanterns and beauty-lanterns chase each other overhead like celestial bodies. Servants push carts replete with teapots and sweets. The Fashion Minister sits on a raised chaise surrounded by people—courtiers, attendants.

"Wait here," the dandy orders.

My hands tremble. "Breathe. Hold it," I whisper to myself, and hope the words sink inside me because a quiver vibrates down my spine as it gets harder and harder to hold the glamour. A headache erupts in my temples. The silvery taste of blood coats my tongue. I'm moments from another nosebleed.

"Just a few more minutes," Edel says.

The dandy leans down and whispers into the Fashion Minister's ear. The Fashion Minister's eyebrows raise, and his gaze finds me.

"Clear the room," the Fashion Minister orders. "Everyone. Servants, too." His command bounces off the walls.

The room empties in less time than it takes for a single grain of sand to fall from one side of an hourglass to the other. As the door clicks shut, the Fashion Minister rushes over to us. I almost collapse into his arms from fatigue.

He holds me up. "Little doll?" His eyes scan over me.

I let the glamour drift away.

He leans back in awe as my skin returns to its regular shade of brown and my hair frizzes, each strand tightening into a curl. Blood streams from my nose.

He hands me a handkerchief, and I nod with gratitude.

"It is you." He wraps me up in his arms like I'm a lost child he's just found. The teacup dragons squeal, causing him to pull back. They peek their heads out of my waist-sash and glare at him, aiming tiny streams of fire at his face, which flame out before they can do harm.

"How adorable," he says, unperturbed.

Edel's glamour disappears.

"Ah, the troublemaking one that Madam Alieas always complained about."

"Alieas was the annoying one," Edel snaps. "And hello to you, too."

"Greetings, troublemaker." He puts a hand on his chest. "How were you able to disguise yourselves like that?"

"Our gifts," I reply with utter exhaustion. He takes my arm.

After settling us onto chaise lounges, he dashes to one of the drink carts and brings us two cups of hot tea. I sip eagerly, the warm liquid restoring strength in my muscles. I have never been so glad not to support my own weight. I let the teacup dragons roam around the room. Three pick at towers of macarons in search of something more savory, and the other three chase the day-lanterns through the cavernous space, tangling themselves in their silk ribbons.

The Fashion Minister stares up at them in awe. "There's a shortage of those. Our newest lady on the throne would be quite eager to get her hands on them."

"Soph—"

He puts his hand in the air, pointing at nearby beauty-lanterns. "Don't say her name. Similar to her blood jewelry, she's using enigmatics, fashioning them to resemble almost anything—fans, keys, royal emblems, even dresses themselves. Rumor has it, she's attached the tiny record-boxes to lanterns throughout the kingdom to be collected by her loyal followers. They target specific words and record gossip. Do you understand?"

We nod.

"Now that I've had a closer look at you both, I can tell you're run-down," he says.

"We need your help with two things—money, if you can spare it, and a way to get into the Silk Teahouse."

Without hesitation, he removes a leas pouch from his inner pocket and hands it to me. The weight of it is a comfort. "The teahouses are locked up tighter than a starvation box until *she* declares them open again. No one other than guards—and servants tending to the Belles—goes in or out."

"We know," Edel replies, then sips her tea. "That's why we're here."

"So, what's your plan?" he asks. "I mean, assuming the teahouse isn't your endgame."

Edel stops mid-sip, her strong gaze darting between me and the Fashion Minister. Her brow furrows with suspicion.

"If I wanted to capture you, you'd already be in chains and headed to that fancy cattle-pen prison," he snaps, before grabbing a macaron from a tiered tray and dipping it into his rose-pink teacup.

"But why should we trust you?" Edel says. "Why are you willing to help?"

He turns to me and blows me a kiss. "I've always had a soft spot for this one."

Edel's eyes blaze. "That doesn't mean you're not an ally of the monster who—"

"Be quiet!" His voice blasts through the room like a trumpet.

Edel blanches. My heart pounds.

"I am no friend of hers. She took my husband." His eyes sheen over with tears. "Under the guise of a job as a milliner, she is holding him against his will. Using him as a way to control me. I need her gone, too."

Edel opens and closes her mouth a few times, but nothing

comes out. I glare at her and will an apology to come from her mouth.

"I'm sorry," I reply.

He reaches for my hand and holds it with a squeeze. "It's fine, my poppet. I am used to being questioned like this. I can prove my mettle and worth." He cranes forward. "Our sleeping beauty is in the Gold Isles and is growing stronger, trying to get well before the ceremonies begin. I can't believe that's coming in four days' time."

My heart jumps. "How do you know?"

"I'm very close with our departed leader's beloved partner." He leans in, waiting for the lantern overhead to drift past, and whispers, "Lady Pelletier."

The pieces of this puzzle begin to shift into place. I glare at Edel, satisfied that this visit has paid off.

"Know our beauty is tucked away like a jewel deep in a mountain."

"Can you help us get to her?" Edel asks.

"And to our sister at the Silk Teahouse?" I add.

A knock pounds the door. "Royal Minister?" a voice calls.

"Yes, to both, but we have no more time for catch-up," he replies. "My duties call and anything that continues to deviate from them will garner curiosity and inspire reporting." He taps my nose. "You must rest overnight. Tomorrow, I'll get you where you need to go. But first, I must rescue your bodies and outfit you in something that won't raise such alarm. Come."

15

The mirrored walls around us fog with steam as we soak in natural hot-spring baths, the water heated from the very heart of the Goddess of Death's caves. We learned in our lessons that her bargain with the God of the Sea required her to allow for heat from her eternal fires to warm these waters.

Skylight windows reveal the midnight stars as they rise. Smooth white stone slopes along my back and bubbles remove the tension in my limbs. Edel only dangles her feet in as her eyes dart back and forth between me and the stone doors behind us.

"We shouldn't have stayed," she says. "We could've gotten Valerie tonight and set off for the Gold Isles. Now, we only have four days until the ceremony."

"Try to relax," I say.

"I still don't trust him," she replies.

"We're in his private chambers. He's sent all his servants and attendants away for the night. If he were going to trap us, he would have already had the guard take us away. It would probably make *her* love him more, and release his husband or make her imprison him. He's taking a risk to help us."

"You trust too easily," she replies. "They wrote about you in the papers, you know. You and her fiancé, Auguste."

A bleeding gash opens on my heart. "What?"

"There were reports in the tattlers about how she was angered by your daliance with him. Is it true?"

My relationship with Auguste replays in my head. His gaze heavy, his eyes with their ability to make me feel as if I were the only person in the room, the only person in the world. The sound of his name stirs painful memories I've worked hard to bury deep inside me, rattling and shaking them like snow in a flipped snowglobe.

"So, is it?" she presses.

"I made a grave error." The admission leaves behind an ache in my heart like the deep prick of a needle. All the secrets spilled between kisses; secrets that allowed his mother to discover sacred truths about the Belles and feed them to Sophia. I'm not ready to face that yet.

"You kissed him?"

"Yes."

"What was it like?" She eases deeper into the water.

"Fine."

She arches an eyebrow. "That's it?"

"I don't want to talk about him." I clamp my eyes shut, trying to erase Auguste, wishing I could remove all the memories of him that I carry.

"Did you love him?"

The question burns. She jostles my shoulder. My eyes snap open.

"What about Rémy? You said you loved him."

"I do. Like the way I love you." I grab her and pull her into the water. She relents.

"I saw the way you look at each other. That love must be different. What is that like?" she asks.

"Do you trust me?" I say, brushing away her question. She's always been a cold teapot, slow to warm.

"Yes."

"Good. The Fashion Minister will help us. In a few hours, we'll get Valerie and she will tell us what to do about the Belle babies and we will all go to the Gold Isles together."

"Don't want to talk about boys, huh?" She dunks her head in the steaming water.

She doesn't resurface for so long I begin to worry, then suddenly she comes up sputtering.

"Are you all right?"

Her skin is blush pink like a teacup pig, and water dribbles out of her mouth. "I will be once we leave here."

"We're getting closer." I grab her hand and squeeze it. "We will succeed. I know we will."

We soak until our skin prunes. Soft nightgowns hang from nearby hooks, awaiting our tired bodies. A side door leads into a small bedroom complete with a large four-post bed. A single night-lantern scrapes its head beneath the bed's canopy, and two carts sit at the foot—one with foods rich with arcana-resetting properties like salmon puffs, beef skewers, bacon-wrapped shrimp, and chocolate squares, and the other with jars of sangsues.

Edel stuffs her mouth with three salmon puffs. "I'm so tired I can barely chew," she grumbles, then climbs into bed and pushes the night-lantern out before pulling the curtains shut.

While Edel's light snores fill the room, I cover my arm with leeches and take out Arabella's Belle-book. Under the soft glow of a single night-lantern, I read through more entries.

Date: Day 3,510 at court

Sophia's beauty addiction has reached new heights. She changed her look for each of her morning activities—brunch with her ladies-of-honor, walking in the winter gardens, meeting her cabinet—and then, again, in the evening for her nightly card games and parties. Before one can join her, she's developed a vigorous beauty test for them. They must stand on a platform to be analyzed and scored. If found to be more beautiful, they are given two options—see me to immediately change themselves, or receive a fine and leave the palace. Most submit to this new routine because they are desperate to be in her presence.

I'm afraid of what's next for Sophia and her grandiose desires.

Date: Day 3,435 at court

Sophia brought in new cabinet members today during the assembly meeting. They filed into the Royal Law Room in the Imperial Library, all eager to be her puppets and do her bidding. I hid in the legal stacks while they met below.

Sophia revealed her imperial cameos—mirror-size and perfect for the walls or vanities—and the advertising campaign intended to sell them to the masses. She said the cameos will connect her to the people of her kingdom, when really they will connect everyone to her obsessive wall. The Royal Beauty Minister, Rose Bertain, challenged her in front of everyone, and the meeting ended early. Sadly, the minister will pay for that.

She's trying to have eyes everywhere. Next, she'll probably institute beauty checkpoints as she continues to turn the palace upside down. She receives a ledger of all visitors to her court now. The Minister of War has provided her with a thousand extra guards, pulling them from posts around the kingdom, despite his protests about the safety of the borders being at risk.

I take a deep breath, her words drumming up even more distress inside me.

A post-balloon putters into the room, sea blue and covered in silk threads. It knocks into the dying night-lantern over my head. I put Arabella's Belle-book to the side and grab the balloon's tail ribbons. It holds a rolled newspaper and a note marked with my name.

I open it:

My dearest owl,

I saw the night-lantern light in your room and figured you were still up. I wanted to tell you again how happy I am to see your face and have you with me. Here's a little something to read. Pay particular attention to the Letter from the Editor column. We can discuss in the morning.

Sleep well,

Gustave

I unfurl the newspaper. My heart squeezes.

The *Spider's Web.*

The white ink rises on the black parchment. A tiny ink spider trots along the border. Under the Night Edition header, headlines appear.

COURTSHIP OFF TO A ROCKY START: QUEEN'S
FIANCÉ STAYING AT SPRING PALACE IN GLASS
ISLES RATHER THAN THE IMPERIAL PALACE

MINISTER OF WAR'S FLEET MOVING THROUGH THE
WARM SEA IN SEARCH OF FUGITIVE BELLES

DANGERS OF BEING GRIS—MINISTER OF NEWS CIRCULATES

NEW PAMPHLETS DETAILING DANGERS AND WARNING

WILL THERE BE A WEDDING SOMETIME THIS

YEAR? QUEEN'S FIANCÉ DERAILS ALL TALKS

AND PLANS DURING PALACE MEETINGS

EYES EVERYWHERE! QUEEN'S NEW DRESS LINE

FOUND TO BE ANOTHER WAY TO CONTROL

AND MONITOR THE BEAUTY OF OTHERS

HOPE REMAINS AS THE FAVORITE BELLE

AND HER SISTER EVADE CAPTURE!

A tiny jolt makes me sit upright.

I find the Letter from the Editor column.

Dear Spiders,

A mandate to all followers!

In the past days, there has been debate about whether or not we, the Iron Ladies, support the Belles.

Despite how we feel about their place in society and their gifts, we back their endeavors. Belles Camille Beauregard and her sister Edel Beauregard remain at large, eluding the queen's efforts. As long as they successfully avoid capture, there's hope we can depose this queen and change Orléans once and for all. With her ego bruised and her attention set on revenge, she's vulnerable—distracted and unfocused on the pitter-patter of spiders' feet. Our sources say the palace has been locked down, with one sole checkpoint allowing entry in and out. Trianon is an occupied city, guards as plentiful as lanterns.

The Belles need our help.

Allies to our cause, we implore all followers to aid them if they come across your path. Share your food, shelter, or money. We pledge to replace all things lost in this noble endeavor and assist in any consequences administered if caught. I will honor them myself.

We are behind the Belles.

We stand in solidarity.

May our threads remain strong and our webs serve us well.

Lady Arane, Leader of the Iron Ladies

My breathing rushes out so loud it feels like words. A surge of adrenaline accelerates my heart.

They support us.

They support me.

I read it once more, tracing my finger over the white letters full of hope and promise and confidence.

I rush to the bed, yank open the bed-curtains, and jostle Edel. "Wake up," I whisper.

She grunts and rolls over.

My eyes cut to the door, and I wish Rémy were there, sitting in a chair beside it. It hasn't been a full day since he left, but the hole he's left behind is quickly becoming a gaping pit. I wish I could share this with him.

I gaze back down at the article, tracing my fingers over the white letters. I glance over Arabella's diary entry again.

The palace checkpoints. Does he know? I think of Rémy trying all the various ways inside the palace and being foiled at every turn. Did he even make it there? What if he's already been captured? I wish I could know if he was all right. I unpack one of the invisible post-balloons Rémy left for us. As the night-lantern light crests over me, the balloon's outline appears and disappears.

I take out parchment, my quill, and an inkpot. After three false starts, I finally quiet my nerves and write to him. It's not *too* early, I tell myself.

Rémy,
Sophia has closed all entrances and exits to the palace save one.
Be careful.

The quill falters before I finish. I think about how to close the letter. Writing the word *love* feels heavy and hard. What does it even mean? I know I care about him and don't want him to be hurt. What if it makes him feel uncomfortable? What if it's too strange a word and feeling to use now?

The hourglass on the table flips over, signaling another hour passed, inching closer to dawn. I scribble the word and fold the note before losing my nerve. I prepare the post-balloon with the charcoal. I pull one of the leeches I've just used from the porcelain jar and pin it inside the balloon.

"Or," I whisper into the dragons' cage. "Wake up, little girl." Her golden scales resemble leas coins. I ease her from the pile of sleeping teacup dragons, hoping not to wake them all. "I need you to find Rémy, petite. I need you to make sure he's safe."

I fetch a piece of bacon from the food carts, then pluck one of Rémy's leeches from my tiny set of labeled jars, and wrap it around the meat. She chomps it down, then coughs out a tiny tuft of fire.

"Not very tasty, I know, I know. Sorry." I tie a silvery ribbon around her neck like a collar, then open the single window in the room. A dusting of snow has fallen, and fog hugs the buildings. The lack of visibility should bode well for little Or. She'll look like nothing more than a fallen star, a tear of the God of the Sky, headed for the ground.

A good omen.

She flies off, and I watch her until she's a pinprick of light in the distance.

16

We wake three hours after the morning star has risen. Edel is in a panic, snatching at the bedsheets and clawing her way out of the massive bed.

"We slept too late," she complains.

I yawn and stretch.

"You needed your rest," a voice calls from the doorway. The Fashion Minister hovers in a leather travel cloak. "It's been so long since you've had such comforts, I thought I might as well let you enjoy them."

"We did," I reply, letting my legs linger in the softness of the sheets one moment longer.

"We don't have time!" Edel yells.

"Please settle down with the theatrics. We aren't in the Grand Opera House. That's been closed for a week, honey. I didn't wake you because I had things to put in place—to *help* you." He dangles another fat leas purse in the air, then sets it on the table beside the dragons' cage. "Get dressed and packed up, then meet me in the adjacent parlor for a late breakfast. You can't do anything on an empty stomach."

We bathe again, quickly this time, and dress in the new garments he's left for us, including thick cold-season veils.

I tuck the remaining teacup dragons, Fantôme, Poivre, Feuille, Ryra, and Eau, into my new waist-sash that is expertly tailored to hold them and even has peepholes for them to gaze out, compartments for each to nuzzle in, and a side pocket that allows me to slip food in and out. I smile. There's even a space for Rémy's maps, and my beauty caisse. I'll have to thank the Fashion Minister later.

"Where's Or?" Edel asks, tying her hair up and away from her face.

"I sent her out last night to deliver a message to Rémy." I fit the sangsues into new travel jars left for me by the Fashion Minister, and parcels of food into my satchel.

"Shouldn't you have consulted with me first?" She flattens the dragons' portable cage and puts it in her bag.

"You were snoring into your pillow," I reply. "I did try to wake you up, I'll have you know."

"You could've waited until the morning to send her." She swipes the second leas pouch from the table.

"And have that glittering little dragon flying about in daylight? No, I thought it better to do it at night."

"Fine. But I like to *know* things."

"Fine. Then I have something to show you." I hand her the *Spider's Web* paper. "I had to warn Rémy after reading it. The Letter from the Editor."

"Little dolls," the Fashion Minister calls from the adjoining room. "The food is growing cold."

I lead the way. Edel follows, her eyes scanning the page, and she crashes into the table.

Beside the Fashion Minister, breakfast carts sit as tall as the hair tower he sports today, laden with tiers of quiches, trays of steak skewers, stacks of honey crepes, and carafes of milk and snowmelon juice. My stomach growls at the sight of the decadent food, erasing the memory of mornings filled with lumpy porridge and hard biscuits at the various bordinghouses.

"I see you got the paper I sent you last night," he says.

"I couldn't sleep," I admit.

"Many throughout the kingdom struggle to as well. They lie awake, panicked with worry. I can't imagine many of us are getting the proper rest." He plucks a strawberry from a warm pile of sugar-dusted crepes.

"Only Soph—"

He tsk-tsks. "Shh, don't forget not to say her name."

I nod and take a caramel-drizzled waffle from the cart.

"And you'd be surprised. I don't think she's sleeping much either. It's hard to try to keep things together when all you have are fear and lies."

Edel gazes up from the paper. "They're tracking us?" she says to me.

"Indeed. Supporting you from afar," the Fashion Minister inserts.

"What will they want in return?" she asks him.

He sits back and narrows his eyes. "I'm not sure I understand what you mean?"

"There's always a price for help. No one does it for free," Edel says. "If they're a group that lives away from the rest of us, rejecting beauty work and tradition, then they can't *really* like us. We represent the things they hate."

"I didn't read it that way," I say.

"Because *you* have hope," she says with a snarl.

"And you have none," the Fashion Minister says. "But resistance comes in many forms and alliances take many shapes. Sometimes it's all fire and storms, cutting off the heads of important people. Other times, it's slow, a crack forming in glass, inching forward sliver by sliver, spreading out across the entire surface." He takes a bite of his strawberry; the juice dribbles down his lips like pale blood. "You don't always have to agree fully to work together. Our stars can align in various ways."

The boom of thunder shakes the room.

Edel and I flinch.

He gazes up at the skylight windows. "The weather's starting to turn. The papers said we'd have thundersnow. The God of the Sky is angry today. He's always a bit fussy as the new year approaches."

Edel stuffs a beignet into her mouth. "I'm ready."

"So, you now have money, and I'm going to take you to the Silk Teahouse. Once you have your sister, be sure to leave by the northwest door. That's the house's pier for deliveries and discreet visitors. A private boat will be waiting to take you to the city of Céline in the Gold Isles. You'll be headed up the Rean Mountains to see our sleeping beauty."

His plan laid out before us invites a calm to settle into me for the first time since I left the palace.

"Do you both agree?" he asks.

I look at Edel, who hesitates a moment, then nods.

I reach for the Fashion Minister's hand. He takes mine and

squeezes it. "Thank you," I say. I wish I could make him understand how much his help means to me, but there's no time.

He rises to his feet. "I have replaced your old travel cloaks, and you can use the veils I left for you. Masks aren't as in fashion here or the Gold Isles. The veils help block all the snow they're plagued with and with all the teahouses shut down, it hides fading beauty, so they've made it into a *thing.*" He sighs.

We drape the dark veils over our heads. The Fashion Minister crisscrosses the ribbons along our necks and drapes my royal emblem on my forehead like the center jewel of a diadem.

The Fashion Minister opens the door and barks to an attendant standing outside the parlor room, "Ready my carriage."

"Yes, sir, Minister," the man replies and bows.

We follow the minister out a side door and into a luxurious imperial carriage the size of three put together. The goldenrod cushions and teakwood paneling enclose us in the front chamber, safe from a heavy snow that's started to fall. Chandelier lamps tinkle as the horses clip-clop over the cobblestones in the aristocratic Rose Quartier of Carondelet.

"She's spoiling me," he says, noticing my eyes taking in the carriage's luxurious interior. "Thinking it'll make me hate her less for taking my husband or somehow win me over. Stamp out my suspicions and doubts."

A servant hobbles around, attempting to serve tea. Instead it drips down her purple servant gown like streaks of mud.

"You should be better at this by now," the Fashion Minister snaps at her. "Steady yourself." He stands to demonstrate.

My stomach twists. I open the carriage drapes and gaze out. Ice coats the window with a delicate lace pattern, and snow scratches the sides of the carriage like sugar grains. Crowds still swell the entrance to the Great Hall as we pass. They're all huddled beneath snow umbrellas with heat-lanterns floating close. Eager faces bear toothy grins and hands clutch leas pouches, ready to admire the dress exhibition and place their orders.

I think about what we might find inside the teahouse. I think about seeing Valerie again, which calls back the pain of losing Amber.

"What's our plan?" Edel asks me.

"We'll go straight in and use our arcana to disarm anyone in our way."

She nods in agreement.

"Don't be so quick to be loud. Try being like a whisper first," the Fashion Minister advises. "Valerie will most likely be very weak."

"Why? What do you know?" Edel asks.

The carriage arrives at the pier before he can answer. Snow-lanterns dot its pathway to a series of lavish watercoaches, like beautiful jeweled swans ready to swim to the teahouse shore. Guards survey the pier, but not as many as when we first arrived. The woman still sits in the Silk Teahouse reception booth, a fire-lantern bobbing over her head and illuminating her face like a tiny sun.

"I've left instructions with my boatman to wait only an hour-glass," the minister whispers before tapping the glass with his cane.

The woman jumps, then slides open the window.

"Sir, Minister, what a great honor it is—"

"Prepare a watercoach. I need to see the house madam," he orders.

She bows her head. "But of course. Would you like me to call ahead so she can—"

"All I'd like you to do is prepare the coach."

"Yes, sir, Minister." She scrambles out and to the pier.

We follow. This time, she doesn't ask for identification. She barely even looks at us.

"I should call for a servant to assist with the pedaling. We are closed, so they're all inside."

"Yes, please. I do not want to arrive disheveled and out of breath," he says.

She scrambles with the circuit-phone and requests a servant to come to the pier. After hanging up, she gazes at him lovingly. "I adore the new dresses—"

He raises a hand in the air, swatting away her enthusiasm like an annoying fly.

The servant arrives in a watercoach. We step onto it and sit beneath an ornate canopy. Heat-lanterns orbit us like bayou birds.

The woman pedals. A wobbly bow-lantern is a beacon as the snow rushes down from the sky. The teahouse is even more beautiful up close. Porcelain replicas of silkworms are curved into spirals and move as the wind hits the building. I glance back at the pier we've left. The small receiving house is blanched by the snow. My stomach dips and knots itself. Will the woman call the house madam and alert her? Will Valerie be removed in the few minutes it took for us to arrive? Will the guards be waiting to arrest us?

The teacup dragons wiggle in my waist-sash. Maybe they can sense growing fear. Maybe they can feel the worries I've been trying too hard to hide.

Edel opens and closes her fists like she always does when she's mad or worried. The wind flaps the canopy, stretching its fabric with the threat of yanking it off, claiming it for its own.

The woman parks the boat and helps us out onto a small pier. Guards hug the teahouse, in perfect formation around its edges like petit plums bordering a sweet cake. Snow collects on their hats and shoulders yet they don't flinch.

I try to count them. Twelve. No, thirteen. No, it could be more. I can't see them all as the snow barrels down. It makes me wonder how many are inside. We would never be able to disarm them all. Are we walking into a trap? Should we have gone straight to the Gold Isles for Charlotte? Perhaps I was too rash in my planning.

The poison bottle in my pocket feels heavier now with the weight of what we are attempting to do.

The double doors of the teahouse open before we reach them. A woman greets us in a garish dress that reminds me of parrot feathers. A crown of black hair is braided on her head and interwoven with winter blossoms. "Sir, Minister, to what do I owe this great honor?"

"Madam Renault." He leans forward and kisses both of her cheeks.

"As you know, we are closed at the moment." She smiles and the rouge-stick on her mouth is painted to resemble a flower in bloom.

"Ah, yes, I was in the room when the very decree came down from our new majesty. However, I have an emergency." We enter the foyer and gaze up into the house. The open levels reveal a guard on each floor. "Let me introduce you to Lena"—the minister motions at Edel, who curtsies—"and Noelle of the House of Rare Reptilians."

I bow.

"They are dragon merchants and traders. I plan to present them to the queen as a surprise, but they need a quick beauty touch-up before going to visit with Her Majesty. It's so close to her Coronation and Ascension ceremony—three days and counting," he says, pressing his manicured hand to his chest. "I thought it was nothing you and your girls couldn't handle."

I pat my waist-sash and the teacup dragons peer out of it.

"How lovely," she replies, then bows her head. "Thank you, Gustave. However, I must see their faces. On the new queen's orders, anyone who enters this teahouse must be registered." She snaps her fingers at a nearby servant. "Bring the ledger."

I glance at Edel, catching the outline of her eyes. She nods.

"You would embarrass them by forcing them to show themselves looking not their best," he replies.

"It's fine," I say.

The arcana send a shiver over my skin. As I undo the veil, I feel my hair and face change. Edel mimics me.

The Fashion Minister nods when we reveal ourselves.

Madam Renault studies our faces. "Still quite pretty."

"But not perfect," I add. "And Her Majesty requires that."

She agrees.

I place the veil back on and let the glamour fade.

"So..." the Fashion Minster says.

"But we have no Belles here, Your Grace."

He takes her hand and strokes it. "You're not a very good liar. I know you must have one or two at the ready. They tell the cabinet members everything."

She leans close to him. "But I'm not supposed to."

"Darling, it'll be our little secret." He winks. "I'll be sure to send you over a dress from my new line. A vivant dress that captures the depth and breadth of your beauty. You have been maintaining it well. I have taken notice."

She blushes and her severe mouth softens. "I only have one Belle available. The other is, well, you know, indisposed."

"One will suffice." He removes an overstuffed coin purse from an inner pocket in his jacket. "For your trouble."

She accepts the money.

"Please note that they like having their treatments done together in the same room. I know you can accommodate. Your teahouse is rumored to be the best, even better than the Chrysanthemum."

She beams. "Those Du Barrys have been running the whole tradition into the ground. There's decorum and order that must be adhered to. No corners cut." She snaps at a nearby servant, "Prepare the large chamber on the fourth floor."

"You are most gracious, my lady. I won't forget this favor." The Fashion Minister grins, offering Madam Renault his arm. They saunter deeper into the foyer.

My heart drums as we follow behind. The Fashion Minister distracts her by telling her about the low silkworm harvest this season and how it's affected the production timeline for the queen's line of vivant dresses.

The teacup dragons in my waist-pouch squirm as if they're responding to the nerves cramping my stomach. I pat them, trying to calm their excitement, as I take in our surroundings. Where could Valerie be? Edel does the same, craning her neck to see down darkened corridors.

An attendant marches out with a young woman. A silver collar studded with diamonds loops around her neck, drops down her chest, and clasps her wrists together. A pillbox hat sits on her head and a short face veil masks her eyes, nose, and mouth with lacy silk. Her skin is the deep crimson of a recently bloomed Belle-rose, ready for plucking, and she has two mouths, a regular one and a small one beneath it.

Du Barry's words haunt me: *"There will be a favored set of Belles, and a secondary set to ensure that the needs of the kingdom are met. Basic supply and demand."*

"Why is she chained?" I ask.

The Fashion Minister eyes me.

"The queen's orders. She sent a new government-mandated Belle guide by official post-balloon last week. After those fugitive Belles left the palace." Her gaze is strong as she searches for eye contact.

The Fashion Minister loosens the purple cravat at his throat.

"What about the Belle from the favored generation? We would prefer her," Edel says.

The Fashion Minister's eyebrows raise with alarm.

Madam Renault pales. "There are no Belles from that generation here." She tugs the girl forward. "This one is very talented despite what her outward appearance might suggest."

The Fashion Minister stares at me, awaiting my response.

"The queen will be doing away with segregating Belles into favored classes and secondary classes. They will all occupy the same sphere regardless of how they turn out. The new Minister of Belles, Georgiana Fabry, will see to it," she adds.

Simply hearing that name—Auguste's last name—stings.

"Ada is very talented," Madam Renault repeats.

The girl steps forward. I fixate on the bright red of her skin tone and that tiny second mouth beneath her bottom lip as it opens and closes. I swallow down my burning desire to scream.

"I will oversee the session," the Fashion Minister replies. "I am consulting on their looks. Giving them a full makeover to please Her Majesty."

Madam Renault grins. "What lucky women." She walks forward, and we follow.

We are swept into a treatment room. The vaulted ceiling is frosted with gold and blue, wide arching windows overlook the water, and beauty-lanterns bathe shelves of beauty instruments and Belle-products. The walls are threaded with white-and-gold silk like a tapestry, and tiny perfume blimps cascade above us.

The memories of a life filled with beauty work and appointments rush back. The ledgers full, Bree helping me with clients, Ivy at my side, the moments with Auguste—and Rémy.

"The room must be cleared for privacy. Only the Belle and us," the Fashion Minister says to Madam Renault.

The servants freeze.

"But it isn't protocol," Ada replies, sounding just as we once did when clients wanted to break the rules.

"It will be today," I say.

"The servants must stay," Madam Renault replies. "House rules. I do hope you understand."

For the briefest moment, I think Madam Renault might be protecting Ada. I know what can happen when we're left alone with the wrong client. Prince Alfred's disgusting face invades my memory. I still wish I could see him stuffed into a starvation box for attacking me.

The Fashion Minister flashes her a weak smile, then looks at us with distress in his eyes.

"The least you can do is give us privacy while we prepare," the Fashion Minister states. "Go fetch us tea or something, and bring a food cart. I'm famished."

The room empties, doors closing behind Renault and the others. Edel starts to speak, but the Fashion Minister shakes his head and points to the doors. We spot the shadows of feet just outside of it. Then he raises a finger up to the ceiling.

Confusion mars Ada's face.

"Enigmatics," he whispers. "Ada, if you'd please prepare."

She nods and rushes around checking the details like Edel and I would: making sure adequate beauty-lanterns float about, setting out pots of Belle-rose tea on the table, adding pastilles to melt on chafing dishes to fill the room with a lavender scent, draping a large table with pillows and linens. As she works, I trace my fingers over the fleur-de-lis Belle-symbols etched onto each item in her sparkling beauty caisse and ponder how different our lives were only a month ago.

I remember the first time my sisters and I sneaked into the Belle-product storeroom. After the house had gotten quiet, we'd stolen night-lanterns and dragged them to the back of the house. The room's wonders had unfolded to us for hours: perfume atomizers and color crème-cakes and rouge-sticks and powders and kohl pencils and golden vinaigrettes and pastilles and potpourri and oils and sachets. The room smelled heady and sweet, and we'd fallen asleep there after powdering ourselves all night. Du Barry made us write one hundred lines each as punishment.

I search Ada's face for something, anything that resembles the connection I have with my sisters. Can we trust her? Will she be happy once we reveal ourselves? Or will she turn us in?

The risk churns in my stomach.

But we have no choice. We must tell her of our plan. But as the Fashion Minister has pointed out, Sophia could very well be listening. Why hadn't we planned for this? I don't even have a spare piece of parchment on which to scrawl out a message. Then I remember another treatment room, another moment I needed to communicate in silence.

"Undress," I say to Edel. "I have an idea."

I know there is confusion in Edel's glare as she stares from behind her veil, but she obliges. I wave Ada closer.

"I want to show you a technique that we both enjoy and would like you to use," I tell her.

Edel disrobes and climbs into the bed.

"Ready?" I ask.

"Just get on with it," Edel mumbles, the frustration stewing just under her words.

I grab a bei-powder bundle, then sprinkle it over Edel's back, coating it evenly with a makeup brush. My hand wobbles.

The door slides open and another servant slips in.

"We need hot towels," the Fashion Minister orders. "Bring them now."

The woman turns back around and scurries out.

I push my shoulders back and wave the brush in the air to get Ada's attention. In the bei powder along Edel's back, I write a message.

Where is Valerie?

I lift my veil and she sees my face.

Ada gasps and falls backward into a teacart. "The favorite," she whispers.

That word cuts across my skin. The Fashion Minister reaches down and puts a hand over her mouths.

"They're always listening," he reminds her.

"Don't say a word," I whisper. "I promise we're here to help. We need your assistance."

Ada nods and the Fashion Minister eases his hand off her mouths. She quickly wipes away my message and writes, *Near Madam.*

I snatch a rose from a nearby vase, then write: *Take us.*

Her eyes fill with fear, her hands trembling at her sides, but she nods.

17

"I'll stay here and distract the servants," the Fashion Minister tells us. "But be quick."

Edel throws her gown back on, and Ada leads us out through the servant entrance. The house is near silent. We tiptoe to a back staircase.

"This only goes to the sixth floor. The seventh is where *she* resides. We go up there when we've made a mistake and need a 'talking to,' as she calls it," Ada whispers. "It's Madam's office."

We follow behind her with our lightest footsteps. The upper floors are filled mostly with a maze of treatment salons and tearooms, but I spot a dining room and game parlor. Unlit lanterns litter the floors. I grip the rose stem so tightly the thorns push into my palm, but the pain is a tiny cut in comparison to the anger rushing through me.

"How old are you?" I ask Ada.

"I don't know."

"What happened to your face? Were you hurt?" Edel asks,

examining the deep red flush that lingers beneath her skin, and the tiny mouth beneath her bottom lip.

"No. It has always been this way."

I've lost track of which floor we're on when suddenly Ada's breathing quickens, and her pace slows. Ahead a man sits in front of a lift, head down reading a newspaper. We press our bodies against the walls, out of sight. His limbs are thin as the bayou reeds from our home island, and his pale skin mirrors the snow falling outside the windows. He whistles softly. The headlines jumble as he quickly turns the pages.

"Stay behind us," I tell Ada, then turn to Edel. "Let's trap him using this rose. We'll turn it into a cage."

Edel nods with a smile.

I close my eyes and the arcana wake inside me. My fingertips tingle. The rose blooms in my mind. I use the second arcana, Aura, to locate its life force; it's weak from being cut and put in a jar of water. Both Edel and I work together to push the rose to grow—the stem splitting into two and slithering along the floor like a pair of thorny snakes. The petals swell to match the man's size.

He shifts his paper down and jumps to his feet, but before he can move forward in our direction, the stem curls around his ankles and the petals swallow him in a red cocoon. His shouts are muffled and his attempts to run thwarted by the binding stems.

"How did you do that?" Ada asks.

"Just how you use the second arcana to grow a client's hair or stretch their muscle tissue," Edel replies.

Ada inspects the massive rose prison we've made as we file into the lift, clearly amazed. She jerks a lever forward. The gilded box sails upward.

"What do we do if she's up here?" Ada's eyes stretch with worry.

"The same thing we just did to him."

She smiles. "I want to learn how to do that."

"We will teach you," I reply.

The set of apartments is empty and dark aside from a single day-lantern hooked to the wall. Edel unties it.

"Now, where did you say our sister was?" I ask.

"Whenever I came up here to be scolded she'd take me to her parlor room. That's where I saw Valerie the first time. There's a bedroom." Ada leads us to a door crested with the Silk Isles' emblem—the silkworm entangled with a royal chrysanthemum.

I push the door open slowly. It's a cross between a tearoom and a small library. High ceilings hold glass windows that gaze down into the belly of the house, with each floor a decadent layer on an expensive cake. Tall ladders slide along mahogany shelves and sets of staircases spiral up to a balcony with more books. Velvet armchairs and tufted couches circle an enormous table littered with replicas of royal emblems sitting on a map of Orléans.

"What is this?" Edel asks Ada.

"She's always plotting and planning and tracking which important people live where. Which courtiers or merchants frequent which teahouses. I've heard her on the circuit-phones. She wants to run all the teahouses. That's her goal."

Beneath the subtle light, the emblems are luminescent and show who has the power in this world. It is only a handful of people.

"This way." Ada pushes through a plain, almost hidden door. Behind it, the room is small, its walls bare, and a bed consumes most of the space.

Its occupant is Valerie.

Edel and I rush to her side. Cerulean healing-lanterns leave strips of light over her face. Vases of flowers ring the bed. Her tawny-brown skin is tough and pruned.

"Valerie?" I whisper.

I touch the wrinkles along her skin. I want to smooth them for her, restore her face to what it once was. But I remember what Ivy said when I wanted to do the same for her—*It will damage your arcana.* I stare at the slope of her nose and the once rosebud shape of her lips and the chestnut of her hair. I can't help but touch her chin.

"What happened to her? What did that woman do?" Edel asks, her voice filling with rage.

"Overuse of the arcana. Ivy's skin looked like this, too," I reply.

"Can we fix it?"

"It's forbidden to work on other Belles," Ada says.

"It's forbidden to do a lot of things," I reply.

Valerie startles awake. "Camille? Edel?" her voice croaks.

My knees buckle, all the worry sliding off me.

Edel and I climb into her bed. The size of it almost swallows us.

"How do you feel?" Edel asks.

Her sluggish eyes brighten a little. "Terrible."

"We've come to take you with us," I say.

"How did you get here?" she asks.

"With a little help," Edel answers. "And we're going to go get Charlotte next and put an end to all of this."

"Where are our sisters?" she asks.

"They've been placed all over Orléans, according to the information I have. Padma is trapped at home, Hana is in the Fire Isles, and Amber is in the Glass Isles," I report.

"Are they all right?"

"We don't know," Edel answers, trying to sit her up, but Valerie's limbs flop every which way and she can barely hold her head straight. "Have you just done beauty work? Is that why you're so tired?"

"I haven't done anything." She fights to keep her eyes open, her lids falling like heavy curtains. "No beauty work in days."

"They're bleeding her. I see the vats of blood being taken to the dock every morning," Ada says.

"But why?" I ask. Valerie is not the aether, so her blood is not being used to grow other Belles.

"I don't know," Valerie says, almost out of breath.

More questions add to the storm brewing in my head. What is Sophia up to?

"We have to get you out of here, and get you well." I push back her once thick hair.

We try to lift her, but she flops back on the bed. I perch over her, wanting my strength to drift into her limbs. The bones in her shoulder push into my leg. A tide of worry rises inside me each time she moans.

"I can't," Valerie replies. "I need to rest for a minute."

"Ada, find some sangsues," Edel says.

I glance up at the hourglass in the room, the sand racing from one side to the other. We don't have much time left to get to the boat.

Edel grabs a cloth from the water basin on the side table and drapes it across Valerie's forehead. "Only for a few minutes, then we have to go."

"Valerie, I have a question." The poison in my pocket almost hums, full of power. "When you looked after the Belle babies, how were they grown? Did Du Barry let you see?"

"Why?" she says.

"Sophia is making more Belles, and I need to know how, so we can stop her."

"She kept two nurseries at home. One for the Gris babies born in the maternity rooms, and one for us." She coughs, then continues, "Sometimes she'd stay up all night, and I'd sneak into the Belle-nursery to see what she was doing. She'd bring a new crying baby inside after the evening star rose."

"Did you find out where they came from?"

Valerie nods. "She digs us up."

"What?" Edel and I say in unison.

"Well, some of us," she pants. "Out of the dark forest. I saw her from the nursery window."

"So much for falling from the sky," Edel snaps.

"No. That's true." Valerie takes a deep and labored breath. "But only one Belle falls. She plants the rest—the favored generation, at least, is grown that way." Her voice grows weaker. "I don't know how she makes the others."

I squeeze her hand and reach in my pocket to wrap my fingers around the poison bottle. "One last question before we try to move you again. Do you think Belle babies can be born without their gifts?"

Edel eyes me curiously.

"Why would you want that?" Valerie asks.

"Yes, why?" Edel adds.

"Sophia plans to sell Belles to the highest bidder," I tell her. Valerie's mouth goes slack with horror. "If we could save the next generation from this fate—"

"Then they could all live normal lives," Edel finishes, nodding in agreement with my line of thought.

I show them the poison bottle. "This might take away the arcana. But I wouldn't know how to administer it. Do you think you could help?"

Valerie's eyes bulge as she runs shaky fingers across the blue bottle. "I believe so...." Valerie starts to drift off.

"Valerie! Valerie. Stay with us," Edel says, rubbing her shoulder.

"Should we try to move her again?" I ask, watching Valerie's eyes flutter.

"Let's check her levels. She's so weak, we might have to cover her in sangsues in order to get her strong enough to move." Edel turns to the side table and retrieves an arcana meter. She plucks needles from the base compartment of the machine and takes Valerie's arm; it's a pale brown branch draped across her lap. Valerie's blood barely fills three vials and slides into the arcana meter's slots.

I hold my breath as I watch Valerie's blood swirl through those chambers. The red liquid bubbles and churns. I wonder what her blood proteins look like now. I wish I could see them beneath Mr. Claiborne's optic-scope. My stomach flip-flops as the numbers begin to illuminate, and reveal her levels.

MANNER: One and a half.

AURA: One.

AGE: Zero.

A knot forms in my throat. She barely has any arcana proteins left in her blood. They are almost gone. This is what will happen to the Belle babies if the poison is successful. Can we survive without our gifts from the Goddess of Beauty? Will she be able to recover?

There's a crash downstairs. "Time to go," Edel says. "We have to move her."

Edel tries to lift Valerie again. I pocket the bottle and help hold up the right side of Valerie's body. She cries out with pain. Edel tries to wipe away a falling tear, but her fingers miss it.

"If she can't walk, we'll be caught," I reply, trying to hide the panic in my voice. "Ada, can you go get the Fashion Minister and bring him to us? We need him."

Fear consumes Ada's face.

I rush to her and take her hands. "He's on our side. He's going to help us."

"What about me?" she asks. "You can't just leave me here."

"We won't. I promise," I say. "Is anyone else here? More Belles?"

"Yes, they're chained on the fourth floor. If I'm not back in a quarter of an hourglass, then..."

"You won't have to worry about that. Just go."

Ada rushes out. We shift Valerie upright, her legs hanging off the bed.

"Good. Almost up," I say. "Just a little bit more."

The teacup dragons shift inside my waist-sash, peeking out, and the dagger at my hip shifts, a half-moon hooked at my side.

"What are those?" Valerie asks.

"Teacup dragons."

"I thought they didn't exist. Du Barry said..." Drool dribbles from her lips.

"Du Barry told us a lot of things," I reply, wiping her face. "They were given to me to help us."

She runs her fingers along their noses as they lick her, then she touches the dagger sheath Rémy gave me.

"All right, let's try to take a step." Edel hoists Valerie's arm around her neck.

"There's so much pain," she cries. "My whole body hurts. It feels like my bones are shattered."

Edel clears her throat and wipes away the tears brimming in her eyes before Valerie can see them. I'm not so quick, and a tear escapes my eye.

"Edel, Camille, I can't." Valerie squeezes my arm with all her strength. "I don't have anything left." Her gaze sears into mine, and her message crystallizes as her hand falls to the dagger at my waist. "Things will never be the same again." She grabs the dagger from its sheath and stabs it into the side of her neck. Her body jerks like a bayou fish caught in a net. She exhales. Her mouth goes soft.

Edel screams.

Not a single drop of blood oozes from Valerie's neck. The wound is dry.

She's empty.

I stumble backward and off the bed, hitting the floor with a thud.

She's gone.

18

"What happened here? I thought we'd embarked on a rescue mission?" the Fashion Minister says, marching into the room with Ada at his side.

"She . . . she . . ." The words won't form.

"She killed herself," Edel says with a sob.

The Fashion Minister perches over the bed. Valerie's body stares up at us—her eyes foggy, glazed like glass marbles. Edel drops to her knees. Tears are a storm of fat raindrops down her red cheeks.

The minister covers his mouth briefly, then says, "We have to go, now."

I can't move. I'm a statue sitting vigil at her side.

"We can't leave her like this!" Edel says.

"She's not *here* anymore."

"She needs a proper burial." Edel's eyes spill over. "So the Goddess of Beauty will receive her."

The Fashion Minister drapes a blanket over Valerie's face. Another sob escapes Edel's mouth. I am too stunned to cry.

"Hush or we'll all be caught. My head will be on a spike after an unpleasant tenure in a starvation box. It's way too beautiful to meet such a fate; I take such excellent care of it. And the two of you will be carted off to Sophia's prison to be milked for your blood— just like Valerie has been. My dandies will keep the body safe, transport it to Maison Rouge under the strictest of instructions. The corpse will be waiting for you to bury her. Now, we must go!"

"Don't forget about me," Ada pleads.

I turn to the Fashion Minister.

He sighs. "Another favor? I can see it all over your face."

"Can you help get Ada and the other Belles out?" I ask.

"And take them where?"

"Anywhere but here."

"More breaking of laws," he says.

"You've always done it one way or another," I remind him. "And when the Goddess of Death weighs your heart at the end of all things, she'll see what you did for us."

He leans forward and plants a kiss on my forehead. "If I keep my head long enough to get my husband back, I want to raise a child to have your spirit—and your looks."

I smile up at him. The thunder of footsteps rises from below and shouts rattle the house.

We scramble.

"I'll set her and her sisters free, but where they go is up to them," Gustave says. "My private schooner is waiting for you. It's not supposed to be out on the open waters, definitely more suited for short-distance travel and through canals and rivers, but we don't have a choice. My boatman is discreet, having served me for many years and having been privy to all of my dalliances. Just stay inside the cabin. He'll announce your arrival at the port, then he'll leave for half an hourglass to give you enough time to disembark in Céline before he returns to me."

"Thank you. I can't tell you—"

Madam Renault and her guards march into the room, choking the space and blocking all ways out. "What is going on here?" She paces in a circle, her little heels clicking along the floor. "I had a bad feeling about your visit, Gustave, but to find the favorite and her sister here? That's another thing entirely."

My heart sinks.

She gazes at Valerie's covered body. "What have you done to her?"

"What have *you* done to her?" Edel snaps, her rage loose and ready.

She laughs. "My duty. But, Gustave, it seems you're caught in something you shouldn't be. Something that might cause you to lose your pretty head."

"You won't touch him," I shout, shaking with anger. The teacup dragons peek out of my waist-sash, irritated and hiccuping fire. "Feuille, Fantôme, Poivre, Ryra, and Eau," I call out. "Burn everything."

I make a whooshing sound, and they mimic me. They bolt out and above our heads. Their tiny blasts of fire quickly ignite the tapestries.

"Arrest them all," Madam Renault orders. "And catch those little dragons."

The guards rush forward.

I pull Rémy's knife from Valerie's neck. The tiniest freckles of her blood mar the silver. The last of her. I prepare to use the dagger, though I don't know how. I think of Rémy. He'd say, *They don't know that you don't know how to use it.* I stab at the guards, pushing them back as the flames grow around us.

Madam Renault fusses with Ada, trying to pull her by the chain. Edel kicks and thrashes at the guards. The Fashion Minister throws anything he can reach in their direction. The teacup dragons' fire spreads through the room, igniting the bed canopy. It collapses, dropping fiery pieces on Valerie's blanket. The flames crawl along her body and catch her thick brown hair.

Madam Renault orders the guards to put out the fire.

My eyes blur from the smoke. The guards cough and choke. I can't see Valerie anymore. I can't see anything.

The Fashion Minister hollers out, "Run!"

I grab Edel and Ada by their hands and do as he says, stumbling from the room. The teacup dragons follow, still spreading their fire.

19

Soft beams of moonlight sweep along the ocean as the left eye of the God of the Sky rises. The Silk Isles' teahouse burns in the distance like a dying star. The edges of the imperial island glare as we sail along its coast—lantern-houses and piers and sill-lanterns in mansions that overlook the waves. The color is so different from the water that surrounds our home. I think of the terrifying stories we were told about the octopus living in the Rose Bayou. But we were never taught what lurked out here, what creatures inhabited the God of the Seas' vast domain.

"We won't get there any faster with you watching," Edel says. "And you're letting in a draft. The dragons are getting fussy."

"All the lighthouses are sending beams of light out. Don't you think that's strange?"

"No," she replies. "But it's freezing."

I close the drapes and turn back to the small but decadent cabin. The Fashion Minister's lavish watercoach feels like a palace apartment set afloat. Plush chaises and couches circle a long table holding all the supplies we've amassed—Rémy's maps, a few stolen Belle-products we haven't had to sell, ink and parchment and a quill, food for the teacup dragons, my beauty caisse full of labeled sangsue bottles, the plump coin purses the Fashion Minister gave us. Fire-lanterns hover throughout, lending their heat to the chilly space. Cabinets boast all manner of treats—roasted nuts, cheese blocks, baskets of macarons, casks of wine and ale. But I have no appetite for any of it. We lost Valerie. We'll never see her again. I can barely hold that truth in my head.

My throat burns, the taste of the fire still on my tongue. "What if all our sisters are in pain like Valerie?"

"We can't lose another sister. We need to find a way to get to them," she says.

"We lost Amber." It stings saying her name.

Edel's face is like stone. "I told you, she's changed."

My frustration, fueled by grief, bubbles over. "You weren't at that dinner party with Claudine. You weren't at the palace. You didn't see what Sophia did to us. She turned everything into a game. She forced me to give a courtier a pig nose, she broke my hand, she poisoned my food. I didn't get to talk to Amber about all the things she'd made her do. Sophia is a monster. She bends you into ugly shapes, and I regret every minute of her being able to do that to me."

"I saw interviews with Amber bragging about being better than us. Better than her sisters. More deserving of the title of favorite." Edel's back stiffens, and her hands ball into fists as she readies herself for a fight. "You can't convince me that she always loved us."

"We all wanted to be the favorite. That means we had to be better than one another," I remind her. "She just wasn't nice about it."

"I never wanted any of that. I never wanted this life."

"Well, good for you for being above it all. But we're not all the same. We're sisters, but we're not the same."

"I don't want to talk about Amber anymore." Edel turns her back to me and reads a newspaper.

We sit in silence for a while, the worries stretching like dough between us. I take Arabella's Belle-book from my travel sack. I trace my fingers across the etched arabella flowers on the cover.

Date: Day 3,657 at court

I found the official Belle registry today. Every Belle who ever lived is accounted for. The favored ones and the non-favored ones. There were ledgers here going back thousands of years. Each generation laid out in family clusters. Names scrawled in parchment alongside their best arcana.

I wonder how many Belles there are now, how many Du Barry grew in my generation, and where they might be. The thought of trying to find them all and make sure they're safe becomes an overwhelming storm. I close Arabella's book to erase the thoughts.

The teacup dragons stir in their sleep just seconds before there's a tap on the window.

Startled, I pull back the drapes. Little golden Or perches on the tiny sill. I push the latch to let her in. She doesn't carry a post-balloon. Instead ribbons loop around her ankle, and she clutches a parchment scroll in her tiny talons.

"You found us, girl." My heart squeezes.

It's from Rémy.

Or lands on my lap. I untie the ribbons quickly and free her to reunite with her brothers and sisters.

Edel darts over to me, almost falling due to the rocky motion of the boat.

My fingers fumble with the note as I try to unroll it. His handwriting is neat, each sentence perfectly placed on the page. I've never seen it before and the sight of it makes me smile. Edel tries to read over my shoulder, but I pull the letter close so only I can read it.

Camille,

All post-balloons are now subject to monitoring if they leave the city of Trianon. The air-postmen have been given strict surveillance orders. They collect them and transfer the messages into ledgers reviewed by the queen and her staff. If approved, the post-balloons can be released for travel. At night, they'll be using sky candles to illuminate the entire kingdom to watch for any alternate forms of communication.

The Minister of News has even developed weather balloons, which release rain down over cities and reveal invisible post-balloons, so don't risk using the ones we purchased. Send all messages with Or using her claw.

I'm still trying to find my way into the palace. Your note was extremely helpful, and I avoided making a huge mistake trying to use the old tunnel network.

My family is being held in apartments rather than dungeons. The Minister of War ensured that, and I am forever grateful. I'm going to break them out in three days' time, the same day as the coronation. I'm putting the pieces together.

Once I secure my family, I will come back into Trianon and wait for you. The festivities will have just begun, and it will be chaos—which is a good thing. Oftentimes, things are missed in a storm. Use the maps!

Be safe.

Rémy

"What does it say?" Edel tries to take the parchment from my hands. "Is it from Rémy?"

"Yes." I pull away. "It was for me. He told me that post-balloons are being monitored and not to send them in the direction of Trianon anymore. To send Or only." I tuck the parchment into my dress pocket, and it feels like a warm bayou rock through the fabric. His words run through my mind.

I will come back into Trianon and wait for you.

Be safe.

She frowns, her mouth pursed with confusion and irritation. "You're being strange."

"Fine." I take the letter out again and shove it at her.

She reads it. "I'm glad he's all right."

"You suddenly like him?"

"I don't *dislike* him." Her eyes burn into mine. "I don't love him like you do."

"He's been good to us. He was there for me at the palace, even when I didn't realize it," I admit. "He's important." The words *I love him* tuck themselves deep down inside me, afraid to be exposed to light and air once again.

The teacup dragons squeak.

"They need to be fed," she says.

"And we should write to Arabella about what happened with Valerie. She's probably heard about the Silk Teahouse burning already."

Edel feeds them salted pork, then hands me my quill, ink, and a small piece of parchment.

I scribble quickly.

Arabella,

Valerie is dead. The Silk Teahouse has burned down. But we've located who we were looking for, and are on our way there. We'll be with you, soon.

Love,

Camille

I read it out loud to Edel, and she grunts her approval. I put the dragons, except for Fantôme, in their cage and drag a cloth over its bars.

"You've got a journey tonight," I say.

Edel feeds her another cube of salted pork. I fish out one of Arabella's sangsues from our jars. Only two remain.

"Stay low." I kiss Fantôme's warm head and send her out the window.

Footsteps draw near to the door. A newspaper slides beneath it with a whoosh.

I grab it—the late-night edition of the *Herald*. The front page shows Sophia and Auguste at the Royal Opera under the headline: TROUBLE BEFORE MATRIMONY. She's all grins and her teacup monkey, Singe, hangs off her tall hair-tower like it's a low-hanging tree branch. Auguste grimaces, his long, tousled hair pulled back. He's grown a full beard and his eyes look sad.

I wonder if soon I won't think about him or remember him, if little moments like this will stop making the cut reopen, spilling fresh blood and pain. His picture stirs memories I'd worked hard to bury deep inside me, rattling and shaking them like sand in a flipped hourglass. How can I still feel this way about him when the thought of Rémy makes me smile?

I close my eyes and imagine arriving at the palace and facing Sophia. I see her surrounded by her pets—both human and animal—wielding her power, and him sitting on the throne beside her, slumped in the chair with a perpetual scowl on his face. I wonder what will happen to him when we stop Sophia from becoming queen. Has he grown to love her? Has he grown to support her?

The boat jerks.

"Drop your anchor," a voice commands.

I peek out from behind the drapes. A sleek black boat slides up beside our watercoach.

"Edel," I whisper hard.

She doesn't stir.

I jostle her arm.

She jumps.

"Someone is outside."

I whistle. All the teacup dragons wake up. I slip them into my pouch, where they curl back together and resume sleeping. I scramble to repack our things. My skin, my heart, my bones all thrum with panic.

There's a rumble as feet hit the ship's deck. Edel and I move to the center of the chamber, standing back-to-back, bracing for whoever comes through the door.

I place my hand on the knife Rémy gave me. Still spotted with Valerie's blood. My fingers buzz with the tingle of the arcana rising inside to protect me.

The door opens.

Three women enter wearing dark gowns edged in white, their faces covered with smiling iron masks. Etched spiders dot across their cheeks. Crowns of strange pink flowers twist around their heads.

"Don't touch us," Edel hollers.

One of the women laughs. "We don't plan on it." She pulls out two small thuribles. The metal burners explode with thick acrid smoke.

Edel coughs and clutches her stomach. The night-lanterns snuff out.

I wave my hands in front of my face as a dull ringing reverberates in my ears, but it's no use. My lungs fill with smoke, and the light disappears as I feel myself falling.

20

I fall in and out of a dream. Maman replaces Sophia. We're in the library at Maison Rouge. The space is dark and somber, furniture upholstered in deep maroons, crimson velvets, and rich golds, with heavy shaded lanterns sitting on each table. Tall bookshelves line the walls, the varnish giving them a bloody glow. Spines reveal legal titles—beauty and toilette laws, city decorum statutes, and royal family protocol—stretching back to the very beginning of Orléans. A large portrait series of Belle generations hangs from a mosaic ceiling by glittering strings. I'm small, skipping behind her from aisle to aisle, chasing her trailing nightgown.

"What are you looking for, Maman?" I ask.

She smiles back at me, her eyes alive with wonder and excitement. "A fairy tale that I want to tell you."

"I thought you knew all the stories." I catch her and slide my hand into hers; it's warm and strong. "You said you did."

"I do, but I need to get the details of this one just right. It's about the Beauty Trials and the everlasting rose. Did Madam Du Barry tell you about that?"

"No."

She smiles. "You'll see."

We sneak through more aisles until she pauses before a shelf of red-spined books. She runs her fingers across them, and I mimic her.

"Aren't they lovely?" she says, pulling out a thin volume.

"Yes," I say.

She cracks it open, sniffs the parchment, then puts it under my nose. "And they smell like..."

"Ink," I reply.

"Magic." She kisses my forehead. "Come, petite abeille." She leads me to one of the cushioned window nooks in the library. We look out over the Rose Bayou to the left—white trees holding their crimson petals and imperial boats navigating the waters to our canopied dock, and the forest behind our house to the right— all-consuming darkness as far as the eye can see.

She opens the book, traces her long white fingers over the calligraphy, and scans the page. "Before the Goddess of Beauty decided to return to her husband, she had to trust someone to take care of us."

"How did she do it?" I ask.

"If you listen, I will tell you." She pushes a finger against my nose. "So many questions before letting the story unfold. She established the Beauty Trials to draw out the right woman who could be trusted to take care of us."

"What's a trial?"

"A test." She points to pictures in the book of the Goddess

seated on a throne made of Belle-roses. "She wanted to make sure the woman would have the right qualities."

"Like what?"

She taps the picture of a line of women.

"Some of the same qualities that you have, little fox. Determination, strength, kindness, loyalty, fortitude, and most of all, selflessness."

My eyes soak in the pictures of various women standing before the Goddess. "What did they have to do?"

"See this chest here"—she traces her finger over the drawing— "it contains objects that start a divine series of challenges."

"Who won?"

"You don't remember the first queen of Orléans from your history lessons?"

I shake my head. She purses her lips.

"Don't tell Du Barry," I plead. "I don't want to have to write any lines."

"Madam Du Barry," she corrects.

I sigh.

"Never. Our secrets are ours." She winks at me. "Queen Marjorie. She was the first monarch of the House of Orléans. The Goddess also gave her an everlasting rose." She flips a page in the book and taps a picture of a black-and-red rose growing from blood-soaked soil.

"What's that, Maman?" I ask, circling my finger over the ink-drawn petals.

"A symbol that represents us," she replies.

My eyes widen. "Do you think she misses us? Do you think she'd ever visit?"

"I think if we needed her, she would come." She taps my nose. "But otherwise I think she's done with this world. She sent us. We are her everlasting roses. Our blood, *her* blood, is what has rescued this world and allows it to thrive."

"Can we call her on one of the circuit-phones? What if we really need help one day?"

She takes my hand in hers, knitting our fingers together like threads of white and brown yarn. "I don't think she'd send us here without being able to protect us if something went wrong."

The light from a single night-lantern is a shock, pulling me out of my dreams and back into this new and strange reality. My surroundings sharpen around me.

A dungeon.

A cage.

Metal bars lock us inside a cave. Long, pointed cylinders push through the stone ceiling like the spikes on a gigantic teacup porcupine.

My eyes are sore, burning with the memory of acidic smoke, but I spot Edel curled up on the floor a few feet away. A cold tremor jolts through my body as I begin to remember what happened. The metallic scent of stagnant water and steam tickle my nose. I lick my lips and wince. My lower lip is split at the corner and the taste of salt stings my tongue.

How long have we been asleep? How long have we been down here?

I touch my pocket. The poison bottle is still buried deep. I touch my stomach. The waist-sash is gone. The dragons gone. The dagger gone. The maps gone. The beauty caisse with the sangsues gone.

Terror drowns me.

"Edel." I touch her shoulder gently. "Wake up."

She groans and turns over, clutching her head. "What happened? Where are we?"

"I'm not sure." I struggle to get on my feet. My body sways as if we're still on the Fashion Minister's watercoach. My skull is light as a perfume blimp.

I stagger to the bars—curved, black, and containing no visible door.

"Who were those people?" she says, agitation sharpening her voice.

"I've seen those masks before, but I can't remember where." I strain to look through the bars. There's nothing but a great pit with water at the bottom of it. The view sends a wave of nausea through me. Sea-lanterns drift about, spreading tiny ovals of light over craggy rocks. The hiss of steam and the plunk of unknown objects falling into water sound in the near distance. A long stretch of black cables disappear into the darkness overhead.

"Hello!" I shout.

My voice bounces off every wall. Edel massages her temples. I shake the bars, and my own headache intensifies. I lean against the cool rock wall and breathe until it subsides.

Edel stumbles as she pushes herself up. She cradles her head. "I feel sick."

"This is exactly how I felt after Sophia tampered with my food."

Edel inspects the bars and tugs on them too. There's no give. Even if we could remove them, there would be no place to go, no ledge to help us escape. We'd fall more than a hundred paces into whatever lies below. That darkness. That water. Those craggy rocks.

"What would Rémy think of what we've gotten ourselves into?" I say.

"That we should've skipped seeing the Fashion Minister—or even Valerie. That we should've gone straight to Charlotte," she replies.

I can't argue with her. But we did need the money to get to Charlotte—not that we have any of it now.

A loud popping makes us jump. Edel and I move closer to each other.

A rickety carriage putters along the black suspension cable. Edel and I hold hands.

The door opens to reveal a snug compartment covered in threadbare velvet and thick navy trim.

A face appears, shadowed by the soft night-lantern—a boy about our age with a crooked grin and a strange excitement lighting his eyes. He inches closer, trying to balance as he leans out, and pushes a slender basket through the bars.

"Where are we? And who are you?" Edel barks.

"That's not a nice way to greet someone who just brought you food," he challenges her. His hair is so dark it could be the night sky itself folded into waves.

Edel kicks the basket aside and its contents spill. "I'm not nice, and I don't have to be. You people are holding us against our will."

He smiles at her. "Well, it's nice to meet you, too. Would you like to know how the weather is?"

"I want to know where we are," she replies.

I gather up the food and inspect it, my stomach growling. A wedge of cheese and dried meat. I scarf down my half while Edel continues to spar with the boy. Her cheeks hold a flush and her hands are balled into fists at her sides. The way they go back and forth reminds me of how I used to talk to Auguste. The memory is a burning knot, and I swallow more food to bury it.

"You're at the mouth of the Goddess of Death's caves. We just call it the Grottos. I grew up on a nearby island—though no one even registers it on an official map of Orléans. If you live out here, you're considered unlucky. Not worth accounting for."

"Let us out." Edel tries to shake the bars again, but they don't budge.

"I'm afraid I can't do that. You're in the web now."

"He's right," a voice calls out.

We look up and spot a woman in an open-top dirigible, the words ORLÉANSIAN AIR-POST on it scratched out and replaced with THE SPIDERS. "Quentin!"

The boy jumps, almost falling. Edel reaches through the bars and grabs hold of him before he tumbles.

"See, I knew you could be nice," he says, earning a scowl from Edel.

"You weren't paid to chat, only to deliver food," the woman says. She's gray like a Gris, her eyes glowing embers with impossibly long eyelashes. Her curly black hair is pinned into an elegant knot, and beautiful. "Scurry along home now. I'd hate to have to tell Lady Arane about this. She'd dock your wages."

"Yes, my lady. May your threads be strong." He bows his head, she nods, then he cuts his eyes back at Edel. "See you around, hopefully." He shuts the carriage door, and it inches its way back down into the darkness.

Edel's eyes are fixed on the woman floating in front of us. I abandon the food and stand at Edel's side.

The woman studies us quietly. "I haven't seen a Belle up close in some time."

"It looks that way," Edel spits out.

"Your commentary doesn't bother me. I've quieted those instincts."

"Who are you?" I ask.

"I am an Iron Lady," she replies.

A glimmer of hope springs up inside me. "You're on our side."

"What?" Edel says to me.

"You support us." I press my face against the bars.

"We support *our* cause, and whatever will help us achieve it." She crosses her arms over her chest.

"And what is that? Locking us up? Why didn't you summon the guards?" Edel grips the bars. "Why torture us?"

"You call *this* torture?" She laughs and motions at the basket of food. "At this very moment, our future queen is finalizing her preparations to turn your favored generation into cows, to live in her farm prison where you shall be milked, your power bottled and shipped around the kingdom. The rest she will dole out to every household that can afford it."

Edel and I exchange glances.

"We are no friends to Sophia. I've read your papers. You know that," I say.

"But you've been used as instruments of power. We must ensure you aren't loyal to her in any way. Proximity to power can distort one's allegiances, can make you align with something that wishes to use you, just so you can be close to it."

"And why should we trust *you*?" Edel says. "You poisoned us and locked us up."

"Sleeping gas. It wasn't poison. Many nurseries use it to help babies fall asleep. You took a long nap. Only a few hours," she says. "We will determine if we can trust each other. You will join me on my dirigible, but once we get to the ground, you must wear these over your head." She holds up two sacks. "If you refuse, you can stay up here until you change your minds. Quentin will not be returning with more food, and hunger may coax you into making the right decision."

Edel and I make eye contact. She grits her teeth. But we have no time to argue.

"Yes," I reply for both of us. "We will come with you."

21

She uses a skeleton key to unlock the cell. Edel rushes forward like a storm cloud eager to burst with thunder and lightning and wind. I grab the back of her dress before she reaches the ledge and hold her close. The rage inside her almost seeps through her skin, a humming tuning fork sending ripples out.

We both gaze down into the darkness below, the expanse of it terrifying, a pit to swallow us whole. My mind fills with all the twisted and dangerous things that might await if we took that plunge.

"There's nowhere to run but straight into the Goddess of Death's teeth," the woman threatens.

Edel jerks back, knocking into me. I tighten my grip around her waist. "Calm down. We're going to get out of here," I whisper to her. "We will find our way."

"If you die down here, you become hers." The woman opens a small door and invites us to board her dirigible. "Ready? Or do you still want to run?"

Edel and I lock eyes, gaining strength from each other, then we ease on board and lower ourselves into two makeshift seats.

"Where are my teacup dragons?" I ask.

"Safe." The woman reaches up and closes the tiny fire hatch beneath the balloon. "For now."

"Is that a threat?" I ask.

"It's whatever you want it to be," she replies.

My stomach swoops as we sink deep into the darkness, the cold wetness turning warmer, the hiss of steam growing louder. When we were little girls, we were told that the Goddess of Beauty hated the Goddess of Death. They'd been sisters who'd fought and fussed over all things until they could no longer exist in this world side by side. Unpopular with the other gods for her unpredictable temper, Death was cast into the depths of the world to hide and deal with the bodies and souls of the dead. The grottos are the entrance to her lair.

We reach a small platform and step off the dirigible. Three masked women approach, gripping burlap sacks, their movements languid like spirits.

My stomach tightens.

"Why is this necessary? It's not like we can see anything down here," Edel snaps.

"Edel," I reply despite my fear. "We agreed."

"Listen to your sister," one of the women says, her voice raspy. "She is wise."

"No one is to know the way in and out of the spiders' lair," another says.

I drop my head forward, submitting to the sack. She pulls it over my head. "Good girl," she whispers.

The light is stamped out and my heart squeezes. Panic starts to overtake me but I try my best to fight it.

Another woman grabs my arm and shoves me forward. We walk along a rocky surface. The scent of water fills my nose, a mixture of the Rose Bayou from home and La Mer du Roi. The hiss of steam muffles our footsteps. *Where are they taking us?*

I take a deep breath and think of Rémy. He would say, "Pay attention. Be ready. You will be all right."

Small freckles of light push through the fabric.

The woman's grip tightens on my forearm, pinching the skin. "We agreed to go with you. No need to be so rough."

"Oh, Princess, I'm so sorry," she says sarcastically.

"We're not princesses," I hear Edel holler back.

"We've never been that," I add.

"Settle, or I'll break your arm," she says, her voice grating against my skin like rough parchment. "And I should for what you did."

My blood runs cold. What I did? How could I have done anything to offend this random person at the edge of the world? "Who are you?" I ask.

"You don't remember?" she purrs in my ear.

"I wouldn't be asking if I did."

"We're almost there," another voice says.

We trample down winding stone stairs. The air around me warms as we venture deeper, like we've stepped into an onsen. A thick, heavy sweat coats my skin.

The sound of applause is so sudden it startles me.

"Our dearest lady, we caught something interesting in our web." The woman elbows me forward, and I hit the warm stone ground with a thud. The sack is yanked off my head.

I look up.

A tall woman in an iron mask peers down at me. It hugs the contours of her face and neck, intricately etched with fine lines shaped into a severe expression. A ruby jewel nestles in the center like a terrifying and beautiful red-bodied spider. Gray robes kiss the tops of her bare feet.

I scramble up, struggling to lift myself upright with the cuffs around my wrists, and glance around. The massive cave is pocked with alcoves fashioned into homes with tiny doors and circular windows and ladders that lead down to long piers. Pavilions float on a blue-green lake, oscillating between small watercoaches. Oblong post-balloons zip around, changing from black to red and back again, their ribbons made of knitted silk to resemble spiders' webs.

A nested underground city. I've never seen anything like it. The strange beauty of it rattles all the things I thought I knew about what the edges and corners of Orléans might look like.

More women step forward, each wearing a mask with unique etchings.

"Who are you?" Edel shouts.

The women laugh, creating a sound ripple.

The tallest woman removes her mask—her skin is as gray as a teacup elephant, her eyes black as obsidian, and her hair white as snow. She almost resembles a wizened spider herself. "Edel Beauregard and favorite Camellia Beauregard, I am Lady Arane, leader of the Iron Ladies, editor of the *Spider's Web.*"

Edel and I exchange a baffled look.

She's the most striking woman I've ever seen.

"We are the Iron Ladies, the Spiders, the Resistance. Welcome to the Grottos!" She spreads her arms wide.

"What do you want from us?" I ask.

"You can't hold us here," Edel says.

"You're free to go if you can navigate yourself out of the Goddess of Death's Grottos. Only a few know the way. Many have tried to leave, and we don't find them until they're reduced to bones. It is a web of tunnels, hence our name." She turns to the women flanking her. "How long would you wager they'd make it in the dark caves, my ladies?"

"Three hourglasses," one says.

"They're Belles, so I'd give them seven hourglasses," another replies.

"Too small and frail. Half an hourglass," a third yells.

Laughter fills the cave, the drone of it turning into a nauseating hum and stirring itself into my anger.

Lady Arane waves her hand to quiet them and smiles. "We don't plan on hurting you, unless you hurt us."

"You're too kind," I reply.

Her mouth flattens into a straight line. "You should be grateful to us. Lady Surielle saved you." The woman who steered the dirigible steps forward and bows before Lady Arane.

"We don't need rescuing," Edel says.

"Oh, but you did. Had your ostentatious watercoach sailed ten more leagues north, it would've run right into a new imperial guard checkpoint at Crescent Hook Lighthouse. They were alerting all fleets for an escaped ship."

Her words settle over me, and I remember the pattern of light hitting the water as we cruised along the edges of the imperial island.

"You would've fallen right into our newest queen's trap before we had the opportunity of meeting and possibly working together."

"Why would we want to work with you?" Edel says.

"Edel," I say through clenched teeth.

She cackles, setting off another cascade of laughter. "It seems you don't understand who we are."

"And your sister owes me." The woman who dragged me here steps forward and removes her mask.

It's Violetta. The servant from the palace. Claudine's lover. An anchor drops in my stomach.

"You killed someone who meant something to me."

The sweaty heat of nausea washes over me. The feelings of responsibility and regret. "I'm s-sorry," I stammer out.

Her face hardens as if we've both shifted back into that memory. Claudine's dead eyes and slack mouth are all I can see. I repeat my apology, but she crosses her arms over her chest.

"Not now, Violetta." Lady Arane nods at Violetta, who retreats, then turns back to us. "Many who resist the world's constraints live down here with us. We've found ways to combat the discomfort that comes with our natural templates. We've learned to harness the madness. We've learned to live without your kind." She paces in a circle around Edel and me.

The women smile at her and clap their hands, or stretch their arms in the air as she talks, waving them about with excitement.

"We are spiders," she calls out.

"Whom others can't see," the women chant back.

"But they will feel our bite."

"They will heed our lessons," they all reply in unison, then assume a tight formation, arms at their sides.

"And experience our venom," Lady Arane says with a smile. "We've been at this work for years, and both of you have just reluctantly woken up and discovered us. Lady Surielle?"

The woman from the dirigible steps forward and bows.

"Lady Surielle is my first disciple. The most agile. The one with the sharpest teeth." Surielle bows farther with Lady Arane's compliment. "Surielle, go and prepare my boat."

Surielle stands, her expression surprised. "Perhaps they need more time in the dungeons, my lady?"

Lady Arane pats Surielle's shoulder, while she holds my gaze. "I think after a tour of our humble abode, they may be ready. We'll dine on board. They will need further sustenance to ask all the questions they will need to have answered before they join our cause."

Surielle nods and leaves Violetta to watch over us, her gaze a hot poker fresh from tending a roaring fire.

I turn my back to her, unable to withstand her glare, and wish there was a way to explain what happened that night. Or better yet, a way to erase what happened.

"This is a bad idea," Edel whispers to me.

"What choice do we have?" I reply. "We must hear them out."

"What if they aren't who they say they are?" Her white cheeks hold a deep pink flush.

"Then we'll try our luck with the Goddess of Death's caves."

Edel holds my gaze. "We can do it."

"I know. We can do anything together." We nod at each other, then turn to watch as a sleek boat slices through the blue-green waters like a black fish. It reminds me of one of the Palace River canal boats but is large enough for a full staff.

"Come," Violetta orders.

We walk down the pier and step into the boat.

Under a dark canopy, modest cushions rim a decorated table.

Sea-lanterns and fire-lanterns knock into one another. A staff of women sets out plates of food—a rainbow medley of sliced vegetables and fresh fruit, a few wedges of cheese, and a small basket of steaming shrimp.

"How did you get all this food down here?" I ask.

"We have figured out ways to survive. With a little hard work things grow in the darkness and the fruit of the sea can be lured into these waters and caught in traps," Lady Arane replies. "With limited resources, the most interesting things can be born."

We all settle at a low table, sitting on plush cushions.

"If I remove the cuffs around your wrists, will you promise to behave?" Lady Arane asks. "I doubt you'd want one of my ladies to hand-feed you."

I nod.

"The question was mostly for the blond one," she says with a wink.

Edel grunts. "Fine!" Her face seems paler, her lips reddened from biting them with hunger and anxiety.

Lady Arane orders the cuffs to be removed. My wrists are grateful to be released. Bruises ring them, dark as the sangsues. Edel and I immediately start to eat.

The boat snakes along the cave river. The rock ceiling crests over us, boasting bright renderings of a night sky. The paintings of all the stars twinkle as if they're actually there. To the left and right, homes are carved into the sides of the grotto; tiny pinpricks of light escape small windows. Women wave and salute at our boat as we pass.

"Everyone who lives in the Grottos takes a vow of simplicity," Arane tells us, sitting back with a cup of tea. "No lavish clothes, shoes, or homes. No decadence, luxury, or excess. We only have what we need. We share most items as a community. We work hard to ensure all are taken care of."

"How long have you been here?" I ask.

"Since I was a young woman. I wanted to be the Minister of War, but was passed over for the position. I fell out of love with the world above and found this community—"

"So, you don't change yourself? Ever?" Edel interrupts.

"We have developed ways to cope. Eye drops to dull the redness. Powders to soften the hair so it's manageable and able to hold on to dye. But we remain gray and proud. We want to reset the world. Change how it deals with the realities."

I hear Maman's words: *"The favorite shows the world what is beautiful. She reminds them of what is essential."*

"With Queen Sophia the usurper in power, we will never stand a chance at this. We're using the *Spider's Web* to influence popular opinion and seed the idea that we don't need to be so intent on escaping our natural forms."

The boat pauses at a pier.

"Come and see."

We leave the boat. Lady Arane leads us along a small incline. It empties at a set of dark curtains embroidered with spiders. She pulls them back to reveal a small room of silkscreens and strange, hulking apparatuses made of wood and brass and bolts.

"What is this?" I ask, gazing all around, my heart lifting with unexpected awe. House-lanterns sail about, illuminating all sorts of instruments—stamps, quills, calligraphy brushes, tiny letter blocks, wooden frames, and color vials. A wall of glass inkpots shimmers, the animated liquid glowing and clawing at their sides, desperate to escape.

"The heart of our web. Our printing press." Lady Arane enters with a flourish and runs her fingers over everything in her path. She points up. Above our heads hang drying newspapers with animated ink racing across the parchment. "This is where my ladies— and a few gentlemen—make our greatest weapon."

"How does it work?" I ask, following Edel as she examines the odd items in the space.

"Violetta," Lady Arane says.

She walks forward, mouth in a grimace. "We create our own parchment and animated ink, catching low-dwelling squids." She takes a piece of parchment from a stack and places it on a long table. "We write our articles and place it in our press." She points at the apparatus. "Just like the ones built by the Minister of News, these produce up to a hundred papers every turn of the hourglass. We've gotten many new followers and lots of support through the circulation of the papers."

Lady Arane touches one of the presses. "I plan to start releasing tattlers to get to those who avoid newspapers, so I can publish works that explore the greatest challenges facing us and make sure the people see the situation as it is, whether they want to or not. Real leaders tell their people the truth, setting the tone for their subjects. Without open leadership and a benevolent queen, Orléans will not survive."

"Princess Charlotte," I say.

"Yes, if she will listen to us, then there's a start. My healers have been visiting her. She's still weak but recovering slowly."

Her words send hope through me that we can remove Sophia from power. "That's such great news."

"You've seen her?" Edel asks.

"Yes, her and Lady Pelletier," Lady Arane answers.

"Where is she? If we can get Charlotte to the palace safely before Sophia's coronation, she can claim the throne and throw Sophia into the dungeon where she belongs," I say.

Lady Arane's mouth breaks into a smile and she nods. Our desires line up like two puzzle pieces locking into one another.

"Why haven't you done that already?" Edel says.

Lady Arane turns to her. "She's not well enough and we don't want to risk being caught before we had a chance to lay our trap. We thought you could help her with your arcana."

"The arcana can't heal," Edel replies.

"You woke her." Lady Arane turns to me.

"We cleaned her blood. Refreshed it, so to speak," I clarify.

"You could make her appear strong enough to face Sophia. She just has to make a legitimate claim to the throne. Sophia thinks she can lie to the world about her sister being dead. There's no telling who she killed and will put on display to get away with this. So, the question is . . . will you help us?"

"Can you also help us?" I ask.

"What do you want?"

"My sisters."

Lady Arane purses her lips. "Yes. We can assist with that. So, do we have a deal?"

"I need to talk to my sister in private first," I say.

Lady Arane nods. She motions for everyone to vacate the room. "We'll be outside."

Once the curtains drop, Edel rushes to me. "I don't think we should do it. Let's just find our sisters ourselves."

"But she knows where Charlotte is! And how will we get out of here if we refuse? I don't think they're going to let us march out and go on our way."

Edel drums her fingers on the table. "But what does she think is going to happen? The whole world will be all right with living the way they do? Gray and without beauty work? What if some people don't want to? They're all going to fight. We've seen how they act at the teahouses. What happens to us? Are we going to be free? Are they going to let us do whatever we want? Or let us do anything other than beauty work? There's no way they're going to just let us go."

I touch her, startling her out of the rant. "I don't know. All I do know is that we don't get rid of Sophia, we will be in chains. We will have to worry about the rest later."

Angry tears well in her eyes and she works hard to hide them from me.

"We will be all right. I promise."

"I don't believe in promises," she replies.

I slip my shaky hand in hers, reaching deep down to stir any bravery hidden there. "When we were little girls and you set off on your wild adventures—like swimming to the bottom of Rose Bayou to find the octopus creature or sneaking out into the dark forest behind our house—I always went with you. No one else would. I told you I would, and I did. Right?"

"Yes," she mumbles.

"I'm telling you right now that we will get out of here and we will get rid of Sophia, then we will get to work on the future. We won't return to the teahouses. We won't let that happen again—not to us, not to any of our sisters. But if we're going to succeed, we need the Iron Ladies' help."

Edel's brow furrows, and she shrugs. Her way of agreeing.

I go to the curtains and snatch them back.

"We're in agreement," I say to the crowd of waiting women.

Lady Arane smiles. She reaches her hand out. "May our threads remain strong and our webs serve us well."

We clasp hands.

The bargain is sealed.

22

Lady Arane's office glows like a sun trapped in a box. Night-lanterns and miniature sky candles warm the space amid the darkness of the caves. Tall bookshelves line three walls with frayed spines of old titles. Maps of the kingdom and its cities along with cameo portraits of Sophia's cabinet and other unfamiliar faces cover the table.

A dozen or more women stand when we enter. They're all various shades of gray, their straw-textured hair styled in different ways and full of multicolored powders, and their black eyes stare back at us with curiosity. They salute Lady Arane. Her presence sends a wave of serious energy through the space.

"Be at ease, everyone, and have a seat. Please welcome Camille and Edel," she directs.

The women nod.

"Belles, these are more of my disciples," she says to us.

The women introduce themselves in rapid succession, and I

can't hold on to all of their names. Two additional seats are brought for Edel and me.

Lady Arane removes her cloak, handing it to a nearby woman. A tiny gavel is placed in front of her. She taps it on a wooden pad. "I hereby call this official meeting in session. Thank you, loyal Iron Ladies. May your threads always remain strong," she says.

"And may your web serve you well," they chant back.

"First order of business is reviewing the modification boxes. Are they still on schedule to be distributed tonight?"

"Yes, Lady Arane," one replies. I think her name is Liara.

"Let me see them. Our trip above was fruitful in many ways." Lady Arane winks at me, then turns back to the woman. "I left more items to be given to all."

One woman stands and returns with stacks of hat boxes. She unhooks their closures and exposes their contents—toilette box items and rudimentary beauty products.

"I thought you all embraced a life without beauty," Edel sneers.

"These are for medicinal purposes. Choosing to live as a Gris person and embracing your natural template does have its challenges. We're not ignorant or untruthful about it. These items help our residents cope with the pain of it all." She lifts a vial. "This is eye serum." She shakes a tub of crème. "This softens the hair to prevent it from falling out." She closes the lid. "Get the point?"

Edel scowls and sits back in her chair.

Lady Arane returns her attention to her people. "Have the latest newspapers gone out?"

"Yes," one answers. "Just an hourglass ago. We sent the newsies and transports. The *Spider's Web* should reach major cities by the time the afternoon papers are distributed."

"Good." Lady Arane nods. "See, girls, what we're doing here?"

She turns to me, her dark eyes burning into mine. "Do you know what we really and truly want?"

"To get rid of Sophia," I reply.

"Yes." Lady Arane nods. "But I'm going to teach you three lessons while I have you. The first, when bargaining, never show your complete hand. Always keep the thing you want most tucked deep down." She drums her fingers on the table. "The ultimate goal is to force the House of Orléans to fall. To trigger another Beauty Trial."

"But I thought you wanted to teach the world of Orléans to embrace a life without beauty," I say. "Not another Beauty Trial. Is that ritual even real?"

The women fixate on me. The heat of their glares sends a nervous ripple down my spine.

"And wouldn't that be up to Princess Charlotte?" Edel adds.

"The people will have their say," she replies. "Even if we do succeed in removing Sophia and Charlotte takes the throne, her newly appointed cabinet won't solve the core issue—changing how beauty work affects this kingdom. We need an eradication of the old way, and new leadership as the first step."

"I assume you mean *you*. That's what this is about, isn't it? Your play for power," Edel challenges.

The women gasp.

"Edel," I say.

"How dare you! Her web is the strongest!" one says.

"She catches every fly—and even lions—in her threads," another barks.

"She is blessed," a third adds.

Lady Arane lifts a hand, silencing the angry women. "I want Charlotte on the throne so she can call for a new Beauty Trial. That is all. I have no delusions of grandeur about her actually dissolving the monarchy of her own volition or deciding that beauty work is killing the world and she should abolish it out of the goodness of her heart. Not all those who demand a change of leadership want to take on the task for themselves. I want a citizen of Orléans to prove that they have what it takes to lead. If we succeed and there's a Beauty Trial, let me enter and prove myself worthy. Let the gods choose me."

"You would make a wonderful leader for Orléans," one woman chimes in.

The others agree with applause.

Lady Arane taps the gavel. "Thank you for your support, but we all must be given a fair shot. The first step is to go see Princess Charlotte and petition her with our desires. See if she plans to challenge her sister's coronation and ascension. We will go see her immediately. There are only two days left until the official ceremonies begin and Sophia reveals that body."

"How will we get to Charlotte?" I ask.

"You will see." She turns to Violetta and Liara. "Prepare our transports."

Violetta and Liara rush out, and, after conferring with Surielle and giving some instructions, Lady Arane gestures at us to follow. We step outside and walk to the end of the pier, where eight wooden boxes sit in a row, their lids flapped open. Three are filled with all manner of goods. The others remain empty.

Edel speaks first. "Are those—"

"Coffins? Yes." Lady Arane gestures to one that is filled with Belle-products. "These are headed to Céline in the Gold Isles. My associates will take them to a warehouse near the pier."

"Why ship them in coffins?" I ask.

"Lesson number two, petite: Never do the expected," she says with a wink. "Port guards don't bother the dead. They're superstitious. Before Sophia began monitoring post-balloons, we'd send the coffins that way—anchor a hundred post-balloons to carry a coffin across the sea—shipping ourselves and our papers throughout the kingdom."

Three of her disciples climb into the coffins and place their masks over their faces. Edel and I exchange glances.

I take a deep breath. "How long is the journey?"

"Four hourglasses. Enough time to sleep, for the midnight star has just come and gone and it will be morning soon."

Edel's eyebrow lifts.

"Get in," Lady Arane orders.

"I'm not going anywhere without my teacup dragons and my knife." I cross my arms over my chest and plant my feet in place.

Lady Arane snaps her fingers.

A woman disappears and returns with a wooden cage. The dragons flit around inside, looking perfectly healthy. I poke my finger in, and they eagerly lick it.

"We did not harm them. They're quite beautiful and rare," Lady Arane says.

Another woman hands me my waist-sash. I quickly tie it. I open the cage. They climb all over me before settling into my waist-sash. Lady Surielle hands me my dagger. Rémy's dagger.

"What about the money that was taken from us?" Edel says.

"Give them back all of their belongings," Lady Arane orders.

Surielle tosses a purse in Edel's direction. It almost tumbles into the dark waters around us, but Edel catches it in time. I bend and rub my fingers across the plush pillows inside the coffin. Belle-products ring the perimeter. The familiar scent of perfumes and crème-cakes finds my nose.

I watch Edel climb into the coffin and the lid close over her. Cold flushes through me.

Lady Arane gestures at the box. "It won't bite. There are no spiders inside."

"How do you travel?" I ask, as all the other coffins are carried off to a boat and not one is left for her.

"I have my own way. Don't worry. You'll have Surielle, Liara, and Violetta, three of my most trusted. They know how to be in contact with me." She winks. "Meet you in Céline. The Gold Isles truly are beautiful. I was born in a small mountain town there. It'll be good to see it once more."

I climb inside the coffin and lie across the pillows. My back presses into them, and they easily take my shape. I barely have time to take one last breath before the lid closes over me and darkness descends.

23

Sweat soaks my back as my heartbeat picks up speed. I try to steady my breathing and calm the flutters in my stomach.

"You will be all right. You will be all right." I whisper the mantra over and over again. "Try to sleep."

The teacup dragons in my waist-sash squirm and adjust. I pat them until they settle. My brain is a tangle of worries: Did we make the right decision to trust them? Will they keep their word and help us find our sisters? What if they ship us straight to Sophia and collect their prize? What would Rémy think of what we're doing?

My vessel is lifted and carried. My stomach flips. I clench my muscles until I feel myself set down. Snippets of Lady Arane's instructions slip inside the box:

"Be gentle with these! We have first-timers."

"Take the southern exit out of the caves."

"Prepare my boat and I'll leave to the east. If we're being tracked, we'll split their attention."

After at least an hourglass's worth of time, the voices quiet and I recognize the oscillating motion of a boat. I feel like a toy caught in the choppy waves my sisters and I used to create in the onsen tubs at home as little girls. Servants would march us into the bathing chambers and tell us to wait at the edge of the largest, bubbling pool, but Edel would leap in first before getting permission and usually pull me in with her. Amber would scowl, then inch her way in, letting her naked body adjust slowly to the temperature. Padma and Valerie would gather the bathing toys and drop them in for us. Hana always entered last, after her request for more bubbles was denied.

I squeeze my eyes shut, trying not to remember those happier times, trying not to think about how we all won't be together again. The space feels bigger as I sink into the darkness of the coffin. I fall in and out of sweaty hallucinations and tumultuous dreams—Sophia's heckling me as we stand in front of her wall of cameos, the pained look on Auguste's face when his true intentions were revealed at that dinner, Rémy waiting for me in Trianon, the dead, glassy eyes of both Claudine and Valerie.

Finally, the lid of my coffin lifts and I feel the relief of a deep breath.

"Is everyone all right?" Surielle asks.

"I am now, thank you." My skin welcomes the cool air. She smiles down at me, her skin glistening like a gray pearl brought from the depths of the Cold Sea. I stretch and try to hold in a yawn. Sleep tugs at my eyelids.

"It's all cargo down here, so you can come out while we travel. It's about one hourglass until we reach Céline and the Gold Isles."

"Where's Edel?" I ask, just before her groan cuts through the space. I turn and find her open casket is behind mine. She's sitting up, her face an awful shade of green. I climb out of my box and rush over to her, scaling over crates and barrels. Surielle follows and together we try to get Edel up, but she cowers.

"I wish we had some barley water," I say, pushing Edel's hair from her forehead.

Surielle rifles through cargo boxes only to discover bottles of wart tonics, cases of wine, and all types of new télétropes.

"What is this? One of your ships?" I ask her.

"No. An overnight cargo vessel from the port of Nouvelle-Lerec."

I notice that Violetta and one other disciple are posted at the door, masks on and daggers in hand. I want to try to speak to Violetta about what happened with Claudine. I want to apologize and try to explain. But Edel moans again and burps up her sickness, and I can't leave her.

"Try to sleep," I tell Edel, helping her lie down again.

She rolls over, cradling her stomach. Surielle brings a cloak to prop her head up. I find a fan and flap a breeze over her until her eyes grow heavy and her breathing softens.

I find a place nearby to sit, a barrel nestled between two crates labeled BEAULIEU'S CHANDELIER-LANTERNS, and let the teacup dragons out of my pouch. They flutter about, stretching their wings while I keep a watch on Edel.

A silence settles over us, only interrupted by the squawk of a seabird or one of Edel's moans or the clomp of a footstep on the deck above.

Surielle steals glances at me, her black eyes combing over my hair and face.

"Have you always been part of this group?" I ask her.

"I ran away from home at thirteen and joined. My mother was terrible about beauty management. She made us change weekly to keep up with the trends. I hated it," she says. "I was in constant pain."

"How did you learn about the Iron Ladies' existence?"

"You have to know where to look. They leave clues. Spiderwebs and cleome flowers—"

"On buildings." I remember the cobwebs and flowers in the shop windows in Metairie. Makes me wonder how many small signs I missed. How much I hadn't been paying attention.

"What happened to you at the palace?" Surielle asks. "We've heard about this new queen for so long and read about some of her antics, but I don't know what is true and what isn't. I want to hear from someone who was there."

"So many things," I reply. "Sophia wants to be the most beautiful woman in the whole world and she will do anything to achieve it."

"But that is impossible. And frivolous."

"That is what she wants." The anger inside me ties itself into a heavy knot. "I thought she'd kill me with beauty work." I close my eyes for a moment. Sophia's wild gaze greets me, glaring. I shudder.

"She will be stopped," Surielle replies. "All of this nonsense will come to an end."

Her words sink down inside me, mingling with the rage simmering. "I know."

Our eyes meet and hold the same purpose.

"Surielle, Liara and I wish to speak with you," Violetta barks. Surielle joins the others at the door.

I take Arabella's Belle-book from my satchel and trace my fingers over the cover until my heart slows. It makes me miss

Maman's Belle-book. I open it and begin to read, hoping it'll make me sleepy enough to rest.

Date: Day 4,128 at court

Sophia carted me to her prison. The last wing is almost complete as she works the builders to the very edge.

Elisabeth Du Barry has been forced to live at the Everlasting Rose prison now. She tried to grow a dozen Belles and many of them were born too damaged to survive. Sophia gave her a guideline for the unfavored class of Belles. The only principle was that they needed to be suitable for beauty work but didn't have to be beautiful themselves. Many were born with too many eyes or without skin, and a few missing their faces.

So many of the babies haven't made it a full day.

My stomach swells with sickness, disgust sending bile up my throat.

"Camille," Surielle says.

I look up.

"Trouble."

She hands me a newspaper, the animated ink racing. An image of the Rose prison twirls like a carousel beneath the headline: CONSTRUCTION COMPLETE IN TIME FOR NEW CORONATION CEREMONY—AND ITS NEW GUESTS! The Fashion Minister's freckled face is pressed up against its pink bars, the iron warped into the shape of roses. His tears glisten as they fall down his cheeks.

My heart slams into my rib cage.

The portrait flickers.

Another face consumes the frame.

Dread fills my insides as the animated ink fills in.

The Beauty Minister. Rose Bertain. Her fingers curls around the bars, and she gives them a purposeless shake. My eyes race

over the article below. The words trip over themselves as I read
with desperation.

*Gustave du Polignac, famed Fashion Minister, and Rose Bertain,
the longest appointed Beauty Minister in Orléansian history, have been
detained and are being held at the Rose until further notice. Regent Queen
Sophia has announced that both individuals have failed her loyalty test
and must be tried before her court to determine if they can remain in her
cabinet for the coming year.*

*"Her Majesty will tolerate nothing but loyalty," the queen's most
trusted advisor reported to newsies. "This quality will be the heartstone
of her reign. A test of mettle will be administered often and without notice,
including time spent in the Rose. These two ministers have been rumored
to be disloyal to the crown, and we will get to the truth."*

*A list of the queen's grievances against the accused will be published
after the Coronation and Ascension ceremonies as the queen institutes
the building of her cabinet.*

My insides are a riot of emotion—rage, sadness, horror, shock,
and regret. All the things the Fashion Minister did to help us
landed him in a torture chamber.

I did this.

I asked this of him.

And now, he won't get to be with his husband again, and he
won't be alive if I don't get Charlotte back on the throne.

The sound of a port bell rings out above us.

"It's time." She shoos me back in the coffin.

Ceiling floorboards creak overhead.

Edel hiccups, then dry heaves. Spit dribbles down her chin.
"We're almost there," I tell her. "Just hang on a little bit longer."

"I don't think I can," she moans. "All I can think about is vomiting. I shouldn't have eaten all of that food."

"Port of Céline ahead. Ready the anchors!" a man's voice drifts below deck.

Surielle and the two others rush back to their coffins. "Everyone in." She closes the lid over herself.

I secure Edel's lid, hoping it will muffle her moans and keep us from being discovered. The door cracks open and my pulse hitches. I whistle. The teacup dragons fly to me. I tuck them back inside my waist-sash, slip into my coffin, and slide the top over me. My rapid heartbeat makes my body tremble. Each time the teacup dragons squirm or burrow, it sends a nervous jolt through me.

The noise of footsteps and scraping pushes through the coffin's thin sides.

"Cargo unloaded first," a man shouts. "Start with the coffins."

I'm lifted in the air.

"I didn't realize dead bodies could be so heavy," someone complains.

"Hurry up! My maman said the heavier bodies carry their trapped souls."

I hear muffled stomping and grumbling and the call of early-morning vendors setting up their stalls for the day. I press my hands to the sides and hold my breath as I'm jostled off the ship. They set me on the ground. Sweat trickles across my forehead.

"We will be all right. We will get out of here." I whisper my mantra to the teacup dragons. "We will find Charlotte."

Outside, gulls caw. I can hear the lulling tempo of waves lapping the pier. Just as I'm feeling slightly calmer, a scream cuts through the air.

Edel.

24

I inch up the lid enough to see, but not enough to draw attention. The pier is a chaotic blur of bodies. Merchants toting their wares, lines of passengers headed to board ships and boats, the loading and unloading of parcels and people and boxes, and a network of fishmonger stalls. The energy of it all creates a nauseating hum of early-morning movement.

"Found a stowaway," a port guard says.

I watch as the men drag Edel from the coffin kicking and screaming. The small crowd slows to a stop to watch. Nearby newsies swarm, sending navy blue story-balloons overhead to capture it all—the first potential headline of the day.

I watch it unfold like a story on a télétrope reel, each picture clicking into its drum, spinning and whirling out of control, the scene growing more and more horrific.

Edel's arms thrash about. The guards struggle to hold on to her.

"Keep a grip on her!" one shouts.

She crashes to the ground and kicks at them. Her foot clobbers a guard in the head. He cowers, grabbing his eye. She tries to run.

Another one grabs her by the waist, yanking her like a rag doll.

"How much is the fine these days?" a port guard asks, taking out a ledger from his jacket pocket.

"Twenty-five leas per mile traveled, plus the port taxes. Ten days in the Céline jail if you can't pay," another adds.

A guard grips Edel's arm. "Why were you on this ship? Who are you?"

Edel vomits all over his clothes, then spits in his face. She's picked up and thrown over one of the guard's shoulders like she's nothing more than a sack of snowmelons. Her wails pierce the air. Each one hits me like an icy wave. She punches his back and more vomit spews from her mouth.

"I'm not paid enough for this," he complains. "It's too early. All these overnight ships are always trouble."

"Search all the coffins!" his cohort barks.

They turn and head straight for me. A punch hits my heart. I want to climb out and follow Edel. I try to keep my eye on her, but they're getting farther and farther away from my sight line. The men kick at the other coffins and bang their tops. They're almost to mine.

"Anyone in there?" one yells. "Might as well open up before we have to wrestle you out."

I close the lid and prepare myself. My hand falls to my dagger. My breath comes out rushed and in pants. The teacup dragons chirp with alarm. I unsheathe the dagger and hold it to my chest.

A series of bells rings out.

"Fire!" someone hollers. "The lighthouse."

"Get to the hoses!" the other one orders. "We'll finish the search after."

The men abandon the coffins and race away.

I push the lid off and it lands on the pier with a clatter. I can't see Edel anymore—only a crowd of bodies buzzing about and headed away from the pier. I gaze out and see the top of the light-house in flames.

One of the nearby coffins opens.

I spot Surielle. She motions for me to get back inside and presses her finger to her mouth in a shush, then closes herself inside again. The noise of approaching footsteps reaches my ears, but there's no way I'm getting back in that box. I have to go after my sister.

I duck and weave between the cargo on the pier, trying to find the men who took Edel. The chaos of bodies blurs. Jackets, dresses, top hats, heat-lanterns, snow parasols, winter veils.

A hand grabs the back of my cloak. "Where do you think you're going?"

I jerk around.

It's Lady Arane.

"You're supposed to be in your transport," she barks.

"They took Edel. We have to get her."

"We have to get to our safehouse."

"But—"

"I'll send one of my disciples out to track Edel. For now, hide. You're about to ruin everything." She points her fingers. "Look! More guards are headed this way. They won't just ignore the fact that a live woman was found in a coffin. They will complete their search. My fire diversion won't last long."

I spot a cluster of uniformed men and women running in our direction.

Reluctantly, I return to my coffin. Lady Arane closes the lid over me, and I lie flat. I rub my waist-sash to calm the agitated tea-cup dragons. Tears burn behind my eyes. I can't get Edel's screams out of my head. I can't believe this is happening again. I tremble with anger.

"I'm here to collect these," I hear Lady Arane state. "They're headed for the warehouse to await transport to the crematory."

My coffin is placed inside something that feels like a carriage. All the light is stamped out as more boxes are loaded up beside me. The teacup dragons free themselves from my waist-sash and spread across my limbs. Their nervous hiccups warm the too-small space, and I feel like we'll all run out of air. My chest is tight with worry.

The carriage moves forward, bumbling over cobblestones, making several turns. I'm jerked back and forth with each one.

I clobber my head on the side of the coffin. The teacup dragons protest as I knock into them. The Belle-product jars crack and spill all over. The perfume chokes us. My breath catches and burns like honey bees are trapped in my throat.

Hot tears soak the pillow beneath my head.

First, Amber.

Then, Valerie.

Now, Edel.

And who knows the fates of my other sisters, Padma and Hana. Or Ivy even.

It feels like hours have passed. My stomach twists with the reality that we're probably very far from the port now, and from Edel.

Maman's mirror bounces on my chest, its grooves sharp and piercing. I wish for her to come back. I wish for her to help me fix all of this. I wish for her strength to help me come out of it alive. All the things I'd planned feel like they've turned to wisps of smoke, each tendril headed in opposite directions.

The carriages stop.

I hear Lady Arane's voice again.

Boxes shift around me.

I am lifted and moved into a cavernous room filled with voices. I can tell how large it is by the way the voices echo. Boxes are set on top of mine. The thud of them makes the teacup dragons fuss.

I shush them and clench my eyes shut. How long will we have to stay in here? Where are they taking Edel? Will I be able to find her? A headache thuds in my temples. The box feels like it's vibrating and spinning beneath me.

I bang on the wooden sides. I can't stay cooped up in here any longer.

"Camille," I hear Surielle whisper.

I knock on the wood. "I'm over here."

I try to push the lid again, but it's too heavy.

Slowly, Surielle and Violetta remove the boxes above me, then yank open the lid. Several morning-lanterns float through the warehouse, scattering strips of light over battered boxes.

I sit up. The teacup dragons fly out, stretching their wings with glee. Stacks of coffins are lined up all around us. The air stinks of rotten flesh.

Surielle helps me out. My arms are shaky.

"Keep watch for our lady," she orders Violetta and the other woman. They pivot and go to the warehouse door.

"Where are we?" I ask.

"A warehouse for the dead," she reports.

"How far are we from the port? We have to go back for Edel," I say, but my voice breaks, and my legs buckle under me.

I'm alone now.

I've failed everyone.

She catches me before I hit the floor. "I got you," she whispers.

"We have to go back to the pier," I mutter, out of breath.

"It's too risky," she replies.

"I can't leave her."

"If you chase her, they will take you—and *us*—and this whole thing will be over. Sophia will win. Do you want that?"

Her words harden inside me.

"Lady Arane is just outside. We are to wait for her. That's the order."

"Edel would come for me. She wouldn't just sit back and let them take me." I collect the teacup dragons, tuck them into my waist-sash despite their protests, and drape my travel cloak and veil over me. "She wouldn't do *nothing*. I need her. I won't lose another sister."

Surielle steps in my path, blocking my attempt to leave. "You can't. I won't allow it." She snatches a dagger from a black sheath. "I'm in charge when Lady Arane isn't present."

Violetta leaves her post and rushes to Surielle's side. She reveals a matching blade. Both catch the light from the floating lanterns overhead. The steel twinkles and shines with the promise of drawing blood.

I put my hand on the knife Rémy gave me. A hot, seething ball of anger amasses in my stomach. The arcana awaken and linger beneath my skin.

Violetta flinches. "She's killed people with her arcana."

"And we've killed people with our daggers." Surielle's eyes blaze with intensity. "We have the authority to cuff you again if you don't cooperate. Bargain or no bargain. But I don't want to have to do that." She flicks her knife at me.

We don't move, each of us as still as a statue.

Newsies rush the streets outside the windows hollering about their midday papers.

My heart races alongside the shouting.

"Get them here. The *Glass Post*, just in. The *National*, arriving soon!" one shouts.

"The Regent Queen reopens the skies to receive coronation gifts. Read about the items she desires in the *Trianon Tribune*. We've got the official list. Be sure to address the post-balloons and set them to land on the Observatory Deck, says newly appointed Minister of Royal Gifts."

"Famed courtiers and kingdom celebrities already headed to the imperial island. Check out our limited edition column for a glimpse of the best dressed and best looks."

"Commemorative beauty-scopes to be sold during the coronation hosted by the *Orléansian Times*. Be sure to get one. They're going to be a collector's item."

The shouting subsides.

"Let me out of here," I almost growl.

The Iron Ladies don't move.

A blimp flies past the dirty window featuring the latest imperial headlines.

We all flinch.

NO MORE SECRECY—WE'RE IN THIS
TOGETHER, SAYS NEW QUEEN!

THE ROSE PRISON TO REPLACE MAISON ROUGE AS
PRIMARY RESIDENCE FOR BELLES—TO ALLOW THE PUBLIC
TO SEE THE INNER WORKINGS OF BELLE TALENTS

LEARN HOW TO GROW YOUR OWN BELLE-GARDEN! YEP—
THEY'RE GROWN LIKE ROSES! READ ALL ABOUT IT

ROYAL WEDDING POST-BALLOON INVITES SENT OUT
TODAY IN TIME FOR AN AUSPICIOUS NEW YEAR!
HOPE YOU ARE LUCKY ENOUGH TO GET ONE!

TWO NEW TEAHOUSES BUILT IN SILK ISLES TO
REPLACE THE ONE LOST DUE TO FIRE

BEAUTY FOR ALL—QUEEN TO PASS OUT NEW PETIT-ROSE
BEAUTY TOKENS TO THOSE WHO EARN HER LOVE

"What's going on here?" a voice calls out from behind us.

We pivot and find Lady Arane standing at the back doorway. She holds her mask in her hands, her gray skin severe in the light.

"She threatened to leave," Surielle reports without moving her dagger.

"Surielle, stand down. All of you," she orders.

"But..."

Lady Arane puts a hand in the air. "I've sent two ladies to track Edel. We should have more news soon."

"I'm going after her." My fingers have grown slippery around Rémy's dagger, but I grip the handle more tightly.

Lady Arane's eyebrow lifts.

"We had a bargain," I seethe. "We help you, and you help me. Now your ridiculous travel arrangements have gotten my sister taken, and I'm supposed to wait patiently?" The teacup dragons circle overhead hissing and hiccuping fire, mirroring my agitation.

She moves closer.

My arcana hum beneath my skin.

"Be careful, my lady," Violetta says. "I've seen what she can do."

"You should listen to her," I say, filling with rage.

"Lesson number three has come faster than I hoped—resisting has a price. And this is the cost. You lose people you love for the greater good of others."

"I need my sister. I've already lost two. I want Edel back."

"That's not true," she says. "You also want revenge. You want Sophia to pay. You want Sophia off the throne like the rest of us. You know that she's poison for this kingdom. You know many more will die if we don't remove her. Once we meet with Charlotte and challenge Sophia, this will all be over. We can free Amber. The guards will release Edel. We will get all of your remaining sisters. None of that can happen if we deviate right now. Some things must wait, however painful. My ladies will track her." She holds her hand up as if swearing an oath.

My promise to Edel drums inside me. That we would get out of this. That we would succeed.

This journey has made me into a liar.

Lady Arane takes another step toward me. My arm quivers, wanting to strike.

"We must go. The longer we delay, the more likely we will be tracked. Our guide awaits." She hands me an iron mask. "You're one of us now."

25

Mountains stretch as far as the eye can see, their snow-capped peaks disappearing into the clouds. They hold layers of gilded mansions, shops and pavilions pressed into their facades, and a bustling port at their feet, as if the God of the Ground poured golden liquid down the sides of these great summits, and it assembled itself into a vertical city. Carriages suspended on glittering cables lift into the air like gold blimps headed for the God of the Sky's lair. They empty beautiful passengers on promenades that circle the mountain like a set of rings stacked on a plump finger. Jewel-box-colored city-lanterns illuminate Céline's vertical quartiers.

The world is bigger and vaster than I could've ever imagined, bigger than Du Barry could've ever described, more wondrous than any depiction in any of the thousands of books in the library at Maison Rouge.

Snow trickles down on us, soft and light, stamping out the sun and collecting on the heat-lanterns drifting behind their owners.

Many of the people around us laugh and giggle and hold hands. My heart pinches thinking of my sisters. The memory of Edel's screams cuts through me. She rarely cried. She was never afraid. She was our troublemaker. She was always the strongest of us.

I swallow angry tears. I remember when Edel and I got scolded for going too far into the forest behind our home. Maman secretly called her the bat of our generation, always drawn to darkness and mischief. Edel had lost a bet, and the consequence was venturing beyond the graveyard's edge. I'd gone with her while our sisters watched from our shared seventh-floor balcony. The endless shadows swallowed us whole as we tiptoed beyond the thumb-shaped tombstones pushing from the dirt at its edge. Du Barry had told us a monster lived in that forest and protected it from unwanted visitors, especially children. We made it ten steps in before Du Barry came running after us like we were headed over a cliff. She toted us back by the elbows like buckets from a well, and we had to write five hundred lines each about why we would never go into the woods again.

"This way," Lady Arane orders.

I snake behind her, flanked by Surielle and Violetta, Liara bringing up the rear. Their faces are covered completely. The light catches glimpses of their masks, but an onlooker might confuse them for silver makeup or a new beauty trend.

Newsies race past us shouting the afternoon headlines:

DEAD PRINCESS CHARLOTTE'S BODY IN TRANSIT
TO TRIANON TO SIT IN MEMORIAM

TWO DAYS UNTIL CORONATION AND ASCENSION CEREMONY!
GET YOUR TICKETS TO IMPERIAL ISLAND, BOATS FILLING UP!

QUEEN'S COUSINS ANOUK AND ANASTASIA
UNINVITED TO CEREMONIES AND FINED FOR THEIR
BEAUTY WORK . . . DEEMED TOO PRETTY!

TAUPE, MAUVE, AND PLUM TO BE QUEEN'S
CORONATION AND ASCENSION COLORS

We cut through the pier crowds and join snaking lines of people waiting to board carriages headed to the city layers. My limbs burn with nervous energy. My thoughts are an overfilled teacup, drowning its saucer. The piercing pitch of Edel's screams ruptures through me. The memory hits me over and over again, then begins to blend with Amber's shrieks from the boardinghouse.

"I will get them back," I whisper to myself.

"What was that?" Lady Arane asks.

"Nothing," I reply.

"Last car on the right," Lady Arane orders. "Get in and spread out. No eye contact."

A carriage porter corrals the line. "Seventh layer. Keep the line tidy. Have your leas ready or you can't board. I'll have no foolishness in my section. Follow directions or be left behind."

We shuffle into the plush carriage behind a couple who can't keep their hands off each other. The woman presses her cold brown cheeks against her companion, who retaliates by pressing his pale white fingers to the crook of her neck. Their infectious giggles fill the quiet space.

I find a seat and look for things to distract me from the chaos of thoughts in my head. Currant cushions and mahogany paneling enclose us, safe from a gathering wind. Heat-lanterns knock into one another over our heads.

"How do those who can't afford the lifts get up to the city?" I ask Surielle.

She doesn't answer, her gaze fixed ahead as if she doesn't know me.

The people around us clear their throats. Some laugh and hide judgmental smiles behind gloved hands.

"The winding path, of course," someone says.

Lady Arane shakes her head at me.

The lift pauses at the market quarter, where shoppers file out, eager to bargain and barter in the stores on this layer. More well-dressed passengers join us, toting hat boxes and lantern carriers and hand trollies bursting with parcels.

We climb higher, pausing at various piers to load and unload people. I stare out the window at the twinkling lights we've left behind, then at Lady Arane and her disciples, who sit like statues. I'm just wondering if we'll be taking the carriage to the very top of the mountain when Lady Arane rings a bell above her head.

"Garden Quartier," the porter announces, as the lift pauses at a level that glows pale green and gold from city-lanterns. Black railings hold winter flower boxes, each bloom wearing a tiny cape of snow.

"We're getting off," Lady Arane whispers.

Surielle waits for me to stand, then takes her place behind me.

We shuffle out and join a crowd on the promenade. Blimps soar in tandem with the crowd's movement, advertising new beauty products soon to be released and the Fashion Minister's vivant dresses. Some feature cameo portraits of Queen Sophia and her promises for new beauty laws. Her hair is all white and loosely curled like a snowstorm trapped around her shoulders. Diamonds dot along the new teardrop curve of her eyes, and she winks at onlookers every few seconds as the blimps circle.

It's almost as if she's watching me. My stomach lifts with panic. Guards patrol the crowds, studying people, but most of the shoppers slip in and out of shops, not paying them much attention.

I glance down at the pier where we began our journey. The lights are tiny pinpricks now, and I feel like we're so close to the sky I could steal a cloud.

I turn around looking for the stairs, but Lady Arane moves forward and I fall into step behind her.

We pass tightly packed shops squeezed next to each other like macarons in a pastry box. Lady Arane stops in front of a door marked CLEOME'S COLLECTION OF CURIOUS FLOWERS. The shop window boasts a miniature greenhouse bursting with colorful blooms.

It's empty of customers.

We enter. A chime sounds. The ladies survey the space. I walk along the edges of the room, running my fingers over a pot of what Maman used to call skeleton flowers in our greenhouse at La Maison Rouge. Her favorite. As a little girl, whenever we'd been tasked to water them, I'd watch in awe as their white petals turned translucent when the liquid hit them, every vein and fiber inside exposed to the light.

I pull one from the pot and put it in my pocket.

Lady Arane whistles.

A pretty clerk peeks from behind a curtain, spots Lady Arane, and nods. Lady Arane approaches a massive bell jar in the middle of the room. It holds a bright cleome flower. A plant-lantern oscillates above, sending down its tiny rays of sunshine.

Lady Arane admires the flower, then whistles again, this time letting the air from her mouth rush into the holes in the bell jar.

The teacup dragons wiggle in my waist-sash, eager to get out, as her whistle sharpens.

"What is she doing?" I ask Surielle.

"Using the key," she says, without taking her eyes off the flower.

The flower curves over and touches the glass. A nearby cabinet inches forward from the wall. Without uttering a word, the clerk hands Lady Arane a night-lantern and Surielle a heat-lantern. Lady Arane slips behind the cabinet, leading the way. Violetta and the other disciple nudge me to follow.

A long winding set of stairs descends down into the dark belly of the mountain. I can't see where they end.

"Welcome to the Spider's Path," Lady Arane announces.

The cabinet closes behind us.

"What is this place?" I ask.

"One of the largest palace fortresses ever built," Lady Arane tells me. "It was called the Yellow Sapphire, but was abandoned by superstitious Queen Jamila because it's believed to contain an entrance to the Goddess of Death's caves. But people say that about many places. Regardless, it's been sealed off and remained unused for decades."

We weave through sharp passageways. The skeletons of post-balloons and night-lanterns scatter the floor. Tapestries of cobwebs coat the walls. The Iron Ladies use their daggers to rip them down so we can continue to pass. We walk for what feels like three hour-glasses. I try to remember all the turns.

Five lefts, and six rights. If I have any hope of trying to make my way back, I have to memorize it.

Surielle hands me a pouch full of water. I gulp it down, then sprinkle some on my fingers, jamming my hand in my waist-sash for the teacup dragons. Their little tongues lick my fingertips thirstily.

Ahead, the silhouette of a man is outlined in the warm glow of a fire-lantern.

Lady Arane whistles again.

The man pivots and parrots her tune.

I freeze. The power of the arcana collects in my hands.

It's Auguste.

26

The sting of seeing him again pins me in place. My legs are weak under me. His hair is cut short and his skin too pale now, the color of eggshells.

Violetta pushes me from behind. "Move forward," she orders, but her words don't register.

My mouth is dry. I feel like all the blood inside me has drained out. I had worked on steeling my heart against this moment. I had trained it against the sound of his voice and let Rémy creep into the crevices left behind. I had thought my feelings for Rémy, combined with my anger, would stamp out any flicker of feeling left inside me.

But they haven't.

"May your threads be strong," he says to Lady Arane.

"And may your web serve you well," she replies.

The cadence of his voice slips beneath my skin.

"Your Grace," she says.

"Please don't call me that." He frowns.

My heart becomes a drum, each beat growing louder and louder, my pulse furious.

"Let me introduce you to my esteemed ladies. My first disciple, Lady Surielle. Second disciple, Lady Liara, and third disciple, Lady Violetta."

They each bow in turn.

The arcana linger right under my skin, reacting, joining the anger inside me. I fish out the skeleton flower in my pocket and sprinkle it with water drops from the water pouch. The petals lose their color and reveal their insides.

"And of course you already know our favorite Belle, Camille Beauregard," Lady Arane says.

I step forward into the night-lantern light.

His mouth drops open and his eyes comb over me. My gaze burns into his. My nerves tingle with revenge. The world around us dissolves. The mountain. The Iron Ladies. The pockmarked lanterns. The teacup dragons.

It's just him and me.

Memories of the night of Sophia's party hit me in waves—the secrets I'd shared with him spat back at me in front of everyone, my private words twisted into unrecognizable shapes and stretched out in the open and subjected to judgment, our closeness exposed to light and air and shriveling like rotting fruit.

His eyes telegraph a thousand apologies.

The teacup dragons gaze out of my waist-sash and cock their heads to the side.

"Camille." My name sounds like a firework when he says it. A loud, popping thing that echoes off the walls. It throws me out of our bubble and back into the long corridor with the Iron Ladies gawking at us.

"What is this about, Lady Arane?" I ask. "Is this some sort of trap?"

"What do you mean?"

"He's an enemy." I grit my teeth.

"Not to us."

"Camille, let me explain…" Auguste starts toward me with his hands out.

I stretch the petals of the flower in my hand until they're the size of the lift carriages we took up the mountainside. Lady Arane and her disciples jump back, shouting in alarm, but I pay them no mind. I cinch the petals around Auguste's waist, trapping him in place. "Don't come near me."

"What are you doing, Camille?" Lady Arane steps closer to me, but I am still as stone. "He's taking us to see Princess Charlotte."

"Step away or I'll snap him in half," I tell her, "and then do the same to you."

"Let us talk in private," he says, his breath ragged as I coil the stems tighter and tighter around his waist and rib cage.

"We had a bargain," she reminds me.

"Our bargain is on hold," I yell.

Anger flares in Lady Arane's black eyes as she glances from Auguste to me. Her jaw clenches and her cheeks vibrate with rage and helplessness. Finally, she nods and her disciples move farther into the passageway, but their daggers remain fixed on me, glinting in the night-lantern light. Ready to stab me at any moment.

Auguste and I stand face-to-face. I hold him pinned like a doll. His eyes gleam.

"Are you going to let me out of this *flower*?" he says.

I tighten it around his waist, thickening the fibers until they're like metal and have the capacity to crush his bones. "Should I?"

"I'm sorry," he stammers out through labored breaths.

"*Sorry?*" I laugh. That word is too small to wipe away the things he did to me. "That's it?"

"I admit it all. I was wrong. At first, my mother had me convinced that helping her was the right thing to do."

"You lied."

"I withheld information."

His expression is anguished, but I can still sense his smugness, like his lips would betray him at any moment and tip into a half-smile.

The memories become a tornado, the turning of a télétrope off-kilter.

The way we argued.

The laughter.

The way he slipped beyond my boundaries.

The sparring.

The way he touched me.

The secret post-balloons.

The way he kissed me.

Sophia's voice rings out between us: "*I've been told you think I'm a monster. That you called me that, in fact.*"

"You told Sophia everything she needed to know to terrorize me and my sisters."

"I didn't know what I was doing."

"You made me love—" My voice breaks, and I clear my throat.

"I loved you," he says. "I still do."

The words are like poison darts to the chest. The betrayal twists into bitterness that feeds the anger.

"I tried to stop it all, but I was too late. The pieces were already in motion."

I don't believe him.

I can't.

"I was just a game token on a board to you."

"No, you were much more," he insists, struggling against his bonds. "I hated having to..."

His words become a vise tightening around my heart, so I force him to feel the pain, too. I tighten the petals around his core, and he lets out a piteous cry.

His words stumble out between gasps for air: "That's why I'm here. When I realized I couldn't stop what I'd started, I convinced Sophia to choose me as her king. I knew I was clever enough to get her to. Then, I could stay close and disrupt all her plans. I've been working with the Iron Ladies for the past month. Right, Lady Arane?"

Lady Arane steps out of the passageway, arms crossed, sweat shining on her gray forehead. "It's true. He's been our palace informant. Integral to keeping tabs on Charlotte and her condition."

"How?" I prod.

He slumps forward. Sweat pours down his face. "I can't feel my legs."

I loosen the petals' grip on his waist ever so slightly.

"After what happened with Claudine, I found Violetta and helped her leave the palace. We kept in touch. When she joined the spiders, I fed her information, and she got me a meeting," he tells me.

Lady Arane confirms his story with a nod.

"See?" he says, his eyes hooded and—I notice for the first time—ringed with bruises from lack of sleep. "I tried to fix what I'd done. I don't expect you to forgive me. What I did was a betrayal, and trust is a thread between people. Once broken it's hard to mend." He sighs. "I know what I did. I know I couldn't possibly make it up to you, or have a second chance."

"No," I spit.

"But I have your sister Padma with me. I hope you'll talk to her and confirm that I've treated her with nothing but the utmost respect."

I lose my concentration and the flower shrivels. Auguste falls forward, crashing to the stone ground with a thud.

"Padma? She's here?" My vision blurs.

"I convinced Sophia to let me take her with me, so I could maintain myself for the papers. But in reality, I wanted to help her find you. And I knew you'd be upset, and I'd feel that wrath." He rubs his rib cage. "Deservedly so."

"*Upset,*" I say, my laugh sharpened by fury. "Take me to my sister."

27

Auguste traverses the tunnels swiftly and silently as if the path is ingrained in his muscle memory. The shape of him is the same, long and lanky, and his stride is confident, his steps pounding like he owns the very ground he walks on.

I ball my hands into fists, trying to quiet every roiling part of me that wants to reach out and hurt him the way he hurt me.

Our footsteps reverberate down the long, winding hall. The cold of the mountain feels caught in the stone all around us, as if the smooth rocks could release snow and wind at any moment. I clench my teeth to keep them from chattering. The Iron Ladies follow behind us, their whispers crescendoing as we snake along.

He steals glances at me.

I glare back.

There's no warmth for him left.

"Violetta first brought me here," he says, taking a left turn. "She showed me the tunnel network. We started working together right after Claudine's death."

The sound of her name still takes the breath out of me.

"I feel horrible about what we did to Claudine," I admit. I don't know how to make it right. I don't know if I can ever fix it.

"So do I," he replies. "I want to fix so many things that have happened."

"I should've stopped it. I should've refused to participate."

"You couldn't have. The rest of us in the room should've challenged Sophia. Stood together against her terrible game. We can't expect one person—or even two—to take the entire burden of resisting on their shoulders. We all have to stand up and say *no*."

I don't know if I ever want to stand with him. Even if he's done the right thing in our time apart. His betrayal is a wound—crusted over, perhaps, but infected and bruised.

"After you woke Charlotte, everything was in chaos. The queen's body needed the ritual treatments to begin its journey to the afterlife, rumors about Charlotte spread everywhere, Claudine's death became newsie fodder, and your escape hit the press like a storm. That, at least, provided the perfect distraction so that we could move Charlotte," he says.

"Well, aren't you a hero?" I snap, the anger inside me loose and ready to hit him once more.

"I'm not telling you this to make you feel differently about me. It's probably too late for that. I don't expect you to forgive me. I don't even know how to ask. But I wanted you to know what happened before you see Charlotte." He nibbles his bottom lip.

I find a pinprick of light ahead to fixate on. I won't look at him. I won't give him any indication of how I feel about any of this.

We turn right. The tunnels smell of metal and iron and rust. Mining-lanterns hang from strings on the ceiling, casting sickly flickering light on the walls.

"Sophia has turned the palace and Trianon into her playground. Installing beauty checkpoints alongside security ones, so she can control everyone."

The image of her shifting blood cameos comes to mind. Then, she was simply keeping tabs on her court. Now, she's found a way to watch everyone, the entire world.

"She tortures those who she deems more beautiful than she. If they don't comply, she locks them up until they relent. She's created new starvation boxes that allow her to watch as their beauty drifts away."

"Sounds like Sophia. She's been given everything she's ever wanted and now, she might be queen." A cold, slippery sensation trickles through my gut. "Who is doing her beauty work?"

"I don't know," Auguste replies.

I think of Ivy and Amber. Of Edel. The things she could be forcing them to do.

The narrow passage opens into a large courtyard before a once decadent palace carved from the belly of the mountain. Gold-and-silver filigree crawls over tall towers. Heat-lanterns and night-lanterns dance around each other, becoming tiny suns warming and lighting the darkness.

"All the passages are plugged with blockades except for this one," Auguste reports.

A set of guards acknowledge him with a nod. They step aside and allow us entry to climb the stairs behind them.

We mount the seemingly endless steps leading to the palace entrance far above. Gilded lifts sit in disrepair with rotten cables. I can imagine the once grand balconies overlooking lavish gardens of mountain flowers, the layers of luxurious private chambers, sumptuous feasts, and overflowing pitchers of champagne and wine, incandescent-lanterns made to capture the light of the outside.

At the top, Lady Arane and Auguste whistle a matching tune. It excites the teacup dragons. They escape my pouch, racing up to the cavernous ceiling and chasing one another like aggravated post-balloons.

I call their names. They dive toward me and tuck themselves back in my waist-sash.

"They're beautiful," Auguste says.

I don't acknowledge his compliment. I don't even look at him. Eyes forward. Shoulders back. Mouth pressed into a frown.

He leads us to an entry flanked by guards. They nod and let us pass. Tunnels branch off in several directions. The remnants of decadent spaces are laid open: skeletal chair frames, broken tables, blankets of dust. I can imagine the cavernous halls filled with light and warmth and bodies and laughter.

We reach a set of doors, and a guard opens them. An old receiving room sprawls out before us. Gold-flecked walls soar to our left and right, touching at high ceilings and lofty peaks. The space is divided into sections—a bedroom, a workshop, and a parlor. Cerulean healing-lanterns leave blue-tinted streaks scattered about. A dark-haired woman hunches over a worktable mixing liquids into vials and pressing herbs along parchment paper. The massive fireplace roars with light beside a bed.

The woman looks up at me, her piercing eyes so pale and gray they shine like silver coins. Deep wrinkles ring her colorless mouth, and gray streaks her hair and lingers right beneath her skin.

Lady Zurie Pelletier. The dead queen's beloved.

"Camellia." She rushes to me, wrapping me in a hug. She smells of medicinal pastes. "What are you doing here?"

"Camellia is here to help," Lady Arane answers before I can.

Lady Pelletier pulls back and inspects me, cupping her warm hand beneath my chin. "We're so glad you're here."

Lady Arane removes her cloaks and orders her Iron Ladies to post at the doors with the other guards.

Lady Pelletier takes my hand. "You're the reason our Charlotte is awake. You must meet Her Majesty now that she can speak."

Hope springs to life inside me. I realize I didn't fully believe until now. She sweeps me forward to the bed and pulls the curtains back. A night-lantern escapes the bed's canopy. "My darling, we have an important visitor," Lady Pelletier says.

Charlotte glances up from reading a book. Her eyes are bright, yellowed by the lantern light and glistening with sickness. Thin brown curls spread over her frail shoulders, and the once bald patches on her head have started growing back in. Lady Pelletier leans down and kisses her forehead.

"Your Majesty," I say with a bow.

Charlotte's eyes drift over me, taking me in. The teacup dragons climb from my waist-sash and onto my shoulders. She marvels at them, and me.

"You look different from the pictures," she replies, her voice soft and so very different than Sophia's.

"Better or worse?" I ask.

A smile plays across her lips. "My sister has a way of making everyone look bad in the papers—and Wanted posters." She reaches out a hand to me. I slip mine into hers, and her bony fingers feel like a pile of twigs. "I owe you my life."

"How are you feeling?" I ask.

"Better but still weak," she responds.

Lady Pelletier stares down at her, stroking the top of her head. "We're doing whatever it takes to get her strong for the days ahead, for her to take her rightful place."

Charlotte takes a deep, labored breath, air rattling in her chest.

"We will get you well, petite." Lady Pelletier pats Charlotte's hand, then turns to me. "Your sister Padma has been using sang-sues to draw the remaining poison out of her."

My heart flickers. "Where is she?"

"She's in the next room, resting. I'll show you." Lady Pelletier sweeps me from Charlotte's bedside.

I follow her into a bedroom reminiscent of our apartments at Maison Rouge. A large bed sits in the back corner beside an open window. Behind a silkscreen, Padma sleeps in a smaller bed, her black hair a mess over the pillows like a spilled ink jar.

I almost trip over my dresskirts as I run to her. "Padma!"

She wakes with a jump. Her sluggish eyes brighten. "Camille!"

I almost fall into her arms, enveloping myself in the scent of her—flowers and powders and home.

I hold my breath to keep from crying, then my words rush out in sputters. "Are you all right?"

She looks fine. Tired but fine. Nothing like the condition in which we found Valerie.

"Yes, I am well," she replies. "And you?"

"Better now!" I tell her. Trembles vibrate through my arms and legs, and I fight to hold on to her, to never be taken from her. A fissure rips inside me, all the worries and stress pouring out of me, all the anger and disappointment and frustration. She strokes my hand. I wish she would tell me everything will be all right like our mamans used to.

But she can't.

We sit in my tear-soaked happiness.

"I saw the news about Amber, then about Edel," she says, pulling back. Tears coat her eyes, which are the same color as mine. "Do you think they're all right?"

"I don't know." I wipe my wet cheeks. "They're being held in the Everlasting Rose. No telling if they're being tortured, if they're surviving whatever experiments Sophia is doing on them."

I open and close my mouth a few times, trying to find the words to tell her what happened to Valerie. But nothing comes out.

Lady Pelletier approaches. "Camille."

I look up from Padma.

"It's time for our nightly meeting. You both must come with me. We're going to put our plan into action."

28

The war room is like a decayed honeycomb. Faded paintings of the great battles in Orléansian history bleed along the walls. Weapons hold rust and cobwebs. Guards are stationed around the room beside every door and window.

The Iron Ladies, Auguste, and Lady Pelletier gaze at a map of Orléans spread across a wooden table along with small replicas of the kingdom's fleet. Newspapers sit in mounds. House emblems are organized under labels—SOPHIA SUPPORTERS or SOPHIA OPPOSERS. A variety of merchant and high houses straddle the line between the two categories.

"More and more pledge support every day." Lady Arane stands, pointing at the royal emblems. "We have two days to get Charlotte to the palace. I say we arrive at the Royal Square and make a spectacle. Our regent queen loves a show above all else."

"We could lure her out of the palace," adds Surielle.

Violetta claps in agreement with this statement.

"We cannot march into the Royal Square with an army," Lady Pelletier replies. "She will just take Charlotte."

"We have the numbers," Surielle says. "We can make a huge and impressive showing. Hundreds alone in Trianon await our call. We can move others in from the isles and cities."

"I agree with Lady Pelletier that this isn't the way," Auguste replies. "She's got her trap set. She's told the world that Charlotte is dead. She plans to present a body and she will. Not many have seen Charlotte since she fell into her unfortunate slumber. They will buy into her lies. They already are. She's used the news and the newsies to her advantage. The *Orléansian Times* ran a poll yesterday and many love her. They will believe that whatever body she trots out is Charlotte."

"But the moment Charlotte shows her face and allows inspection of her identification marker, the world will know the truth," Surielle says.

The table grows quiet.

"What is the *truth* in Orléans?" Lady Arane says, then turns to me. "You and your sisters spent your entire existence altering appearances, shifting reality, catering to the most shallow whims. This world was born out of a rotten, poisonous seed—and now, the framework is laced with it. Everyone spends all their time trying to look like something else. The masses will believe what is presented to them, as long as it's compelling and beautiful. Thanks to you, they no longer have any idea what's real—what's true."

Her words sting and rattle me, the truth of them pressing beneath my skin as I begin to understand exactly what she thinks of us. Padma squirms at my side. I attempt to get the conversation back on track.

"Sophia will expect us to make a big show," I state calmly. "She will have planned for it. She is most likely counting on it. I think we should be like a whisper." I use the Fashion Minister's words, the image of his smile cascading through my mind.

"I agree," Lady Pelletier replies, leaning across the table and pulling out the map of the palace grounds. "I've known this child my whole life. She craves spectacle and assumes everyone else thinks the same way she does."

"I've been told there's only one way into the palace now," I say, boldly repeating Arabella's warning about the main entrance.

"You've *heard*..." Lady Arane replies with suspicion.

"I have my own supply of information." I sit up a little straighter.

"Camille is right," Auguste says. "It's not known to the public, but the northern entrance to the palace serves as the checkpoint in and out. The other three gates have been closed citing 'repair' and are being closely monitored. She has plans to have them shut permanently once the construction on the Everlasting Rose is complete."

The mention of the prison sends a shudder through me. The images of the Fashion Minister and the Beauty Minister are ever present in my mind. I can't close my eyes without seeing the anguish in their eyes and the pain in their faces. So many people are suffering, and it's up to us to end it.

Lady Pelletier taps her finger on the table. "We should go in through the queen's tunnels and bypass the single checkpoint." She turns to me. "That is how Arabella smuggled you and Amber out after you woke Charlotte."

Lady Arane purses her lips and considers. "The element of surprise....Hmmm..."

"Sophia has discovered those passageways," Auguste

interjects, sucking all the hope out of the room like air in a pierced post-balloon, sending it plummeting to the ground. "As Regent Queen, she was briefed on the tunnels, as is protocol."

"We don't have time to send someone to find the right way in and report back. Once the coronation happens, Orléansian law is clear. We will have to topple the entire cabinet," Lady Arane says.

"Maybe it needs to be erased and remade!" someone else shouts.

The group explodes with opinions. Their voices agitate the teacup dragons in my waist-sash. The various ideas swirl around me, none of them settling or feeling like the right thing to do.

I wish Rémy were here. His quiet determination. His ability to see all aspects of a problem. His ability to present his ideas and then listen to others patiently, without arguing. His ability to remain calm. My brain is a chaos of thoughts on how to get into the palace, growing louder over the arguing voices. Only one thing is clear—one or all of us will have to walk straight through the front doors of the palace. What kind of person would Sophia be unable to refuse? All the moments spent with her shift through my mind—her insatiable desire to be the most beautiful, to be feared and loved by all, and to have the most attention in every single room.

I let the irritable teacup dragons out to explore. They knock over the house crests, making a mixed-up mess of the Iron Ladies' chart—those they have identified as Sophia supporters and opposers.

The door slides open. A guard pushes Charlotte into the room in a wheeling chair.

"Your Majesty," Lady Arane says.

Everyone stands to greet her.

"So happy to have you join us." Lady Pelletier rushes to her side and places a hand on her cheek, then moves her to join us at the table.

"I could hear you down the hall. But this person you speak of..." Charlotte begins to say, her voice wobbly. "It doesn't sound like my sister. Not the one I knew. Sweet, always in pursuit of adventure, a lover of gifts and trinkets, and full of laughter. My mother used to tell us stories of our births. My sister loved hers. Maman said there were shooting stars the day she came, and she was destined to bring light. But all I've seen is darkness since I've woken."

"She is changed." Lady Pelletier takes the princess's hand.

"I've been reading about what has happened in Orléans since I've been asleep, none of it good." She sighs and leans back in her chair. "The world has twisted her. Warped her."

"More than just that," I say, but no one looks up, and they launch back into sharing their various plans. Their voices rise over one another, each trying to drown out the next, each thinking their idea is better, more sound.

"We can alter the course the world is on," Lady Arane says, striking the table with confidence. "We can make sure Charlotte is queen." She looks at the princess and steadies her voice. "The *rightful* queen."

"I need more time to recuperate. If Sophia is as bad as you say, I'll need all my strength to do what needs to be done," Charlotte replies.

"Queens don't rule alone. You will have counsel and support," Lady Pelletier assures her. "We will make sure you're ready. This is what your mother would want."

"Do I look like a queen?" she asks the table.

Her eyes gleam with sickness beneath the night-lantern light. A soft cloth swaddles her head and her hands fight stillness, tremors moving them without her control. The light brown of her skin fades, gray seeping in along the edges of her face.

"We thought bringing Camille here could help with that," Surielle interjects. "She will make sure you appear strong."

Everyone turns to face me.

"Yes. I will make our rightful queen appear healthy and formidable," I tell them.

"And then what?" Charlotte asks. "How are we to enter the palace?"

I close my eyes and see Sophia on the throne, her teacup pets racing around her as she tortures women standing on dress blocks. I see the Sophia from my dreams, laughing and sneering beside her imperial blood cameos. I see Rémy and Edel and Amber and Valerie. An idea surges through me, the hope of it blazing bright and revealing what I must do from the pits of my heart.

"I will be her wedding gift," I say, my voice slicing through the room, pouring out louder and sharper than I intended.

"What did you say?" Lady Arane demands.

"I will march through the front doors," I announce.

"Excuse me?" Surielle asks.

"Auguste, you will write to Sophia and tell her you're sending a dragon dealer to the palace in honor of the upcoming Coronation and Ascension. She needs teacup dragons for her menagerie. They're lucky and auspicious. She will be able to meet several and pick one."

"That doesn't solve the issue of how *we* will get inside the palace. One person can't topple an entire kingdom," Lady Arane fires back.

"But one person can start a fire," I reply. "Sophia loves nothing more than a beautiful gift. You just said so, Your Majesty." I gesture at Charlotte. "One of the newsies said Sophia is reopening the skies to receive offerings in celebration of her coronation. You are adept at moving cargo no matter the method of transport. So send your entire army in a set of gift boxes via post-balloon. They're being collected on the Observatory Deck, I believe. Someone get the latest papers."

Lady Arane lifts a suspicious eyebrow and looks at Auguste. "What do you know of this?"

"That it's brilliant," he replies.

I don't let his compliment make me smile, though his confidence in my plan strengthens it. I sit up a little taller and push my shoulders back.

"I remember going there as a child to look at the stars through the gigantic optic-scopes with my father," Charlotte says.

"Violetta, go get the papers," Lady Surielle orders.

Violetta nods and scurries out.

The table stares at me, waiting, anticipating. I will my thoughts to settle into coherent shapes. I take a deep breath and continue. "I will make sure the doors from the Observatory Deck to the inside of the palace are open so you can come down into the palace. And that whoever watches over the gifts . . . cannot effectively do so anymore." The words are thick on my tongue. My willingness to harm a stranger feels so easy and wrong, and not a choice.

"The Ascension Ball starts after the midmorning star in two days. It's an all-day affair according to the latest papers," Surielle says. "If we arrived that morning, we'd be able to infiltrate easily. The palace will be in the chaos of preparation."

"We will forge special masks for the occasion and join them

only to…" Lady Arane rubs her fingers under her gray chin, considering my proposal. "Yes, yes, I think I like this."

"But the question is…" Surielle perks up. "How will you just march into the palace without being recognized? Your face is plastered all over the kingdom."

I close my eyes.

The arcana are a small throbbing tendril under my skin, a reluctant thread buried deep that I pull to the surface with an angry tug. A cold prickle crawls up my spine.

I hold a portrait of Maman in my head.

My body changes.

Everyone gasps.

I hold a portrait of Lady Arane in my head.

My body changes.

I hold a portrait of Surielle in my head.

My body changes.

A headache pulses in my temples. Blood trickles down my nose.

"What…how…?" several voices say.

Padma stands, slipping her hand in mine. "How did you do that?"

I lose the glamour. She gazes at me, her eyes brimming with questions. "I'll teach you. Edel taught me."

I wipe my nose, then turn to the table. "I know Sophia. I have experienced her torture. I know what to do." I clasp my hands together. "Your Majesty, Padma and I will work together, if you feel well enough, to make sure you look strong and beautiful to face her and the people of Orléans."

"I will stay and help Charlotte travel," Padma offers.

A hush comes over the room. Lady Arane cups a hand over her mouth. Excitement thrums in their veins—I can feel it.

"Are we all in agreement?" I ask, the power of the bargain swelling around me.

"Yes." Auguste stands.

"Yes," Charlotte replies. "That is what we must do. We will plan to arrive by sundown before the ceremonies begin. We will meet you on the Observatory Deck."

"I'll leave in two hourglasses. Prepare a transport," I order.

"May our threads remain strong and our webs serve us well," Lady Arane says. "And may you, Camille, trap our enemy."

The treatment rooms in the subterranean palace resemble a painting plucked straight from the Belle history books in the Imperial Library. Grand pools stretch out in each direction, water ravines sloping through the mouths of massive fireplaces. A constellation of cracks decorate each empty hearth—mosaic images of the gods fractured. Candelabras clutch half-burnt candles bearded with rotten drippings.

Lady Pelletier pushes Charlotte into the first private chamber. She unties three night-lanterns from the back of Charlotte's wheeling chair, and sets them afloat. They drift about, their pleats of light revealing a long table covered in a blanket of dust. Moth-eaten pillows cling weakly to the remains of their intricate embroidery. Cabinets contain decayed Belle-products.

"Your Majesty," I say, and turn to her, "maybe we should do your beauty work in the receiving room where your bed lies."

"I couldn't bear to do it out in the open with all those people," she replies.

"We could clear the room," Lady Pelletier adds.

"No." Charlotte raises a weak hand. "I can handle a little dust."

Lady Pelletier starts clearing the table. She coughs as dust clouds explode around her. One of her attendants helps Charlotte from her chair. She wobbles before taking her first step toward the bed.

"Should we lift you, Your Majesty?" the woman asks.

"No." Charlotte straightens her back and takes a second step.

Padma and I exchange glances.

How will she be ready to face Sophia?

How will the kingdom support her claim to the throne?

I take a deep breath and point to the cabinets. "There's probably nothing we can use here."

Lady Pelletier produces a few of the Belle-products Edel, Rémy, and I had stolen from the Spice Teahouse.

"Glad to see those haven't gone missing," I reply.

"We don't like these circulating in our dwellings for fear of triggering old habits and stoking old impulses from our followers."

Padma takes them from Surielle. She sets out the few Belle-rose elixir vials, four miniature skin-paste pots, and one small bei-powder bundle. "It'll have to do."

We unbutton the thin gown Charlotte wears. Gray rises from beneath the brown of her skin, swallowing it. Her bones protrude, and I resist the urge to count her ribs.

Padma and I nod at each other. She coats the princess in white bei powder.

Lady Pelletier tips the vial of Belle-rose elixir to Charlotte's mouth, easing the liquid down her throat.

"Do you have a desired look?" I ask her.

"Make me look the way my mother would want me to."

Her request tightens my throat.

"I'll focus on her hair and face," Padma says. "And you her skin and body."

I nod. "We must go slow. One thing at a time." I remember my first beauty session with Princess Sabine and all the treatments I tried to complete all at once, almost killing her. I hear Ivy's words and feel the pinch of missing her too. Hopefully I will see her and all my sisters soon.

Padma and I stand on opposite sides of the table. We reach across it and hold hands. Padma's arms quiver with nerves. I squeeze her fingers tighter and close my eyes.

Princess Charlotte's body appears in my head—frail, almost gray.

The arcana hisses through my veins with warmth and familiarity.

"You first," I whisper. "Hair."

A patchwork of frizzy brown curls sprout from Charlotte's scalp; the scars left behind from Sophia's poisoned comb zigzag across the soft flesh, barely healed, but the new growth of hair covers them.

"You next," Padma says.

"Your Majesty, are you all right?" I gaze down at her.

She nods.

I run my fingers over her skin, deepening the brown so she matches her beautiful mother, Celeste.

Padma fattens her cheeks, the outline of her skull no longer visible. I do the same to her body, thickening her muscles and plumping her frame, fortifying her bones, and giving her the shape of an hourglass.

Sweat soaks through my clothes.

Charlotte starts to resemble the young woman I saw in portraits before she fell into the long, poison-induced sleep.

The doors snap open.

"Camellia!" Lady Arane says. "I'm sorry to interrupt." She clutches a newspaper. "You must go right now."

She holds the paper out. The headlines scatter. The words *torture* and *guard* and *Rémy Chevalier* scramble.

Chains crisscross over his bare chest. Blood drips down his dark arms, gashes oozing and pulsating.

I rush to her and grab the pages from her hands. The headline reads:

CAMELLIA BEAUREGARD'S TRUSTED GUARD CAPTURED

AT PALACE—TO BE EXECUTED IN THE ROYAL SQUARE

29

I fall back on the bed, all the air rushing out of me. White spots stamp out my vision. Worry and anxiety drum through me.

"Camille, what is it?" Padma asks.

She helps me up, the grip of her brown hands comforting but not enough. I think of Rémy, of his strength, of the fact that he needs me, and I pull myself together to stand up straight.

"She's right. I have to go."

"But we aren't finished—"

"I will send word when I'm safe." I kiss her cheek, and she pulls me into a hug. "I love you."

"I love you, too," she whispers.

I swallow down tears. Being with her made me feel a little less alone, a little more confident that everything would be all right. But I will see her again. I have to believe that.

In a nearby chamber, I dress quickly, pack my belongings, and gather the teacup dragons. I walk out expecting Lady Arane only to find Auguste leaning against the wall.

"What are you doing here?" I snap.

"I've arranged for one of my boats to take you to Trianon. The imperial fleet will grant you safe passage if you sail under my flag. I've sent word ahead of my travel plans, and the gift I'm sending to my fiancée—a dragon dealer named Corrine Sauveterre."

The words *thank you* can't form in my mouth.

I nod.

"I've already started having the gift boxes made to fit each one of the Iron Ladies," he adds. "They'll be beautiful on the outside and—"

"I don't need to know the details—just that they're being sent. I need to go."

"Yes, of course." Auguste leads me back through the winding network of tunnels. The teacup dragons fly above us, their scales catching the light from the single night-lantern he carries. The melody of their flapping wings and the pounding of our footsteps are the only conversation between us. I constrict like a corkscrew, knots coiling tighter and tighter as the unspoken words are a set of knives twisting inside me.

The throbbing gashes on Rémy's body appear over and over in my mind, thoughts of him being tortured drowning me.

Auguste's eyes search for mine in the subtle darkness.

I march forward, picking up my pace. The tunnels grow colder as we snake through them, the outside close. The scent of snow and ice replaces the stench of stagnant water and rust.

He whispers my name.

I ignore it.

He touches my arm.

"Don't!" I snatch it away.

"I'm sorry."

"You think that word can fix it?" My teeth clench. "Do you know how small that word is? Too tiny to fix what you did. Too easy to try to sweep away all the things you set in motion."

"What can I say? What can I do?"

"Nothing. It's impossible for you to erase this. It would be like asking for the sun to leave the lair of the God of the Sky. Or asking the ocean not to rush the shore." I run ahead, hoping it's the right direction. "I don't have time for this. I have to get to the palace."

"I know there's nothing I can ever do to make you trust me again," he shouts out behind me. "But I've been trying to do *something—anything* in my power to right this wrong."

I stop and whip around to face him. "You gave her exactly what she needed to destroy me! Me *and* my sisters!"

My voice booms off the cavernous walls. I don't care who hears me. My anger transforms into something that could live outside of me, a windstorm bursting from my chest made of thunder and lightning and furious rain.

"I didn't know." His hands shake at his sides.

"That answer will never be enough. It will never be all right." My glare burns into him. I wish it would reduce him to nothing, show him how I felt after I discovered what he did to me. "Valerie is dead. Amber and Edel and Hana are under Sophia's control. Who knows what she's doing to them?"

"We will stop her," he says. "I can fix this."

"*I* will stop her. *I* will fix this. I will end this," I say through clenched teeth.

We lock eyes. The deep brown of his irises is rimmed with red like chocolate malt candies dipped in cherry glaze.

"Are you done?" I shout.

I harden into stone as his shoulders shrug forward. "You're

still the most beautiful girl I've ever met, and even more so when you're mad."

His compliment stirs into the fire inside me. "And you're still an ass who thinks charm and compliments are bandages."

"No, just sharing the truth." His voice breaks. "If I have to... and if something happens, if things don't go as planned...I will make sure no harm comes to you, and that...she doesn't survive as queen. Neither you nor your sisters will ever suffer again. I'll do whatever I can to make this right. You have my word."

"And it's worth a grain of sand."

"I know, but you have it nonetheless." He tries to take my hand.

I pull it away from him. "Just make sure you hold up your side of the deal. Make sure Padma and Charlotte and the Iron Ladies get to the palace safely. That's all I want from you. I will take care of Sophia. I will take care of the rest."

"Understood."

We start walking again. He makes a left at a fork in the tunnels. Nothing is left between us.

Auguste's boat, the *Lynx*, skims the top of the ocean like the dragonflies that soared across the Rose Bayou back home. I wander around his private chambers. Sea-lanterns hang from hooks, and his desk is tucked into a corner. Maps cover the walls between the porthole windows. The scent of him lingers everywhere. The teacup dragons all nuzzle on a large horseshoe-shaped couch in the center.

I remember when I first met Auguste outside the palace, and he smugly reported that this was his boat. The memory is a hard lump in my stomach. I want it to burn a hole straight through and take with it all the memories of him.

The darkness outside the windows suddenly lights up, the sky filling with sparklers and star-shaped wish-lanterns as the God of the Sky and the Goddess of Beauty receive the kingdom's desires. It must be midnight. A new year has arrived.

"Happy days to come." The new year's blessing drifts down into the office from the deck above.

"The Year of the Goddess of Love always brings something sweet."

I hear the clink of glasses and more cheers.

I plop down on the couch with the dragons. They tuck themselves into the folds of my skirt and release tiny snores. I close my eyes and think back to this time last year. I spent the whole day making candy houses with my sisters. We lit tea candles and sat them inside our little creations, then placed them at the windows of Maison Rouge to call forth blessings from the God of the Ground. He'd find sweetness in this house and leave behind his goodwill and a fortune box for each sister. At midnight, our mamans had given each of us a wish-lantern and a slip of parchment to write down our heart's desires. I'd scrawled along mine: *I want to be the favorite.*

That wish is now a nightmare. So much has changed in just a few months. All those little girl hopes evaporating—wish-lanterns destroyed by winds. If only I'd known what my life would become.

I jam my eyes shut to prevent angry tears from falling. The smooth rocking of the ship lulls me to sleep, my body sinking deeper into the softness of the couch. But soon I am snatched into violent dreams.

I'm falling through the sky. Cold air catches every fold and layer of my dress, ballooning it like a pavilion bell. My limbs flap around me, unable to help me slow down. I fight to open my eyes, the wind pushing tears down my cheeks.

I look ahead and spot a shock of red hair like the crimson tail ribbons of a festive kite.

Maman.

I scream her name, but the syllables are lost in the howl of the gale.

We tumble forward, the speed of our bodies accelerating.

I try to catch her. I try to stretch out my fingers to grab the end of her dress. But she's just out of reach.

The dark tangle of the forest behind Maison Rouge lies ahead, the thick branches ready to engulf us, every naked skewer primed to stab through our insides. I scream and thrash about as Maman crashes into the boughs, their black fingers piercing her flesh.

"My lady," a voice whispers.

My eyes snap open. I leap to my feet, hand on Rémy's dagger.

Auguste's guard thrusts a pale orchid fortune box at me. "For you. Sweet days to come and good fortune."

"Thank you," I say, a little embarrassed.

I take it, the paper soft and supple, almost like skin, and slip it into a secret compartment in my waist-sash. It will be the only fortune box I'll receive tonight.

"Who is it from?" I ask.

"Mr. Fabry," he replies.

I suddenly want to shove it back into his hands, but he smiles at me like he's so happy to deliver this pretty box. I don't want to offend him.

"We'll be docking in Trianon in less than an hourglass. Prepare to disembark." He bows, then exits.

I tuck each one of the sleeping teacup dragons into my waist-sash. They fit like small jewels in their favorite compartments. I ruffle the long layers of my travel dress, pull on my cloak, and affix a veil over my face.

I call the arcana, letting the three gifts rush to my fingertips. Just in case.

The city of Trianon appears in the distance, its outline glittering and the city-lanterns tiny pinpricks of light like stars in a dark swath of sky.

I will burn it all, if I have to.

30

"Take Lady Corrine to the address as instructed," Auguste's guard orders a carriage driver.

The royal pier sits away from the busy port. The remnants of wish-lanterns scatter along the cobblestoned streets and skim the harbor waters like debris coughed up by the God of the Sea. Ivory streaks scar the early-evening night sky as the fireworks taper off and those celebrating the coming of the new year have most likely had their fill of sweetbread and champagne and chocolate coins.

A gale freezes my cheeks, joining the deep chill shooting through me as I hold a glamour. The port guards don't even flinch as I climb into the carriage. Eyes straight ahead, arms at their sides, bodies frozen in place.

Strange.

"May your threads be strong," Auguste's guard whispers to me. I don't have time to ask questions before he closes the carriage door, and the horse clip-clops forward.

The space is cold and empty, the fireplace absent of wood and the small servants' quarters vacant. I cover myself with a veil, let my glamour disappear, and wipe the small trickle of blood from my nose. Carefully, I inch back the drapes covering one of the carriage windows.

The pier market is desolate, blue-lanterns snuffed out, stalls boarded up, and the twisting lanes empty. Wooden booths sit at the market entrance marked CHECKPOINT. A guard shouts through a voice-trumpet: "Invite-only into the imperial city of Trianon. Have your papers ready!"

The carriage slows, and a pair of guards approach. Their shiny black uniforms and the gray stripe down the middle of their hair make me think of Rémy.

I hold my breath and close the curtain.

I hear low gravelly voices.

An anxious hum ruptures through me—the wonder of how long it will take me to find him and what condition he might be in and if he's all right... and still alive. I brush that thought away.

The carriage moves forward again. They didn't even inspect it. Auguste's word holds such a great deal of power. Even though I would have preferred to live my entire life without seeing him again, I must admit that Lady Arane made a wise choice in taking his help.

We enter the Garden Quartier, where shops sit like stacked pastry and hat boxes, one after another, so high they disappear into snow-swollen clouds. Gold blimps circle overhead like fat, sun-kissed raindrops. Animated ink whips along their middles with a message—*Smile! Look Your Best for the New Queen Because She Is Always Watching!* Light-boxes drop from their bellies and flash beams of light every few seconds.

Sophia has eyes everywhere now.

The carriage pauses at another checkpoint, then moves forward. The driver taps the wall, and I flinch as he slides back a panel. "Prepare for arrival, my lady."

"Thank you," I whisper, adjusting the veil over my face and taking a deep breath.

It all begins now.

Finally, the carriage stops before a closed shop called Larbalestier's Bawdy, Bodacious Bowlers, Bonnets, and Mischievous Millinery. Post-balloons float behind the windowpanes carrying all manner of hats—bowlers, pillboxes, ferronnières, miniver caps, toppers, bonnets. The oscillating movement oddly soothes the rapid beat of my heart.

I enter. A bell chimes. The foyer smells familiar—roses, charcoal, and sugar.

Home.

I spot bundles of Belle-rose flowers tucked into the brims of many of the display hats.

"Hello?" I call out.

Tables are littered with supplies. Shelves hold proud hats that resemble jewels in the subtle darkness. An abacus sits on a ledge; the red and white beads catch the lantern light. The cashier table is spread over with newspapers.

Their headlines shimmer:

ORLÉANS CABINET PASSES ONE LAW BEFORE NEW
YEAR'S—SET TO REMOVE THE WAIST SIZE RESTRICTIONS

LADY RUTH CARLON, HOUSE EUGENE, ACCUSED
OF BEAUTY MIMICRY AND FINED 20,000 LEAS

Gossip tattlers glow, drawing my eye to the *Parlour of Titillating Tidbits* and *Speculations of the Foulest Kind*, their reports teasing onlookers:

SOPHIA TO TAKE A MISTRESS AFTER MARRIAGE;
LONG-TERM LOVE DUCHESS ANGELIQUE DE
BASSOMPIERRE OF HOUSE REIMS SEEN MOVING INTO
SPECIAL PALACE APARTMENTS YESTERDAY

RUMORED LOVE CHILD OF KING FRANCIS SLATED
TO BRING A CASE BEFORE THE MINISTER OF
JUSTICE TO OBTAIN A TITLE AT COURT

QUEEN'S BETROTHED WON'T BE AFFECTIONATE
WITH HER; OVERHEARD WHILE INEBRIATED TELLING
A COURTIER HE'S IN LOVE WITH ANOTHER

Auguste.

A woman marches out of the back of the store. She has a large hourglass shape, her curves fitting beautifully into a robin's egg–blue dress cinched at the waist with a golden sash, and her hair is pulled so tightly into a bun at first I don't notice its curly texture and streaks of gray. "You're right on time."

"I am Corrine—"

"I know who you are. You can get rid of your veil. We have much work to do. You are to meet our future queen in less than an hourglass's worth of time."

"And you're Justine, I'm guessing?"

"Never guess. And no, Justine is not here. She's off chasing materials for her latest hat. But you don't have to hide any longer. Or attempt to run."

A shiver prickles up my back. The familiarity of her voice seeps beneath my skin.

"You are Camellia Beauregard. You were seven stones when you were born," she says.

Her words startle me. "My name is Corinne Sauveterre from the House of—"

"It's me, Madam Du Barry," she says, reaching out her arms.

I stumble backward. "No."

"Camille, I could never get you to follow rules, you always wanted to do the opposite of what I asked—always in the name of curiosity." She pulls down the sweetheart collar of her dress and reveals her imperial identification mark, the cursive letters of her name—*Ana Maria Lange Du Barry*—spelled out in permanent ink.

My mouth drops open.

"It's really you," I say, reaching out to touch her, and she grabs my hand, squeezes it, and pulls me into a hug.

I crumple in her arms. Even though I spent most of my life fearing this woman and the past few months uncovering all the lies she told us, her scent wraps around me like a cozy blanket. The comfort of her quiets the anger. I'm a little girl again.

The teacup dragons inch their way out of my waist-sash and start to whiz around, spraying their tiny coughs of fire at the bigger one in the hearth.

"What happened to you? Where did you go?" My eyes search her body and face, her outside so different and foreign from the shape of her I've always known. But her eyes—they always keep the same eyes. I can see her in there.

She leads me to chairs in front of the fireplace. "We don't have much time. But while your bath is being prepared, I will tell you what I can. When the queen's death was imminent and Sophia's behavior ever more unpredictable, I'd caught wind that she was planning to replace me and topple our traditions. There was a rumor that they planned to hold me in the dungeons, so I tried to take Elisabeth and leave the palace right after you did, but they'd already taken her. So I had to go on my own. It is something I've regretted ever since that day."

"She was in the prisons with us for a while. How is she faring at the palace?" I ask, remembering the sound of her voice on the other end of the circuit-phone at the Silk Teahouse. My anger toward Du Barry cools slightly, seeming so silly now after all that's happened.

"She's been sending me information when she can. Sophia won't let her go. She threatens to put my daughter in one of her new starvation boxes—allow the whole kingdom to see her nude body and watch it turn gray." Her voice quavers, but she quickly coughs, pours tea, and hands it to me.

"Thank you." The heat warms my hands.

"Elisabeth sends me letters every week if she can," she says, pulling a wad of parchment out of her pocket, and handing it to me. "She helps me track information and inform the Iron Ladies."

I purse my lips. "How did you meet them? And why? You are a guardian. We were a business to you. And it was profitable."

"It was our way of life."

"But you lied to us. You kept so many secrets from us," I say.

"And I'm sorry for that. I truly am. But I know that apology might be too little and too late." Her eyes gleam with tears in the firelight.

"I spent most of my life being angry with you."

"And I'm sorry."

That word again. It means nothing.

"You weren't children for very long, but I should've done things differently than my maman. I mimicked what was in the Belle-manuals, what my maman and grand-mère had done." She puts a hand on her face. "Camille, you have to understand...this was the way it was always done. Since the beginning of time. It wouldn't even have occurred to me to do anything differently than what *my* maman had trained me to do. But then, I saw the way Sophia treated Amber, and then you...It was clear something had to change. Perhaps the Iron Ladies' way is the better way. I met them while evading Sophia's network of guards.

"I know you've seen Sophia's pods. I never appropriately explained the other Belles that you discovered at the Chrysanthemum Teahouse. I should've told all of you about how you were born. I regret not being forthright. Adhering to the guide, I foolishly didn't realize that you having knowledge would keep you safe if things were to ever go wrong." She knits her hands in her lap. "I should have shown you how it worked."

The memory of Sophia's glass contraption slides into my head. "Were we all born from those pods?"

"The favored generation isn't." Her voice cracks.

"Why not? How did we grow?"

"From the goddess."

"Is she even real?" Anger chokes in my voice.

"That story has some truth. The Goddess of Beauty used to send Belles down from the sky like rain, and they'd burrow into the ground as seeds and grow under the protection of the dark forest behind Maison Rouge. They were beautiful bulbs. When I was a little girl I'd go out there with my mother to tend to the Belles. I used to think the bulbs were diamonds—their outer shells glittered in the darkness. We'd make sure they were covered by the rich soil and pour the blood of the previous generation over the them for nourishment."

My heart races alongside her story. It sounds like madness.

"Guardians were tasked to tend to that forest. Protect it. Keep it holy. Keep it hidden."

"The one you forbade us to enter."

"But the one you were always drawn to. You thought I didn't know when you and your sisters would sneak out there." She stares off into the fire. "Over many weeks, thick stems would push out from the soil, holding the babies in petal-like cases covered with thorns."

I open and close my eyes. The images her words etch in my mind are like scenes plucked out of dreams and nightmares.

"Once you were born, we'd pair you with one of the Belles who returned from court. To help raise you and prepare you for your duties. Over the centuries, fewer Belles dropped from the sky, and the guardians had to adopt radical methods to keep up with the growth in Orléansian population."

Du Barry purses her lips.

"What did you do? What did the guardians do?" I ask.

"I'm ashamed to tell you these guardian secrets. Saying them out loud solidifies just how wrong they've been all these years," she says without looking up.

"I want to know. I deserve to know." My anger is a teapot boiling over.

DuBarry takes a deep breath and lets it out slowly, staring into the fire. "My great-great-great-grand-mère figured out a way to extract some of your blood, parts of your tissue, and replicate the growing process in controlled pods. But this created greed and more demand." She reaches out to touch my shoulder. "To be honest, I don't think she really knew what she was doing. She thought she was solving a problem, but she only created more."

I clench my jaw and say nothing. What was there to say?

"What she discovered, over time, is that there is one Belle in each generation whose blood is stronger than the rest," she continues.

"Me," I say, and she blinks, surprised. "Arabella."

"Yes. You are the aether, as the guardians call it. Or as I thought of it as a child, the everlasting rose."

Sophia's cruelty in naming her prison after us burns afresh. "That's not how the story goes."

"It never is."

She pauses and leans closer to the crackling fire in the hearth. Her eyes gaze at the wild flames.

"This world doesn't deserve Belles," I yell, standing up and pacing around the room.

"You are right to be angry."

She stands and reaches out a hand, but I avoid her touch.

"Angry? That word is too small to describe how I feel." My muscles tense and my fists ball. I want to knock every hat from every perch and punch every post-balloon until they crash to the ground. "Sophia has Amber and Edel and Ivy and all the other Belles you lied to us about, like Delphine. And Valerie is dead."

Du Barry flinches, clutching her heart and stumbling backward into her seat. "What?"

"You heard me. She's gone. Sophia bled her to death, and she couldn't handle it any longer."

Du Barry holds her head in her hands. "I'm so very sorry."

"I don't understand why this all happened—how the world

could treat us like this. How could you lie to us over and over again?"

"You need to understand the value of beauty and how it creates deficiencies in the world. Deficiency is weakness. Beauty is power. It creates need and desire and want. Not having it creates a market." Du Barry looks up at me, her eyes watery and her cheeks tear-stained. "I can never be sorry enough."

"I've heard too many sorrys and none of them change anything."

An hourglass on the mantel flips. A long silence seeps between us. It seems there is nothing more to be said. Eventually, Du Barry clears her throat.

"Your imperial carriage will be back to get you and take you to her," she says, all business. It is a tone I recognize. "It's time to get ready."

Time to face Sophia.

31

"This arrived moments before you did. Lady Arane had it made," Du Barry says, holding a small box in one hand as I stand before a mirror. "I don't know how they got it into this tiny thing. It's not bigger than a hatbox."

She hands it to me and I open it, removing a card on top of the soft paper wrapping. It reads: *Pull the ribbon and wait for the dress to reveal itself.*

"Where did the Lady order this from?" I ask.

"The shop next door—Lili's Marchande de Modes. Very popular on this street."

I peel back the paper covering to reveal a thick red velvet ribbon. I pull it. The box flattens and I jump back, startled.

Bolts of turquoise-and-gold fabric unfurl, tumbling out like an ocean wave. Glittering sequins coat the fabric like scales. It starts to assemble itself upright. A row of black-and-white bows dot the center of the fitted bodice. The neckline dips into a sweetheart with champagne beadwork and a graceful train. The skirt ruffles alternate colors, and tiny golden cages push through. Finally, an oversize matching hat appears atop the box.

I gasp, circle it, and touch its edges. "It's perfect! Sophia will be intrigued."

The teacup dragons fly around the dress.

"There's a compartment in the bustle where you can store your things so you can travel lightly. Any luggage you might bring would be inspected, and your identity quickly uncovered." She shows me the small space almost the size of my satchel.

Du Barry's attendant whistles to get the dragons' attention and lures them into a low basin to wash the fireplace soot from their scales.

"Do you want their collars back on?" she asks me.

"No, thank you," I reply.

"Prepare her veil as well, Mia," Du Barry orders.

"I don't need one," I say with confidence, stretching upright.

"She will recognize you."

"No, she won't," I reply. I can't tell her about the glamours. Edel would never forgive me for divulging her discovery to the woman who lied to us our entire lives. "Please trust me."

"You must take it just to be safe. It's a new style called lace-skin." She holds up a tract of lace, shaped with the contours of a face, and rubs it against my skin. The thin black material spreads around my cheeks and down my neck like the intricate frosting on a cake. "All the ladies at court wear this now, to shield themselves from Sophia's gaze and hide their beauty for as long as they can."

Du Barry's attendant gingerly places each teacup dragon into its cage on my dress. They gnaw at the bars, hiccup fire, and stamp their talons in protest.

A bell chimes.

"It's time." Her eyes take me in and she touches my cheek. "You look extraordinary. If we never see each other again, I want you to know how much I do love you." Her voice cracks, and she clears it. "Don't lose sight of the *real* enemy."

"What's that supposed to mean?" I ask.

"Sophia is an enemy because she hurt you, hurt all of us. But the *real* enemy is inside every Orléans citizen. Cutting off Sophia's head—and trust me, I'd love to see it displayed in all its glory in Trianon's Royal Square—will do nothing, because another head will replace it. Stick to your plan. You must be a whisper in a field that turns to a roar right before she can sense it." She kisses my forehead like she did when we were little and earned high marks. The warmth of her mouth is the same. "I hope to see you again."

She presses the official imperial invitation into my hand, the paper thick with promise and danger.

The palace is awash with light, and the sky above it filled with snowflakes and pretty post-balloons headed to the Observatory Deck carrying gifts for the new queen. I smile for the first time in weeks, thinking about the Iron Ladies and Charlotte headed this way soon.

Courtiers spill out of gilded carriages pausing at the palace checkpoint. Revelers stumble with excitement and clutch the remnants of candy houses and empty champagne flutes. They sing traditional blessings and wish each other well. They shout their names, the syllables stretched with slurs and excitement.

I join the crowd. A set of imperial guards collects invitations and checks a parchment scroll. They let some courtiers in and reject others.

I walk up and hand the guard my paper. "Corrine Sauveterre."

"There's a star beside her name," one guard says.

"The queen has been waiting for her most of the night," the other replies. "We must rush her in before the others and send word ahead."

A golden post-balloon bursts from the checkpoint building. Its ribbons snap and flicker in the wind. I wonder what the note inside says. If she believed Auguste's offer of a gift. If she is excited to meet Corrine Sauveterre, premier dragon merchant, here to let her have her pick of dragons for her upcoming coronation.

My heart shivers under my rib cage. The teacup dragons protest in their new cages, their wings batting against the bars, irritated at being jostled around.

The guards lead me onto the palace grounds. The topiary maze is now a garden of flowers fashioned from jewels—roses with ruby petals and emerald stems. Perfume blimps making spritzing sounds skate over the fake flowers. Black gossip post-balloons stalk the gardens as if they've been calibrated to find information and sniff out stories in dark corners. The palace rivers are chockfull of newsie boats. They send fleets of story post-balloons up to the entrance like a storm of navy birds. A newsblimp weaves in and out of the palace turrets holding banners of new year's wishes.

All I want to do is take out Rémy's maps and let the ink reveal where the dungeons are. All I want to do is ensure his safety, then, first thing in the morning, I'll go to the Observatory Deck to make sure the Iron Ladies and Charlotte can arrive undetected. All I want to do is execute this plan without any problem.

I walk into the receiving room, and it has been transformed into a menagerie. Gilded cages descend from the high ceiling, made of fine porcelain edged in gold, holding every teacup pet one could imagine. A unicorn sports a tie. A pack of wolves wear tiny hair bows. A wall-length aquarium holds teacup fish, where a small narwhal chases a teacup shark. A family of teacup penguins shuffle an egg back and forth.

A flood of memories follows me into the foyer of the main entrance, and I am transported back to the night Amber was declared the favorite. High-backed chairs flank the long carpet. Onlookers sport monocles and press eyescopes to their faces and lift up ear-trumpets. Light pushes through the ceiling glass; threads of it stitch across my path, creating a tapestry of orange and gold.

We enter the throne room and I'm stunned in place, feet heavy and leaden.

Sophia is just ahead, perched on her throne, singing at the top of her lungs out of tune, her blond hair tower full of teacup swans. Her ladies-of-honor surround her. They look the same as they did weeks ago when I was here. Gabrielle, closest to her, with beautiful dark brown skin, rich and coated with glitter, then a new girl with hair the color of black soil who has replaced Claudine fawns over a teacup sloth, and little Henrietta-Marie with her nose in a book.

The sight of them fills me with rage. The arcana wake inside me, each skill a small, throbbing curl melding with my simmering ire. I'm not sure I can keep it contained. Sweat dots my brow and dampens the lace-skin Du Barry put over my face. With each breath I take, the anger bubbles up, clawing at my throat and eager to escape my mouth.

Sophia's new royal emblem banner hangs proudly from the ceiling. Her ladies-of-honor perch on pillows at her feet, watching and goading her on. Courtiers shout blessings and sweet nothings at her, desperate for her attention.

The room is chaos. I focus my attention ahead, not removing

my eyes from Sophia, wishing each glance could leave burns across her porcelain-white skin.

I move forward. Each footstep I take, I use my arcana to create a glamour. The cold pain claws up my spine. I deepen the brown color of my skin, stretch myself a touch to be taller, and darken my hair.

The taste of blood coats my tongue, slivery, metallic, and sharp. I hope I can hold off a nosebleed.

The attendant removes a voice-trumpet from his jacket. "May I introduce Lady Corinne Sauveterre, daughter of Alexandra and Guillaume Sauveterre of the House of Rare Reptilians in the Gold Isles," the attendant announces. "She has brought you gifts from your fiancé, Auguste Fabry of House Rouen."

The teacup dragons hiccup fire from my dress. Sophia notices and squeals. I reach the throne platform, my anger threatening to consume me as I get closer and closer to her.

Sophia races down the stairs, her favored teacup pets nipping at her heels.

"Your Majesty," I say, deepening my voice and bowing as she approaches.

"Welcome to my court," Sophia says, then turns to her ladies-of-honor. "Ladies, this is our new guest. She's brought me dragons."

I bow to her ladies as well.

"This is Gabrielle, Lady of All Things, a princess du sang and my very best friend," she says.

"This is Rachelle, my new Lady of the Dresses to replace the unfortunate loss of my friend Claudine de Bissay."

They all bow their heads in mock sympathy.

"And my little Henrietta-Marie, Lady of the Jewels," she adds.

Henrietta-Marie doesn't look up from her book.

"Pleasure to meet you all," I reply.

Gabrielle eyes me with discerning interest.

"Just look at these dragons!" Sophia gushes, reaching into one of the cages to try to pet my little golden Or, but she evades Sophia's fingers. Sophia's elephant, Zo, kicks her feet up at me and pushes her tiny trunk at my skirt. She squeals with delight.

I panic. Mr. Claiborne's warning pulses through me: *There's a natural perfume you have. Different than ours.* What if Zo or her teacup monkey, Singe, recognizes my scent?

"Let me see you," Sophia demands, facing me.

"Of course, Your Majesty. As you wish." I remove the lace-skin Du Barry gave from my face.

My heart beats against my sides as her gaze combs over me, her odd rainbow-colored eyes full of curiosity like a teacup cat nosing around a room in search of a mouse. Who is doing her beauty work now, and how absurd has it become?

"Do we know each other?" she asks.

"No, Your Majesty. I haven't had the pleasure to come to court before today." I bow.

"You are a beauty," she says.

The crowd claps.

"Though never as beautiful as you," I add, earning a smile from her.

She blushes. "Of course."

Zo trumpets at my feet, and I try not to flinch.

"Oh, Zo's very friendly," Sophia says, looking at the tiny elephant lovingly. "And it seems she likes you already." Her eyes drift all the way up me, inspecting each and every inch. "This bodes well for our potential working relationship."

Singe does a lap around me but keeps his distance.

"You will give me all of those glorious teacup dragons, correct? That's what Auguste said. My fiancé knows me so well." Her gaze fixates on them. "You saw the horrifying news about the loss of my other ones? Happened a week or so ago."

"I did. It was most unfortunate," I say with mock sympathy.

"Indeed. Most unfortunate. Once the perpetrator is caught, I will make them wish they'd never been born." She pauses to look out over the crowd of courtiers. "Even though Pearl, Sapphire, and Jet will always be remembered, I must replace them. The Goddess of Love was rumored to keep dragons, so I must have them all, and any others you're currently tending."

"That's not quite how it works," I say, steadying my voice.

Her court gasps.

"What does that mean?" Her pale blond eyebrow lifts with surprise.

"If you aren't present for their birth, my breed of teacup dragons must choose their owners. They must deem the person worthy. You see, they're very noble creatures. Exceedingly rare. All dragons are said to have come from the womb of the Goddess of Love. Their affection, loyalty, and disposition mirror exactly what love should be."

The crowd oohs.

Sophia scowls. "I am a queen. I was born deserving and worthy. My lineage and bloodline make it so."

"Of course," I say, and add a little bow to keep her from seeing me seethe. "But the dragons will have their say."

My words sizzle and crackle in the silent room.

Her rainbow-colored eyes burn into the top of my head. Sweat rises from my skin, cold and clammy. Maybe I pushed too hard, said too much. I swallow and try to hold on to the glamour. A headache blossoms in my temples. The taste of salt fills my mouth. The nosebleed will come any second.

"I enjoy a challenge," she snaps, reaching for Or's golden tail. Or lets herself be caressed, then curls back into a corner in the cage. "I always win."

"You are blessed by the God of Luck, and we will see which dragon chooses you."

Her mouth parts, but she closes it and grins. "Until then, you shall remain here as my honored guest." She waves a nearby attendant over. "Prepare the guest apartments in the east wing."

"Pardon me, Your Majesty, I don't mean to question your hospitality, but I must be in chambers nearest you. My breed of teacup dragons must acclimate to your scent. Bond, if you will. So that one or two may connect." I let a clever smile play upon my lips, hoping she takes the bait and puts me in Charlotte's chambers.

Her eyes widen. "I want them all to love me. So, yes, whatever is necessary shall be. I'm prepared to give you all the leas you could ever want, and spintria, too, if you prefer it." She turns to another attendant. "Give her my darling and dearly departed sister's room."

Courtiers flap their fans wildly as if a flash of warm-season heat stormed through the room.

"I couldn't possibly stay in Princess Charlotte's apartments. I am not of noble birth. Would it not be inappropriate?"

"She has passed on." The lie tumbles from her pink lips without effort. "At sunset tomorrow, I will present her body and we will mourn her officially. I cannot be queen until she is sent to the afterlife properly to be with my maman." She presses two fingers together and taps her heart, a sign of respect for the dead. The entire room mimics her. "I'm having a pavilion built in her honor on the palace grounds. It is my desire that you and the teacup dragons are as close as can be. I make the rules and I can break them."

I nod and bow. "As you wish."

"I do. I do." She takes my hands; hers are sticky and shaky. I try not to flinch or pull away. The rosewater scent of her sends a tangle of revulsion and rage through me, making it hard to hold on to my glamour.

"Your nose is starting to bleed." She hands me her own personal handkerchief embroidered with her initials and the House of Orléans emblem.

I quickly wipe my nose, the beads of blood soaking through the expensive fabric. "The cold season and travel have exhausted me."

"You must rest. The Coronation and Ascension Ball starts the day after tomorrow, and you must attend as my honored guest. You can wear one of my latest vivant gowns." She whips around to another attendant. "See that she's settled properly and all her needs are met."

"You are most gracious," I reply.

"And you are most welcome to my court."

I bow.

An attendant rushes forward with a sealed letter. "Your Majesty, this just arrived."

Sophia snatches it.

I stand up and see the words *Gold* and *Charlotte* and *spotted* before she rips up the note.

"I have to excuse myself," Sophia says, rushing off.

My heart pounds in my throat.

I must warn them.

32

Sophia's attendant walks me down a familiar hall to Charlotte's former apartments. The glitter of the night-lanterns and the scent of fresh cold-season flowers and the sounds of nearby laughter hurtle me back into the past. Memories of the night we left slice in like nightmares with each step I take. Rémy carrying Amber. Arabella's trunk and dragon eggs. It feels like both a lifetime ago and just yesterday—all spinning in my head to the beat of panic.

I need to find Rémy. I need to find Arabella. I need to figure out how to get to the Observatory Deck first thing in the morning. Trembles of exhaustion quiver through me, and the pain of holding the glamour sends more blood trickling out of my nose. I wipe it away as best I can, but it streaks the front of my gown.

The attendant pauses before a set of apartment doors. Charlotte's royal emblem is now absent, the wood naked, her presence erased. Mourning balloons carry cameo portraits of the "deceased" princess and her royal emblem. They carry tiny sound-boxes hissing out wails and cries every few minutes.

"Are you all right, my lady?" the attendant asks.

"Just tired."

"Time to rest."

I am ushered into the foyer, where a kneeling servant awaits.

"Lady Corrine, I leave you here to become acquainted with your chambers and your appointed help while staying with us." She turns on her heel before I can reply and leaves the room.

"Good evening," the servant says while standing. "May your new year be sweet!"

Her voice sends a shiver across my skin and stirs up thoughts of Bree buried deep down inside. It feels like shaking a snow globe. "And also yours," I reply. "What is your name?"

Her ponytail is a ribbon of honey down her back. I start to ask her if we've met before, but this is supposed to be my first time at court.

She looks up. Her eyes large and stretched, her skin dotted with star-shaped freckles. She looks like a doll from a shop window in Trianon.

She sets down a tray. A teapot, cup, and plate of sweets sits on top of a spread of newspapers and magazines. "I thought you might want something to read . . . and there's a note." Her voice drops an octave.

My heart knocks around in my chest.

"The queen's rooms are nearby. Hopefully, close enough for the teacup dragons to familiarize themselves with her scent." She launches into a detailed explanation of all the things I will find in these lavish apartments and shows me down familiar corridors. I don't care about any of it anymore.

I nod at the eager woman, trying to pretend I care, trying to keep from running straight out of here to find Rémy. The scent of

Charlotte lingers despite the perfume blimps drifting about. Just days ago, the ceiling was filled with cerulean healing-lanterns and a large four-poster bed containing her sleeping body.

"The bathing onsen is down the left corridor." She points. "And a small library to the right."

I gaze into the darkness of those halls, thinking of Rémy and Arabella, both tucked away somewhere in this expansive palace. Close yet so far away.

"Her Majesty has—"

Another trickle of blood escapes my nose. "Thank you. I must lie down and put my teacup dragons to bed," I say, cutting her off.

"Oh, yes, of course. I'm sorry." She bows. "Do you need additional help?"

"No," I reply, more clipped than I intend. "I'm just so tired from the journey."

"Understood." She nods and slips out.

I let the glamour fade and unhook the teacup dragons' cages from the dress. They eagerly stretch their wings, inspect the room, then settle on the perch of the bed canopy. Fantôme and Eau quickly fall asleep.

I push my hand into the dress pocket and remove the poison bottle, which I set on the vanity before removing the cumbersome dress. I unpack Arabella's Belle-book, Rémy's maps, the bottles of sangsues, and the case of eye-films.

Despite exhaustion, I rush to the room's desk and find parchment and ink.

I write to Padma:

P,

She knows that Charlotte is alive. She has been spotted in the Gold Isles.

Get in the air as soon as possible.

Love,

C

I whistle to Poivre and feed him one of Padma's leeches. "Find her. You're the fastest." I open a window and look out on the palace grounds. The Golden Palace River is filled with newsie boats and jovial courtiers singing and laughing and guzzling champagne.

I nudge the red teacup dragon out.

He disappears into the mass of wish-lanterns and post-balloons floating up to the sky. I turn to Rémy's maps. They almost hiss as I flip the pages and wait for the ink to settle. I trace my fingers along the drawings as they reveal each wing and its various chambers. My eyes droop with sleepiness, but I try to focus and search for the Observatory Deck and the dungeons, my heart torn about what to do first. I need to figure out the best way to get to the deck tomorrow so I can make sure Charlotte and the others can enter through it. If my plan doesn't work, there's no way in. But Rémy is somewhere in this palace being tortured.

I pace around. My hands shake at my sides. The indecision is a landquake inside me. If I find Rémy first, he can help me make sure that the Iron Ladies can enter.

My heart squeezes, giving me the answer to my question.

I have to find him, then I'll go to the deck.

I flip through the maps until the dungeons are shown beneath the receiving room.

I stir Or from her perch. "I need your help." She yawns but perks up. I take the last of Rémy's leeches and hold the writhing creature between my fingers. This is my last connection to locating him. "We need to find him, little friend. Don't let this gamble be a waste."

I pull on my cloak and the lace-skin again, and grab a night-lantern by the tails. I listen for the noise of servants before exiting the chambers. Adrenaline propels me, or maybe it's delirium from exhaustion.

Or flies in a circle above my head.

"This way, girl."

The teacup dragon hesitates.

"This way out."

Her big eyes grow large as glass marbles.

"Why are you confused? I will get us to the dungeons, and then, you take it from there." I whistle. She finally obeys, diving into the corridor.

I take out the map and navigate my way from the palace apartments to the receiving room. Jeweled chandelier lanterns hold frosted candles. Animated frescoes shift through the portraits of queens and kings, goddesses and gods. I used to love everything about this place—the bustling, beautiful bodies headed to the game rooms and tea salons, the scent of sweets escaping the golden carts of the royal vendors, lavish furniture spilling from every room.

But now, I see it for what it really is—a beautiful shell masking rottenness.

I skulk through the halls, hiding as guards patrol and courtiers stumble about looking for the exits to the Palace River piers or the carriage-house. Or drifts ahead, sometimes circling back as if she wants to return from where we came. I direct her to move forward.

Cold-season chrysanthemum trees grow up from the belly of the palace wing, their branches almost finding me as I race over the gilded walkways from one side of the palace to another. Empty chariots glide along the lattice cables. I race down a massive set of stairs and make a left at the entry fountain. Gleaming leas coins litter the bottom like drowned stars. It would almost be peaceful and settle the erratic beat of my heart, if I wasn't so terrified.

Footsteps invade the quiet. The doors of the receiving room swing open as I pass by.

I panic and find a dark corner to hide.

Servants carry a palanquin with a sleeping Sophia sprawled over the cushions. Her hair hangs in a tangled nest; her rouge-stick is smudged all around her mouth. Her teacup monkey, Singe, rubs her cheek. The heady scents of too much champagne and perfume linger as she passes.

Zo trots behind the small procession, trying to catch up with the palanquin. The miniature animal pauses, spots me, and cranes her neck. I duck deeper into my hiding place, but she trundles over and puts her little feet up on my nightdress. She wears a tiny jeweled crown that matches Sophia's. Her toenails are painted a bright mulberry. She sniffs my dress with her tiny gray trunk. I feel her fluttering heartbeat on my leg as she tries to climb it.

I try to shove her away. "Go on, now."

Or hisses at Zo, but she doesn't back off. Instead, she traces her slimy trunk along my wrist, sniffing the perfume ointment wiped there.

I push her away and lose the tail ribbons of my night-lantern. It drifts off.

One of the imperial guards yells, "Who is there?"

I turn back to the map and dart down the nearest corridor. Zo marches behind me making a tiny trumpet noise like an alert.

The guards pause, Sophia's palanquin perched on their shoulders.

This is it. I'll be caught, and all because of Sophia's ridiculous pet obsession.

"Shh. Go."

Zo's trumpeting grows louder, threatening to bring the entire imperial guard my way.

"Fetch me my beloved," Sophia shouts, her voice thick and heavy with champagne. "Do it *now!*"

I glance back down the hall. Sophia slaps the nearest guard across the face, then spits on top of his head. Revulsion pools in my stomach. The desire to hurt Sophia bursts inside me. Her evil, sadistic face flashes in my head like a télétrope reel.

Her laugh.

Her smile.

Her voice.

I think about squeezing her skull until it collapses, her hand until it breaks, her heart until it stops.

I see nothing but her.

I hear nothing but her laugh.

I feel nothing but the pain of her breaking my hand.

Rage churns in my heart.

Angry tears storm down my cheeks.

My vision blurs. My skin warms. My body prepares to use the arcana. I can't make it stop. I fumble with Rémy's maps, my tears soaking the parchment as I try to see the ink-drawn diagrams. I scramble to find one of the entries into the dungeons as I dart ahead.

Zo runs at my heels, chasing me like this is a game.

Sophia's high-pitched shouts hit me in waves as she barks at the guards. Zo's tiny heartbeat fills my ears like the flutter of a hummingbird's wings, followed by the noise of the blood rushing through her small body. I sink to the floor at the dungeon's entrance. The heat in my hands, the drum of my heart, and the movement of my blood create chaos in my stomach.

Zo climbs into my lap.

"Go away. Go away. I beg you." My refrain coils around me like a vise. I clamp my eyes shut. A headache throbs in my temples. My cheeks burn.

I slow Zo's heart.

I can't stop. I collapse forward, out of breath.

Zo lies on her back, eyes open, heart still.

A hand jostles my shoulder. The servant from earlier gazes down at me. "My lady . . ." A pair of familiar eyes stare back, but I still can't place them.

The woman removes the tiny elephant from my lap and places her aside, then helps me to my feet. "What are you doing here? I came to your chambers to make sure you didn't need anything before bed. I followed you."

"It was an accident," I pant. The truth tumbles out: "I was looking for my friend and the elephant—"

"The queen doesn't keep her most important possessions in the dungeons. Too easy to be plucked."

I search her eyes. "Who are you?"

"Trust your dragon. He's been moved." She lifts Zo's tiny lifeless body, tucks it under her arm, and leaves me where I stand.

33

I watch Or as she flutters overhead, dodging coral and butterscotch coronation post-balloons. We head back in the direction we came— to the royal apartments. I run behind her, my hand on Rémy's dagger, the arcana hissing just beneath my skin, and my nerves ready to help me do whatever it takes to find him. What did she mean when she said he would be too easy to pluck from the dungeon? Is it really so simple to get into this fortress? If he's not there, then where is he?

The questions pound inside me, in time with my footsteps.

Blood trickles from my nose, and I wipe it away without stopping to pause. My arcana prickle inside my veins, achy and like nothing I've ever felt before. Maybe a sign of trouble. We dart back up the stairs and over the gilded walkways. But as we reenter the royal wing, Or turns left, away from the apartments and down another long corridor.

"Why are we going this way?" I ask her, wishing she could answer me.

Worries drum inside me, piling one on top of the other. Have the sangsues gone to waste? Is she confused? Why is she leading me this way?

My exhaustion makes it impossible to think and another nosebleed starts. I know I need to rest and to reset the arcana. I've done too much.

Or pauses out front of Sophia's workshop. The House of Inventors emblem of cogs and gears and chrysanthemums glows in the darkness.

I take a breath and open the door. A sleeping guard is slumped over snoring, two empty bottles of champagne at his feet and new year's sweets smeared down his chest. I tiptoe past him.

The room holds even more items than it did the last time I was here. Moonlight escapes the glass ceiling, its beams leaving an eerie glow over the space. Beauty-boards perch on easels and litter the floor at the foot of the treatment table. Every wall displays a collection of blood cameos now. The portraits shift and morph alongside the noise of blood whooshing through brass piping.

Or zips ahead, hovering over a closet door.

I untie the single night-lantern from its hook.

Or leaves tiny scratch marks in the wood.

I open it.

My heart does a flip at the sight of him. Rémy is tied up, arms suspended in ropes, head slumped forward. His shirtless body is covered with lashes and brands—the wounds oozing with blood, swelling with infection, and smelling of burnt flesh. The deep brown of his skin is split open. A cut in his lip drips with blood, and his skull is now bald and covered in wounds.

I rush to him. "Rémy," I whisper, and cradle his head.

He jerks back. One of his puffy eyes opens as wide as it can.

"It's me." I pull off my lace-skin mask. "It's Camille."

"You here to rescue me?" he croaks out.

"Yes." I wrap him in a hug, all of my relief with it.

He grunts but lets his head rest in the crook of my neck.

"We've got to get you out of here." I pull away, take out the dagger he gave me, and cut the ropes. His body slumps forward, almost crashing to the floor, but I catch him.

"I can't leave my family here," he mumbles.

"We won't. I promise." I try to keep my voice from breaking. A pinch in my stomach grows hotter. The pain of seeing him like this threatens to consume me.

I muster all my strength and help him stand.

We hobble out of the closet. I take some dress-making fabric from a nearby table and wrap it around his body. "The guard is asleep."

Rémy drags himself ahead. "Where are you staying?"

"They gave me Charlotte's old apartments."

"Then we should take the—"

"You're not in charge this time," I tell him. Keeping him on his feet is taking all the strength I have. I reach down and grab one of the bottles at the guard's feet. "You're a drunk courtier who lost his clothes in the game rooms, all right?"

A painful half-laugh escapes his lips.

Or circles overhead. He tries to look up at her.

"I should've trusted her," I mutter. "I would've found you sooner."

Rémy and I ease past the snoring guard and amble into the hallway. I hold his weight on one side and pretend to fuss at him about drinking too much.

The hall is empty aside from a few servants who have just gotten the opportunity to celebrate tonight.

We turn left and right.

His legs grow weaker and his breathing more labored.

"We're almost there," I tell him.

The sound of footsteps ahead stops me.

I pull him into one of the salon rooms. He slumps against the wall. I watch as three male guards pass, chasing after three courtier women. Their kissy noises echo, then fade.

I stare at him. Rémy Chevalier, son of Christophe Chevalier, decorated—and now disgraced—soldier from the Minister of War's First Guard.

"Can you make it? We're just outside the doors," I whisper.

He grunts a yes back.

I grip his waist and drag him into Charlotte's apartments. I lay him across the bed and use the water in the basin to clean the burns on his chest—Sophia's emblems carved into him. The sight of them flares my anger. He winces each time I touch him.

"What did they do to you?" I ask.

"Everything."

I rest my hand on his cheek.

He takes it and kisses it. "Don't worry about me."

"You're covered in blood and burns and you're telling me not to worry." I put pressure on a cut on his shoulder.

"I've been trained to withstand it." He turns his head to avoid the wet cloth. "What's happened since I left you? Did you find Charlotte?"

I hold his head still and continue to wipe away his blood. "Yes. Remember those newspapers you got for us—the *Spider's Web*?"

He nods.

"We found the Iron Ladies. Well, they found us." I choose to leave out the part about the capture. "They have been helping to keep Charlotte safe. They're on their way here."

"How will they get inside?"

"The Observatory Deck," I say with pride. "Via post-balloon."

He struggles to smile. "Your idea?"

"Yes."

"But I need to go find the route to the Observatory Deck, so I can get there easily before the midmorning star and make sure the door from the deck to the interior is unlocked and unobstructed. They'll arrive and wait until everyone is at the Ascension Ball to attack."

He remains silent. I try to search his eyes for what he thinks about my plan. "What do you think?"

"It's smart—and unexpected."

His encouragement fills up the tiny holes of doubt inside me. He tries to sit up but leans back against the pillows again.

"Here. Stay still."

"How did you get here without her knowing?" he asks.

"Auguste sent me and the teacup dragons as a wedding gift."

He stiffens.

A silence crackles between us, the noise of the fire in the hearth heightening it.

"You've seen him?" Rémy's swollen mouth purses.

My stomach becomes a tangle of nerves.

"He's been working with the Iron Ladies. Supplying them with information and help."

"You forgave him?" he asks.

"I took his help. Now, rest."

"Go open that door," he says, then traces a shaky finger along the edge of my face. "I missed you."

"And I you." I nuzzle my face into his shoulder and try to hold back the storm of tears wanting to break loose from my chest.

I lie there until his breathing slows and he drifts off to sleep and I know that he's going to be all right. But before I head back out again to find the route to the Observatory Deck, the bedroom door eases open.

34

"Camille," a voice whispers from behind.

I leap up from the bed at the sound of my name. It's the servant from earlier. The one who took Zo's dead body.

"It's me."

And just like that, I finally recognize her voice.

"It's Bree."

I race to her and wrap my arms around her. "I knew it," I whisper into her hair. "I knew when you were trying to show me around the apartments. Your eyes. I felt it. But I had to keep my disguise."

"I couldn't tell you at first. I didn't want to alert anyone and didn't think I'd be able to keep it all together," she says. "But after what happened with Zo . . . I wanted to get rid of the body first and make sure it was safe."

I squeeze her tighter. "What happened to you?" I comb over her, touching her cheeks and arms. "Are you all right? I was so worried. They told me they put you in a starvation box."

"They did, but then when you disappeared from the palace, Elisabeth Du Barry came and got me out."

"She did?" I say, shock rattling me. Elisabeth Du Barry did something that didn't benefit herself?

Rémy coughs.

"Who is there?" she asks.

"Rémy."

Fear flashes in her eyes. "She will know."

I squeeze her hand.

"She has the guards lash him every few hours. If they find him gone, they will search the entire palace for him."

"That's why we have to work fast," I say. "Do you know where I can find Arabella? I need to see her, then get to the Observatory Deck."

Bree looks startled by the question. "Well... yes. She's right next door."

"What?" I gasp. I glance into a slit in the bed-curtains at Rémy. His mouth is slack with sleep, and the blood on his bandages is drying. His wounds no longer leak fresh blood.

"He will be fine here," Bree replies. "We'll close the bed-curtains. Any servants who come in will assume it's you. I'll make sure he remains hidden. Give strict orders to the other servants—as I'm a premier servant now—not to disturb you."

I nod, trusting her.

Knots of pressure and panic tighten throughout my body as I place the lace-skin mask Du Barry gave me back on my face. The anticipation of seeing Arabella again—of having help—is almost too great.

"Let's go. The apartments are connected."

We slip through a network of servant corridors. I hold my

breath until Bree stops walking. What if Arabella is ill like Valerie? What if she is unable to help?

"Ready to go in?" Bree waves me forward.

My stomach knots. "Where are we?"

"One of Sophia's tea salons."

"This is where she keeps her?"

Bree nods.

I imagine a sleeping Sophia passed out, smelling of champagne and macarons and flowers, and Arabella being forced to tend to her beauty work. Bree fumbles with her keys until she finds the right one. She jams it in and turns. The door opens. A chill drifts down my spine.

The room is tiny and dark with a single night-lantern whizzing about and a low fire in the hearth.

"Arabella?" I whisper.

Bree closes the door behind us. "We have to be quick. One of Her Majesty's favorite and most loyal servants oversees her."

I nod and tiptoe closer to the bed.

"Arabella?"

No answer.

I inch back the bed-curtains. Arabella lies there, propped up on the pillow. Her arms and neck are covered with sangsues, the little leeches pulsing black, then flushing red as they fill with her blood and share their proteins. The skin on her face is creased like parchment and so thin and pale that all the veins are visible beneath her skin. Her brown pigment has lost its depth and richness. My heart aches at the sight of her. It's even worse than I feared.

I reach out to touch her, my hand hesitating and pulling back like she's a stove too hot to touch.

"Arabella," I say a little louder.

She stirs and her eyes pop open. She presses back into the pillows.

"It's me, Camille."

She wipes her eyes. "I've been waiting for you. I tried to get to you earlier when I heard the announcement that Corinne Sauveterre, famous dragon merchant from the Gold Isles, had come to see the soon-to-be new queen. But they never let me leave these chambers, no matter what I do or say."

"What has she been doing to you?" I ask, as Bree brings over a tumbler of fresh water.

"Draining me of blood to send to the Everlasting Rose..." Arabella says.

The cruelty of the name still twists like a knife inside me. Arabella sips at the cup, and water dribbles out the corner of her mouth.

"To grow more Belles." She sighs and leans back into the bedding, waving the water away. Bree takes it, shooting me a nervous glance, and I squeeze her free hand.

"She did the same to Valerie until she had nothing left. And now she's dead."

Arabella shrugs, as if this news doesn't surprise or bother her. "She's been experimenting," she says. "She brought your other sisters back to the prison after the Silk Teahouse burned down. All except Amber."

"What do you mean? Where is she?" My heart rises in my chest threatening to bubble up.

"She's here," Arabella says.

I gasp. "At the palace? How? Why?"

"I don't know. But I heard her voice the other day. I thought, at first, that it was a recording or something for the newsreels

Sophia has been orchestrating, but it's been more frequent. I can't do Sophia's beauty work anymore—and she won't allow any of the other Belles from the unfavored generation to work on her—so I knew it would be just a matter of time."

My eyes dart around the room as if Amber were hiding beneath a beautiful piece of furniture.

"She has my focus on the few Belle babies here as she tries to find out how the favored generation is born. Her scientists have made so many mistakes. So many Belle babies have already died." She gathers her strength, sits up, and reaches for me. "Let me show you the favored Belle-pods."

I turn to Bree. "Watch the door, please."

She nods and takes up watch at the front of the room, clutching her hands nervously.

Arabella's entire body quakes as I help her slide open the door to the next chamber. The night-lantern follows us, illuminating hundreds of glass cradles etched with tiny golden roses. In each, a brown baby floats. Small hourglasses affixed to each pod are marked with animated ink that snaps across the glass with the labels *first cycle*, *second cycle*, and *third cycle*.

I run my fingers over the glass and peer in. Tiny feet and legs and hands and tight curls suspended in liquid and time.

I gasp. "They look like me."

"And me," Arabella adds. "Eventually, she wants to sell them to the highest bidder. Enable Belles to be kept like teacup pets and also use our blood to make beauty products."

"We can't let this happen," I say. Arabella takes my hand and squeezes it. The skin of her fingers is so thin, and her bones feel like sticks. "I can take care of these babies and ensure no more will be made."

I take my hand from hers and drop it into my pocket where the poison sits.

"What is that?" She takes it from me, fingering it, her watery eyes tracing its details.

"It takes away the arcana."

Her mouth falls open as her eyes find mine. "How?"

"It hardens the arcana proteins. But the amount has to be right, otherwise it could cause death." I watch her examine it as if its secrets lie on the edges of the bottle. "What if we both drank a bit of it, so that neither of our blood could be used to make more Belles?"

The heat of the question radiates between us. Arabella uncorks the bottle to sniff it. My heart skips.

"Be careful," I say, remembering the rapid destruction of the blood cells in Claiborne's optic-scope. "I believe I could also make sure that the aether of the next generation couldn't be used either."

She puts a drop of the poison on her finger and tries to inspect it.

"Arabella..."

She takes a gulp.

"No!" I grab the empty bottle from her.

Arabella's eyes bulge. She coughs—a gurgling, ragged sound. Her skin wrinkles in a blink, line by line covering her forehead to her cheeks to her throat, the brown shriveling like dried-out clay.

"Arabella!" I scream.

Her body hits the floor.

35

I can't hear the screams being ripped from my mouth. My ears clog and spots stamp out my vision. But the piercing rawness of my throat is real.

Bree claps her hand over my mouth and her other arm around my waist. "We have to go. Someone has probably already heard you." She tugs me away from Arabella. "Sophia will discover you're here."

"But I can't leave her." The sight of her body—another dead Belle body—sends another scream reverberating inside me. She is me. I am her. The aether. And now she's dead and the poison—my only chance to save us all—gone. The empty poison bottle falls from my hand. The glass shatters, each jagged shard a realization of how careless and reckless this whole thing has become.

"You have to. Someone is going to come check on her soon if they haven't been alerted by your screams already. You can't be here when they do." She pries me away, almost having to carry me, my limbs heavy with regret and anger and sadness and frustration and most of all, exhaustion.

Hope sputters out of me like the air of a dying post-balloon. First, it was Valerie, and now, Arabella.

How can I ever fix this?

How can I ever make things right?

She hustles me into the apartments. Rémy's gentle snores alternate with the hiss of the fireplace.

"Sleep," Bree whispers.

"How can I possibly sleep now?" My breath catches in my throat and my heart races. I put my hands on my head, trying to make everything slow down. I'm caught in a whirlpool. Even too tired to cry. "How could she do that? What was she thinking? I needed her help."

Bree tries to console me with tea.

I shove the pot away but burn my hand. The pain sears and I ball my fist and bite back another scream.

"You need to sit, Camille. So you can focus." She forces me into the chair beside the fireplace. "Let me look at your hand."

"It will—"

"Let me see it," she urges.

I flash her my palm.

"It will need a little ointment."

"It's fine," I say, even as it throbs.

"You will have to dance tomorrow at Sophia's ball." She goes to a recently delivered service tray and begins mixing honey with ice. "The invitation balloon is on the door hook."

I look over and spot it bobbing—its golden edges glittering in the subtle darkness. The sight of the pretty bauble, after what I've just witnessed, is absurd.

"I need to get to the Observatory Deck. I should've already gone. They will be arriving in the morning."

Bree kneels before me and gently coats my palm with her poultice. "You will. You will," she replies, her voice softening to barely a whisper. "I'll be sure to wake you, and help you get there. I promise."

Her vow is a temporary comfort. "Is it true that Amber is here at the palace? Can you get a message to her that I'm here?"

Bree's face twists. She tears a bit of fabric from a bedsheet and wraps it around my hand. "You rest first."

"What's wrong?" I ask. "Have you seen my sister?"

"Nothing is wrong." Bree stands and backs up.

"Please just tell me. Is she all right? I can't bear to lose another person I love." My heart lodges in my throat. "I need to see her."

"I'll find out where she's being held and get her a message," Bree assures me. "But only if you go to bed."

There's no way I can possibly sleep. I open my mouth to argue. Her eyebrows lift.

I stand. My skin buzzes, but the pain in my hand is already beginning to calm. I climb into the bed beside Rémy and lay my head on the pillow next to him without hesitation. The perfume of his skin has seeped into the fabric.

Bree ties a night-lantern to the bedpost hook and draws the curtains around us. "See you in the morning. I'll be in the servants' quarters just near the apartment's tea salon. I'll keep watch."

I nod at her, then turn my attention to Rémy. I study him in the soft dark. I run my fingers over his bandages and check them for blood. His cuts are crusting over.

He grunts and lifts his hand to touch mine. "Stop fussing over me. I'll be all right."

"Those wounds were deep."

"I know. I feel the bruises down to my bones," he says with a grimace as he tries to turn to his side.

"Don't move."

"You're very pushy."

"Yes, and you must listen to me."

He smiles weakly, then takes my hand, letting the pad of his thumb trace my palm. "I'm already feeling stronger. I promise." He stares at me. "What's wrong?"

"Nothing." I want to tell him everything, but it's too much, and I don't want to burden him. Not while he's still weak.

"I thought we established that you can't hide the things on your face." His brown eyes are full of concern.

"Please sleep. I'll tell you when you wake."

His eyelids flutter, heavy with sickness and pain. He outstretches his arm, offering me his shoulder to lie on. I nestle against him and find a spot on the bed canopy to stare at, knowing I won't sleep much tonight.

36

Bells chime through the belly of the palace, snatching us awake. My head pounds after getting only tiny bits of troubled sleep. A voice-box on the side table announces, "Palace on heighted alert! All apartments, chambers, rooms, and persons will be searched before the ceremonies commence. Security measures in place!"

The teacup dragons bolt from the bed canopy, spraying agitated fire. I call their names and try to get them to calm down. Rémy moans as he tries to sit up. The bedroom door bursts open.

Bree dashes in out of breath. "She knows Rémy's missing, and they found Arabella's body." She almost collapses forward. "She's on a rampage looking for her teacup elephant Zo, too."

An anchor drops in my stomach. I glance back at Rémy on the bed. I put a hand on Bree's back. "Are there more guards inside the palace?" I ask. "Do you think they suspect me?"

"No more guards than usual," she says. "But they're watching and checking everyone. They will be going through every single apartment, including this one."

"I have to hide him," I tell her. "I have to get to the Observatory Deck before the midmorning star. How much time do I have?"

She pulls an hourglass from her pocket. "One hour," Bree says, "and the ball starts right after it, so you must get ready. She will be expecting you, and if you don't arrive on time, she'll suspect something. Your dress is here, too."

As if on cue, a gold-and-cream post-balloon ambles through the door. Its sides glow with Sophia's soon-to-be official emblem. At midnight tonight, she will be queen according to Orléansian law. The court will celebrate all day in anticipation.

If we don't stop her.

The post-balloon's tail ribbons haul a polka-dotted dress box with a note. The teacup dragons attack the balloon until it crashes to the ground.

I fetch the note.

Corinne,

Ten a.m. sharp.

Imperial Ballroom. We shall celebrate the start of my Coronation and Ascension ceremony and say a final farewell to my beloved sister. Hoping you bring your teacup dragons. They deserve to join us.

—Sophia Regina

I crumple the paper, balling it in my fist. "You have to hide him?" I say to her.

"I know where they won't look," Rémy calls out from the bed.

"And so do I," Bree replies.

I rush to Rémy's side and help him out of bed. He's groggy and slow-moving. "Where will you take him?"

"Somewhere safe, I promise," she says.

"I know how to hide," he grumbles.

"When you're not recovering. Please listen to Bree. You both know this palace well. And you're both so important to me." I take his hand.

He yanks me close, the strength of his motion a shock. Our foreheads touch. "Be safe. The Observatory Deck is on the top floor of the northern wing. Take one of the chariot lifts."

I kiss his cheek. "I will."

I turn to Bree. "I'll get ready for the party when I'm back."

She nods.

I pull on one of the simple day dresses in the apartment's dress salon, part of me wondering if these once belonged to Charlotte or if Sophia had all traces of her sister erased.

How can she so easily erase a sister?

The pain of losing Valerie—and now Arabella—is seared into my skin like an identification mark never to be removed. I squeeze any tears down inside me. They're quickly replaced with anger and determination.

Rémy and Bree are gone from the bedroom when I return. I snatch the voice-box from the side table and take it with me, then put the lace-skin over my face.

The hallways swell with bodies—servants toting gift boxes or pushing carts, attendants ushering excited courtiers in the direction of the festivities, royal sweet-vendors advertising their goods. And guards. Guards seem to be everywhere.

I join the chaos and grab one of the chariot lifts taking people across to the different palace wings.

"Where to?" a porter asks.

"Observatory Deck."

"That's for palace officials only," he replies.

"I am a guest of our future queen and I want to make sure her gift is delivered and placed with the others." I hold it up and lift my chin as if I'm the most important person in the world. "And I would *hate* to have to complain to her tonight of all nights." The confident threat beneath my words is enough to get him to close the door and shift the handle.

We sail over the belly of the palace. I keep my eyes down to avoid inviting more suspicion from the man. Below, I spot courtiers stealing kisses in dark corners and newsies rushing over gilded balconies and walkways with their navy story-balloons in tow and crowds of bodies making their way to the Imperial Ballroom. Mourning balloons putter about, complete with Charlotte's picture. They buzz along the corridors and walkways, leaving a sad trail of tear-shaped glitter and tiny wailing cries. Sophia's really added all the right touches to convince people of her lies. In a newsreel playing on the sides of the balloons, she describes how my experimentations led to her death.

One follows the chariot and the noise of it stokes my anger. Sophia must go. Our mission must succeed. Finally, the chariot stops at a platform near the very top of the palace.

"The Observatory Deck," the man announces, opening the door. "Ring the bell when you're ready to leave and I'll come back to get you."

I nod and thank him, then step off.

The deck is a glass bridge that smiles over the western wing of the palace. The walls are made of multicolored shards like a gigantic prism from the God of Luck. It catches the morning sunlight, shattering rays of indigo and ruby and turquoise and canary across a maze of gift boxes. Beyond the glass, post-balloons land on a balcony, one after another.

I scan the space.

Three guards. One on the deck itself. One beside the platform. One in the far corner.

Sweat beads in my temples. I didn't account for there being guards to watch over the gifts. But of course there would be. To watch for thieves.

I gulp down the sudden swell of nerves rising inside me. Another complication.

A woman with a parchment board and quill hunches amidst the sea of boxes. She glances up. "May I help you?"

"I have a gift for the queen. By the looks of things, it seems like she probably doesn't need another."

"Her Majesty loves presents above all else."

She loves beauty more.

"Guests are not allowed up here. There's a gift table in the Imperial Ballroom," the woman says.

I wait for the guards to turn in our direction, but they don't. Instead, they stand fixed in place. I walk in a zigzag, stepping over gift boxes both large and small, some covered in winter-season flowers and others exploding with velvet bows and silk ribbons.

"I am an important guest of Her Majesty. And I wanted to speak to you because I need my gift to impress. You must have the best sense of what she's gotten so far." I lift my royal emblem. I feel terrible about the fact that I'm going to need to hurt her, but I walk closer. A riot rises within me. My heartbeat overwhelms my entire body. My stomach twists with guilt and regret. A sticky sweat seeps out of my skin. "Can I show you the gift, and you'll let me know if it is good enough?" I ask.

Her blue eyes light up, and a primrose pink sets into the white of her cheeks. "Yes, it would be my pleasure. But quickly, I will get in trouble if you're found up here. I don't know how you got the porter to bring you up. It's forbidden."

"Our new queen said I could. He was following orders," I lie, and turn my back to her, set the box down, and remove the lid. She inches closer and leans forward. I wrap my finger around the voice-box, its brass edges warming beneath my fingertips. My hands itch with anticipation.

When I see the blond of her hair, I clobber her with it. She stumbles, croaks, touches her head, then collapses.

I hold my breath and wait a moment, hoping the nerves settle and that she isn't dead—just asleep for a little while. Enough time for the Iron Ladies to arrive.

One of the guards turns in my direction. "What's going on over there?"

His voice startles the others into action.

"She fainted," I lie.

"Show us your identification ink," one demands.

"You should call for a nurse from the Palace Infirmary."

They run in my direction.

I gaze down and grab a box covered in holly. Anger collects in my fingertips, the fire inside me loose and uncontrollable.

I grasp for the arcana, my three gifts just beneath my skin, at the ready. I stretch the waxy leaves until their edges are as sharp as Rémy's dagger at my hip.

These men will not get in my way.

Not now.

Not when I'm this close.

Two of the guards stumble backward with alarm. One clobbers his head and loses consciousness.

"Who are you?" the other one yells.

I catch the third as he tries to grab me, forcing the holly plant to coil around his torso. I press one of the thickened leaves at his throat, pushing the pointed edges into his skin. I tell the other guard, "Leave or I will kill him."

I let the holly plant dig a little harder into the man's flesh, and draw a teardrop of blood. The other guard's face pales and he puts his hands up. "I'm just here to watch the gifts. I don't even want to be a soldier," he stammers out, then scurries off like a coward.

I turn the holly leaves into a coffin, covering the guard's entire body until he resembles one of the hedges from the topiary maze on the palace grounds. No one will find him for a while or hear his shouts. I grab the woman's wrist and hunt for a pulse. It's faint. I exhale. She'll hopefully be out for a little bit.

I drop to my knees. The weight of what I've done couples with exhaustion from last night.

The sound of post-balloons bumping and thudding the glass is the only melody around me as they beg to be let in, their tail ribbons taut with the weight of their parcels.

I go to the Observatory Deck doors and slide one open a crack. Not enough for a passerby to notice. Not enough to cause alarm. A tendril of cold air cools the clamminess of my skin.

I look out at the horizon at a snow-white sky full of battalions of beautiful gift boxes and post-balloons. Many of the crates are so huge they require ten post-balloons to carry their weight. Ribbons in gossamer and amethyst and emerald and plum ruffle in the wind.

I hope they're full of Iron Ladies.

37

I walk with Bree to the Imperial Ballroom in the heavy gown sent by Sophia. The whole palace—its domes, gardens, turrets, spires, and pavilions—is aglow. Snow-lanterns bathe every possible corner with light. Gentle snowflakes dust the shoulders of men and women who dance under the snow-lanterns. People try to point out shapes before they shift into a myriad of new patterns. The cavernous room is thick with men in tuxedos and women in jewel-toned dresses.

With each footstep I take, I wonder what Sophia is going to do. Who is she going to present as Charlotte? Did she capture her sister? Did she kill someone? I push away any doubt. I have to believe our plan is moving forward.

"Did you find Amber?" I whisper to Bree before she leaves.

"No. Sophia must be hiding her. I'll keep looking."

I take a deep breath, touch the emblem around my neck, and hold the glamour in my mind. There's been no word from Padma or Auguste or any of the Iron Ladies in the last hour. But if Sophia can convince everyone that Charlotte is dead, she will be queen by the end of the day. I can't let that happen. Even if I have to stop her myself.

"Happy snow. Happy love." The cold-season blessing flutters through the room followed by kisses and the clinking of glasses. "May the Goddess of Love bless you. May you find sweetness in the new year. And most of all, may you always find beauty."

The ballroom is a jigsaw of bodies: men in top hats and women in gowns that swish and swirl as they spin in diagonals, dancing to a waltz being played by a small orchestra. Tiers of crème tarts and milk macarons sit on jeweled carts.

Courtiers pass by, locked in the fever of gossip.

"Did you see Colette Durand with her too-dark eyebrows? Looking just like the court jester. She thinks tinting them will work. That trend is long gone. Now, she just reeks of the elderberry juice she used to color them herself," one says.

"And Aimee Martin smells of skin paint," another adds. "She could've at least gone to the trouble of wearing a pomander or carrying a scent box. She's even gone and drawn veins onto her neck and face like she's a walking portrait or something."

The women burst with laughter.

"Inès Robert needs a skin treatment. She thinks taffeta patches will cover up those pocks," a third woman offers. "Thank god the teahouses will reopen soon. Our new queen will deliver on her promises."

"If I had Josette Agulliard's unfortunate bone structure, I'd have a Belle completely rebuild me from the bones out," the first says.

Black gossip post-balloons swarm overhead, listening to every word. Imperial attendants use tall poles and nets to swat them away, but they adeptly dodge and soar higher up to the grand ceiling, seeming to revel in a game of cat and mouse.

My nerves are on edge as I wait for Lady Arane, Surielle, Charlotte, and Auguste. I try not to fixate on the door for fear someone might ask me who I'm waiting for.

Sophia sits on a throne at the top of the room. Her teacup pets each have their own matching chair. Her ladies-of-honor sit at her feet on bright cushions.

An attendant announces me as I approach.

"And where are my teacup dragons?" Sophia whines to me.

"Resting. They don't like parties. Too many people cause anxiety," I improvise.

"A pity. We will have to train them out of it, now won't we?" She stares at me with a perfectly portioned smile on her face. "I don't think I'll be able to choose just one."

I bite down hard to avoid saying something nasty. When I look at her all I see are Remy's bruises, Arabella's dying breaths, a dagger in Valerie's neck. I don't know how long I can keep up this charade. Or this glamour.

Her attention flitters away from me and to the crowd. "I've always loved a ball at this time of year," Sophia says. "The cold weather is perfect for dancing."

"It's incredible tonight," Rachelle replies, gazing up at the snow-lanterns above her.

"Do you like it, Corinne?" Sophia pats a cushion beside her throne for me to sit on.

"Yes," I answer, sinking down beside her, hoping I can swallow my rage. "I can't wait to wander around and look at each snow-lantern. The newsies say each one is unique."

My body is alert with anticipation, hoping the Iron Ladies have come down into the palace. Any second now and the game will begin.

"It's a pity it'll turn into a funeral tonight," Rachelle says.

Sophia tries to hide a chuckle. "With the sweet comes the bitter."

I steal glances at her, wondering if she did capture Charlotte. I search for a sign, anything to know if Charlotte is all right, if she will show today as planned.

"We will dance and feast all day long, then you will say good-bye to your sister, and at midnight become queen," Gabrielle says proudly. "As it should be."

I pretend to watch the dancing as I keep my eye on the doors. Graceful dress trains swish and slap the floor. Men hold women's waists and turn them like pastel spinning toys.

The music shifts.

Sophia's old suitor, Alexander Dubois from House Berry, strides up. His jacket is lined with the brilliant silvers and reds of his house emblem, and under all the lights, his bald head shines like a copper ball. "Happy snow, Your Majesty."

"And to you," she says.

"May I have the next dance?" He presents his hand.

She glares at it.

"No," she says.

His face crumples with disappointment.

"I'll send for you when I'm in the mood."

He bows low and retreats.

"His hands used to get so wet they'd soak through my gloves," she complains. "And he always smells of cheese."

Her ladies giggle.

"And why is he bald at such a young age?" one asks.

Sophia shrugs. "I'll have my favorite Belle give him a tiny crop of hair."

Her words send a flicker up my spine.

"You are about to be married, anyway. He shouldn't ask you to dance anymore. You didn't choose him. Where is Auguste?" Rachelle asks. "Shouldn't he be here by now?"

I was just wondering the same thing.

Sophia stiffens. "My betrothed is on his way. I received his post-balloon not too long ago," she snaps. "And how dare you question it?"

Gabrielle glares at Rachelle. Anger stews inside me like a storm and triggers a headache to pulse in the back of my head. Pressure builds in my nose, signaling the start of another nosebleed. If I'm going to last all day, I need to take a break from holding the glamour.

I stand.

"Excuse me, Your Majesty. I am slipping off to the powder room," I lie with a quick bow. "Be back momentarily."

I don't wait for a response from Sophia or the others. My pulse flies as I weave in and out of the crowd. Before leaving the room, I stuff myself with tiny apple blossoms and fruit tarts and chocolate ganache from golden trays, hoping they will help reset my levels as I desperately hold on to this glamour.

Women steal glances at me. Snippets of gossip escape their carefully cupped hands. I rush past the windows, heading for the door.

A vendor hands me a cup with a hot sugared square of dough. "For you, my sweet."

I take it from him and force a smile. At that moment, the doors to the veranda are thrown open to let out a bit of the heat, and there it is—the Everlasting Rose. The building is massive. Its exterior glows, a sea pearl on a dark watery cushion. I crush the square in my hand like the head of a flower. The crumbs litter the floor beside me. The faces of my sisters and the other Belles flutter through my mind like the shuffling of a deck of cards.

Ivy

Edel

Hana

Amber

Delphine

Ada

Where are Charlotte and Padma and Auguste and the Iron Ladies? They should have been here by now. I duck through the crowds. I need to go back to the Observatory Deck. Maybe the woman woke up. Maybe she alerted other guards. Maybe they've all been taken.

A trumpet blares.

The room freezes.

"Ladies and gentlemen, please turn your attention to Her Majesty, Sophia, the next queen of Orléans," an attendant says.

Sophia stands. Everyone bows. I drop my head reluctantly.

"My loyal court, as we begin my Coronation and Ascension ceremony, I'd like to introduce you to several *loyal* people who made this whole thing possible. First, the newly titled Minister of Belles, Georgiana Fabry, and my *favorite* Belle, who will help me usher in this new age of beauty," she replies.

A chill wraps its arms around me.

The side doors burst open. Palace morning-lanterns rush in, scattering jewel-shaped shadows over the floor. Auguste's glamorous mother, Georgiana Fabry, strides into the room. Tall and stately, she towers over most in the crowd. Her yellow dress shimmers around her like sunlight woven into silk, and behind her, a rolling platform holds a life-size bell jar. Inside the jar is Amber.

38

The beat of my heart mirrors the rapid movement of the platform wheels. Amber's hands press against the walls of the glass; she's a trapped butterfly. Chains loop around her wrists like strands of golden pearls and her corseted dress holds her in place. Her pale and freckled arms wear jagged gashes.

I jerk forward, almost forgetting my disguise. The cold pain of the glamour pools with my rage. I duck and move through the crowd of bodies, trying to get closer to my sister.

Sophia springs up from her throne, her eyes wild as she gazes at Amber. "My favorite!" she taunts Amber, walking around the glass cage. "I have lots of new plans for the Belles, as evidenced." She motions to the veranda and the view of the Everlasting Rose. "Now, my petite Amber, if I take you out of this jar, you must promise to behave." Sophia traces her pointed nails along the glass, tapping it to make Amber flinch. "They're slowly learning their place."

The crowd chuckles.

Amber nods. "I promise." Her eyes spill over with tears, and are ringed with bruises.

A single guard removes the glass. Another hands Sophia a silver whip. She snaps it at the courtiers and several of them yelp. Sophia laughs, a deep belly laugh.

Angry tremors work their way through every part of my body as acid rises up my throat.

"Minister of Belles, tell this esteemed group of my most loyal courtiers some of the things they have to look forward to once my Coronation and Ascension are complete."

An attendant hands Georgiana a voice-box. "Good day to you all. I am so happy to join you on this auspicious occasion as we usher in this new age. Soon, I will set in place the Belle Codes, a new body of laws governing beauty work and—"

"Tell them about the facials," Sophia interjects with a squeal.

Georgiana purses her lips. "Yes, Your Majesty. We will offer Belle-blood facials as one of our newest treatments. We're unlocking the science of their blood. If you inject Belle blood into the top layer of your skin, you can defeat the gray."

The crowd oohs and ahhs.

My stomach dips and knots itself into a tangle. I must do something. I must help Amber. But what can I do? There are dozens of courtiers gathered about, and I can feel myself weakening after holding the glamour for so long.

Another door flies open. My heart jumps with hope that it's Padma and Auguste, Charlotte and Lady Pelletier, Lady Arane and her army of Iron Ladies.

Instead, more courtiers flood inside.

"Shall we demonstrate?" Sophia asks. "Wouldn't you all like to see how Belle blood transforms the skin?"

The crowd shouts with excitement.

Sophia pivots back to Amber. "We're going to show them our new trick."

Amber almost shrinks into herself. She pulls her arms in tight and drops her gaze.

Rage hums in my bones, urging me to help her. I step a little closer. Only a few paces more. Sophia motions for a nearby attendant, who steps up on the platform with my sister. Amber jerks away.

"I thought we were going to be agreeable today." Sophia twists the whip, then slaps it on the ground.

The sound reverberates through the room, the noise cutting deep inside me. My eyes burn with tears, my throat tight with disgust.

"I don't want to have to use this," Sophia says, but her anticipatory grin tells another story.

"Don't touch her," I shout.

The courtiers nearest me gasp and turn to stare.

"Who said that?" Sophia spins around.

I step out of the crowd.

We glare at each other. A knot coils tighter and tighter, the unspoken words between us twisting inside me like a set of knives.

"Corrine?" Her eyes flicker over me.

"Let her go," I demand.

A dead, haunting silence stretches through the room.

Amber stares at me.

The cold pain of maintaining the glamour sends blood pouring from my nose. I release it. I'm tired of holding on to it, tired of hiding. I want Sophia to know it's me. The disguise disappears.

Gasps explode in the room. The whole world seems to still.

"Camille?" Amber cries, that one word suffused with so much relief and anguish, hope and fear, it almost kills me.

A grin slowly curves along Sophia's mouth. "Dragon merchant." She begins to clap slow at first, then descends into a fervor. "Well done. You tricked me. I didn't know you could change yourselves."

"There's a lot about our gifts that you don't understand—will *never* understand and will *never* know!" I snap. "No matter how many of us you lock up or poke or prod."

I watch for the guards. They inch closer.

"Give me my sister."

"She is not my prisoner," Sophia replies, her eyes inspecting every inch of me.

"She is chained."

"Only because she tried to break our deal."

"What deal?" I spit.

Sophia jumps with glee. "Oh yes, oh yes. We have a deal, and deals are binding." Her gaze cuts back at Amber, who begins to sob. "Should I tell her? Or do you want to?"

She waits for an answer. Amber's cries deepen and her whole body shakes. I want to go to her. I want to tell her that everything is going to be all right, that I will get us both out of here even if no one shows up to help. She swallows over and over again like she has something stuck in her throat. Beads of sweat race down her face.

"This pretty little mouse sent me all sorts of messages about you," Sophia reports. "As soon as she told me what I needed, I staged her capture."

My pulse throbs, counting down the moments. Hate simmers inside me, sharp, hot, and pricking.

My fists ball. I clench my jaw.

I glare at Amber. She won't look at me. Edel's suspicions of her lock into place. The betrayal is thick and painful. I don't know why she would feed information to Sophia. Not even the hint of a reason can form in my head. It has to be something. Blackmail. Coercion.

Sophia motions to the guards. They unlock Amber's chains.

"After I caught this pretty little mouse, she promised to be my personal Belle until my new generation had reached maturation. She even said she'd give them lessons. Teach them everything those wretched Du Barrys taught you." Sophia's eyes gleam in the snow-lantern light. "Oh, and there's more." She pirouettes, her ballgown billowing around her slender frame. "She knew you'd come for her. She agreed to lure you here." She blows me a kiss. "Some sister that is."

"Amber, we're leaving. Let's go," I shout, not believing a word coming out of Sophia's lying mouth.

Amber gazes down at the platform.

"Amber?"

Sophia watches like a cat ready to pounce on its prey. "Amber, please bring me one of your flowers."

Amber sobs and hands one to her.

"Amber?" I say.

"Amber, bow to me."

Amber drops to her knees.

"Why would you do this?" I say, imploring her to look at me. The words taste sour as they leave my throat.

"Will you be going anywhere?" Sophia asks Amber, cupping her chin. Tears rush down my sister's reddened face. "So much for sisterly love." Sophia blows another kiss at me.

"I've seen *your* sister," I hiss at Sophia.

The crowd bursts again into a frenzy of whispers.

She frowns. "My sister is dead."

"She is not. She's alive and well, actually."

Sophia shrugs. "The gods will welcome her home soon, and I will be crowned queen."

"Whatever poor soul you'll be presenting to these people, her identification mark will prove she is no princess."

Sophia paces around me, then leans in to whisper, "To whom? No one in *my* cabinet. No one in *my* guard. I am adored. Any challenger, any usurper will be put down." She waves a hand in the air and turns back to the watching crowd.

The arcana is a small throbbing hum inside me, a reluctant ribbon buried deep, one I wasn't sure I wanted any longer, but I summon it to wake up again. The memory of what I did to the guards and the woman watching the gifts rushes back. I close my eyes and picture Sophia just as she is standing before me. My skin ignites, my limbs stretch, my curls straighten, and my dress changes to match hers.

"What are you doing?" Sophia yells. "Guards! Guards!"

We're identical now. I take a breath and attack, leaping on her with every ounce of my rage coursing through me. We toss and turn, thrashing across the floor. I slap her and shake her, and she bites and kicks.

The onlookers scatter to the edges of the room, cowering and screaming and trying to get away from us.

She shoves me away.

We scramble to our feet.

"Arrest her," Sophia orders, pointing at me.

"Arrest her," I parrot back, pointing at her. My first arcana—Manner—helps me perfect her pitchy voice.

The guards stand stunned.

"Did you hear me?" Sophia says, her voice now a shrill. "She's the fugitive Belle. A traitor."

They move in my direction.

I repeat her words.

They freeze.

Sophia's jaw tenses. "Fine! You want to play this game?"

I mimic her.

We circle each other, ready to fight again. I focus on holding the glamour and don't dare look away from my enemy. Her fingers twitch, and so do mine. I lick my lips, salivating to lash out, to end this once and for all.

I realize a second too late that our circling has brought Sophia within inches of her whip. Before I can move, she scoops it up and, with a flick of her wrist, it curls around Amber's neck, cuts a deep gash, and snaps it.

Amber doesn't even scream. Her eyes flutter, lashes batting like butterfly wings, and she tumbles forward.

"No!" I scream, falling to my knees.

The crowd erupts in horror.

39

"I win. I win. I win," Sophia says, parading around the now silent room.

I rush to Amber, cradling her head in my lap. Her vacant eyes stare up at me. My heart is still. Frozen in my chest. Maybe never to beat again. The glamour slides right off me, and with it more blood pours out of my nose and down onto Amber's forehead. I can't loosen my arms around her to wipe it.

"Now, take her, but don't be too rough. She's the one I really need," Sophia says.

The guards snatch me away from Amber. Her body slides off me and hits the floor again with a thud. A river of blood leaks from inside her. They loop chains around my wrists and lift me to my feet.

I can't fight them. My hands and arms are numb.

Sophia does a lap around me. "Now, I'm going to take all those teacup dragons of yours and add them to my collection. I'm going to keep you in my prison, for you will be *my* true everlasting rose, and I'm going to kill that traitorous guard you love so much. What's his name? Reim ... no ... Raine ... no ... Oh, Rémy. That's right."

The sound of his name hits me.

"You will learn to be loyal." I jerk forward, but the guards pin me in place. The edges of the room lose focus. "One way or another."

She laughs and I shiver. A cold settles into my veins like I'm about to create another glamour. But instead, Sophia and each guard appear in my head. The erratic beat of their hearts floods my ears. Their pulses are racing melodies. My anger mingles with the arcana twisting their portraits into unrecognizable shapes.

They all drop to their knees. Sophia screams. Her skin crinkles like parchment. Her eyes drift to the sides of her face like fish's. Her mouth is an O shape of anguish. I can't hear what she tries to say. I can't stop.

I focus on the hearts of everyone in the room. I slow them down, beat by beat, until there's only a faint murmur. The guards turn pale, and Sophia grabs at her chest. Her eyes begin to roll back. Everyone drops. Hundreds of people. Their screams are a chorus, echoing off the ceiling.

Blood rushes down my lips and chin and neck, the salt of it seeping into my mouth. My nerves are raw with power; all three arcana gifts sear through me.

I could kill them all. Not one of them helped Amber. Not one of them tried to stop Sophia.

The room almost dissolves around me. A carousel of light and shapes spinning as the heartbeats slow to a stop.

The door opens. "Stop!" a voice hollers.

It's Charlotte. She hobbles forward with a cane to support her. Her curly brown hair towers over her, thick with magnolia flowers, and her eyes hold strength. "You don't want to do this!"

The Iron Ladies stand proudly in their masks. Padma and Auguste edge into the room and stare at the horror I've unleashed.

"You aren't this person," Charlotte says.

"I am," I reply. "It needs to be over."

Sophia's body jerks forward and rolls around the floor. Her breath is ragged, and she starts to hiccup.

"Valerie is dead because of her. Arabella. Amber. She's hurt so many," I say. "She will keep doing it. She will never stop."

"And she hurt me," Charlotte says. "But I want her alive."

"Why? She poisoned you. Kept you asleep for six years."

"She's my sister." She looks down at Sophia with tears in her eyes. "Just like you forgive your sisters for their mistakes, I will forgive mine. Let me deal with her." She steps closer to me. Her hands reach out to touch my shoulder. "You don't want her death on your heart, and the rest of these people are innocent—complacent, maybe, but not evil. I need you to help me fix the problems she's created."

Padma cautiously approaches me and puts a hand in mine. "Just let go, Camille. Just breathe."

The rage inside me fights to get out. I close my eyes. I don't know if I can stop it. The portraits of the guards and Sophia are a swirling tornado. The blood is a river gushing from my nose still.

"You can," she whispers.

I release everyone in the room. All around me people gasp for air. I collapse forward. Sweat streams down my face and arms and legs. More blood pours from my nose and over my lips. All the light in the room disappears.

40

I'm swept into tumultuous dreams of our very last beauty session before the Beauté Carnaval. Back when we were still little girls. Back when we didn't know anything outside of the walls of the space we were born into. Back when we thought we were divine instruments to be treasured instead of used. Du Barry had us listen to visiting courtier women and their complaints about their bodies. We noted how they asked us to reset their insides, shifting the bone and marrow into new shapes more beautiful than their natural template.

My sisters and I hovered around a long treatment table like a ceremonial fan, gawking down at one woman's limbs. She'd traveled over six golden imperial bridges and on one canopied river-coach through the Rose Bayou to get to us from the Silk Isles. Tiny clusters of beauty-lanterns drifted over her like midnight stars. Perfect balls of light revealed how the gray of her skin made her look like a piece of fish that sat out all night.

We'd been so eager to use our beauty caisses for the first time and the items on the carts that the servants had wheeled in: tiered trays bursting with skin-color pastilles and rouge pots, brushes and combs and barrel irons, tonics and crèmes, bei-powder bundles, waxes and perfumes.

The woman's soft moans stretched out like an anxious bubble between us. Tensions were high during our final session before we traveled to the imperial island, before we displayed our talents for the queen, before we found out who would be named the favorite, before we were told which one of us was most important.

There was a woman waiting on the table. There would be people at court waiting to be changed, and anticipating perfect results. There would be expectations.

My sisters and I exchanged nervous glances. Edel had turned as pale as the white lesson dresses we all used to wear. Padi's black Belle-bun always caught the beauty-lantern light as she nosed around with careful and cautious curiosity. Hana had gotten in trouble for giggling when we'd catch a glimpse of certain body parts, and her long black braid hung down her back like a rope, swishing left and right as she trembled with laughter. Amber's cheeks had been permanently red from intense focus. Valerie always rubbed her hands together with a smile, antsy to make sure she did whatever she could to make someone's dreams come true.

We'd been all together. We'd worked together. We'd go through this experience together.

I'd felt like I had swallowed bayou butterflies that day.

The sound of humming pulls me awake, slow at first and then all at once. My eyes startle open, sore and watery as the light hits them through gauzy bed-curtains. The memories of where I am and what happened slide into my mind and a wave of nausea hits me. Sophia. Charlotte. The Iron Ladies. The Coronation and Ascension Ball.

I try to move, but my arms are threaded with needles and tubes, and my limbs hold the deepest soreness I've ever experienced.

I attempt to speak, but words come out in croaks.

"You sound terrible," a voice says. "You should just *not* speak."

I turn my head to the right and see Edel's grinning face. Tears spill out the sides of my eyes.

"Ugh, don't cry." She inches closer, then clutches onto my arm like it's the edge of a cliff and she needs to keep us both from tumbling off it. "I'm all right, and you're all right."

The bed-curtains open. "Did you wake her? You weren't supposed to," Padma says, carrying a morning-lantern. The beams illuminate the rich brownness of her skin like honey drizzled on a square of chocolate.

She climbs in on my left.

"Where's Hana?" I ask.

"I'm here. I'm here." She peeks her head through the bed-curtains. She looks different, so skinny she might be whisked away if a snowy wind became too strong. A soft day gown drapes her now wiry frame in the color of ginger and squash, and her black Belle-bun holds glass ornaments.

"Are you all right?" I reach for her.

She finds a space on the bed. "I will be. I arrived last night from the Fire Isles."

When we were little girls living at Maison Rouge with our mamans, we'd pile into bed together just so we'd be able to wake up near one another. We all had our positions: Edel would have to be on the edge so she could get out if she needed to, Hana loved being in the center, Padma along the foot, Amber in the middle where she could control everyone's movements, and Valerie closest to Edel, her favorite sleep partner out of all of us. I was happy wherever, as long as I was with my sisters.

The memory stings—the bed once snug with a tangle of legs and arms and warmth, and now, so few.

I start to ask them if they're all right and if we're going to be all right, but we each make eye contact and lie there in silence. I hold their hands and trace my fingers over their skin and gaze at them, ensuring that my few remaining sisters are intact. I am filled with regrets and unrequited wishes.

The doors open and Lady Pelletier pushes Charlotte in a wheeling chair followed by Lady Arane, Surielle, and Violetta.

Hana, Padma, and Edel sit up.

I struggle to rise.

"Please don't move, Camille," Charlotte says. "Rest."

Lady Pelletier pushes her close to the bed, then leans down and kisses my forehead. I swallow down tears. The softness of her lips reminds me of Maman.

"You look better," Charlotte remarks.

"Her levels are almost back to normal," Hana reports. "A few more days of rest, and she should be back to her old self."

I don't even know who that is anymore.

"You saved us," Lady Arane says to me. Her black eyes hold joyful tears as she gazes into the bed. "You opened the Observatory Deck and then created the perfect diversion."

"It didn't feel much like saving," I admit.

"But you did it," Charlotte adds, her voice strong and clear.

"What happened? How many days has it been?" I ask, trying to piece together the rest of the night after I fainted.

"It's been three days. I've freed all the Belles, plus the Fashion

Minister and Beauty Minister, from the Everlasting Rose and put my sister in her own prison, where she will stand trial for her crimes and get the help she needs. I don't know if she will ever truly understand the damage she's done, but I will spend my days impressing this upon her."

She purses her lips. "You missed my coronation," she teases.

"You are a beautiful queen," Lady Pelletier adds with a smile. "Your mother would be proud."

We all kiss our two fingers and tap our hearts to show respect for the dead. I let my hand linger there, thinking of Valerie, Amber, and Arabella.

"Where are the other Belles?" I ask.

"I've seen a few of them," Edel interjects. "They're here at the palace."

"We've released them from the teahouses as well and given them accommodations." Charlotte takes a breath. "And we'd love it, Camille, if you'd stay with us, and be our advisor on all matters related to Belles as we figure out what beauty work will look like going forward."

Lady Arane clears her throat. "Living without modifications does take adjustment and patience. The Iron Ladies will be moving our headquarters to Trianon to assist those who wish to make the change," she assures me.

The proposition stirs around inside my head. This last year I've felt like I've been trapped in a snow globe, shaken and jostled until the glass fissures and all the water leaks out. Before, all I ever wanted was to live at the palace forever in one of the beautiful apartments. But now, all I want to do is go home. Or to whatever is left of it.

"Your Majesty, it would be an honor to help you with this and

to be here with you, but I don't believe it's the right path for me,"
I tell her. "I want to go back to Maison Rouge and take any Belles
who want to come with me. While things are still settling across
the kingdom, it will be a troublesome time for us. I need to be in a
place that I know is safe, and I need to keep my sisters safe. And,
if I may . . . I must also grapple with the things I've done—and the
losses I've suffered."

Charlotte smiles knowingly. "I understand. I respect your
decision. But I will still need your help. All of your help." She gestures at Hana, Edel, and Padma.

"I'll stay behind," Edel says, surprising us all.

"You will?" Padma replies.

"I won't ever return to another teahouse," she declares. "And
if things are going to change in Orléans, I want to be a part of that
change."

She reaches for my hand and for Hana's. I can feel her pulse
thrumming beneath her skin.

"If I accomplish one thing in this life," she says firmly, "it will
be to ensure that the old way of doing things is done."

41

A week later, the journey home from Trianon feels a thousand moments longer than the one that first brought me and my sisters to the imperial island. Our hearts buzzed with the promise of being true Belles, stepping into our destinies, being chosen and placed. The two days drifted past us before we knew it, our fates sprawled out before us like paths to unknown places, full of promise.

The horses' pace quickens as the carriages travel north across imperial bridges connecting the main island to outlying ones. The ride home is shadowed with worries, a tapering storm that may reignite at any moment.

We sit in silence. The noise of the road among us. Padma thumbs through Arabella's Belle-book. Hana reads a stack of newspapers and tattlers. Rémy sleeps, his arm in a sling and his foot propped up. Bree stokes a small fire. The absence of Valerie, Edel, and Amber is like a cold weight in my chest. At least Edel is well. She's taken her place at the palace at Charlotte's side.

I glance out the window at our procession—several carriages carrying Belles released from the Everlasting Rose and the teahouses—all those who wished to come.

The city of Trianon disappears in the distance, fading to a mere smudge. I crane to see its outline, wondering if I will ever return, if I'll ever want to. I wanted nothing more than to be the favorite and to stay in Trianon and the royal palace forever, but I had no idea what it would be like, all the horrors that would come to pass. A dream turned nightmare.

I curl into a little knot, limbs and body lost in the folds of my dress, and sink into the weight of all that's happened.

"More newspapers and tattlers," Bree says, sliding one stack into my lap and another into Hana's.

"Sit with me?" I ask her.

"I need to prepare tea."

"You're no longer an imperial servant."

"I know, but—"

I pat the cushion beside mine. "Just sit with me awhile."

She concedes.

We sit in the window and go through the headlines in the *Orléansian Times*:

MINISTER OF BELLES FLEES! GEORGIANA FABRY MISSING

THE LEADER OF THE IRON LADIES INVITED TO
MEET WITH HER MAJESTY QUEEN CHARLOTTE

LOCKED IN A TOWER OF HER OWN MAKING!
DISGRACED ALMOST QUEEN SOPHIA HELD IN
THE EVERLASTING ROSE TO AWAIT TRIAL

RIOTS AND UNREST SPARK IN THE SPICE ISLES!

"What do you think will happen?" Bree asks.

I turn the page and the headlines scatter. "I don't know."

"Will things go back to what they once were?"

"Can anything go back? All I know is that we will take care of one another and those with us, and help Charlotte." I trace my fingers along the underside of my wrist, the veins there a reminder of the arcana. And a choice.

She opens the *Trianon Tribune* and reads silently.

I close my eyes. Images circle inside my head with nowhere to go, like flies in a jar. I drift in and out of sleep. Time passes, more than three hourglasses' worth. The world outside the carriage gets quieter and quieter.

The wheels sink into soft earth. I recognize the feeling and know we're close to home. When I was younger, I loved the mud between my toes and the tiny worry that you might drift down and through the center of the world. If we were the slightest bit dirty, Du Barry would send us for a scrub treatment, and it was never pleasant. I miss those little-girl days before I was so excited to leave home—to crash into the world and discover its secrets.

We rattle along the wooden bridge to the carriage-house, and I hear the familiar late-night noises of the Rose Bayou—the hum of crickets, the bleat of frogs, and the buzz of fireflies. Above me a quilt of branches is heavy with snow-white moss.

The carriages are parked inside the brick carriage-house, which sits on a platform in the middle of the bayou. Behind me, the wooden bridge pulls away, returning to our closest island neighbor—Quin. During the warm months, rows of fruits and vegetables in every color, shape, and size grow along high hills and mountainsides, and we could see teams of workers tending to the millions of plants from my bedroom window.

Would everything settle back in place like a reset bone?

As the bridge disappears behind me, so does the path to the outside world. Maybe that's a good thing now. Maybe time away from the world will help.

I gaze ahead across the water. Home hides among the Rose Bayou's cypress trees. The newspapers used to say the Goddess of Beauty placed Belles on an island of milk and blood because of these white bark trees and their red leaves.

I wish the sight of them gave me the relief I crave, but it doesn't. What will it feel like to be here without Amber and Valerie? Will I be able to do all the things that need to be done?

Bayou boats arrive at the carriage-house pier.

We climb in.

Snowflies skip along the surface of the water, their little bodies white sparks brightening the dark. I want to plunge my whole hand in, like I did when I was a little girl. I want to see if the water is still the same.

The warning Du Barry used to give me rings out in my head: *"Sit up, Camellia, and hand out of the water. This bayou is full of the unknown."*

I leave a sliver of the window open to watch as we pass through a dense thicket of cypress trees where the boats slow to curve around their trunks. I want to reach out and pluck one of the roses growing out of the dark waters, but the feeling of Du Barry's eyes upon me lingers. Even if she isn't here.

Maison Rouge appears ahead. The pointed roof rises above the trees. Sill-lanterns sit in each window and cast red light over the island. Stone crypts freckle the land, and the Belle-graveyard seems endless, spilling into the dark forest that lurks in the mansion's shadow. Maman and I used to play hide-and-seek in the graveyard when she wanted alone time for us away from the other mothers and little girls. We'd zip around those vaults and fill the space with laughter instead of death. Back then, I wasn't afraid of dying, and I never thought there'd be a day when Maman would be placed in one of the graves. They were just stone pyramids to hide behind until my mother found me. Now, they feel real and used. Ready to receive the bodies of my sisters.

The boats are tethered to the dock, and the servants help us onto the platform. We follow a path of stepping-stones along the walkway to the house. Twisted cypress trees block the stars. The noise of our feet adds to the melody of the bayou. I jam a key into the lock just as Du Barry once did.

I slide the entryway doors open with both hands. The floors are warm beneath my feet, and the walls and corridors and rooms carry the scent of charcoal and flowers. The familiar smell of home.

Ivy stands there waiting. Her face has settled back to its original shape. She opens her arms, and I fall into them.

"It is so good to see you," I say. "How did you get here before us?"

"Always asking questions."

Her words make me smile. "It's good to see you, too."

"Welcome home, my little fox."

"Are we going to be all right?" I ask.

"Yes," she replies. "Together we will."

Epilogue

I open the double doors of Du Barry's office. The wood whispers beneath my feet, and I'm a little girl again, bracing myself to get in trouble, waiting for her to step out of the circuit-phone booth in the corner, expecting her to appear behind me, and say, "What do you think you're doing in here? Fetch your parchment and write fifty lines."

The scent of her lingers—rose water, cloves, and a touch of sugar—and it makes me wonder where she might be now. The windy season is here, and it's been three months since Charlotte locked Sophia in the Everlasting Rose.

Du Barry's high-backed velvet chair is still creased with the memory of her shape. Her abacus perches on the side like a tanager bird. The walls boast portraits of her ancestors—eight generations' worth, all stemming from the grand-mère who found the first Belle as she emerged from the dark forest.

Nothing has changed. All of it is frozen in place, anticipating her return, anticipating all things to settle back into place like they once were.

But everything is different now.

I sit at her desk, my legs finding the grooves left behind by her body.

The house bell rings. I glance out the window that faces the front. Padma ushers in more of Sophia's pods. The growing Belle babies slosh in their cradles as they're lifted inside. Hana follows behind, her arms full of supplies.

I step into the hallway. The lesson rooms are filled with small Belles examining flowers and products, the pitch of their voices bordering on squeals. Day-lanterns sail over the room like floating stars.

The foyer buzzes with activity as the nursery chamber welcomes the Belle-pods from the palace. Nurses rush in and out, following Ivy's orders.

I leave the house through the back doors. The dark forest lies ahead, spread out across the rest of our island like a blanket of night. The Belle-graveyard sits along its edge, headstones poking like thumbnails from the rich soil. The three freshest graves hold the bodies of Amber and Valerie and Arabella, but already the earth around them has settled. They barely look new anymore.

My heart pinches.

I glance up at the sky, wondering if new Belles will actually fall from it one day. Will my sisters be replaced? What will happen in the weeks and months and years to come?

A warm and familiar hand slips into mine. I look up and meet Rémy's eyes. "When did you get back?"

"Just now."

"How are your sisters? And mother and father?"

"Better," he says with a sigh of relief. He presents a ruby post-balloon. "This arrived from the palace."

I rip open the back of the balloon, fish out the letter holder, and unroll the parchment. Rémy reads over my shoulder.

Camille,

I hope everything is all right at home.

I have news that you should know in case it leaks to the papers. I still don't trust anyone here at court. Charlotte plans to abdicate the throne once things settle down. She wants to call for a new Beauty Trial.

It could be two months or two years from now. I don't know.

But I'm looking forward to what comes next.

Be safe, and write me.

Love,

Edel

PS: Hi, Rémy!

Rémy and I exchange glances.

"What does that mean?" he asks.

"Maybe chaos. Maybe an end to beauty work for good." I glance back at the house. "I don't know. One can only hope our new leader will be wise and just, and nothing like Sophia."

I look up at the post-balloon, and then at the sky as a streak mars the blue.

His hand finds mine.

"What would you say if I asked you to go into those woods with me? Would you be afraid?"

He turns my face toward him. "Anything for you."

We walk forward into the shadows, hand in hand.

ACKNOWLEDGMENTS

I have so many people to thank for helping me cross the finish line with this book. It was a struggle and a roller coaster, because during the writing of this book I was diagnosed with a very large, noncancerous liver tumor. Through numerous medical appointments, biopsies, and MRIs, I wrestled with this book and its plot and all my deadlines, and the reality that my quest for perfect skin was the reason I had this medical emergency. After spending several decades on oral contraceptives to control my cystic acne, I discovered it gave me a parting gift—a tumor the size of my hand. Beauty has a price, and I am learning the cost now.

It took a team to help me get this book to be its best. A list of thanks in no particular order:

My badass agent, Victoria Marini. Thank you for keeping me together. You are a superhero!

My amazing editor, Kieran S. Viola. Thank you for rescuing me. Always. Thank you for your patience as this medical crisis interrupted our normal editorial process. Thank you for helping me organize the chaos.

My amazing champion, Emily Meehan. Thank you for your vision and your support. I love being part of the Freeform family.

Marci Senders, brilliant cover wizard, you continue to amaze me with your cover-making powers. They just get better and better.

Maz Zissimos, best publicist in the freaking world, thank you for keeping me all together and making sure I get cool opportunities to talk about my world. You are amazing, and I feel lucky to also call you a friend.

Thank you to the whole Freeform team—Seale Ballenger, Holly Nagel, Dina Sherman, Mary Mudd, Shane Rebenschied, Elke Villa, Andrew Sansone, Patrice Caldwell. You are the dream team.

Thank you to my friends, my love nests, my group chats, my Slack channels, my covens. All those who keep me human. You know who you are. This was a tough year, and I barely made it through. Thank you for listening to me complain and whine and cry, and for keeping me all stitched together. Thank you for the chicken broth and the flowers and the tea and the steak. ☺

Thank you, Mom and Dad, for everything. Always, and forever.

And thank you to the readers. Thanks for coming down this dark rabbit hole with me.

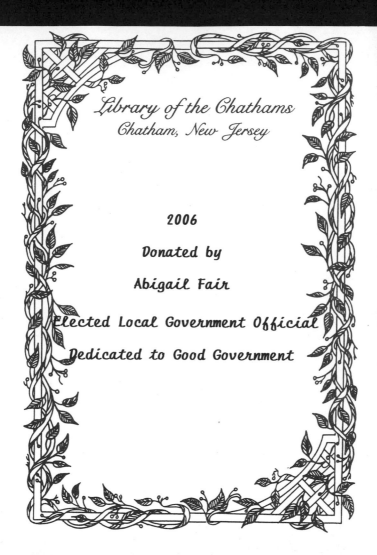

DEMOCRACY

DEMOCRACY

A History

JOHN DUNN

Atlantic Monthly Press
New York

First published in Great Britain in 2005 by Atlantic Books,
an imprint of Grove Atlantic Ltd.

Printed in the United States of America

FIRST AMERICAN EDITION

Library of Congress Cataloging-in-Publication Data

Dunn, John, 1940-
    Democracy: a history / John Dunn.
      p. cm.
    Includes bibliographical references and index.
    ISBN-10: 0-87113-931-6
    ISBN-13: 978-0-87113-931-3
    1. Democracy—History. I. Title.

    JC421.D85 2005
    321.809—dc22   2005058861

Design by www.carrstudio.co.uk

Atlantic Monthly Press
an imprint of Grove/Atlantic, Inc.
841 Broadway
New York, NY 10003

Distributed by Publishers Group West

www.groveatlantic.com

06 07 08 09 10   10 9 8 7 6 5 4 3 2 1

For Ruth

ACKNOWLEDGEMENTS

This book is no one's fault but mine. But many people have put them-selves out to help me as I wrote. I am extremely grateful for the patience, lucidity and directness of Gill Coleridge throughout my efforts to plan and complete it. At Atlantic Books, I should like to thank Toby Mundy, who brings to publishing a combination of consideration and zest of which authors vainly dream, and Bonnie Chiang, who has been consistently encouraging and helpful. I have had prompt, generous and effective aid over particular points from many colleagues in Cambridge and beyond: notably Robin Osborne, Simon Goldhill, Stephen Alford, Paul Cartledge, Basim Musallam, Gareth Stedman Jones, Tim Blanning, Bela Kapossy, and Michael Sonenscher. The experience of writing it has reminded me vividly of old intellec-tual debts which can never be repaid, above all to Moses Finley and Bernard Bailyn, of the intellectual companionship over decades of Michael Cook, Quentin Skinner and Istvan Hont, and of the help and encouragement in a variety of settings of many friends: Bianca Fontana, Bernard Manin, Pasquale Pasquino, Adam Przeworski, Tony Judt, Richard Tuck, Cynthia Farrar, Sunil Khilnani, Sudipta Kaviraj, Tom Metzger, Ian Shapiro, Andrew Barshay, Takamaro Hanzawa,

Takashi Kato, and most recently Guillermo O'Donnell, who has devoted his life to fathoming democracy's fate. I owe very special thanks to Raymond Geuss, with whom I have taught now for over a decade, and who has been the truest of friends.

My colleagues in the Department of Politics have shouldered many burdens to give me the chance to work on it. I am especially grateful to Helen Thompson and Geoffrey Hawthorn for their help and solidarity. The University of Cambridge gave me the sabbatical leave which enabled me to begin it in reasonable calm; and the Arts and Humanities Research Board, once again, gave me the final term of research leave which I needed to complete it.

Three figures particularly have given me hope and nerve over the last few years in pressing the questions which I try to answer. Edward Said by his warmth, his glowing vitality, and his unforgettable generosity of spirit, as the shades closed in. Janet Malcolm by her grace and luminosity on the page, and by the ear of the Recording Angel. Dr Kim Dae-Jung, the one unmistakably great political leader with whom I have had the privilege to talk at length, to whom his country owes far more than it has yet begun to realize, by his singular courage.

King's College, Cambridge, October 2004

*We used to go down on our knees before the people
in power, but now we have got to our feet.*
NADIA BEREZOVSKA

(middle-aged postmistress, amongst the crowds in central
Kiev who forced the holding of a fresh election on Ukraine's
incumbent President)

[Stefan Wagstyl & Tom Warner, 'We used to go down on our knees
before the people in power, but now we have got to our feet',
Financial Times, 21 December 2004, p17]

CONTENTS

Preface

WHY DEMOCRACY?

This book tells an astonishing story. It is the story of a word of casual origins, and with a long and often ignominious history behind it, which has come quite recently to dominate the world's political imagination. Over the course of the book I try to show how little we yet understand that remarkable ascent, but also how we can learn to grasp its causes and significance altogether better.

Why does democracy loom so large today? Why should it hold such sway over the political speech of the modern world? What does its recent prominence really mean? When America and Britain set out to bury Baghdad in its own rubble, why was it in the name of democracy of all words that they claimed to do so? Is its novel dominance in fact illusory: a sustained exercise in fraud or an index of utter confusion? Or does it mark a huge moral and political advance, which only needs to cover the whole world, and be made a little more real, for history to come to a reassuring end?

This book sets out to explain the extraordinary presence of democracy in today's world. It shows how it began as an improvised remedy for a very local Greek difficulty two and a half thousand years ago, flourished briefly but scintillatingly, and then faded away

13

almost everywhere for all but two thousand years. It tells how it came back to life as a real modern political option, explaining why it first did so, under another name, in the struggle for American independence and with the founding of the new American republic. It shows how it then returned, almost immediately and under its own name, if far more erratically, amid the struggles of France's Revolution. It registers its slow but insistent rise over the next century and a half, and its overwhelming triumph in the years since 1945. In that rise we can see how strong the continuities remain, but also how sharp the breaks must be, between its Greek original and any modern democratic state. We can grasp what it is about democracy which equipped it to evoke such vital allegiance, but which also guarantees that it will continue to arouse intense fear and suspicion, and open intellectual and moral scorn. Within the last three-quarters of a century democracy has become the political core of the civilization which the West offers to the rest of the world. Now, as never before, we need to understand what that core really is. As do those to whom we make that offer.

In this book, accordingly, I try to answer two very large questions. The first concerns an extremely strange fact about modern politics. The second concerns the single most unmistakably momentous political outcome of the last three-quarters of a century. I know of no serious attempt to answer the first question. Few even care to pose it in a clear and reasonably frank way. Answers to the second question, by contrast, are two a penny. They litter the pages of serious newspapers and form a commonplace of contemporary political commentary. Most, however, are plainly wrong; and once the question is considered with care, it becomes all too clear that it is exceedingly hard to answer. I believe that the answers to these questions are closely connected, and that, between them, they show something of immense importance about modern politics. But readers may judge otherwise, and still, I hope, learn for themselves from the challenge of trying to answer each.

The first question has two distinct elements: the existence of a single cosmopolitan standard, and the term selected to express it. Why should it be the case that, for the first time in the history of our still conspicuously multi-lingual species, there is for the present a single world-wide name for the legitimate basis of political authority? Not, of course, uncontested in practice anywhere, and still roundly rejected in many quarters, but never, any longer, in favour of an alternative secular claimant to cosmopolitan legitimacy. This is a startling fact, and clearly requires explanation; but in itself it is not necessarily any stranger than much else about the world in which we now live. What is very strange indeed (in fact, quite bizarre) is the fact that this single term, endlessly transliterated or translated across all modern languages,[1] should turn out to be the ancient Greek noun *demokratia*, which originally meant not a basis for legitimacy, or a regime defined by its good intentions or its noble mission, but simply one particular form of government, and that a form, for almost two thousand years of its history as a word, which, it was overwhelmingly judged by most who used the term, had proved grossly illegitimate in theory and every bit as disastrous in practice.

The first question, therefore, is in part a question about the history of language (the vocabulary of modern politics, and its historical antecedents). But it is also a question about the history of political thought and argument, and about the history of political organization and struggle. Why should it be this word that has won the verbal competition for ultimate political commendation across the globe? What does it carry within it to gain it this smashing victory? How did the ideas we now take it to imply, in the end and after so very many centuries, face down the variety of ideas which for so long dominated it with such apparent ease? How did it shake off its lengthy notoriety, adjust its register from dispassionate or disabused description to confident and committed commendation, and pick up the oecumenical allure which its Athenian inventors never intended, and could not distantly have imagined?

At the core of this story is the intensely political history of a very political word. But the word itself cannot answer our questions. Once it was there (as far as we know, summoned into existence precisely to name the regime form which Kleisthenes pioneered for Athens, for his now largely inscrutable reasons, very late in the sixth century BC), that word could be carried laterally in space, and aimed backwards as well as forwards in time. It could be deployed to designate communities which had never heard of Kleisthenes, or even Athens, and practices, whether earlier or later, which were clearly quite unaffected by anything the Athenians ever did, or anything else which we know them to have said. But for over two thousand years it remained a noun designating a system of rule. Not till very late in the eighteenth century, very close to France's great revolution, and apparently largely in and because of it, did *democracy* transform itself into a noun of agency (a *democrat*), an adjective which expressed allegiance and did not merely allude to it (*democratic*), and a verb (to *democratize*), which described the project of refashioning politics, society, and even economy in their entirety, to meet the standards set by the idea of popular self-rule. Ancient Greece had partisans of democracy as a regime. But, as far as we know, it did not exactly have democrats: men (or women) who did not just favour democracy in a particular setting within a given conflict, but were also confident of the clear illegitimacy anywhere of every rival political form, and relatively clear just where the superiority of democracy lay. Certainly, no Greek thinker or political actor ever either defended or explained their political aspirations as efforts to raise distinct aspects of political, economic or social arrangements to the exacting standards which democracy implies.

Athens gave democracy a name, and worked out an elaborate, highly distinctive and astonishingly thoroughgoing interpretation of the political conditions required to achieve it. But it took the French Revolution, well over two thousand years later, to turn *democrat* into a partisan label and a badge of political honour, and first lend imag-

inative credibility to the idea of transforming human collective life, anywhere and everywhere, to fit those requirements. Only after 1789, as far as we know, did any human beings begin to speak of *democratizing* the societies to which they belonged.

For us, democracy is both a form of government and a political value. We quarrel fiercely, if confusedly, over how far the value vindicates or indicts our own practices of government; but we also quarrel over how far the same value is practically coherent, or desirable in its prospective consequences in different circumstances, on any scale between an individual family or domestic unit and the entire human population of a still painfully disunited globe. When we do so, we largely recapitulate Greek arguments between local partisans of democracy as a form of rule, and intellectual critics who invented political philosophy, alongside other genres of critical reflection on politics, in their attempts to call its merits into question.

With the French Revolution, democracy as a word and an idea acquired a political momentum that it has never since wholly lost. Its merits, both moral and practical, have been contested vigorously throughout, as they still are today. But despite these blatant and endlessly reiterated vulnerabilities, it has become ever clearer that, whatever its limitations, there is something irresistibly potent about democracy as a political rallying cry, and that any hope of halting it permanently in its tracks is utterly forlorn. The political potency of democracy as a word is no guarantee of its intellectual potency as an idea. But its political force is no standing miracle. It cannot issue merely from a meaningless or unintelligible buzz of sound. Democracy has won its present prominence, and even the degree of reluctant deference which it now enjoys, in ferocious competition with very many other words, and not a few other ideas. Today, it is plainly a source and embodiment of political power in itself; and its cumulative victory, however disappointing or hollow if judged against loftier aspirations of its own or others, has itself been a sustained display of political power.

In this book I tell the story of democracy's passage from parochial eccentricity and protracted ignominy, seek to capture its main metamorphoses along the way, and show what its long, slow and wholly unexpected victory really means for the political world in which we all now have to live. In tracing that vast arc across space and through time, I try throughout to do full justice to two clear perceptions which most students of democracy have found it uncomfortable to combine: the startlingly insistent power lurking in this apparently drab word and in the ideas which it has come to evoke, and the speciousness of applying it at all literally to the organizational and governmental structures of any human population early in the third millennium. It is easy to grasp democracy by suppressing either perception. But, if you do, what you grasp must always be drastically other than what is really there: a cynical truncation of that reality, or a stupidly ingenuous gloss upon it. (It is not hard to be an idiot in politics. We are all strongly tempted to political idiocy quite a lot of the time.)

The citizens of Athens in the fifth and fourth centuries BC, to a now bewildering degree, governed themselves. What they meant by democracy (which was originally their word) was the extraordinary complex of institutions which enabled them to do so. No modern population can govern themselves in the same sense; and we lose all feeling for political reality when we strive today to see in America or Britain, as they prepare for war or draw up their public budgets, instances of either people governing itself in even a mildly opaque way. When any modern state claims to be a democracy, it necessarily misdescribes itself. But that is very far from rendering the misdescription inconsequential, and cannot credibly be viewed merely as deliberate self-deception. There is every reason for today's citizens to insist that their own state describe itself in these terms, and choose its friends and commit its power and resources largely alongside other states which also choose to do so. There are, as we shall see, very practical advantages to doing so over time, even if most of them

might be furnished just as reliably for a bit under a more clinical vocabulary.

But the label of democracy does more than affirm a clear duty for states to provide their citizens with these practical advantages. It also expresses symbolically something altogether different: the degree to which all government, however necessary and expeditious, is also a presumption and an offence. Like every modern state, the democracies of today demand obedience and insist on a very large measure of compulsory alienation of judgement on the part of their citizens. (To demand that obedience and enforce such alienation is what makes a state a state.) When they make that demand in their citizens' own name, however, they do not merely add insult to injury, or perpetrate an evident absurdity. They also acknowledge their own permanent potential for effrontery in levying any such demands, and offer a slim measure of apology for the offence inherent in levying them. With that offer, they close the circle of civic subjection, and set out a framework of categories within which a population can reasonably think of itself over time as living together as equals, on terms and within a set of presumptions, which they could reasonably and freely choose. Everywhere that the word *democracy* has fought its way forward across time and space, you can hear both themes: the purposeful struggle to improve the practical circumstances of life, and to escape from arbitrary and often brutal coercion, but also the determination and longing to be treated with respect and some degree of consideration. What we mean by democracy is not that we govern ourselves. When we speak or think of ourselves as living in a democracy, what we have in mind is something quite different. It is that our own state, and the government which does so much to organize our lives, draws its legitimacy from us, and that we have a reasonable chance of being able to compel each of them to continue to do so. They draw it, today, from holding regular elections, in which every adult citizen can vote freely and without fear, in which their votes have at least a reasonably equal weight, and in which any

uncriminalized political opinion can compete freely for them. Modern representative democracy has changed the idea of democracy almost beyond recognition. But, in doing so, it has shifted it from one of history's hopeless losers to one of its more insistent winners.

My second question, then, is what exactly it is, embodied in or centred upon this novel state form, that has given this very old and much reviled word the stamina and drive to win through in the end.

This book, then, tells three remarkable stories. It tells in the first place the story of a word. But it also tells alongside it the story of an idea, by turns inspiring and ludicrous, and the further story of a range of widely varying practices associated with that idea. One broad family of those practices, the governmental forms of the modern representative capitalist democracy, now dominates the world through its wealth and confidence, and through the quite unprecedented powers of destruction which it has at its disposal. The first two stories are long, complicated, and closely intertwined. The first two sections of the book, accordingly, tell them in the boldest outline. The third is far briefer, but also much denser and more complicated: the very core of the political history of the globe over the last half-century. It is not clear that it could yet be told as a story at all, let alone told convincingly at endurable length. In this third section, therefore, I attempt not to record what has happened, but to explain why it has done so.

This is a story, all too obviously, about us: the story, at the very least, of the historical backcloth to the lives of an ever-growing majority amongst us.[2] The question I try to answer here, the book's second question, is why this particular state form, the modern representative capitalist democracy, has for the present won the global struggle for wealth and power. This is a hard question; and I cannot claim to have answered it conclusively. What I hope to show is why its answer cannot be either of the two conclusions which we are endlessly urged to draw from it (because it is evidently just and

because it works reliably in practice), and where, instead, that answer must lie. If these judgements are right, they imply at least one simple conclusion: that our own need to understand the political reality of the world in which we now live is still every bit as urgent as the need which prompted the Athenians to invent and deepen that very distant system of self-rule. For them, it was a price they chose to pay to protect their freedom, as well as an expression of that freedom in itself. We cannot protect our freedom in the same way. But we too, if we care to, can see how pressingly that freedom still needs protection, judge how best it can be protected amongst the many claimants who volunteer their services for the purpose, and choose for ourselves the price we are or are not willing to pay to protect it as best we can. We too, if we choose, can use this antique word, not in theft and mystification, but to focus the challenges which history sends us, and face them alertly together.

Chapter One

DEMOCRACY'S FIRST COMING

Out of the dark and from very long ago has come a word. Like every word which carries authority for human beings, it began its life somewhere in particular. Today that word reaches out almost everywhere on earth where humans gather together in any numbers. Wherever it goes, it presses a claim for authority and a demand for respect. Everywhere, still, these claims remain sharply contested. In some settings they are brushed effortlessly aside, and all but cowed into silence. In others they are affirmed sonorously enough, but heard by most listeners with a hollow groan. Virtually nowhere any longer, even in the most brutal of autocracies, are they merely unintelligible as claims; and in remarkably few sites by now are they simply and permanently inaudible: excluded or erased from public speech by the sheer ferocity of repression. (Note, for example, what was first to respond even for Iraq in the summer of 2003 when the United Nations Security Council demanded its submission, before America launched its invasion. It was not the tyrant who had ruled the country with such murderous brutality and for so long, and whose image dominated every Iraqi public space, but what passed for a national representative assembly: a Parliament. It was they, not their real master, who

showily declined to submit. Within the week, their real master, less showily, had decided quite differently. Or so, at least for a time, it seemed.)

As it travels through time and space, the word democracy never travels all on its own. Increasingly, as the last two centuries have gone by, it has travelled in fine company, alongside freedom, human rights, and perhaps now even, at least in pretension, material prosperity as well. But unlike these companions, democracy stakes a claim which is disconcerting from the outset: the claim to be obeyed. Every right constrains free action. Even freedom necessarily intrudes on the freedom of action of others. But democracy is itself a direct pressure on the will: a demand to accept, abide by, and in the end even submit to, the choices of most of your fellow citizens. There is nothing enticing about that demand, and no guarantee ever that accepting it will avoid fearsome consequences and may not involve hideous complicities. In many ways, and from many different points of view, the authority won by this far-flung word is strange indeed.

This is a story with a beginning. Democracy began in Athens. Not anything whatever which anyone today might reasonably choose to call democracy,[1] but something which someone first in fact, as far as we know, did. Today democracy has come to be used, with sufficient gall, to refer to almost any form of rule or decision making. But when it entered human speech, it did so as a description of an already existing and very specific state of affairs, somewhere in particular. That place was Athens.

What exactly did democracy describe when the Athenians first used the term as a description? What did they mean by describing it in this way? To see what was happening in that first act of naming (or labelling), it helps to begin by listening to the Athenians as they addressed one another about the experience which they hoped to capture. Consider two voices, one very much speaking on democracy's behalf, the other writing of it without enthusiasm and in a more confiding and enquiring fashion.

The first is famous and imposing, the voice of Pericles himself. The grandest celebration of ancient democracy comes not from a poet or philosopher (or even a professional orator),[2] but from the great political leader who led Athens into the war which all but destroyed her. It evokes, and claims to report, a single momentous historical ceremony, held late in the year 430BC. True, we do not know that Pericles himself ever spoke a single word of it. But Thucydides, the mesmerizing historian who certainly composed virtually all of it, assures his readers that it, like the many other speeches of his *History*, conveys not merely what Pericles should have said but also what he would have meant.[3] Thucydides, as he tells us himself with some pride, intended his story to last for ever;[4] and Pericles by that point had led his city state in war and peace for longer than Abraham Lincoln or Winston Churchill, and done so under conditions which often tested the skills of domestic political leadership as exactingly as America's devastating Civil War or the grim struggle to withstand and overthrow the Third Reich. He also led it (and could only have led it), to a degree that has never been true in any modern Parliamentary or Presidential regime, by convincing, time after time, a majority of the citizens present on the occasion by the speeches which he made. He held power by oratory,[5] and did so steadily and tautly enough for Thucydides himself to describe Athens at the time as being ruled by a single person.[6] We need not be surprised at the lasting power or resonance of this remarkable witness.

It was a speech for a proud sad occasion: a eulogy to the war dead of Athens in the opening year of the long drawn-out Peloponnesian War, delivered, as at every Athenian public funeral of its fallen (with the single exception of the victors of Marathon),[7] before their common grave beside the loveliest approach road to the city walls. In it, Pericles spoke not at all of the individual exploits or daring of his heroes,[8] though he left his hearers in little doubt that many had done finely. What he spoke of, incomparably, was Athens itself, the community for which each had made their final sacrifice. He spoke of its

singular glories and its unique claim to such ultimate devotion. Thucydides was no sentimentalist, and no one since he wrote has judged the political conduct of the Athenians in those years more searchingly. What he makes Pericles say in praise of Athens at that point, in vindication of the choices of those who went out to die on its behalf, begins from and centres on its political regime, and the political and spiritual lives which it freed and prompted the Athenians to live together:

> *We live under a form of government which does not emulate the institutions of our neighbours; on the contrary, we are ourselves a model* (paradeigma, *or paradigm*) *which some follow, rather than the imitators of other peoples.*[9]

This regime, which is called democracy (*demokratia*), because it is administered with a view to the interest of the many, not of the few, has not merely made Athens great. It has also rendered its citizens equal before the law in their private disputes, and equally free to compete for public honours by personal merit and exertion, or to seek to lead the city, irrespective of their own wealth or social background.[10] Pericles praises it for the mutual politeness and lack of spite it fostered between those citizens, for the deep respect for law it inculcated, and for drawing to the city the fruits and products of the whole world. He praises it, too, for the military superiority it had mustered, for its determined openness in face of every other people, and the stalwart courage nurtured by its way of life. But he praises it, equally, for its taste and responsiveness to beauty, its sobriety of judgement and respect for wisdom, its pride in its own energy, discretion and generosity. Athens, he boasted in summary, is an education for the whole of Greece.[11]

Democracy for the Athenians began (and even acquired its name) before the category itself carried or expressed any clear or special value. Yet within a few decades of picking up the name, it had come

to mean for some not just a way of organizing power and political institutions, but a whole way of life and the inspiring qualities which somehow suffused it. At the core of that way of life lay a combination of personal commitment to a community of birth and residence, and a continuing practice of alert public judgement on which that community quite consciously depended for its own security:

> *For we alone regard the man who takes no part in public affairs, not as one who minds his own business, but as good for nothing; and we Athenians decide public questions for ourselves or at least endeavour to arrive at a sound understanding of them, in the belief that it is not debate which is a hindrance to action, but rather not to be instructed by debate before the time comes for action.*[12]

There has never been a fuller or saner expression of the hope which lies at the very centre of democracy as a political ideal.

The speech which Thucydides gives us is a historian's presentation of a dutifully partisan and highly political performance. It is also an epitome of the ways in which the citizens of Athens had come to wish to conceive themselves as a community.[13] To other Athenians at the time, just as earlier and later, democracy naturally meant something very different, as it presumably did to many inhabitants of Attica – slaves, women, *metics* – who could never become full citizens.[14] With the critics of democracy there is a wider range of voices to listen to, not all of them cultured despisers like Plato.[15] Especially striking is the figure whom British classical scholars, for reasons now largely forgotten, have come to call the Old Oligarch, author of a terse study of *The Constitution of Athens*, long attributed to Xenophon.[16] For the Old Oligarch, writing in all probability before the Peloponnesian War even began, Athens's democracy was no occasion for applause;[17] but it certainly was a coherent political order, with many elements well calculated to sustain and strengthen it over time. It gave power to

the poor, the unsavoury and the unabashedly popular,[18] and did so quite deliberately at the expense of those of wealth, nobility of birth or social distinction.[19] This distribution of power[20] had entirely natural consequences,[21] benefiting the former mercilessly at the expense of the latter. What made the distribution viable was the main source of the city's military power, its citizen navy, drawn overwhelmingly from the poorer sections of Athens's population, unlike the heavily armed hoplites who dominated its land armies.[22] In the eyes of the Old Oligarch, it was true in every country that those of greater distinction[23] oppose democracy, seeing themselves as repositories of decorum and respect for justice, and their social inferiors as ignorant, disorderly and vicious.[24] In the face of these attitudes, the poorer majority of Athens's citizens are very well advised to insist on their opportunity to share the public offices of the city, and their right to address their fellow citizens at will,[25] and especially well advised to allocate those public offices on which the safety or danger of the people depended,[26] the roles of general or cavalry commander, not randomly across the citizen body but by popular election of those best equipped to hold them (inevitably, the wealthier and more powerful).

For Pericles, as Thucydides makes him speak, the democracy of Athens was a way of living together in political freedom, which ennobled the characters and refined the sensibilities of an entire community. It opened up to them lives rich with interest and gratification, and protected them effectively in living out these lives with one another. It would be hard sanely to ask for more from any set of political institutions or practices. For the Old Oligarch, in stark contrast, the democracy of Athens was a robust but flagrantly unedifying system of power, which subjected the nobler elements of its society to the meaner, transferred wealth purposefully from one to the other, and distributed the means of coercion clear-headedly and determinedly to cement this outcome and keep the nobler elements under control.

*For the people do not want a good government under which
they themselves are slaves; they want to be free and to rule.*[27]

No one could miss the clash between these two views. What is harder
to assess is how far they really conflict in judgement and not merely
in taste, and, where they do conflict in judgement, which better
conveys the way democratic Athens really was.

Anyone who tries to see that reality for themselves faces three very
different obstacles. The first is intrinsic to assessing the politics of
anywhere at any time. It comes from the ambiguities of politics itself,
above all the permanent tensions between its two principal components.[28] Every political community is an elusive and unstable blend
of human purposes and the (principally unintended) consequences of
human actions. Those purposes can be extremely narrow or very
widely shared. They can flicker for a day or two, or congeal into well-
defined institutions or rules of action, and carefully interpreted conceptions of why both institutions and rules are or are not appropriate. Any
picture of politics which focuses principally on institutions, practices
and values starts off from the official face of a political community, and
registers its aspirations and pretensions. A picture which attempts
instead to pin down what actually happens as a result of how particular
men and women choose to behave is all but certain to present that
community in a less sanguine or generous light. It is likely to conclude
that the aspirations enunciated on its official occasions are often bogus,
its institutions grossly at odds with their official justifications, and the
values invoked within it to sanction one line of political conduct
against another little more than tools of deception.[29] What must be
true, however, is that neither picture can ever be adequate on its own
and neither, therefore, ever wholly beside the point.[30] With Athens,
more clearly perhaps than with General Mobutu's Zaire or the
Wahabite Kingdom of Saudi Arabia, the need for each is very clear.

The other two impediments to seeing Athenian democracy the way
it really was are less intimidating but every bit as inconvenient. The

first is the sporadic and often capricious character of the evidence which is still available to us. Much of this does not consist of elaborate descriptive texts.[31] But all of it is still very much in the shadow of a relatively small number of extremely striking texts, above all works of history, philosophy, drama or oratory. All of these, in one way or another, press upon us their own picture of that very distant reality, and do so for purposes of their own, many hard, or even impossible, now to identify. We have works of painstaking institutional description, like Aristotle's *Constitution of Athens*, comedies and tragedies from Aeschylus to Aristophanes, probing histories from Herodotus and Thucydides, passionately engaged speeches by prominent political advocates like Demosthenes or Isocrates, unexcelled enquiries into the meaning of human life and the place of politics within it from Plato and Aristotle. Between them these disparate texts make some things arrestingly clear; but they also leave a great deal which is now wholly out of view. These large gaps in our knowledge do nothing to blur the realities of the distant past,[32] or weaken our reasons for straining to grasp them as best we can. But they offer a salutary warning of how easy it will always remain to deceive ourselves about the sources of our own views of those realities: why we see them, and feel about them, the way we do.

The third obstacle is the lengthy and surprisingly continuous history which has led us to see them this way, a history largely carried by the historical transmission of exactly the same texts. There is, as we shall see, little direct relation between the political institutions and practices of ancient Athens and those of any human community today. But there is unmistakably at least one connecting strand, which runs without interruption from the texts of Aeschylus to the present day. What is transmitted along this strand is seldom, if ever, firm structures of power or definite institutional practices. What travels along it, often with great vitality, is conceptions of what to value and aim for, and why and how to act on the basis of those conceptions. Conceptions of this kind (values, ideals, visions of life) never

determine the outcome of the politics of any community, and change constantly as they shape and reshape purposes along the way. But no community can exist even fugitively, let alone persist and extend across long spans of time, except by courtesy of just such conceptions, and the complicated tissue of institutions and practices which they inform and sustain. (The law of any society is an ideal setting in which to see the weight of this simple consideration: an endless battleground of contending force, but also and just as necessarily a seamless canvas for enquiry and interpretation, the play of intelligence and even the impact of scruple.[33]) As we peer back towards the democracy of Athens, through the murk of history, and quarrel endlessly about what was ever really there, we largely recapitulate Greek arguments. We do so partly because of an obvious continuity in subject matter: because the reality we are trying to grasp was to such a large degree what those arguments were about; and partly too because recapitulating Greek arguments was what for almost two thousand years Europeans, and later North Americans, were tirelessly trained to do. But we also do so because of the enduring power of some of those arguments, itself a testimony to the power of the way of life from which they first came.[34]

What then was Athenian democracy? Of some things we can be quite certain. For the Athenians themselves what it was remained fiercely contentious from its beginning to its end. It could scarcely have been less like the anodyne political recipe which democracy readily seems today, an almost wholly unreflective formula for how things ought to be politically almost everywhere and almost always (anywhere and any time, at least, at which it does not very urgently matter).[35] What the Athenians disagreed about, of course, was what happened in and through and because of their democracy, and what their regime therefore meant. They had far less doubt about what its principal institutions were, or when it had come into existence, or when, eventually, it had come to an end. What divided them, as it divides every human community, was how they saw one another's

political actions, and the purposes which lay behind these, and the forces and interests (conscious or otherwise) which in turn lay behind those purposes.

Throughout its history, the democracy of Athens had bitter enemies as well as committed partisans, both at home and abroad. It may have come to be, as Pericles boasted, a proudly shared way of life in a conspicuously splendid setting; but that way of life itself attracted hatred and scorn as well as love and admiration; and the hatred and the love flowed out over and enveloped the institutions and practices of the democracy itself, and the balance of competing groups, social interests and political energies which it reflected and secured.

Democracy in Athens arose out of struggles between wealthier landowners and poorer families who had lost, or were in danger of losing, their land, and who therefore risked being forced into unfree labour by their accumulated debts.[36] It did not arise, directly and self-consciously, through that struggle itself, by unmistakable victory of the poor over the rich, but through a sequence of political initiatives which reshaped the social geography and institutions of Athens, and endowed it with a political identity, and a system of self-rule which equipped it to express and defend that identity. The most important of these initiatives, the reforms of Solon, were put in place before Athens had in any sense become a democracy.

Solon was an Athenian nobleman (*Eupatrid*), chosen magistrate (*Archon*) for the year 594BC, and given full power to reorganize the basis of land ownership, credit and personal status amongst the Athenians, and give it lasting legal form. He codified the laws, revised the levels of property on the basis of which wealthier Athenians were eligible to hold public office,[37] modified the structure of law courts, greatly improving access for the poor, freed those already enslaved for debt and abolished debt bondage for the future. He firmly refused to redistribute the land.[38]

By these means Solon tamed the brutal dynamics of appropriation, land hunger, debt and potential enslavement amongst the Athenians

themselves, and showed them how Athens could hope to conceive itself, and keep itself together as a community, while the world changed round it. What he failed to do was to establish a political mechanism through which the Athenians could act together to realize that hope. His reforms were a remedy for a dire trouble between the Athenians themselves. It was yet to become a remedy in their own hands.

The next key initiative, the conventional date for democracy's inauguration, came almost a century later and after much intervening political turmoil. Solon was a real historical person; but he was also a figure of legend, one of the two great Lawgivers (Legislators) who haunted the political imagination of Greek communities, and have obsessed their would-be successors ever since.[39] What the Lawgiver did was to focus the fundamental challenges facing a particular community clearly in his mind's eye,[40] set out a framework which provided a durable solution for those problems and define this through the medium of law. Kleisthenes, who brought to Athens in 507BC what the Athenians in due course came to call democracy, was also a historical figure, a nobleman (*Eupatrid*) like Solon; but he has never become a figure of legend. None of the historical sources presents him as setting out from a clearly articulated conception of the fundamental challenges Athens faced, or carefully selecting democracy for their remedy. Democracy, indeed, was not merely as yet unnamed.[41] It was not even a pre-specified formula, applied to solve a clearly defined problem. What Kleisthenes did, as Solon had done before him, was to reorganize Athenian social geography and institutions to resolve a set of immediate problems and build a stable framework for Athens as a community around that would-be resolution. To do so, he needed to win power in the first place; and democracy, as it turned out, was both an initial means to do so, and in due course a consequence of having done so. What was different about his solution was that the framework he established was from its outset a way of organizing political choice which took it outside the ranks of the well-

born and relatively wealthy, and assigned it clearly and unapologetically to the Athenian *demos* as a whole.

Herodotus presents Kleisthenes's adoption of this approach, not as an instance of intellectual or moral conviction, but as a practical expedient to muster support against his aristocratic rivals and their Spartan allies.[42] But even at the time the motives and aspirations which led him to select it may not have greatly mattered, once he had done so. What mattered more even then, and still matters to this day, is that in many ways and for a surprisingly long time the expedient worked.

As it continued to work, it acquired a name of its own (*demokratia* – rule of, or by, or, more literally, strength or power in the hands of, the *demos* – the people as a whole, or, in the eyes of its enemies, the common or non-noble (non-*Eupatrid*) people). It also fashioned a developing institutional form to express that rule, and a steadily deepening sense of its own identity and point. Pericles's speech was delivered (in some form) some three-quarters of a century after Kleisthenes won power in Athens through and for democracy; and Athens remained a democracy, with two brief but destructive interruptions, for a further century afterwards. When democracy came to an end in the city, what ended it was not Athenian political choices (or even their unintended consequences). It was foreign military power: the armies of the kingdom of Macedon.

Throughout this century and three-quarters, Athens, a community of some third of a million inhabitants with a large and increasingly resplendent urban centre and a substantial rural hinterland, was very often at war, initially against the Persian empire, but usually against other Greek city states (above all, its great rival, the warrior kingdom of Sparta), and eventually and decisively against the only quasi-Greek kingdom of Macedon. There were close ties, as there were in every Greek community, between its military (or naval) organization, its political institutions and the balance of social groups within it which supported or threatened these institutions. The Athenians liked to

think of themselves as more historically continuous and more firmly rooted in their own territory than other Greek city states,[43] contrasting the depth of their commitment to the more opportunistic and nomadic attitudes induced by more fertile parts of Hellas.[44]

By the time that Pericles had finished with it Athens had become a rather grand city, full of fine new public buildings (many still there to be admired) and magnificent statuary (much of which, for one reason or another, is now elsewhere). But except when directly threatened in war, when most of its rural inhabitants chose to retreat behind its Long Walls, the majority of Athenian citizens did not live permanently in the city itself but continued to own and farm land elsewhere in Attica. The citizen population of Athens was never very large, perhaps 100,000 in all,[45] of whom about 30,000 would have been full citizens, all adult males and most of them Athenian by descent for several generations. In addition there were some 40,000 resident aliens (*metics*), men, women and children, a few of whom could hope in due course to become citizens themselves, and a much larger number of slaves (perhaps 150,000 in all).[46] The full citizens therefore represented little more than a tenth of the population.[47]

Most of these citizens, naturally, did not spend all their time attempting to rule the city, or fighting in its endless naval or military campaigns. Many, for the century after Kleisthenes,[48] could not conceivably have afforded to, since they did not own slaves themselves, and drew such income as they had, and secured much of their household's food supply, from the produce of their own small farms. Some lived too far away from Athens to attend the meetings of the Assembly with any frequency. But all had the right to attend whenever the Assembly met, as it did with increasing frequency as the democracy evolved over time, whether at pre-arranged intervals or to deal with particular eventualities – a diplomatic or military emergency, a major trial.[49] They also had the right not merely to vote on all proposals coming before it, and thus to determine together its outcome, but also to address it themselves, if they could muster the

nerve, on any issue which came under discussion. They held these rights as equals, whatever their own level of personal wealth or education, the social standing of their families, or the prestige of their occupations. We do not know how many mustered the nerve, or just what emboldened them to do so. But we certainly know that a majority of them for nearly a hundred and thirty years remained firmly committed to, and took a deep pride in, the conspicuous core of personal equality which these arrangements expressed and asserted. For success in Athenian politics personal wealth, family background and even costly education were just as helpful as they are in the United States today (or most other wealthy capitalist countries). As far as we know, no Athenian was surprised that they should have proved so, or embarrassed when they did. What was surprising, and remained disconcerting to some throughout Athens's history as a democracy, was how robust the assertion of equality eventually became, and how clearly it set the terms on which the pressures of wealth, family background and educational embellishment could continue to exert themselves.

Besides the Assembly itself, which took all the great decisions of state for the Athenians, made war or peace, despatched armies or navies, and passed or rejected each new law, there were several other key institutions, which kept the main direction of Athenian political life firmly in the hands of its citizens as a whole. There was the Council (the *Boule*), 500 in number, which drew up the agenda for every Assembly meeting.[50] This met each weekday, co-ordinating other public bodies and effectively conducting the foreign relations of the *polis* throughout. It was drawn from all the 139 territorial units (the *demes*) into which Kleisthenes had divided the Athenians for political purposes, its members selected by lot from those who chose to offer themselves for the purpose.[51] Within the Council a tenth of its members served as a continuing executive body, rotating throughout the year, chaired on each occasion by a fresh individual, selected again by lot from the tenth in question for twenty-four hours at a time.[52]

There were also the popular Law Courts, in effect juries drawn from an annual panel of 6,000 citizens, all of whom had volunteered for the service and sworn a formal oath to do justice within it, and who were paid a modest daily fee for providing it. These courts heard every significant case brought to trial in Athens and decided its outcome by their verdict, without benefit of (or impediment from) professional judicial advice. They held every magistrate to account for the conduct of their office, most decisively of all in the great political trials which any prominent Athenian political leader might have to face at any point, and which often endangered not merely their reputation or personal fortune but their very lives.

It is not hard in this picture to pick up some of the fierce directness of Athenian democracy, and the formidable dispersion of personal power and responsibility across the citizen body which it made possible. What remains hard to see clearly is quite how this startling immediacy in Athenian politics, and the permanent and intensely personal accountability which it enforced, nevertheless fitted with and modified the continuing role of its political leaders. If Pericles ever in any sense ruled Athens as a single person, he certainly did so by continuing courtesy of, and with the clear consent of, most of his fellow citizens who took an active interest in the matter; and even Pericles in due course found himself the target of a menacing prosecution, and sentenced to pay a heavy fine.[53] Where the leaders made their mark, and laid themselves open to such acute personal danger, was by setting themselves forward to champion major changes in the law, or defend one line of policy against another, principally in the field of foreign war, and by competing to lead the armies or fleets sent off to fight in these incessant struggles. To do the first, they had to win the consent of the Assembly, and do so without the backing of an organized personal following which could ever have mustered a substantial proportion of the votes required. (Contrast any modern legislature in action.)[54] To do the second, they had to get themselves elected for the purpose. The election of the Generals,

strangely to our eyes, was widely recognized as the least democratic feature of Athens's political arrangements, a clear concession to the massive importance of warfare, and the dire potential costs of losing at it.

We can picture this political regime most clearly when at its most public and dramatic, in the great set-piece debates in the Assembly at which it took its most momentous decisions. We see it above all, whether we wish to or not, through Thucydides's glittering portrayal of the trajectory of the Peloponnesian War: in the savage punishment willed upon Mitylene and almost immediately regretted, or the launching of the Sicilian expedition which ensured Athens's ultimate defeat. We know almost nothing of the ceaseless mustering of influence or flow of persuasion which gave its main leaders their followings and helped them sway their huge audiences. In so far as it did work, we do not really understand why, or quite how, it did so. All that we can plainly see is that in many ways and for a long time it just did.[55]

Looking at it from today, what we most want to believe is that Athenian democracy somehow worked because it should have done so, because, within its own narrow confines,[56] it organized power in essentially the right way, assigning it, within those terms, on the right basis, and allocating it in the right way. It is above all that conviction, however confusedly, which we locked into place, when we turned the noun which initially described it into our own name for the sole basis on which it is decent to claim political power over time in any modern political community. Quite how and why we chose to effect that transformation is what this book is about. Most of the answer must lie very far from ancient Athens either in time or in space. It might in principle even be true that none of the answer had any real connection with that vastly distant experience. The passage of the word itself might mean no more than that. It might be just an accident in the patterning of letters or sounds, across languages and territories, over a huge span of time. But that at least we clearly know to be false. The survival of democracy as a word, its penetration from ancient

Greek into a wide range of later languages, and still more its enforced translation over a much briefer time-span into the language of every other substantial human population across the globe, came less from its continuing capacity to elicit enthusiasm than from its utility in organizing thought, facilitating argument and shaping judgement.

This is extraordinarily important. It means that democracy entered the ideological history of the modern world reluctantly and facing backwards. It won its vast following not by evoking a golden past, or reminding its hearers of a glory for which they consciously longed, or with which they already urgently identified. It did so just by referring, and in less than seductive terms, to possibilities now opening up before them. Initially at least, when it did this, it helped them not merely to talk more clearly to one another about these possibilities, and the rewards and hazards which they might carry, but also to think more clearly about whether to pursue these possibilities, and at what prospective cost. Two millennia and more later this is not a role which the term can still readily play. Today the term democracy has become (as the Freudians put it) too highly cathected: saturated with emotion, irradiated by passion, tugged to and fro and ever more overwhelmed by accumulated confusion. To rescue it as an aid in understanding politics, we need to think our way past a mass of history and block our ears to many pressing importunities.

What survived from ancient democracy, for at least the next two thousand years, was not a set of institutions or practical techniques for carrying on political life. It was a body of thinking which its creators certainly envisaged (whatever else they may have also had in mind in fashioning it) as an aid in understanding politics. Its most powerful elements can be found principally in three books, by three separate authors who overlapped with one another in time: the historian Thucydides, and the philosophers Plato and his pupil Aristotle. All three spent an appreciable portion of their lives in Athens itself. None was an open partisan of democracy as a system of rule; and Plato was as harsh a critic as it has ever encountered. But all were

evidently more concerned to understand what democracy was and meant than they were to sneer at it or try to subvert it.[57]

The least explicit of the three in his ultimate judgement, Thucydides, was also in some ways the most informative, and still gives by far the best sense of what the democracy was like in action. (Aristotle's most informative text on ancient democracy was not his systematic treatise the *Politics*, but his historical study of the *Constitution of Athens*, which made little or no attempt to reach an overall assessment of its merits.)[58] It was Thucydides's *History* above all on which the most committed and influential modern interpreters of Greek democracy have drawn for their most evocative evidence of what it was like, from George Grote in mid-nineteenth-century England up till today.[59] Plato and Aristotle make little attempt to convey anything of the kind. For all their differences with one another, each viewed the democracy at work through an elaborate and enormously ambitious conception of what a political regime is, or should be, for. Each, accordingly, judged the democracy of Athens and found it to some degree wanting, because its principal elements and natural operating dynamics laid it wide open to purposes of which they keenly disapproved, and largely closed it to considerations and forces which they valued far more highly.

Much of the continuing political and moral thought of the western world has been a sequence of arguments about what conclusions to draw from these three writers: naturally about many other matters too, but increasingly over the last two centuries about democracy in particular. What claims should we and should we not accept about it? In what respects should we place our trust in it, or decline to do anything of the kind? For far the larger part of this span of time, the conclusions drawn remained more or less sharply negative. Democracy, on the Athenian evidence, was not a set of institutions or techniques for conducting political life in which any community would be well advised to trust. The experience of Athens, no doubt flamboyantly misreported, was grossly discouraging. It was an

experience, too, which had ended in humiliating and permanent defeat. And well before this, less than halfway through its political lifespan, it passed through the long trauma of the Peloponnesian War, staged, by a writer of superlative political intelligence and literary force, as a story of the due punishment of overweening pride, greed and deeply corrupted judgement.[60] Scholars disagree to this day over how far Thucydides was in the end an enemy to democracy itself, and how far he was merely a particularly subtle and clear-sighted analyst of how it operated in Athens over one of its darkest times and in face of its single most unnerving challenge.[61] What is certain is that many later European thinkers read his *History*, as Thomas Hobbes did as he worked through his translation in the anxious decades before England's mid-seventeenth-century Civil War,[62] as the definitive diagnosis of the malignity of democracy as a political regime. To see in Thucydides a case for democracy you had to look for it, as the great Victorian historian George Grote did, with some care. To find that case today is as hard as ever, not least over democracy's suitability as a way of conducting the foreign relations or choosing the defence strategies for a community in immediate peril, as Athens was, and we are sure to continue to be.

But it was not the text of Thucydides which preserved democracy as a format through which generation after generation of Europeans sought to understand politics. What preserved it for this purpose, and kept it durably available as an instrument of practical thought, were the more politically explicit and intellectually demanding texts of Plato and Aristotle. It is not, of course, because Plato so detested it that we have all become democrats today (however sheepishly, however evasively). To reject democracy today may just be, sooner or later, to write yourself out of politics. It is definitely to write yourself more or less at once out of polite political conversation. But there is a deep connection between Plato's open scorn and the salience of this term in all our political vocabularies. The connection is not obvious, and it is far from clear what it means. It does not run from democracy,

either as an idea or in the forms in which the Athenians institutional-
ized and realized that idea, to a set of conclusions which the idea or
its institutional embodiments simply enforce upon anyone. Instead it
runs from the experience of democracy over time, to the occasion
which that experience offered them, and the opportunity which it
provided them, for reflecting more or less accountably with others on
just what it does mean to institutionalize power in one way rather
than another, and seek to realize particular political goals through
one such institutional form rather than another. More bemusingly, it
runs from the drastic force of the conclusions reached about each
question by these two remarkable thinkers. When they gravitated
back to the vocabulary of ancient Greek classifications of forms of
government (democracy, aristocracy, oligarchy, monarchy), what
pulled successive generations of Europeans back, time after time, was
the imaginative tug of these two political assessments.

At face value, Plato's *Republic* is not a book about democracy.
Perhaps, as it says itself, it is principally about justice, or acting as one
should, or about the nature of goodness and why human beings have
sound reasons to try to see that nature clearly and respond to it with
all the imagination and energy at their disposal. It certainly discusses
good and bad forms of government for a city state (*polis*) community,
ending up by defending the exotic conclusion (as implausible then as
it remains to this day) that in the best form of government philosophers would rule. But it at least appears to do so principally in order
to clarify the grounds which every individual human being intrinsi-
cally possesses for living well rather than badly: as they should, and
not as they emphatically shouldn't.

Except in its physical setting and its cast list, furthermore, the
Republic is not obviously even a book about Athens: more a book, in
aspiration, for everywhere, as Thucydides's *History* was to be a book
for all time. But, despite the modest portion of the text devoted to
democracy and what it means, it is no distortion to see the *Republic*
as a book against democracy, and at least in part therefore in the last

instance against Athens precisely because it was so ebulliently a democracy.

There are many reasons why Plato might have disliked democracy, and held his dislike against his own community of birth and residence. It might have been simply a matter of social background, since Plato himself came from one of the grander Athenian families, forced collectively to surrender power to it over the preceding century, very much against their will. He belonged unmistakably in the ranks of the losers from democracy, as the Old Oligarch saw them: *to beltiston* (the best bit).[63] But this must be too simple, since the same was true of Pericles, as it had been of Kleisthenes before him, by no stretch of the imagination enemies to the democracy. It might have been a more immediate matter of personal milieu, the circle of friends, or even lovers, some of whom proved their enmity towards democracy in all too practical and conspicuous ways. It might, more narrowly still, have been a response to the bitter fate of his great teacher Socrates, sentenced by a democratic court to kill himself for his impiety, and for corrupting the city's youth (once more drawn principally, if not exclusively, from its grander families). Probably, it was partly all three. But none of these, not even the judicial murder[64] of Socrates, that primal stain on democracy's honour, does much to explain what Plato held against democracy, what he saw as ineliminably wrong with it.

Socrates himself had been a deliberately disturbing presence at Athens for many decades, before the Athenians at last turned on him and chose to kill him. He disturbed by challenging the terms in which his fellow citizens thought, above all about how and how not to live. As a citizen he carried out every duty required of him (above all on the battlefield) over the course of a long life; and at the end, when only deserting Athens could still save that life, he elected to stay in prison instead and kill himself as ordered, because he had no wish to go on living anywhere else, and saw the very idea of taking flight as the betrayal of a lifetime's commitment to a place, a group of fellow citizens and his deep respect for the community to which he had

belonged throughout that life and striven to serve to the utmost of his own courage and imagination.[65]

This proud choice was the clearest message which Socrates left behind him; and Plato turned it, with whatever embellishments, into a text of singular power, the *Apology*.[66] In so far as Plato's case against democracy was merely a denunciation of the killing of Socrates, that denunciation is carried far more clearly and directly in the *Apology* and the *Crito* than in the *Republic* itself. The Athenians chose to kill Socrates, as far as we can tell, for a number of different reasons. One was the affront which he gave to their religious sensibilities in the hectic conditions at the end of the Peloponnesian War. Another, almost certainly, was his intimate relations with some of those who most harmed Athens during those terrible years: above all with Alkibiades and Kritias. Alkibiades was the glittering, haughty, ruthless orator and general most responsible for launching the disastrous invasion of Sicily, who eventually betrayed his fellow citizens most flamboyantly by deserting to the enemy. Kritias was the most brutal and domineering of the oligarchic leaders who crushed the democracy at the war's close and tyrannized over their fellow citizens, until they too were overthrown in outrage in their turn. These were not, in retrospect, friendships which it was easy to excuse. But Socrates himself was no advocate of tyranny or treason. When Plato set out the lessons which he had drawn himself, in the more elaborate and searching explorations of the *Republic*, what he too offered was in no sense a defence of tyranny,[67] or even of the social, political or economic privileges of the loftier elements in any existing society.

In all its elusiveness and power, that offer centred on a defence of the need for rule and order, and the steady recognition of what genuinely is good, and on an uncompromising rejection of the democracy's claims to provide any of these, except by sporadic and fleeting accident. *The Republic* is a book with many morals. It is also a deliberately teasing book, and open to an endless range of interpretations.

But no serious reader could fail to recognize that it comes down firmly against democracy.[68]

Plato makes many charges against democratic rule, and the way of life which forms around it and arises out of it. He sees it in essence as an all but demented solvent of value, decency and good judgement, as the rule of the foolish, vicious, and always potentially brutal, and a frontal assault on the possibility of a good life, lived with others on the scale of a community. The principle of democratic rule is equality, the presumption that, when it comes to shaping a community and exercising power, everyone's judgement deserves as much weight as everyone else's. That presumption in turn implies that there can be no lasting shape to a democratic community, and nothing reliable about the ways in which power is exercised within it. What this means, as Thomas Hobbes pointed out two thousand years later, is that in a democratic community there can be no real security for anyone or anything except by sheer fluke.[69]

Exactly the same principle applies, with equally calamitous effects, within the individual personality and in the individual life.[70] For the democratic man (the individual personality formed by and appropriate to a democracy) there is neither order nor compulsion (*taxis oute anagke*) in his life.[71] For him it is precisely this shapeless unconstraint which makes a life free and sweet and blessed (*makarion*: the key word of the Beatitudes in the Sermon on the Mount).[72] Plato acknowledges the vitality of this way of life, and sees how enviable its colour and diversity can readily make it.[73] But for him the rage for liberty[74] which accompanies and corresponds to its commitment to equality ('Anyone free by nature could see only a democratic *polis* as fit to live in')[75] will infallibly undermine democratic rule and dissolve every form of authority within it. It disrupts and in the end destroys the ties between teacher and taught, father and son, children and parents, young and old, foreigners (*metics*) and citizens, free persons and slaves, even human beings and animals.[76] Any constraint at all comes to be seen as slavery.[77] The chaos which this unleashes must end

ineluctably in arbitrary rule (tyranny): a precipitous descent from democracy, the height of liberty, to the fullest and harshest slavery.[78]

Plato's assault was not an astute prediction of the democracy's future over the next two generations. It captured nothing of what in due course brought democracy to an end in Athens itself. But it raised the stakes in assessing political regimes to an unprecedented height. Democratic Athens shrugged Plato himself aside without discernible effort. But the challenge which he levelled at the democracy's preferred conception of what it meant remains as potent as ever today, in a world which has chosen to embrace at least the word and some aspects of the idea in preference to any of its innumerable competitors across the ages. How can this of all political ideas in the end make any stable sense? How can it claim allegiance and win loyalty, while it endlessly takes to pieces every other form of order or basis of inhibition around which groups of human beings have tried to organize their lives?

Plato saw democracy above all as a presumptuous and grossly ugly idea, whose demerits could be read clearly in its erratic passage through the Greek world. The chaos of the idea itself was realized in the political disruptions of the communities to which it came, and the disorder of the ways of life which it sanctioned. While not a reliable recipe for the worst life, as tyranny was,[79] it all but guaranteed a bad life to any community that chose to adopt it, and effortlessly subverted every attempt to lead a good life together in close association with a community of others. This was an extreme view, and clearly derived not from careful study of what did or did not occur in many places over a long period of time, but from brooding on the idea itself.

Aristotle, Plato's most gifted and least dependent pupil, had far less confidence in what can be judged about the human world merely by considering ideas in themselves. He set himself as well to assess the merits of contending political formulae by identifying what did and did not occur in most cases in the human world when they were

applied to it. The lessons about democracy which he drew from these enquiries were far more extensive and complicated than Plato's verdict in the *Republic*.[80] They are also far less conclusive in their ultimate implications. Plato loathed democracy and did so without inhibition. Some have seen, in his entire conception of knowledge, a systematization of that overwhelming distaste. Aristotle was more sober, less carried away by his feelings and more open to the judgements of others in the conclusions which he eventually drew. For him democracy (*demokratia*) was not itself one of the good forms of rule,[81] since it amounted to government not in the interest of the community as a whole but merely of the poor (*ton aporon*). But government by the many (*to plethos*)[82] could nevertheless prove a good form of government, provided only that it was exercised for the common good. When he thought it was, Aristotle himself chose to call it not democracy but *politeia* (polity or, more informatively, constitutional government). *Politeia* was distinguished from democracy not merely by a difference in purpose and disposition (a commitment to collective good rather than group advantage), but also by a different and more elaborate institutional structure. The purpose of this structure was not to enforce the will of some upon others at the latter's expense (like oligarchy, or at the extreme tyranny), but to distribute powers and responsibilities as far as possible in accordance with capacities, and thus draw on a far wider range of energies and skills, and elicit a correspondingly broad range of sympathy and loyalty by doing so.

Politeia is not the only form of government which aims at the common advantage[83] and is therefore compatible with justice. Monarchy and aristocracy, the government of a single person or a superior group, might in principle set themselves the same goal and vindicate their claim to justice in so far as they contrived to reach it. But their success or failure depended quite directly on the virtue, discernment and luck of the rulers themselves. Only in the case of *politeia*, Aristotle suggests strongly, does the prospect for realizing

justice in practice in the government of a community depend largely on the institutional organization of power and the resulting division of responsibilities within it.

Aristotle does not seem ever to have supposed, as later followers of Thomas Hobbes or Jeremy Bentham often did, that the institutional organization of power, or the predictable workings of individual interest within it, might somehow furnish dependably just outcomes, without the need to pass through and engage the purposes of human agents, who took justice for their own goal and accepted the constraints which it inevitably imposed upon them. He did not think of political institutions as a substitute for personal virtue, but more as a way of eliciting and sustaining it, and a means for economizing on what might always prove a very scarce good.

Aristotle, it seems clear, did not draw the distinction between democracy and *politeia* from current common usage. He developed it to bring into focus a key contrast. The point of that contrast was to answer two large and pregnant questions: what is the point of human beings living together in substantial numbers? And how exactly must they organize their lives together to best secure that point? The point, as he saw it, was to explore and define together compelling conceptions of how it does and does not make good sense to live, a search that depended profoundly upon language, imagination, and the balance of sympathy and antipathy between human beings; and then, to realize the more compelling of these conceptions to the highest degree possible in the living of real lives. Even as Aristotle himself envisaged it, this proved an open-ended and somewhat centrifugal task.[84] It has lost greatly in imaginative force, and ceded much ground in recent centuries to the very different enticements of the quest to enhance material comforts and multiply personal amusements. But, like the latter, the principal dynamic of our own economic energies, Aristotle's goal too can, without mistranslation, be described as the pursuit of happiness.[85] What is striking for us in how Aristotle saw

that quest is not the value he attached to experience and the will to shape a life, but the extent to which he viewed a system of participatory self-government as an aid in its pursuit, and the peculiarities of the Greek *polis* as a special opportunity for attaining it.

Because of the massive impact of his book *The Politics* on the thought of Europe, and then the world, both idiosyncrasies have proved to matter. The special eligibility of the *polis* as a setting in which to pursue the good life together is an elusive and confusing theme[86] which need not concern us. But the idea that a system of participatory self-government will aid its pursuit provides the central strand of the story we need to follow for most of the next two thousand years. Two elements in Aristotle's view are especially important. One is the far juster and more careful assessment of the merits of government by the multitude, where this is based on the acceptance of a common good, and on some willingness to pursue it together, and where it is also organized in a way that uses the capacities of its citizens and restrains their more malevolent and dangerous characteristics in an effective way. The second, in the end less decisively, but for a very long time every bit as consequentially, was Aristotle's decision not merely to contrast a healthy with a pathological version of rule by the multitude, but also to reserve the term *demokratia* for the pathological version.

The Greek champions of democracy praised and fought for rule by the multitude (*to plethos*), by a broad array of political arrangements. But, unlike Aristotle, they either did not choose to write books, or failed to ensure the preservation of any books which they did write. Their picture and their case have largely passed from the earth, leaving the scantiest traces behind.[87] *Politeia* for Aristotle we might say (using a device of Hobbes) was simply democracy liked, while *demokratia* (democracy to you and me) was democracy keenly misliked. Not only was the word itself marked negatively; still more insistently, it was marked in a way and through a set of thoughts that explained all too evocatively just why it deserved such suspicion.

Democracy in Aristotle's final vocabulary, the vocabulary he eventually handed on to medieval Europe and thus to modern understandings of politics, was a form of government which simply did not aim at a common good. It was a regime of naked group interest, unapologetically devoted to serving the many at the expense of the wealthier, the better, the more elevated, the more fastidious or virtuous. As they took their bearings through the vocabulary which Aristotle had passed on to them, it is not hard to see why generation after generation of European thinkers shied away from this word. Not only was democracy violent, unstable and menacing to those who already held wealth, power or even pretension, it was, Aristotle taught many centuries of European speakers to mean, ill-intentioned and disreputable in itself through and through.

Why then have we now, so recently and yet so completely, changed our mind? (Or, if not our mind, at least our verbal habits, and the feelings which we attach to them?) The first of those questions is blunt, and perhaps not too difficult to answer (though it is hard to pluck a plausible answer off the library shelf). But the second – just what lies behind our selection of the term *democracy* itself as privileged vector for political legitimacy and decency across the globe – is more elusive. To grasp this, we need to see a good deal more than how and why we have reversed the values attached to that word, shifting it back from pejorative to neutral, and then, more tentatively, onward to all but untrammelled enthusiasm. Such shifts in the evaluative connotations of political words occur during most protracted political struggles and often serve to register their outcomes.[88] The real question is not why we feel more warmly towards democracy today, or why our greater warmth has crept into our vocabulary choices. It is why we have chosen, somehow, out of the entire prior history of human speech, this single, for so long so baleful, Greek noun to carry this huge weight of political hope and commitment. Why should we have chosen a Greek word at all? Why should we (that large majority of us who are not Europeans) have chosen a European word? Why

should it be this of all Greek words? Why is it this set of letters and this loose blur of sound on which we have come to place this vast gamble?

No doubt, if we see the matter quite like this, we must be grossly in error, either in understanding what we are doing, or in placing the bet itself. It cannot possibly be sane to entrust the destiny of the species[89] to an arrangement of letters or a set of sounds. But that, of course, is not what we suppose ourselves to be doing. What we believe ourselves to be doing (no doubt correctly enough) is to place our trust in what that word picks out, however vaguely, in the world: in a more or less coherent approach to assigning power and acknowledging responsibility within the ever more complicated network of political, economic, social and legal communities to which we belong and on which we have no real option but to depend.

Democracy has come to be our preferred name for the sole basis on which we accept either our belonging or our dependence. We may not embrace either with joy, or even ease; but, at least on this proviso, these might be communities which on balance we can accept rather than repudiate. It is, above all, our term for political identification: we, the people. What the term means (even now, when that so clearly is not how matters are in the outside world)[90] is that the people (we) hold power and exercise rule. That was what it meant at Athens, where the claim bore some relation to the truth. That is what it means today, when it very much appears a thumping falsehood: a bare-faced lie. Much of the history of modern politics has been a long, slow, resentful reconciliation to this obvious falsehood, a process within which democracy has often proved a far from preferred term for political identification.[91] Across this struggle, with all its swirls and eddies, and stagnant backwaters, the vicissitudes of democracy have often been of negligible importance. There is no special reason to believe that to focus on it will give either clear or economical guidance on what exactly has been at stake or why the battles have come out as they have. Where there has proved to be something very special about

democracy is in the lonely eminence it has now won. In that outcome, however temporary or precarious it may prove, we can see quite clearly, there is something of immense importance which we reasonably can (and perhaps now must) set ourselves to try to understand.

One side of the story, the embrace of this one word, has, for all its intricacy, a single relatively clear shape in space and time. It is, we have already noted, a story with a beginning. It is, too, a story with a single heroine. (*Demokratia* is a feminine noun.) Or, if that seems too literal-minded a way of putting it, a story with a single collective hero, the *demos*, first of Athens and now, potentially, of anywhere in the world where a set of human beings cares to think of themselves as belonging together by right and responsibility, and through and because of who they are.

The other side of the story, the words not chosen, has no shape at all. It has no discernible beginning and no self-identifying sites: not even a definite cast list, let alone a manageable array of heroes or heroines. Much of it, obviously, is too unheroic and inconsequential to bear telling. There cannot be a story of all the myriads upon myriads of unchosen words which fall by the wayside.

We cannot think about the casting aside of potential rivals, or passing them by on the other side, all at once and through a single evidently appropriate structure. Still less can we sift consecutively through all these interminable rejections or evasions in any coherent way. All we can readily do is to recognize the different shapes of enquiry appropriate to these three questions we have already raised. Why firstly a European word? Why secondly a Greek word at all? Why thirdly this of all Greek words?

The main brunt of the answers to the first and third of these questions falls clearly on the last two centuries or so of world history. They are facets of the answer to a very different type of question: why is it that one way of organizing and competing for power, the capitalist representative democracy, has had such overwhelming competitive success over the last sixty years? It was this Greek word, of all

Greek words, because it names something about that now dominant political format which is closely (if perhaps misleadingly) tied to what gave it that awesome competitive edge. It was a European word because, in the end, it was European powers and not China which forged the world capitalist economy, and built the successive empires within and through which that economy was largely shaped, and because, once their power had ebbed, it was the United States of America, very much an heir to the language of European politics, and in no small part built through that language, which stepped commandingly into their abandoned shoes.

To get beneath this somewhat glib level of understanding, we would need to view the history of human life on earth as a single blind amorphous struggle between human beings to get their own way, and see right across it and with steady detachment why exactly the balance of advantage has tilted endlessly towards some and against others along the way. It is not hard to see why the global name for legitimate political authority does not come from the language of the San Bushmen or Evans-Pritchard's Nuer in the Southern Sudan,[92] their homeland now seared by decades of repression. But there is no crisply convincing way to see why it should have been Europe rather than China[93] which made the world a single crowded painful common habitat for our species, and so made Europe's bigotries and parochialisms a global world-historical force, instead of a mere local deformity or a continental stigma. To see the place of the words not chosen we must take many things as given, above all the densely over-lapping histories of capitalism and imperialism, the shapers of the world in which we all now belong.

The odd one out in these three questions is why the privileged European word which has come to enjoy this startling world-historical destiny should have been a Greek word at all. It might have come instead from further north or further east, from a Norse or Teutonic or Turkish language. It might, still more plainly, have come from slightly further west, from the language of Greece's Roman

conquerors, or the later Romance languages which in due course stemmed from these. All of these languages recognize some form of authorization through popular political choice. Some for a time loomed large within Europe itself, and even beyond it in the global struggle for wealth and power. But, whatever would have happened by now if the Third Reich had somehow won the Second World War, only one of these languages looks today like a truly formidable rival, the Latin language of Rome's great empire. That language still gives us a large proportion of our vocabulary of political evaluation: citizenship, legality, liberty, public and private, constitution, republic, union, federation, perhaps, directly or at one remove, state itself.

What it does not give us is the word *democracy*. And that, not because *democracy* does not happen to be a word which the Romans themselves went to the trouble of borrowing. Not only is democracy not a classical Latin word. It is not a Roman way of thought. It does not express how the Romans (any of them, as far as we know) envisaged politics. It is not that the Latin word *populus* (people) is at all a bad translation for the Greek work *demos*. Nor is it that the Romans in no sense conceived the Roman *populus* as the ultimate source of Rome's law, and hence of political authority within Rome. It is simply that they never conceived that *populus* as ruling directly itself, unimpeded, and within a framework of authority which it was permanently free to revise for itself.[94] The unit of political authority in Roman public inscriptions (of which there were many) was the Senate and People of Rome (*Senatus Populusque Romanus: SPQR*). In that formula (and by no means only in that formula), the Senate came first.

There is much else to say on this question, some of it powerfully argued over the last few decades in Oxford and elsewhere.[95] There were, perhaps, other possible futures for the Roman Republic than the military subversion and imperial subjection in which it came to its bitter end.[96] There could perhaps have been another outcome to the struggles of the champions of the *populus*, the brother Tribunes,

Tiberius and Gaius Gracchus, than the political murders to which they succumbed. Perhaps it might even have been possible to keep the Republic in being, alongside the armies with which it conquered most of the world it knew, and for Rome's empire to have been an empire only for the rulers whom it overthrew.[97] For almost fifteen hundred years the political thinking of European communities repeatedly circled back to brood on these possibilities, and try to summon them back into life.[98] But that was not the history which in fact occurred. It was not the history that forged the world in which we live. It has nothing to tell us about why democracy should now be our name for duly exercised political power.

The Romans themselves, as far as we know, never used the term democracy to interpret or assess their own political arrangements,[99] or indeed anyone else's. It was, however, used about them by at least two sophisticated Greek analysts of Rome's historical development as a political community, Polybius and Cassius Dio.[100] Of these two, Polybius was the loftier thinker. He drew systematically on the accumulated resources of Greek political thought to analyse the basis of Rome's rise to mastery over the Mediterranean world and explore its future prospects.[101] In many ways his *Histories* remained, for well over a thousand years, the most systematic attempt to grasp the dynamics of Rome's remarkable rise. In it, Polybius also made some effort to grasp the relations between the basis of this extraordinary ascent and the internal vulnerabilities to which, many centuries later, it, like any other human community, was eventually bound to succumb.

Polybius saw Rome from a singularly instructive angle. Born and raised in a leading political family in Megalopolis, the effective capital of the Achaean League, he was brought back to Italy as a hostage in his youth, following the Roman conquest of Greece in 168BC by the Consul Aemilius Paullus, and lived for decades in close contact with his conqueror's household, for at least part of the time as tutor to one of his sons. That son, Scipio Aemilianus, more than twenty years later, was to be the Roman general who finally defeated

and sacked the city of Carthage, Rome's leading rival for Mediterranean domination for a full century beforehand, and half a century earlier, under its own great general Hannibal, very close indeed to being its final destroyer. Amongst other qualities, Polybius had a fine sense of historical occasion and records with some éclat the tearful response of his distinguished pupil, looking down over Carthage in flames, to the recognition that one day (as it happened over five hundred years later), Rome too would fall for ever.[102]

In some ways the picture which Polybius painted of Rome's political order is now hard to read. Large parts of his text have not come down to us. His book was composed over an extended period of time and, like Aristotle's *Politics*, it probably changed significantly in its central subject matter from the author's point of view in the course of composition. As far as we can judge today, it is also reasonable to conclude that some aspects of his thinking never became entirely clear or coherent. But what is unmistakable is that it seems never to have occurred to him that Rome in the period after it ceased to be a monarchy, several centuries earlier, had at any point become a democracy. Viewed from one of the city's principal political families, suppliers of Consuls for generation after generation, this was not surprising. Like Aristotle, if a trifle less clear-headedly, Polybius fully acknowledged the practical value of a democratic element in the organization of a political community, and in his case more particularly in the organization of Rome's Republic. But, again like Aristotle, he was at pains to insist that this value depended strictly upon its firm restraint by two further elements, aristocratic and monarchical, which restricted power of initiative over many issues, in the Roman case above all to the Senate and Consuls.[103] It would have been extremely odd for a client of Scipio's family to see Rome as a democracy, even if the prospects for its male members to win high political office continued to depend on their capacity to get elected by citizen assemblies.[104]

A simple comparison between the composition, authorization and practical powers of the Athenian Council (*Boule*) and Rome's Senate shows just how implausible any such equation is,[105] as it plainly was to Polybius himself. What is striking, however, was Polybius's judgement, not that Rome already was (or could readily be conceived by anyone as being) a democracy, but that in the long run, and disastrously, it might in due course become one. If and when it did, Polybius warned, that condition could not last long, and must inevitably destroy the city itself.[106] If the flames of Carthage were the portent of a final foreign conquest, a sack of Rome, like Alaric the Goth's, Polybius himself also contemplated the possibility of a purely domestic end to Rome's great journey: the coming of democracy.

At this point in his analysis, Polybius's vocabulary muddied somewhat, and democracy was retitled, following a Platonic precedent, *ochlocracy*[107] (the very worst sort of democracy, the rule of the lowest and most disorderly component of the *demos* or, as the English later put it, the mob). But this was more the deepening of an insult than a refinement in diagnosis. The political structures (*politeia*) which had enabled Rome to conquer most of the world it knew, with its deft, if wholly unplanned,[108] balance of contending elements, might all too readily end in the unrestricted exercise of power by just one of these elements, with a loss not merely of all external restraints upon that power, but also of every internal inhibition amongst those who then exerted it.

Polybius's portrait of Rome disappeared from view completely for a millennium and a half. But before it did so, and when it came back into view in the aftermath of the Renaissance, it could hardly have done less to recommend democracy as a promising regime form to the world at large. Seen through his eyes, democracy was the worst nightmare or the final ruin of by far the most imposing historical model of which any European was even aware: both a symbol and a potential mechanism for the doom of an entire civilization. Who would have thought that this word, of all words, was due to conquer the world?

The word *demokratia* entered the Latin language, as far as we know, in the 1260s, in the translation by the Dominican Friar William of Moerbeke of Aristotle's *Politics*,[109] the most systematic analysis of politics as a practical activity which survived from the ancient world. (It is important for the intellectual history of Islam and the political history of the modern Middle East that it had not already entered the Arabic language, with the very elaborate and substantially earlier reception of Aristotle's thought in the great centres of Islamic civilization.)[110] Once duly latinized, it became available, and has remained so ever since, as an aid in assessing political practices and possibilities. In this guise, it soon proved its utility, less because there was a throng of sovereign democracies to hand to consider, than because, as Aristotle had carefully noted, very different sorts of political regimes may each have some democratic aspects. The self-governing city states of a thirteenth-century Italy had their own conceptions of the purpose of their internal organization and used the Roman language of republican liberty extensively to explain and commend it in all its turbulent variety.[111] Some cities combined relatively broad citizen bodies with elective magistrates and a clear legal framework for the exercise of power. But none of these chose to adopt the new-fangled Greek vocabulary of Moerbeke to vindicate the merits of its own regime. Ptolemy of Lucca, the continuator of St Thomas Aquinas's book *The Rule of Princes*,[112] recognized the second-century BC creation of the office of Tribune at Rome as adding an element of democratic primacy (*democraticus principatus*) to the unmistakably aristocratic primacy in its republican regime, epitomized by the Senate and Consuls.[113] Bartolus of Sassoferrato, a leading civil lawyer writing at much the same time about city regimes (*De Regimine Civium*) and with his eye very much upon contemporary Italy, distinguished, as Aristotle enjoined, between good and bad versions of the rule of a few (*aristocratia* and *oligarchia*) and good and bad versions of the rule of the many (*politia* or *democratia*).[114] But no medieval or early modern

Italian writer bluntly described any Italian city government of which we know as a democracy; and anyone deploying Aristotle's vocabulary in Latin (or any other language into which it came to be imported) could only have been insulting the city in question, by doing so.

It took a good three centuries for the term to recapture some of its Greek descriptive neutrality and simplicity, and shake off the stigmatizing company of its more respectable Aristotelian twin *politeia*. Even once it had begun to do so, *politeia* (polity) at least retained its strong positive connotations: not merely a mixed form of government, which somehow combined the best of monarchy, aristocracy and democracy, but a structure which contrived to constrain democracy in ways which could reasonably hope to keep it on its best behaviour.

Only in the seventeenth century does the term at last begin to shake off these negative connotations and be used, slowly and with much hesitation, to defend and justify existing political arrangements or insist on the urgent need for new ones. It does so in several different settings. The opportunity was clearly there for a Catalan early in the seventeenth century. The Perpignan lawyer Andreu Bosch firmly insisted that Catalonia under its existing constitution with the two core institutions, the Cortes and the Generalitet, was in fact governed on a democratic basis, as, according 'to common law, in all republics and towns, the government simply is the people' (*es lo govern lo poble*).[115] On this occasion the opportunity to describe the regime itself roundly as a democracy does not seem to have been taken up. But, as the century went by, it at last began to be so, most strikingly in the powerful, commercially dynamic and quasi-republican regime of the United Netherlands, in stray places in the tough, disabused writings of Johan and Pieter de la Court,[116] in Franciscus Van den Enden's *The Free Political Propositions and Considerations of State in 1665*,[117] and above all in the deep but obscure reflections of the dissident Jew Benedict de Spinoza.[118]

Even at this point the term *democracy* was far from serving as a rallying cry. In the great seventeenth-century struggles which it is natural for us to see as blazing a trail for democracy, and most of all in the Leveller drive to use a greatly broadened franchise to hold England's government to the active consent of its subjects,[119] the term democracy plays no public role. Where it does begin to appear, more and more insistently, is in anxious conservative responses to the great seething mass of rebellion which shook England's state to its foundations. Thomas Hobbes himself placed the blame for the Great Rebellion and the regicide itself on many different factors, not least the translation of the Christian Bible into the vernacular,[120] the development of Protestant theology and the endless proliferation of priestly ambitions. But pride of place amongst his villains falls to the 'democratical gentlemen' of the House of Commons, puffed up with the cheap and silly learning of the Universities,[121] and giddy with the republican indiscretions of the ancient world.[122]

When Hobbes described the Members of the Long Parliament as 'democratical', he was certainly not using their word, and scarcely providing a fair description of any beliefs which they actually held. But in the long run he was perhaps right to be so confident that he could see more clearly than they did, not merely into the sources of the beliefs and attitudes which they held, but also into the political implications which ultimately followed from them. Perhaps by the time of the English Civil War, and certainly by the time that it became available for recollection in anything but tranquillity, the potential of this pejorative analytical term to pick out potent sources of allegiance was at last in clear view. From then on, its rise to world mastery, at least at a verbal level,[123] was to be just a matter of time. In the centuries since the printing of Hobbes's *Behemoth* (1676), allegiances have come and gone and regimes have risen and fallen. But all the time, and ever more insistently, one word has worked its way forward. It has shaken off its esoteric and shame-ridden past and claimed an open and proud future. This is much more than its due, and a very

poor description of the real basis of its triumph. But it is a striking and consequential enough shift in human experience to require recognition in its own right.

By the beginning of the next century this shift in its apparent powers of attraction becomes easier to pick up. It appears first very much in private self-description. We find, for example, the still relatively youthful Irish Deist John Toland, illegitimate son of a Catholic priest and already author of the widely execrated *Christianity not Mysterious* (1696), boasting in 1705 of his exploits in publicizing the lives and editing the works of James Harrington, John Milton and other advocates of 'democratical schemes of government'.[124] But this was firmly in the context of a private letter, and far from frank even in its own terms. Toland was a figure of disorientating charm and legendary indiscretion, who maddened everyone who had to deal with him, from the loftiest aristocratic patrons to the grubbiest fellow hacks. He was also indefatigable in his own self-advancement and notably unfastidious in the techniques which he was willing to deploy in promoting it. Yet even Toland would have hesitated to proclaim his political allegiances in public with such unflinching clarity.

To see what made the shift possible, we need steadier and franker views. For these, it is hard to do better than turn back to two of the seventeenth century's greatest political thinkers, Hobbes and Spinoza. Hobbes wrote at some length against democracy and did his pungent best to pin down its principal demerits once and for all. He saw it, as his ancient sources encouraged him to do, as disorderly, unstable and intensely dangerous. But he also saw it very much in his own way, as combining much of the insecurity of the state of nature (a condition of comprehensive and standing peril) with a level of mutual offence only conceivable in a setting in which human beings were expected to listen to one another patiently and at undue length. It was a paradise, especially, for orators (or those who fancied themselves as such), and also in effect a form of tyranny by orators: of subjection against one's will to the force for others, not of the better argument, but of the

more potent speech.[125] Hobbes captured better than anyone before or since the pain of oratorical defeat, and the centrality of these feelings within democratic participation for anyone who cares about what is at stake but has no particular oratorical flair:

> *some will say, That a* Popular State *is much to be preferr'd before a* Monarchicall; *because that, where all men have a hand in publique businesses, there all have an opportunity to shew their wisedome, knowledge, and eloquence, in deliberating matters of the greatest difficulty and moment; which by reason of that desire of praise which is bred in humane nature, is to them who excell in such like faculties, and seeme to themselves to exceed others, the most delightfull of all things. But in a Monarchy, this same way to obtain praise, and honour, is shut up to the greatest part of Subjects; and what is a grievance, if this be none? Ile tell you: To see his opinion whom we scorne, preferr'd before ours; to have our wisedome undervalued before our own faces; by an uncertain tryall of a little vaine glory, to undergoe most certaine enmities (for this cannot be avoided, whether we have the better, or the worse); to hate, and to be hated, by reason of the disagreement of opinions; to lay open our secret Counsells, and advises to all, to no purpose, and without any benefit; to neglect the affaires of our own Family: These, I say, are grievances. But to be absent from a triall of wits, although those trialls are pleasant to the Eloquent is not therefore a grievance to them, unless we will say, that it is a grievance to valiant men to be restrained from fighting, because they delight in it.*[126]

The key egalitarian prerogative of the Athenian *demos*, the equal right to address one's fellow citizens as they take their sovereign decisions (*isegoria*), has always been offset by the less agreeable (but accompanying) duty to hear out the persuasions of every fellow

citizen who chooses to exercise it, and by the still more painful duty to accept whatever these fellow citizens together then proceed to decide. Under the conditions of a modern commercial society, the rewards of this egalitarian prerogative were not merely offset but effortlessly outweighed by its evident inconsequentiality for the great majority and by the ever more prohibitive opportunity costs of exercising it. Modern liberty (as Benjamin Constant assured the audience at the Athénée Royale in 1817 in the wake of Napoleon's fall and the Bourbon Restoration), the liberty to do what you like for at least a substantial proportion of your life, now made almost everyone an offer it was all but impossible to refuse. Ancient liberty, the opportunity to do your best to bend the sovereign judgement of your fellows to your own will by pressing your views upon them in public, promised almost nothing in practice. But in the nightmare months of the Terror, the ghost of that ancient promise had raised the temperature of politics to fever pitch.[127] Better a quiet and enjoyable life, even under a monarchy of some absurdity. To pursue ancient liberty under the conditions of modern commerce was to clutch at a mirage, to suffer in return a penal weight of irritation and ineffectuality, and to run in addition a considerable and pointless risk of extreme danger.

As Constant pressed the point in the wake of the Jacobin Terror, it came out as a demonstration of the superiority of modern representative democracy over ancient participatory democracy. In Hobbes's hands, however, the main thrust of the case was still against the dispersion of political power across the adult membership of a political community and in favour, by contrast, of the superiority of monarchy over every other form of regime. Even Hobbes, though, conceded not merely that democracy was a plausible basis on which for political society to have begun, but also that it was in a sense equivalent to the establishment of a political order in the first place. Since a political order can only be created through the choices of individual human beings, it must at its inception simply be their own personal agreement to accept a common structure of authority over

themselves. It was that agreement which made them into a People, a single entity, capable of ruling and exerting authority, and not a mere multitude of quarrelsome individuals.[128]

Once converted into a People and rendered capable of ruling, any People could choose to rule itself,[129] through a 'Councell' of all the citizens with equal rights to vote (a *Democraty*), or to have its rule done for it by 'Councells', where the right to vote was more narrowly restricted (an *Aristocraty*), or by a single person (a *Monarch*). In each of these, Hobbes strikingly insists, the People and the Multitude remain quite distinct.

> *The* People *rules in all Governments, for even in* Monarchies *the* People *Commands; for the* People *wills by the will of* one man; *but the Multitude are Citizens, that is to say, Subjects. In a* Democraty, *and* Aristocraty, *the Citizens are the* Multitude, *but the* Court *is the* People. *And in a* Monarchy, *the Subjects are the* Multitude *and (however it seeme a Paradox) the King is the People.*

For his contemporaries it certainly was a paradox to equate King with People, and a paradox viewed either way round. The equation incensed Charles I well before the People (or those who claimed to act in its name) placed him on trial for his life and took it on the scaffold.[130]

Hobbes was too eccentric a thinker and too independent a person to find tact easy; but he viewed the turmoil of mid-seventeenth-century England from a highly privileged angle, as tutor briefly to the young Charles II at his exiled court in Paris, on tour with a miscellany of young aristocrats of varying educational susceptibility, and as long-term tutor and secretary to the Cavendish family.[131] No one could have mistaken him for an advocate of 'democratical schemes of government'. Spinoza was distinctly less well connected (except with other intellectual luminaries),[132] but, as even Hobbes noticed, if

anything was even less disposed to tact.[133] Born as the second son of a prosperous Portuguese Jewish family in a fine merchant house in the centre of Amsterdam,[134] his worldly prospects were transformed for the worse by the destruction of its extensive foreign business by English maritime predators and Barbary pirates, and ensuing bankruptcy[135] and his own vituperative excommunication from the Sephardic community at the age of twenty-three, for his evil opinions and acts, his abominable heresies and his monstrous deeds.[136] The philosophical basis for these heterodoxies seems to have been laid remarkably early; and it gave him a considerable underground reputation for intellectual originality and incisiveness, which lasted from his late twenties until his death and well beyond. He appears from that time onwards to have lived principally on earnings from grinding optical lenses, with some pecuniary help from his friends,[137] and to have devoted the bulk of his energies to developing a remarkable intellectual system, which set the life of human beings as a whole within the order of nature with unique steadiness and resolution.

The political implications of this system were summarized in two works, the scandalous *Tractatus Theologico-Politicus*, published surreptitiously in 1670 (which cemented his reputation as an atheist by offending every extant religious confession within range), and the *Tractatus Politicus*, left unfinished at his death and published only posthumously.[138] Both texts say many appreciative things about democracy (as well as some less appreciative things). The *Tractatus Politicus* breaks off with a brief (and notably perfunctory) defence of the view that there is no pressing occasion to treat women as political equals. (They have less physical strength; and treating them as equals will aggravate men's already dismaying tendency to inane sexual competition.) But before it does so,[139] it certainly appears on the point of settling down to defend an egalitarian and participatory democracy as the ideal political order. It is not clear quite how this defence would have run, nor how it would have fitted with his earlier acknowledgement that no states have proved less lasting than popular or

democratic ones, and none as apt to be disrupted by sedition.[140] What is clear, however, is that Spinoza abhorred political disorder and fought hard and consistently throughout his life for the primacy of the human need for freedom of thought and expression. This commitment was clearly central to both his major political works; and he was at pains to insist that the need could be satisfied as readily and securely under a sound monarchy or aristocracy as in a democracy, and would pose no more threat to the viability of the former than to that of the latter. Human beings need to think freely and express their thoughts without fear. They also need a clear and effective framework of authority to protect the lives which they live together. Neither need necessarily encroaches on the other, and neither has any clear priority over the other.

Democracy is a state in which sovereignty (the authority to make and repeal laws and decide on war or peace, the key prerequisite for every commonwealth) is exercised by a Council composed of the common multitude.[141] A commonwealth holds and exerts the power of a multitude led as though by a single mind,[142] a union of minds (*animorum unio*) which does not make sense unless the commonwealth itself (*civitas*) aims to the highest degree at what seems, to sound reason, useful for all men.[143] If democratic commonwealths are shorter lived and more disrupted than their aristocratic or monarchical counterparts, the overwhelming verdict of the tradition on which Spinoza drew, this union of minds was scarcely more likely to persist in a democracy. Nor was there any obvious reason why Spinoza should have seen democracies as wedded any more dependably to freedom of thought or expression. All he clearly believed in this respect, like Hobbes and virtually all other natural law thinkers, was that democracy was closest in structure to the basis of all political authority, the universal agreement, whether historical or presumptively rational, of the human beings over whom it was to be exercised. In this sense democracy was, as Spinoza insists in several places, the ultimate source of all political regimes,[144] and in just the

same sense the most natural of all regimes. Democracy, the *Tractatus Politicus* concludes, is the third and completely absolute type of state.[145] In it all children of citizens, all native born inhabitants, and anyone else whom the laws choose to recognize, have a natural right to vote in the supreme council of the state and hold public office, a right which they can lose only through personal crime or infamy.[146] Democracy in this sense is[147] the most natural of regimes. It comes closest to preserving the freedom which nature allows to each human being. No one transfers their natural rights to anyone else so completely that they are never consulted again; but each transfers these rights to a majority of the community to which they belong. 'And so all remain, as they previously were in the state of nature, equal.'[148] In both works the potential disadvantages of transferring these rights to smaller numbers of people or to a single individual are explored in a variety of ways.

Spinoza at no point played a public role in the politics of the Netherlands. The exiguousness of his means and the notoriety of his opinions would scarcely have permitted him to do so even had he wished to. But he was for a time a clear partisan and may even have been a personal acquaintance and potential client of Holland's greatest seventeenth-century statesman, the Grand Pensionary Johan de Witt. On the day when the two de Witt brothers were dragged from prison and lynched by their fellow citizens, an *ochlocratic* moment if ever there was one,[149] Spinoza himself was living just across the town in the Hague. Four years later, he confided in person to the philosopher Leibniz that only his Lutheran landlord's understandable insistence on locking the house up had prevented him from sallying forth the same day to put up a placard denouncing the murderers as utter barbarians, and being promptly torn to pieces himself.[150] Some intellectuals can stretch a point in retrospective accounts of their own heroism on such occasions; but everything we know about Spinoza suggests that, if he said this at all, he can only have been telling the simple truth.

What exactly was he trying to tell his contemporaries about democracy? He was not, quite certainly, seeking to assure them that liberty of thought and expression, for him the most urgent of all distinctively human needs,[151] was any safer in a democracy than anywhere else.[152] He cannot have been telling them that democracy gave them any more solid guarantee of their individual physical security than its more potent rivals. He was scarcely telling them that democracy was a particularly effective form of state in face of armed threats from foreign enemies,[153] let alone boasting, like the English republican Algernon Sidney,[154] of the superior capacity of any form of republic, democratic or otherwise, to level armed threats of its own at everyone else. The clearest practical merits which he ascribed to it were in direct comparison with the competing state forms which had supplanted it throughout the civilized world: aristocracy and monarchy. While no inhabitant of the Netherlands during Spinoza's lifetime as an adult could have seen his judgement that democracy was more at home in peacetime as a practical advantage,[155] they could perhaps have seen some connection between the military advantages of its more successful competitors and their uglier domestic political consequences. Spinoza was no rhapsodist of democracy's edifying spiritual impact on the ruling *demos*; but he was an acute and forthright critic of the corrupting effects of personal power upon aristocrats and monarchs, a subject matter on which there was then considerably more extensive and recent evidence. It is hard to see in his ultimate verdict, broken off abruptly,[156] any clear claim for the superiority of democracy on grounds of security or liberty (then, as now, the most evocative bases on which to vindicate a political regime). What there is, and what can only have disconcerted as cool a political judge as Johan de Witt,[157] was a consistently disabused view of the limitations of every form of government and a sharp assertion of the special tie between democracy and equality.

The significance of that tie is still as hard to judge after over three centuries of practical exploration. But the tie itself goes back to the

beginning and lay at the heart of the vision and practices which the Athenians evolved to realise and secure democracy.[158] The relation of freedom or liberty to any state form can be specious (at the mercy of persuasive definition, or brazen mendacity). In every state, freedom and liberty by necessity must be defined in the end, however intricately and courteously, on the state's terms and by the state itself.[159] But equality, whatever equality lurks in nature itself (the way we simply are, irrespective of what subsequently happens to us) does sound like an external limit to the state's claims, and perhaps even ultimately to its powers. If democracy expresses human equality (whatever equality comes with simply being human) better than any other regime could, then that might well prove, sooner or later, a comparative advantage of some weight. Perhaps in the end it might come to seem a *decisive* advantage?

But can a state really express equality? Is not a state the most decisive and, at least in aspiration, the most permanent erasure of equality? And one backed, too, by an effective monopoly of the means of legitimate violence? How can whatever equality lurks in nature itself survive within a structure of uniform and relatively effective subjection, in which some in the end will always be deciding who is to be coerced by whom, and others in due course carrying out the coercion required? How can equality be more than a cruel dream in a world in which some own and control and consume vastly more resources than others? How can it be so when they own and control these resources on a basis which, unless ceaselessly and skilfully overridden, ensures that the inequality re-creates and magnifies itself into an indefinite future?

What we affirm today, when we align ourselves with democracy, is hesitant, confused and often in bad faith. It becomes less convincing, almost always, the more clearly we bring out the premises which lie beneath our own values and the more openly we acknowledge the realities which make up the institutions which we take them to commend. Where we have become clearer, more frank and more

confident as time has gone by is in what we deny when we take our stand on democracy. Above all what we deny is that any set of human beings, because of who or what they simply are, deserve and can be trusted with political authority. We reject, in the great Leveller formula, redolent of England's seventeenth-century Civil War, the claim (or judgement) that any human being comes into the world with a saddle on their back, or any other booted and spurred to ride them.[160]

C h a p t e r   T w o

DEMOCRACY'S SECOND COMING

As it entered the eighteenth century, democracy was still very much a pariah word. Only the most insouciant and incorrigible dissidents, like John Toland or Alberto Radicati di Passerano,[1] could take their political stand upon it, even clandestinely or amongst intimates. Anyone who chose to do so placed themselves far beyond the borders of political life, at the outer fringes of the intellectual lives of virtually all their contemporaries. Yet, within a century, something had changed decisively. We can pin down with some confidence where the change first became apparent. What is harder to judge is what caused it to occur.

What brought democracy back to political life, late in the eighteenth century, was two great political crises on either side of the North Atlantic. The first arose in the mid-1760s amongst the set of British colonies in North America which had never fallen under French rule; the second, some two decades later, in metropolitan France itself. The two settings could scarcely have been more different. The thirteen British colonies which chose to revolt formed as fluid a society and as dynamic an economic milieu as any in the world, opening out on to a vast and still largely unknown (if far from

uninhabited) landscape.² *Ancien régime* France (as it soon came to be called) was the proudest and most self-consciously civilized state in continental Europe, locked in a century-long struggle with England for world mastery. It was the epitome of absolute monarchy, the formidable heritage of the Sun King Louis XIV; but its haughty rulers found themselves challenged increasingly by an assertive society, ever more suspicious of their political intentions and ever less reconciled to their own effective exclusion from political choice. In America's War of Independence, France threw its military and diplomatic weight behind the revolting colonies. For a time these two arenas meshed, leaving by its close a new nation and a high water mark for France's naval and military triumph, but also a burden of governmental debt which neither the organization of France's economy nor the structure of its state was equipped to handle. Six years after the war ended, France too found itself in revolution, a domestic struggle so drastic that it gave the world a new and uniquely disruptive political conception – the modern idea of revolution itself – that spilled irresistibly across the continent of Europe and beyond.

The two crises differed in their causes, their rhythms and their outcomes; but each has marked the history of democracy ever since in indelible ways. The term democracy played no role at all in initiating the crisis of the North American colonies, and no positive role in defining the political structures that brought it to its strikingly durable close. Where it featured at all in the language of America's political leaders in the course of their great struggle, it did so most consistently and prominently as the familiar name for a negative model, drawn from the experience of Athens, of an outcome which they must at all costs avoid. Only in retrospect, as America's new constitution was put to work and the new nation went on its way, did the perspective alter sharply. When it did so, the familiar practices of England's own representative government, above all the election of a key body of its legislators (in North America, usually on a far broader franchise than in most English parliamentary constituencies), found

themselves rechristened in the language of the ancient world. Once they had been so, Americans began to see themselves, in the mirror of their protracted colonial past, as having long been democrats already without knowing it. The classic rendering of that picture was given not by an American author but by a young French aristocrat, Alexis de Tocqueville, writing some half a century after America's independence, and explaining the Americans not merely to his fellow countrymen and European contemporaries but also to themselves, more insinuatingly than anyone else has ever done before or since.[3] The key to America's experience as Tocqueville saw it was also the source of its exemplary force in due course for every other future human society across the globe, the pervasiveness throughout its ways of life and forms of awareness of the brooding presence of democracy itself. In Tocqueville's book *Democracy in America*,[4] we find for the first time the recognition that democracy is the key to the distinctiveness of modern political experience and that anyone who hopes to grasp the character of that experience must focus on and take in just what it is that democracy implies.

America's Revolution was an anxious response to a widely perceived threat to liberties long enjoyed, the very liberties which, as time went by, were to form the evidence for its protracted democratic past.[5] Once those liberties had been successfully defended, or won back by force of arms, the constitutional order which the Americans constructed to secure them in future came in retrospect to seem a uniquely clear-sighted exercise in thinking through the requirements for political liberty and implementing the conclusions of this remarkably public process of deliberation. Nothing quite like it had ever occurred before; and no subsequent episode in constitution making has fully matched the acumen in diagnosis shown by the new nation's political leaders, still less the remarkable longevity of the remedies on which they settled. Ninety years later William Ewart Gladstone, Queen Victoria's great and infuriating Prime Minister, described the product of their efforts as 'the most wonderful work ever struck off at

a given time by the brain and purpose of man'.[6] In the aftermath of America's savage Civil War, the grimmest evidence of the limits to diagnosis and to remedy, this was a generous assessment. But it scarcely conveyed the levels of effort, the range of participants, or the fluster and animosity of the process of decision-making which had made it possible.

The Constitution was initially drafted in a secret Convention held in the city of Philadelphia between May and September 1787, through an elaborate process of manoeuvre and bargaining.[7] The resulting draft was first made public on 17 September 1787, and put to the twelve State ratifying Conventions, for their approval or subsequent emendation. For the next ten months it was debated publicly State by State. By July of the following year, all but North Carolina and Rhode Island had duly chosen to ratify it. During the opening session of the First Congress which met under its auspices, between March and September 1789, as Revolution accelerated in France, two fundamental elements were added to it. A Bill of Rights, the first ten Amendments to the Constitution, drafted by James Madison on the basis of scores of recommendations from the individual State Conventions, was sent back to the States for their approval; and a Judiciary Act, creating the Federal court system, and endowing it with the requisite powers, was passed by the Senate.[8]

The most intense phase in this process followed the initial publication of the Constitution. It involved not merely the 1,500 delegates to the State ratifying Conventions, who worked over its entire text, but a volume of public and private discussion, in pulpit, newspaper press and personal correspondence, which reached across the entire nation.[9] Through this hubbub of assessment and argument, one text in particular now looms with extraordinary authority. It appeared at the time as a series of anonymous newspaper articles by three already prominent political figures, James Madison, Alexander Hamilton and John Jay. Hastily written week by week, and barely co-ordinated between the three authors, whose views differed appreciably from one another,

it intervened boldly and effectively in the ratification debate. The case which the *Federalist* made for the merits of the new system of government, while it failed to convince a great many amongst its immediate audience,[10] rapidly became the barely disputed rationale for the basis of America's Republic ever since. It was a case for the need for, but also for the safety of, a strong central government, which could raise revenues, control naval and military forces, and sign treaties with foreign powers like any other state, but do so in a way which posed no threat to the personal liberties which the Americans had won back at such peril from their former colonial masters.

The case for America's Revolution had been exaggeratedly simple: that unrestricted power was a mortal threat to personal liberty, and that Britain's imperial government was moving deliberately and with some energy to dismantle all restrictions upon its power. More than half of the *Federalist* was written by Alexander Hamilton,[11] one of the most economically sophisticated of America's leaders and uniquely sensitive to the commercial and strategic threats and opportunities which it was sure to face in the centuries to come. But the essays which have given the *Federalist* its unique authority were not written by Hamilton. Their author was the shy, diligent, unabrasive elder son of a Virginia planter, thirty-six years of age as the Constitutional Convention opened in Philadelphia, James Madison. By May 1787[12] Madison had played an active part in America's struggle against Britain and in the tangled politics of the new nation for over eleven years. He brought to the Federal Convention an elaborate set of proposals on how the American Confederation, with its single-chamber Congress, could be reconstructed as three independent branches of government, with a two-House legislature with distinct responsibilities, elected on contrasting bases of representation.[13] The first delegate to reach Philadelphia from out of State[14] and one of the very few present on the day when the Convention was due to begin, Madison, together with his colleagues from the Virginia delegation, seized the opportunity of this forced

interlude to draft a fifteen-point Plan of Government around which all subsequent debate revolved. Characteristically, he also set himself, once the Convention formally opened, to the enduring gratitude of historians, to take a full record of its debates.[15] His main purpose in doing so was to ensure his own grasp of an extraordinarily complicated and consequential agenda. The Plan of Government was not the work of Madison alone; and the constitutional draft which emerged from the Convention's deliberations clashed in places with some of his strong convictions. But in his steady, patient, unhistrionic and wonderfully thoughtful way he did more than anyone to give it its ultimate shape.

The central purpose of that shape he set out and defended with exemplary clarity in the most celebrated of all the *Federalist Papers*, number 10, echoing the arguments of a letter composed a month earlier to his fellow Virginian and close friend, Thomas Jefferson, drafter of the Declaration of Independence. The tenth *Federalist* sets out a remedy for the violence of faction, the key weakness of popular governments[16] and source of the 'instability, injustice and confusion' which plague their public councils, 'the mortal diseases under which popular governments have everywhere perished' and 'the favourite and fruitful topics' of the adversaries to liberty. Faction cannot be eliminated except by eliminating liberty itself. Its latent causes are 'sown in the nature of man', in the variations in human faculties, the contrasts in the ownership of property, and the consequent divisions of society into different interests and parties. The sources of party identification are endlessly variable; but the most potent and consistent of them is the 'various and unequal division of property'.[17] The propertied and those without property 'have ever formed distinct interests in society'. (The immediate back-cloth to this perception in 1787 was the issue of whether to honour or repudiate the vast debts, always to individual creditors, which every American State had run up in the course of winning its independence.) How were these sharply opposed interests to be balanced justly against one another?

The causes of faction, Madison was very sure, cannot be removed. All that could reasonably be hoped for was to control its effects.[18] A minority faction could provoke endless trouble; but within a republican government it ought never to find an opportunity to impose itself through the law. Where a faction forms a majority, however, popular governments give it every opportunity to sacrifice both the rights of minorities and the public good to its own passions and interests.[19] The key challenge to popular government was to secure both public good and private rights against the threat of a factious majority, without at the same time sacrificing the spirit and form of popular government. (A 'pure Democracy', Madison insisted,

> a Society, consisting of a small number of citizens, who assemble and administer the Government in person, can admit of no cure for the mischiefs of faction. A common passion or interest will, in almost every case, be felt by a majority of the whole; a communication and concert results from the form of Government itself; and there is nothing to check the inducements to sacrifice the weaker party, or an obnoxious individual.[20]

That is why such democracies have always been so turbulent and contentious, have always proved incompatible with personal security or property rights, and 'have in general been as short in their lives, as they have been violent in their deaths'. Theoretical partisans of democracy, accordingly, have had to presume, in Madison's view absurdly, that reducing men to perfect political equality would at the same time render them perfectly equal in their possessions and uniform and harmonious in their opinions and passions.

In place of that perilous project of levelling and homogenization, Madison offered a different model which promised to provide a cure for the ills of democracy: 'a Republic, by which I mean a Government in which the scheme of representation takes place'. A Republic in

Madison's sense differed from a pure Democracy in several ways. 'The two great points of difference between a Democracy and a Republic are, first, the delegation of the Government, in the latter, to a small number of citizens: secondly, the greater number of citizens, and greater sphere of country, over which the latter may be extended.' The Union of American States covered a vast territory and took in a very substantial population. It required a scheme of government which could encompass both in a way that 'Democratic Government' plainly could not. It was compelled to choose, therefore, a relatively small number of representatives to act on behalf of a very large number of citizens; and this very selectivity, Madison optimistically assumed, would ensure the quality of the representative so chosen. The scale of its territory and the size of its citizen body would create a wider variety of parties and interests, and lessen the risk of majority coalitions intent on encroaching on the rights of other citizens. Even where such coalitions did arise, the need to operate politically on a far larger stage would itself impede the co-ordination of surreptitious and plainly disreputable policies. Religious bigotry, 'a rage for paper money, for an abolition of debts, for an equal division of property, or for any other improper or wicked project' are far less likely 'to pervade the whole body of the Union' than they are to infect a particular State, just as they are more likely to taint a particular county or district than an entire State.[21]

The extent and structure of the Union, therefore, could and would provide 'a Republican remedy for the diseases most incident to Republican Government.'[22]

Three and half months later, in *Federalist* 63, Madison returned to this judgement, qualified one aspect of it but reaffirmed its central element. The principle of Representation formed the pivot of the American Republic.[23] There were elements of representation even in the purest of Greek democracies, in the election of public officials who held executive power.[24] 'The true distinction between these

communities and the American Government' was '*the total exclusion of the people in their collective capacity* from any share' in it,[25] not the comprehensive exclusion of popular representatives from the administration of the *polis*. Successful representative government would have been impracticable in these small and all too intimate communities. But on the scale of the American Union, the evident need for it could and would provide it with enough political support for it to operate with sufficient calm and for long enough to make its solid advantages very clearly apparent.

Even though we use the term democracy so differently today, the force of Madison's insistence on the total exclusion of the people in their collective capacity from any share in the American Government still comes as something of a shock. For Madison himself, however, it was the clearest evidence how unlike the democratic city states of classical Greece the new state which he was struggling to defend really was, and the proof that it, unlike them, was not a democracy at all. In his vocabulary, as in Plato's or Aristotle's, a people totally excluded in their collective capacity from the government of their community could not conceivably be thought to rule it directly themselves. What controlled it in the end was the will of the majority of its citizens. But immediate control over it rested somewhere quite different. Whatever else the new American state might or might not be called, it could not properly be termed a democracy.

A representative government differed decisively from a democracy not in the fundamental structure of authority which underlay it, but in the institutional mechanisms which directed its course and helped to keep it in being over time. These depended for their effect not solely on the legal precision with which they had been defined ('parchment barriers against the encroaching spirit of power'),[26] but also and more decisively on the practical relations between them and the political energies on which they could hope to draw. In a democracy, 'where a multitude of people exercise in person the legislative functions, and are continually exposed by their incapacity for

regular deliberation and concerted measures to the ambitious intrigues of the executive magistrates', the threat of tyranny might come principally from the executive. But in America, the principal threat came from the legislature, the threat, as Jefferson had put it in his *Notes on the State of Virginia* three years earlier, of 'elective despotism'.[27]

As the Americans moved towards Revolution in 1774, John Jay, a young New York aristocrat, and in due course co-author of the *Federalist* and future Secretary of State, described them with pardonable exaggeration as 'the first people whom heaven has favoured with an opportunity of deliberating upon and choosing forms of government under which they should live'.[28] At this stage the opportunity seemed exhilarating, and the risks associated with it (in stark contrast to those of defying the British) relatively negligible. If the term *democracy* carried no particular inspiration, it held little or no immediate menace. Even such a hardened political sceptic as John Adams felt confident that 'a democratic despotism is a contradiction in terms'.[29] The new State constitutions redrew the boundaries of electoral districts to make them more equal, insisted on annual elections, widened the suffrage, imposed residential requirements on electors and representatives alike, and empowered constituents to instruct their representatives.[30] In doing so, they reinforced and sharpened a key contrast between American and British experiences of political representation, with the Old World emphasis on historical continuity, the sovereign unity of a single community, and the symbolic and virtual character of the links between represented and representer discarded firmly for an insistence on actuality, choice, consent, and an ever fuller and more equal participation.[31]

In the immediate aftermath of the Constitutional Convention this process of deliberation and choice was still very much in train; and there were no surviving public advocates of a less participatory or egalitarian basis on which to approach it. What had become drastically more salient were the risks of failing to reach a firm conclusion,

and the substantial contribution which democracy itself could and almost certainly would make to aggravating those risks.

At this stage the Americans had in essence four options. They might have chosen to repudiate the most democratic elements in their new state, the uniquely prominent place which it gave its free male population for wide popular participation in conditions of near political equality in framing and taking public decisions. In continental Europe, even a century later, there were still many prominent (and sometimes powerful) defenders of this response; and between the two World Wars, in Europe and also in Japan, Fascist governments sought to implement some aspects of it, with devastating consequences at home and abroad. But in America, with the defeated Loyalists fled to Canada or across the Atlantic, it had no surviving public advocates.

They might also, as Madison noted, have chosen instead to press the principle of political equality (still confined to males, and still juxtaposed with little apology to a very substantial slave population) boldly forward, so that it clashed with and overrode the claims of property, abolished debt, redistributed large land holdings and remade a society to be equal all through. Here too, at this point, there seem to have been no advocates amongst the Americans for this more drastic, and potentially equally destructive, alternative.

More realistically perhaps, they might also very readily have failed to choose at all, recoiling from any strengthening of the central power of America's new state for fear that this must re-create the alien and always potentially tyrannical structure from which they had just escaped at such a high cost. In effect this would have been the immediate practical upshot of the victory of the Antifederalists, a passive acceptance of the existing forms of government, as these had already emerged under the Articles of Confederation, with no effective overarching structure between the individual State governments.

The option they chose, in broad outline the option which Madison and his fellow authors pressed upon them, was embodied in the new Constitution, as this survived the ordeal of ratification and amend-

ment, and then of implementation in Washington's first Presidency. That option gave the Americans, and in due course the world, a great deal. It failed to reconcile a regime of political liberty (at least for men) with the widespread ownership of slaves, a reconciliation effected only partially even three-quarters of a century later in the convulsions of Civil War. Even today there is as little agreement as ever over how far that reconciliation has since been carried, or what hope remains that it will ever be completed. What is certain is that the option taken in 1787 has conspicuously failed to eliminate the egalitarian impulse from America's continuing political imagination. But it has given that impulse a distinctive cast, rendering it far less vital, insistent or prominent an element within the American imagination than it has proved in most other societies across the globe over the following two centuries. It secured the new Republic extremely effectively, and, as we now know, for a very long time. In doing so, it turned the United States into the most politically definite, the best consolidated and the most politically self-confident society on earth. It also, over time and to the vast prospective gratification of its raffish and impatient Secretary of the Treasury, Alexander Hamilton, opened the way for it to become overwhelmingly the most powerful state in human history.

When Madison looked back on the making of the Constitution in his old age,[32] evoking 'the distracted condition of affairs at home, and the utter want of respect abroad' which surrounded its birth, he still saw every reason for pride in 'a constitution which has brought such a happy order out of so gloomy a chaos'. No human government could eliminate the risk of the abuse of power. But America's federal republic, on the evidence of over a third of a century, had cut those risks to a bare minimum.[33] It had not done so by embracing the claims of democracy without reservation; and Madison himself shows little sign of warming to the term in later life. But he did recognize how deep the inroads of the new conception of democracy now were, and how futile it was to resist them openly. By the early

1820s, property qualifications for the suffrage, which had seemed so obviously benign at the time of the Convention, had become a point-less anachronism.[34] A more obdurate conservative like Chancellor James Kent of New York might still not hesitate to argue overtly for their key role in taming 'the evil genius of democracy'.[35] But for Madison by this point, where a propertyless majority threatened a propertied minority, this was not a danger which could appropriately be handled by excluding that majority from the franchise. To exclude a majority from the suffrage 'violates the vital principle of free government, that those who are to be bound by laws ought to have a voice in making them'.[36] It also establishes a basis for governing which was certain in practice to destroy any free government: 'it would engage the numerical and physical force in a constant struggle against the public authority, unless kept down by a standing army, fatal to all parties'.[37] Instead, Madison placed his hopes, over and above the internal restraints of the Constitution he had done so much to create, on the ameliorative impact of education. In its sobriety, his conclusion had much in common with the verdict, delivered fifteen years earlier by the prominent architect Benjamin Latrobe, in a letter to Jefferson's Italian friend Philip Mazzei: 'After the adoption of the federal constitution, the extension of the right of Suffrage in all the states to the majority of the adult male citizens, planted a germ which has gradually evolved, and has spread actual and practical democracy and political equality over the whole union.'[38] The results were undoubtedly impressive: 'the greatest sum of happiness that perhaps any nation ever enjoyed'. But they did have their costs: 'our state legislature does not have one individual of superior talents. The fact is, that superior talents actually excite distrust.' This general erosion of deference and social distinction had 'solid and general advantages'; but 'to a cultivated mind, to a man of letters, to a lover of the arts', he noted frankly to his equally fastidious correspondent, 'it presents a very unpleasant picture'.[39] Henry James was waiting in the wings.

What presented this distasteful picture was a democratic politics become wholly routine, an entire way of political life, with its own logic and its own all too pervasive culture. Once become in this way a matter of routine, democracy might still be threatened by the bitter struggle between South and North over slavery, or perhaps even by the depths of the Great Depression almost seventy years later, seismic pressures on the foundations of the social order or the economy which sustained it. But, within politics itself, democracy had come to dominate the landscape. It faced no surviving rivals and was seldom under much pressure to reflect on its own nature, let alone defend itself against a real challenge to its ascendancy. For Americans, from then on, it filled the horizon of politics; and anyone who chose to reject it publicly simply rendered themselves politically impotent. In America, the battle for democracy, as Americans had come to understand it, was won effectively by default, even if much of its substance had been won much earlier and with much effort under very different names.

It was in Europe, late in the eighteenth century, that the term first figures in the speech of political actors, struggling to transform a state, and seeking to explain the basis on which they were planning their strategies and coming to understand the implications of their goals. In this guise it made its initial entry, sporadically and very much on the margins, in the Patriot Revolt which revitalized the faded political life of the Dutch Republic in the 1780s. At the outset this revolt was diffuse in its goals and more than a little confused in its political strategies.[40] But between 1785 and 1787 a number of the Patriot leaders at times shook themselves free of the hallowed squabbles between the wealthy urban oligarchs and the House of Orange, which reached back to the origins of the United Netherlands, and set out a novel and consciously egalitarian political platform.

The institutional key to the most radical aspects of their challenge lay in the urban popular militias of the Dutch Provinces, the

Free Corps,[41] which met in regular assemblies from December 1784 onwards, usually in Utrecht.[42] As the far from egalitarian Patriot leader, Baron Joan Derk van der Capellen tot den Pol, noted: 'Liberty and unarmed people stand in direct contradiction';[43] and by December 1784 the Patriot movement had taken up arms. At the peak of the movement, a delegate of the Delft Free Corps proclaimed ringingly:

The Burgher, dear comrades, no longer wanders in the shadows. He can show himself fearlessly in the light of our fiercely breaking dawn. The Sun of his freedom and Happiness shines more strongly from hour to hour, and we can assure you on the most powerful grounds that before she reaches her zenith there will be no more Tyrants of the People to be found in this land. The Armed Freedom will blot out their very name.[44]

The Provinces of the Dutch Republic split bitterly between Patriot and Orange parties. By 1787, suppressing the Patriot movement required the intervention of a Prussian army, despatched to rescue Princess Wilhelmina of Orange, a Hohenzollern princess who had had the temerity to set out to travel to the Hague to raise the Orange flag and the misfortune to be apprehended en route by the Gouda Free Corps, and treated brusquely and with some indelicacy by her irritated captors.[45] By September 1787, the Prussian forces, under the command of the Duke of Brunswick, had restored the rule of the Stadholder at the Hague; and by 10 October, the last bastion of Patriot resistance, the city of Amsterdam, surrendered to him.

The Patriot movement did not at any point define itself as a movement for democracy. Its goal, in so far as it had a coherent and common one, was to establish a constitutional order for the Dutch Provinces which represented their inhabitants at large, and freed them from the control of a potentially oppressive Orange monarchy, or a

wealthy and entrenched urban oligarchy, equally intent on usurping the people's powers.

In seeking to define a less oppressive and more appropriate form of representation for the Dutch nation, the Free Corps leadership found themselves on at least two occasions adopting a position which it was entirely natural to describe as democratic. The third Free Corps assembly, held in June 1785 in Utrecht, drew up an act of Association,[46] pledging its participants to defend a true Republican constitution to the last drop of their blood, to restore the lost rights of the burghers and to strive for a 'People's government by represen- tation [*Volksregierung bij representatie*]'. A few weeks later, a Free Corps assembly in the Province of Holland adopted a still more revo- lutionary manifesto, the Leiden Draft. Its preamble stated boldly that: 'The citizens of a State, above all of a Republic founded on Liberty, confer this on each of them, head for head... Liberty is an inalienable right, adhering to all burghers of the Netherlands commonwealth. No power on earth, much less any power derived truly from the people... can challenge or obstruct the enjoyment of this liberty.' Its Articles affirmed the sovereignty of the People, the responsibility of elected representatives to their electors, the absolute right of free speech as foundation for a free constitution, and the denominationally impartial admission of all citizens to the militia (the effective coercive guarantee of their continuing freedom). Taken together, they formed a compelling expression of 'the ideas of a Republican popular sover- eignty'.[47]

In the aftermath of its military suppression, the Patriot movement was soon caught up inextricably in the international political and military maelstrom of France's great Revolution. As it disappeared into this swirling chaos, its presumptive heir, the Batavian Republic of 1795–1805, shed any trace of national autonomy and came to seem a mere puppet of the French state in the latter's rapid metamorphoses. At its nadir, the Emperor Napoleon was rude enough to describe the Netherlands as an alluvium washed down by 'the principal rivers of

my empire'.[48] But the Dutch themselves naturally retained a keener interest in their domestic disagreements. As they strove to define these more clearly, they found themselves increasingly attracted to a vocabulary drawn largely from Paris. In the course of these efforts, *democracy* and *democrat* won an unprecedented prominence in Dutch political programmes and identities. By 1795 Amsterdam boasted a leading newspaper *De Democraten*, and a political club whose goal was the winning of a '*democratisch systema*'. By 1797 France's own Directory was assuring its Holland agent that what the Dutch wished for was a 'free and democratic constitution'. In January of the next year, a third of the members of the Dutch Constituent Assembly duly signed a petition for 'a democratic representative constitution'; and in the succeeding month a committee of the same assembly unwisely boasted to the French agent that the Dutch were 'capable of a greater measure of democracy than would be suitable to the French'.[49] By this point, aristocrats had long surrendered the centre of the stage. But in Holland, as in France itself, it had been *Aristocrats* who first served to define a political grouping, well before *Democrats* could come to do so. In 1786 Gijsbert Karel van Hogendorp, a long-term partisan of the House of Orange, described his country in French to a correspondent as troubled by a cabal, which people say 'is divided into aristocrats and democrats'.[50] Van Hogendorp himself was certainly by Dutch standards very much an aristocrat, even before he became Pensionary of Rotterdam in 1787. He moved in elevated circles; and it was his son who provided the immediate stimulus to Princess Wilhelmina's ill-judged escapade.[51] He was also a practised caballer in his own right, and was still intriguing vigorously on behalf of the Orange cause at the time of the Orange restoration a quarter of a century later.[52] But in 1786 his perspective on Dutch factional squabbles still aspired to be external, detached, cosmopolitan and sophisticated: a painstaking exercise in political judgement. It was not itself a political act; nor was it cast in terms intended as either domestic or distinctively Dutch.

The first setting in which the term democrat does appear incontestably as a pole of domestic political affiliation in Europe's (or the world's) modern history was not in one of the more advanced states, economies or societies of the continent (in Holland, France or Britain), but in what is now Belgium and was then the Austrian Netherlands. The provinces of the Austrian Netherlands, all subject to the Austrian Emperor, formed the southern half of the Low Countries which Spain contrived to reconquer after the sixteenth-century Revolt of the Netherlands. As a result of that reconquest, and in drastic contrast to the Provinces which got away, it was still solidly Catholic, and effectively excluded from international commerce by the closing of the river Scheldt to sea-going traffic, enforced by the terms of Dutch independence. Within it, the Church dominated political and economic life to a remarkable (and somewhat stifling) degree, making it a virtual 'museum of medieval corporate liberties'.[53] The Dutch Patriot refugees who fled across its borders in 1787, as the Duke of Brunswick reimposed order, found it 'backward, superstitious, priest-ridden and oligarchic'.[54] Belgium's awakening from its political slumbers came very much from the outside, and in response to the spirited reform initiatives of the Emperor Joseph II, the archetype of the Enlightened Despot. Joseph first set himself, with characteristic vigour, thoroughness and lack of tact, to reform the penal law by abolishing torture, to rationalize the activities of the Church (dissolving a number of religious houses, regulating pilgrimages and the timing of popular festivities), challenging the guild monopolies, deregulating the terms on which masters could employ labour, and opening up public offices to non-Catholics.[55] In 1787, he went on, more drastically, to reorganize the entire administrative and judicial system of the Provinces. This was seen across Belgium, accurately enough, as an assault on the old order, and duly resented as such. The nobles of Alost, unabashed aristocrats to a man, complained forcefully that: 'Our right to judge is our property, Lord Emperor. We do not hold it by grace, but have received it from our fathers and bought

it with blood and gold. It should not be taken from us against our will.'[56] The lawyers of Brussels, less grandly but no less cogently, remonstrated that they had paid good money to secure the positions they held, and done so, and laboured to acquire the knowledge needed to discharge their responsibilities, in the confident expectation of supporting their wives and children on the proceeds.[57] Their rights to do so rested on the historical foundation stone of the Province's liberties, the celebrated *Joyeuse Entrée*, issued by the Duke of Brabant over four centuries earlier in 1355.

Late in 1788 the Estates of Brabant and Hainault refused to pay taxes to the Emperor, and Joseph II responded by repudiating, over four centuries since its initial proclamation, the *Joyeuse Entrée*.[58] The two main leaders of the revolt, Van der Noot and Vonck, were each Brussels lawyers. Van der Noot was wealthy and at least related to the aristocracy, Vonck the son of an appreciably poorer farmer. Van der Noot assailed the Austrians in an incendiary pamphlet, but promptly fled abroad and busied himself with unavailing efforts to persuade the House of Orange to intervene and reunite the Netherlands. Vonck drew the moral of Brunswick's brisk suppression of the Dutch Patriots, and set himself instead, along with a group of Brussels friends, to organize a secret society *Pro Aris et Focis* (For Altars and Hearths), to co-ordinate groups of youthful volunteers to travel abroad for military training, and link these to a clandestine network of sympathizers within Belgium itself. Vonck attracted many followers across the entire range of Belgian society, from the abbots of the wealthiest monasteries to the grandest of the secular nobility.

On 18 June 1789 Joseph responded by dissolving the Estates of Brabant and annulling the *Joyeuse Entrée*. By this time France's own Revolution was well on its way and the Estates General had begun to meet in Versailles.[59] Only the day before, the representatives of the Third Estate proclaimed themselves the National Assembly.[60] In August, Revolution broke out too in the Prince-Bishopric of Liège,[61] and young Vonckists flooded across the frontier to prepare themselves

for the armed struggle. In practice, little struggle was required, since the Austrian authorities gave up without a fight in one province after another. The network of urban revolutionary committees which Vonck had established set itself to reconstruct the patchwork of medieval liberties as a single sovereign national government. Vonck's allies in this task 'were called Vonckists by their enemies, but democrats by themselves'.[62] These enemies, unsurprisingly, included not only the earlier followers of Van der Noot, but also most of the major beneficiaries of the established order, with the great Abbot of Tongerloo now prominent within their ranks:[63] 'The abbots as a group represent the secular and regular clergy, and indeed they represent the whole rural country as well, being the largest landowners; and, finally, usage has always been this way, and should remain so, since it is constitutional, and the Constitution cannot be changed.'[64]

It was an unequal fight. The Vonckists found themselves tarred with the menace of France's Revolution, especially after March 1790, when many of their leaders were arrested, and the remainder, with numerous of their followers, found themselves forced to flee into exile in France itself. They also found themselves portrayed, not entirely erroneously, as catspaws of the new Austrian Emperor Leopold II, whose reform plans, if less draconic in style than those of Joseph II, were every bit as out of sympathy with the hallowed customs and whimsical privileges of Brabant. Neither alignment was reassuring to the foreign champions of the other; but the two together, however inconsistent the combination, were more than enough to unite a large majority of the Belgians against the Democrats. In June 1790, in a rehearsal for the bloodily suppressed counter-revolutionary rising in the Vendée three years later,[65] the parish priests of rural Brabant roused their devout peasant congregations by the thousands, and marched threateningly, week after week, into the centre of Brussels, carrying the insignia of their threatened faith, and brandishing an unnerving array of agricultural weaponry.[66] Vonck himself, who came from just such a parish, had

never thought it wise to adopt a public programme for the democratic reconstruction of Belgium as a state. His followers did not see
themselves as democrats, because they had chosen from the outset to
pursue a clearer and more extreme version of France's national
reconstruction. They did so because the immediate enemy they faced
was a far denser and an even more arbitrary array of aristocratic
privileges than those of France's first two Estates, and because this
enemy was backed by much wider popular support than their French
equivalents proved able to draw on. In Belgium, as in Algeria a little
over two hundred years later,[67] a democratic outcome chosen by a
majority of the adult inhabitants would certainly not have meant the
establishment and consolidation of a secular and democratic
republic. The *pays réel*, given the opportunity, would have voted any
such democracy down without a moment's hesitation. No one
thinking through the implications of the Vonckist movement and its
fate in retrospect could possibly have inferred from it that the cause
of democracy was destined to sweep the world.

To see why democracy faced that future, we certainly need to bear
in mind its fate in North America over the next century, and the
majestic rise of America's economy under its aegis. But, beyond the
Americas, the impact of these experiences on the politics of other
countries was still quite modest until the First World War, and did not
really come into its own until the aftermath of the Second. Before
then, democracy's unsteady dispersion across the world was no testimony to American power, and not much even to the force of
American example. If anything, it testified, rather, to one of two
things. It might be evidence of the intrinsic power of democracy itself
as an idea (odd for a political term which had not even begun its life
as a conception of the politically desirable, and which had long served
to label the quite evidently politically undesirable). More plausibly,
but still quite puzzlingly, it might instead be testimony to the force of
another and far more obtrusively ambiguous historical example, the
awesome Revolution which overwhelmed France.

What happened in France in the few short years between 1788 and 1794 changed the structure of political possibilities for human communities across the world almost beyond recognition. It did so, for reasons we still very vaguely comprehend, both radically and permanently. Even when it was over, with Robespierre's overthrow in Thermidor in 1794, or Napoleon's rise in Brumaire 1798, or on the plains of Waterloo, quite close to Brussels, in 1815 when Napoleon fell for the last time, it left a different conception of what politics meant, a new vision of how societies can or must organize themselves politically, and a transformed sense of the scale of threat which their own political life can pose to any society and all within their reach. It was within this new conception that democracy forced itself, slowly but inexorably, upon one community after another. It made these inroads, once again, not through its prominence in the speech of the Revolution's leading actors, or through the names adopted to pick out political groupings, factions or institutions. Those names – Jacobins, Girondins, the Mountain, the Left – all had their own history. Some, in due course, cast lengthy shadows over distant corners of the world. But none of them ever competed, even momentarily, for the role of world-wide basis for political legitimacy; and none ever offered a comparably firm standard for political authority to live up to. The democratic legacy of the Revolution was very much the product of its intense and often devastating political struggles. But it was no echo of its public symbols,[68] nor of the language in which those struggles were openly conducted. Only at a handful of points was the category of democracy deployed explicitly to define what was at stake within them, and even then only once at the storm centre of the struggle itself. Only in retrospect, as the most detached and analytical categories through which Europeans had striven for centuries to grasp what politics means and why it operates as it does were set to work to fathom just what the Revolution as a whole really had meant, did democracy slowly begin to emerge as its central issue, and do so in its own right and under its own name.

At this point, it linked back to one of the most intriguing visions of France's political predicament earlier in the century, the *Considérations sur le gouvernement ancien et présent de la France*.[69] The *Considérations* was the work of a prominent aristocrat, René-Louis de Voyer de Paulmy, Marquis d'Argenson. D'Argenson came from a long line of royal officials, and his father had been the Paris chief of police.[70] He served himself in several elevated positions, most notably as Minister of Foreign Affairs. But he was too brusque and too independent to be a practised courtier; and in many of his loyalties and much of his social imagination he was a traitor to his order. The *Considérations* was first published, anonymously and from a highly imperfect manuscript, in 1764.[71] It set out a plan for the political reconstruction of France which D'Argenson had already advanced as early as 1737, and which he for long hoped to persuade the King to permit him to carry out himself in the role of First Minister. In manuscript form, and subsequently in print, it had, as his son boasted in a Preface to the greatly augmented second edition twenty years later, left its mark on most of the great French political works from the middle of the century onwards: the Physiocrats, Quesnay, Mirabeau, Montesquieu, Turgot, Rousseau, Mably.[72]

D'Argenson's plan was a striking expression of the *thèse royale*, the perspective on French government, economy and society which saw in an enlightened monarchical reform the best hope for reshaping and rationalizing France as a state and society, and serving the interests of its people as a whole.[73] But D'Argenson approached the task of reform, as the title of his manuscript made clear,[74] not by seeking merely to restructure the royal administration, but by asking himself 'how far democracy could be admitted into monarchical government'. This was scarcely the sort of question calculated to win cheap popularity at the court of Versailles. In later decades, as the royal government clashed with its principal constitutional courts, the Parlements, D'Argenson at points modified the sharpness with which he sought to exclude the aristocracy from the strategic niches

which enabled them to obstruct royal power.[75] But what marked him out throughout his political life was the extent to which he believed it essential to introduce democratic procedures and institutions into the way in which France was governed. What made these procedures indispensable, in his eyes, was less the difficulty of enforcing the common good through a purely monarchical structure of power, or any prospective divergence between the interests of the monarch and those of his people, than the sheer difficulty of locating what the common good was in the first place. For this latter task, democratic institutions and procedures enjoyed unique advantages. He put this point with particular clarity in his (equally unsuccessful) submission for the Academy of Dijon's 1754 prize competition which elicited Jean-Jacques Rousseau's *Discours sur les origines de l'inégalité parmi les hommes*. Nature

> *is divine and dictates to us only laws which are easy to execute. But you must listen to her to follow her; she makes herself heard only among equal citizens and friends. In these conditions, contradictory interests control and conciliate themselves, sharpness softens, difficulties are levelled [s'aplanissent] by what is evident, and the common good discovered. It is thus from equality alone that good laws come to us. It is through the assembly of men equal among themselves that their implementation [manutention] can be assured.*[76]

In the Plan of the New Administration which D'Argenson proposed for France,[77] the public good, the supreme law, was to guide a well-organized monarchy, with the aid of a well-understood democracy which in no way encroaches upon royal authority.[78] This left very little room (and no need whatever) for an intermediary power between king and people.[79] D'Argenson argued that the sole inconvenience of democratic authority was that it was too divided to make itself obeyed. It must therefore be regulated and directed by a single

spirit which bears upon the entire body of the state but has no interest aside from the general interest. Such was the role of royal authority.

The role of democracy was to enlighten the sovereign, who, as all French monarchists stoutly maintained, had no interest of his own apart from those of his people, and so no motive for betraying them,[80] but who could all too readily fail to ascertain what their interests were. Any sovereign therefore needed the help of his subjects to identify which of their interests were truly common, just as urgently as the people in their turn needed to be aware of one another's judgements to distinguish particular interests from the general good. Nowhere did the monarch need this aid more urgently than in the assessment of the level and distribution of taxation, an ever more contentious issue as the costs of global military and naval conflict mounted inexorably, and the government's debts rose precipitously along with them.[81] Under D'Argenson's Plan, the administrators who set the tax levels in every district of France must be chosen from then on from men who resided and owned property within the district, by majority vote and through secret ballot.[82] They were to be subject annually to renewal or replacement at elected Assemblies of the district. Besides offering a belated political basis on which to meet France's spiralling fiscal crisis, this democratic choice of administrators would also help to intensify French agriculture, ensuring that all land was cultivated by its owners.[83]

In itself, D'Argenson's conception of democracy was conventional enough: 'Democracy is popular Government, in which the whole people shares equally, with no distinction between nobles and commoners.'[84] He distinguished in the classic fashion between true and false democracy:

False Democracy rapidly falls into Anarchy. It is the Government of the multitude, as when a People revolts. Then the insolent People scorns the Laws and reason. Its tyrannical

Despotism shows itself in the violence of its movements, and by the uncertainty of its Deliberations.

True Democracy acts through Deputies, and these Deputies are authorized by the election of the People. The mission of those chosen by the People and the authority which supports them constitute the public power. Their duty is to insist on the interests of the greatest number of citizens to protect them from the greatest evils and secure them the greatest goods.[85]

On the first appearance of his book in 1764, D'Argenson notes at this point that a democracy of this kind was, or should have been, the Government of the United Provinces. By 1784 he (or more probably his son) felt free to replace this assessment by the bold claim that the only true Democratic States in Europe at the time were the popular cantons of Switzerland.[86]

D'Argenson was an unabashed monarchist. He fully accepted the French monarchy's exclusive commitment to the Catholic Church, whatever his reservations may have been over the manner and timing of Louis XIV's Revocation of the Edict of Nantes and subsequent persecution of the Huguenots. For him democracy was a valuable adjunct to the monarchy, not its rival or potential replacement. But he differed sharply for most of his life from theorists of mixed government, then or earlier, who saw the political aftermath of European feudalism as a system of government uniting monarchical, aristocratic and democratic elements in careful balance against one another, and savoured, to varying degrees, the restraining influence on royal wilfulness of the intermediary powers of the aristocracy. In France this meant above all the *noblesse de robe*, who staffed the French constitutional courts and saw themselves as the dedicated custodians of the laws.[87] For D'Argenson the crying need of the French monarchy was not restraint but guidance; and neither aristocracy nor Church had the least capacity to provide that guidance in a dependable form.

D'Argenson was a frustrated monarchical reformer, who feared that a French monarchy left unreformed must collapse in chaos in the relatively near future. Although he had been dead for many years by the time that it did, his picture of its fundamental flaws was notably acute, and his sense of what was likeliest to hasten its end uncommonly prescient:[88]

> *If ever the nation were to recover its will and its rights, it would not fail to establish a universal national assembly [une* Assemblée nationale universelle], *dangerous to royal authority in quite a different way. It would make it necessary and always in being. It would compose it of great lords, deputies of each province and of the towns. It would imitate in every respect the Parliament of England. The nation would reserve legislation to it and would give the king only a provisional* (provisoire) *right to implement it.*

What broke the monarchy in the end was its own political clumsiness and bad luck, a wholly unpredictable succession of maladroit Ministers, failures of nerve, vagaries of judgement, and sheer mishaps. But what placed it within reach of catastrophe was less any special infirmity in the person of the reigning monarch, or even the acute unpopularity of his Austrian wife, than the obstinacy, conceit and ruthlessness of D'Argenson's key adversary, the French nobility, the order from which he came. France's Revolution was a revolution against aristocracy well before it turned against the incumbent monarch. As far as we know, none of its prominent native actors[89] was a convinced democrat (either in their own vocabulary or in ours) until well after it had unmistakably broken out. Even those who did most to foment it, like the Abbé Sieyes himself,[90] for long championed its democratic elements solely as complements to the continuing and effective authority of its monarchical government.

As with the making of America's Constitution, what drove the reconstruction of the French state was the crippling burden of war debt, and the political challenge of finding a basis on which to discharge it without openly repudiating it. In America what this principally required was the design of a system of government safe from capture by irresponsible enemies of property, a firm barrier to democracy's most notorious weakness, or to what D'Argenson called 'False Democracy'.[91] But in France the immediate obstacle to handling the debt effectively was the very partial and obstructed fiscal reach of the royal government and the elaborate tissue of exemptions, province by province and order by order, which served to limit it. All these exemptions were a matter of law, in most cases law of many centuries' standing. As they faced a government forced to live ever more desperately beyond its means, every one of them was a kind of privilege, a special form of legal immunity, or private legal right to elude the law as it bore on other French men or women. France was not a single kingdom, with one law for all its subjects. It was a vast archipelago of overlapping jurisdictions and endlessly differentiated statuses, all fiercely defended, and all at least pretending to centuries of antiquity. It defied systematic comprehension, let alone coherent excuse, every bit as obdurately as the customs of Brabant had defied Austria's reforming Emperors.

The two most prominent blocs of privilege belonged to the Church and the nobility, the First and Second of the three Estates, who, in the understanding of virtually all France's population who interested themselves in such questions, made up the French Nation. Neither Church nor nobility was ranged solidly against the interests of the royal government, let alone the French Nation. Between the year of America's Independence and 1789, each provided leading Ministers who struggled to persuade their recalcitrant fellows to surrender at least some of their tax privileges in order to bring the debt back under control. But Church and nobility both firmly refused, in one setting after another, to comply with these proposals.

The Ministers, noble or ecclesiastical (or in one case both), soon fell; and by August 1788, France's increasingly anxious King, Louis XVI, found himself forced to turn once more to a Minister who was neither a noble nor a Prince of the Church, indeed not even a French subject, the Genevan Protestant banker Jacques Necker.[92] More disconcertingly still, and even before his hapless Minister Loménie de Brienne had handed in his resignation, Louis found himself compelled to agree to summon the Estates General of France, for the first time for a full century and three-quarters. Brienne himself epitomized the political limitations of the *ancien régime* at the end of its tether. Archbishop of Toulouse at the time of his appointment, he had had the conspicuously poor taste to take advantage of his position to arrange for his own transfer to the considerably more remunerative Archbishopric of Sens; and his tactless and indecisive handling of the Provincial Estates greatly aggravated suspicion of the royal government throughout France.

Because it had not met for such an immense span of time, no one knew quite how to summon the Estates General, even once the decision had been taken; and no one could be certain quite how its members were to be selected, let alone what they would be commissioned to concede or demand. No one even knew what forms it would meet in once its members did duly assemble. Brienne himself belatedly recognized the need to fix the procedures for the election of its members, invited evidence and opinions on how it had last been, or should now be, constituted, and lifted the censorship, so that the answers could be properly considered. The result was overwhelming.

Throughout France, in the months from July onwards, busy archival research in one place after another probed into the question of how things had been done back in the distant days of 1614, with varying and confusing results. Every rank in French society was to be invited to take part in one forum or another, whether, like the grander aristocracy or the bishops, in the select company of their peers and

with some hope of commanding attention for their views, or in the local rural assemblies in which even those of the peasantry with the nerve to take it were to be given their brief say, and permitted to cast their votes, before the outcome was filtered upwards. In each setting, lists of grievances (*cahiers de doléances*) were drawn up, as preconditions to the acceptance of any fresh taxes needed to refloat the French Treasury, or bargaining counters in the allocation of the new tax burden amongst different groups of the population.[93]

Amidst all this excitement, and the spontaneous optimism which it both prompted and reinforced, one particular public decision sharpened the inchoate contours of social and political interest and redefined suddenly the muddled struggle between nation and royal government as an open confrontation between the Third Estate and its two privileged counterparts. One of Necker's opening acts as First Minister was to reconvene in September 1788 the Parlement of Paris, the principal institutional challenger to royal authority in recent decades, summarily evicted only four months earlier from its ancient role of registering the public law of France and all royal edicts which covered the whole kingdom, in favour of a judicial body appointed by the King himself. Only two days after its triumphant return to Paris, the Parlement gave its decisive verdict on how the Estates General must meet: in the forms of 1614, as three distinct Orders, and with the Third Estate having no more and no fewer representatives than each of the other two. Two months later Necker reconvened the Assembly of Notables to see if they could be persuaded to reverse this outcome, with equally little success, and was able to secure a doubling in the number of Third Estate representatives only by a decree of the Royal Council at the end of December.

By this time the damage was well and truly done.

The Parlement's decision ensured that the population of France would be forced, as never before, to choose between the accumulated routines of its long past and a vital attempt to redefine itself, through political choice, as a single national community fully

equipped to assume responsibility for its own security and destiny. Many able and well-placed figures throughout France held huge stakes in that past. Like the monarch himself, every French subject was deeply inured to seeing in it the source and basis of much of what made life worth living, and the ground of every practically serviceable right which they were fortunate enough to enjoy. But very many of them had also come to have at least a shadowy aware-ness that this way of viewing their lives over time made imperfect sense, and that it had a certain obvious shabbiness and absurdity to it. The crushing burden of the debt, the manoeuvres of the old regime's beneficiaries to shirk responsibility for meeting it and the debilitating squabbles over who was most to blame for the steady worsening in the predicament of both government and nation focused on the nobility, the Church and eventually on the Monarch himself, an unprecedented weight of ideological odium. In the end all three buckled beneath it. For the next five years, through turbulent political exploration and struggles, intense legislative deliberation and enactment, and bitter civil and international warfare, the French nation set out to endow itself with a new legal identity. It also set itself to design and implement a fresh set of institutions through which to live together without either ignominy or absurdity, and on a basis which guaranteed liberty and security to all its citizens. It remains almost as hard to see that convulsive effort clearly and calmly today as contemporaries found it at the time. The attempt to reconstitute France as a society and a state through political action was often nightmarish in its consequences, and as cruel, hypocritical, muddled and disorientating as the very worst abysses of the *ancien régime*. It ended, on its own terms, in failure: military dictatorship, a *parvenu* empire, and, a quarter of a century later, in the reluctant restoration of the dynastic monarchy. Before it had done so, it devastated the continent of Europe and ruined the lives of countless millions of its inhabitants. (Think of the imagery of Goya's *Disasters of War*.)[94]

But the same attempt to reconstitute France through political action also in due course defined a new universe of political and legal practices for every other human society across the globe, with the single and glaring exception of the United States of America. Many of those societies have yet to be forced to submit to its requirements. But none of them, not even Britain, France's global military, political and economic rival, which did most of all to bring the Revolution to its exhausted close, has since been able consistently to ignore it.

Given the depth of the nightmare, and the awesome impact of the Revolution's blood-stained wars, some of the models drawn from it, inevitably, were negative rather than positive – precedents to avoid or catastrophes to insure against at virtually any expense. Revolution and counter-revolution were born together, and have proved, as Edmund Burke promptly warned,[95] practically inseparable ever since. It is hard to tell whether the unintended consequences of the attempt to reorganize a society rationally for the benefit of its members have had any shallower an impact than the more edifying of the political goals which its leaders adopted and pursued in their uniquely conspicuous setting. The harms which it perpetrated over time did not stem solely from excess of audacity on the part of its partisans. They issued just as forcibly from the galvanizing effects of that audacity on its more obdurate enemies, and on the political entrepreneurs who traded in their fears. If Robespierre and the Terror looked forward to Stalin and Mao Tse-Tung and the vast famines which each unleashed, they also gave the cue for the extremities of struggles to arrest or reverse the threat of revolution for more than two centuries to come, to Fascism, the Third Reich, and perhaps even truly Islamic revolution.

One figure did more than anyone else to draw the battle lines and unleash the Revolution. Emmanuel Joseph Sieyes was a surprising candidate for the role, and in many ways ill-equipped to finish what he had started.[96] He was not one of the Revolution's great orators like Mirabeau or Danton, who could hold sway over the Assembly for a

time by the sheer power of their words; nor did he have Robespierre's gift of assurance in arranging to have his political enemies killed. Forty years old when the Estates General was summoned, Sieyes had earned his living from within three years of his ordination by serving as secretary, first to the Bishop of Tréguier in Brittany, and then, following his patron's fortunate posting in 1780, to the far wealthier and less secluded see of Chartres, with its majestic cathedral and ready access to Parisian intellectual and political circles.[97] Once in Chartres, Sieyes became in turn vicar-general of the diocese, a canon of the Cathedral and in 1788 Chancellor of the Chapter. He also began to make his mark in a variety of the Church's representative bodies.

In 1788, under the pressure of events, he wrote in quick succession three striking pamphlets. The first to be composed (though last to be published) was a relatively cool and systematic analysis of how the Estates General could now best set about rescuing France from the deep quagmire of its political past: *Views of the Executive Means Available to the Representatives of France in 1789*. It drew extensively on the many years of careful reading and hard thinking which Sieyes had devoted to working out the political needs and opportunities of the highly commercialized society which France, like Britain, had long been. Behind it lay close study of what he called 'social mechanics':[98] the contribution of some of the most powerful economic, social and political thinkers of eighteenth-century Europe, and most decisively of all of Adam Smith. Sieyes's key insight was the shaping influence throughout this novel kind of society of a radical division of labour, guided above all by the single criterion of effectiveness.

This was not in itself an evidently democratic line of thought. Indeed, for Plato, over two thousand years earlier, it had served as the central ground for rejecting democracy en bloc for its brazen indifference to the demands of justice: 'distributing a certain equality to equals and unequals alike'.[99] But for Sieyes, far from flouting these demands, a political order could be dependably just or effective, if and only if it

viewed and treated the human beings who made it up as equal bearers of rights, and organized itself to protect and benefit every one of them. Sieyes was as alert as Adam Smith[100] to the need for authority in any human community; but, like Smith, he believed that a state could hold its authority legitimately only by dint of meeting the needs of its own subjects. This did not make him a democrat, any more than it made Smith one. For Sieyes, democracy was neither a rhetorical rallying cry, nor a favoured political paradigm. (Neither, given its long history, could it have been one of his characteristic neologisms, deployed, like the interminable coinages of Jeremy Bentham, to pin down the shadowy worlds of politics and law with new clarity and precision, if seldom widely taken up by anyone else.) But, if Sieyes was no democrat, he was no simple enemy of democracy. Even in *Views of the Executive Means* he insisted robustly, as D'Argenson had done before him, on the need for every legislature to be refreshed by the democratic spirit,[101] and on the consequent need to minimize the number of levels which separated the inhabitants of the local communities who made up the nation from the successively elected representatives who would in due course legislate on their behalf. It was the scale of France as a society which necessitated an elaborate structure of representation: 'In a community made up of a small number of citizens, they themselves will be able to form the legislative assembly. Here there will be no representation, but the thing itself.'[102] Representation serves efficiency; but it also carries great dangers:

> *every human association has to have a common aim and public functions. To carry out these functions it is necessary to detach a certain number of members of the association from the great mass of citizens. The more a society advances in the arts of trade and production, the more we see that the work connected to public functions should, like private employments, be carried out less expensively and more effectively by men who make it their exclusive occupation.*[103]

Sieyes plainly viewed public administration as a thoroughly worthy employment for the talented; but it is less obvious that he had any clear conception of what a career in electoral politics was likely to involve. One point which he certainly did grasp, however, was that those who carry out this work, in whatever form, readily develop an interest of their own, which may be sharply at odds with those of their fellows. They come to see their role as a right and an item of property, and no longer as a duty to others. When they do, they dissolve the bonds of political community and establish a form of political servitude.[104] France as it was in 1788 was less 'a nation organized as a political body' than 'an immense flock of people scattered over a surface of twenty-five thousand square leagues'. To turn it into a politically organized nation, what it needed was not to probe into its murky and benighted past.[105] It was to heed the lessons of reason, draw boldly on the recent findings of social mechanics, and endow itself, all too belatedly, with a sound constitution, the sole means which could guarantee citizens the enjoyment of their natural and social rights, consolidate the elements in their common life which worked for the better, and 'progressively extinguish all that has been done for the bad'.[106] In the remainder of his pamphlet Sieyes set out carefully just how the Estates General must view and organize itself to provide France at long last with that constitution, and do so without allowing itself to be sucked back into the political whirlpool of the debt which had prompted its summons in the first place.

Unlike the *Views of the Executive Means*, the first of Sieyes's pamphlets to reach the public, in November 1788, the *Essay on Privileges*, was an immediate response to the Parlement of Paris's fateful September decision and an open call to arms. In his bitter tirade against the claims of privilege,[107] Sieyes broke openly with the nobility of France as an order and set himself to demolish the entire edifice of conceit and pretension which held its world together. The very idea of privilege (the basis on which the first two Estates held their formidable powers of political obstruction) was lethal to any

good or happy society. The essence of privilege is to place its possessor 'beyond the boundaries of common right',[108] either an exemption from the prohibitions on wrong action which face every other citizen,[109] or the gift of an exclusive right to do what the laws would otherwise leave open to anyone. 'All privileges... from the very nature of things, are unjust, odious, and contrary to the supreme end of every political society.' Not only was privilege deeply wrong in itself, it was also profoundly corrupting of all who benefited from it. Privilege was not an honourable quest to earn the admiration of fellow members of society; it was a constant spur to insolence and vanity: 'You ask less to be distinguished *by* your fellow citizens, than you seek to be distinguished *from* your fellow citizens.'[110] It was a secret sentiment and an unnatural appetite, 'so full of vanity, and yet so mean in itself', that all who feel it seek to cloak it in feigned concern for public interest. The idea of country, in the heart of the privileged, 'shrinks to the caste to which they belong'. They come to seem to themselves 'another species of beings'.[111] This apparently exaggerated opinion, while in no way implied in the idea of privilege itself, 'insensibly becomes its natural consequence, and in the end establishes itself in all minds'. The effects were ludicrous, turning the imaginations of the nobility endlessly back towards a distant and ever more practically irrelevant past. They were also intensely pernicious, fomenting an *esprit de corps* and a relentless party spirit within their ranks.[112] The inheritance of privilege broke any possible link to desert,[113] and left its presumed beneficiaries to a life of intrigue and mendicity, of 'privileged beggary', at the expense of their fellow citizens.[114] It nurtured also in the scions of the nobility formidable skills in this ignominious competition for self-advancement. The inevitable result was to spread the corrupting example – 'the *honourable* and *virtuous* desire of living in idleness and at the expense of the public'[115] – throughout society.

The third, and far the most famous, of Sieyes's trio of pamphlets appeared next, in January 1789, turning this tirade into an open

programme of revolution, and handing on to the young Karl Marx half a century later the classic formula for revolutionary consciousness.[116] We do not really know quite what gave this forty-year-old cleric his visceral hatred of aristocratic pretension. It may have reached back to his childhood as son of a minor royal official in the modest Provence township of Fréjus. It may have been nurtured later, in the course of his reluctant training for the priesthood in the Parisian seminary of Saint Sulpice, a career for which many besides Sieyes himself subsequently noticed his drastic lack of vocation. (As a boy he strongly preferred the prospect of life as an artillery officer or mining engineer.) What we do know is that, when he came to express it definitively in public early in 1789, the resulting text lit a fuse which raced across France. A year earlier, no one would have been likely to find 'What is the Third Estate?' evocative as a title, or even especially stimulating as a question. By January 1789 the summoning of the Estates General had made it the political question of the hour.

It was Sieyes's answer to that question which turned political crisis into Revolution. As they entered 1789 the first two Estates were still very much the fair sisters, pride and glory of a long and singularly self-assured history.[117] The Third Estate was at most their drabber and more nebulous adjunct, the Cinderella of France, with its claim even to belong to the same family eminently in doubt.[118] Both the first two Estates had a conscious solidarity, a sense of collective identity, a commitment to that identity and a confidence in its own power, dignity and worth. To enquire 'What is the First Estate?' was to ask how to see and understand Christianity itself, and the Church which embodied and interpreted it on earth. In France at least, that Church was well organized to answer the question on its own behalf, and free to draw on the resources of a long history of self-consciously continuous thought and devotion and a practised fluency in political self-assertion. To enquire what the Second Estate was was to ask how to view Nobility, again a question with many centuries of rhetorical effort devoted to working up flattering answers, if for the most part on

the basis of distinctly less strenuous intellectual exertion. In his *Essay on Privileges*, already, Sieyes had highlighted the imaginative fragility of this carefully cultivated tradition of self-regard. In *What is the Third Estate?*, he turned the tables decisively on his smug and over-bearing antagonists, and set out a quite new basis for political authority in what was already a very old state. He began, notoriously, by giving an astonishing answer to his title question. The Third Estate, he proclaimed brashly, is 'Everything'.[119] Up to then, in the existing political order of France, it had been 'Nothing'. It had carried no polit-ical weight, and received no formal recognition. The King's Ministers and the Privileged Orders had acted in its name and on its behalf, if at least presumptively for its benefit. In doing so, they had not been, as they fondly imagined, displaying a generous and attentive paternalism. They had simply usurped powers which legitimately belonged to it, and robbed it of the place which was its rightful due.[120]

To survive and prosper, a nation requires private employments and public services.[121] It must work the land, manufacture everything which its inhabitants require, and distribute these products to their eventual consumers. It also requires a huge variety of personal services from the loftiest to the most menial.[122] At present all the most rewarding and honorific of these services are monopolized by the first two Estates. But there is not a single one of them which could not perfectly well be provided by the Third. Already the latter carries out all the really hard work, while receiving virtually none of the honour. The Third Estate contains 'everything needed to form a complete nation'.[123] It is 'Everything; but an everything that is fettered and oppressed. What would it be without the privileged order? Everything; but an everything that would be free and flourishing. Nothing can go well without the Third Estate, but everything would go a great deal better without the two others.' The exclusion of the Third Estate from every post which carries honour is 'a social crime' against it.[124] It reflects a 'state of servitude',[125] which, however long it may have lasted, can only have arisen in the first place from conquest

and can no longer be sustained against a people which 'is strong enough today not to let itself be conquered'.[126]

> *They may try in vain to shut their eyes to the revolution which*
> *time and the force of things has brought about: it is real for all*
> *that. There was once a time when the Third Estate were serfs*
> *and the nobility was everything. Now the Third Estate is every-*
> *thing and nobility is only a word. But beneath this word, a new*
> *and intolerable aristocracy has slid in, and the People has every*
> *reason not to want any aristocrats.*[127]

The political consequences are clear. The nobility has separated itself from the rest of the nation and made itself a people apart.[128] Its insistence on exercising its political rights on its own has made it 'foreign to the Nation by virtue of its principle, because its mandate did not come from the people, and second, by virtue of its object, since this consists in defending, not the general interest, but particular interest'.[129] The aristocracy monopolize high office in army, Church and magistracy. They form a caste which dominates every branch of the executive power. They side instinctively with one another against the entire remainder of the nation. Their usurpation is total. Truly they reign.[130]

The battle lines are sharply defined and already foreshadow civil war: 'the Privileged show themselves no less enemies of the common order than the English are of the French in times of war.'[131] By excluding themselves from the common ranks of citizens and insisting on their privileges, they have forfeited the political rights which only citizenship can carry, and made themselves 'enemies by estate of the common order'.[132] They form a caste which clings to the real nation like the vegetable parasites 'which can live only on the sap of the plants that they impoverish and blight'.[133]

'No aristocracy', therefore, must be the rallying cry for all true friends of the nation.[134] But the enemies of aristocracy are in no sense

democrats. We 'will repeat "No democracy" with them and *against* them... representatives are not democrats;... since real democracy is impossible amongst such a large population, it is foolish to presume it or to appear to fear it.' What is all too possible is a 'false democracy' in which a caste of birth, independently of any popular mandate, claims the powers which the body of citizens would exercise in a real democracy. 'This false democracy, with all the ills which it trails in its wake, exists in the country which is said and believed to be monarchical, but where a privileged caste has assigned to itself the monopoly of government, power and place.' For Sieyes, his immediate political antagonist, the Second Estate, fighting tooth and nail as a single agent to preserve their privileges, forms a 'feudal democracy'.[135]

For Sieyes, democracy as such could pose no real threat in France, however deep its crisis, since it was simply impracticable. In a country as large as France, the *demos* could never assemble together to shape itself into an effective political agent. To act at all, it must be represented. A select and separate group, small enough to co-operate effectively and be capable of action, must act on its behalf. But, to act with its authority, that group must first be chosen by it.

As 1789 dawned, the aristocracy of France still had the presumption to claim the authority of the French people, and the coherence and solidarity to abuse that claim to press their own private interests. Sieyes was very sure that their time was gone: 'During the long night of feudal barbarism, it was possible to destroy the true relations between men, to turn all concepts upside down, and to corrupt all justice; but as day dawns, so gothic absurdities must fly and the remnants of ancient ferocity collapse and disappear. This is quite certain.'

Even in *What is the Third Estate?*, however, he was sometimes less confident of what exactly would replace it: Shall

we merely be substituting one evil for another, or will social order, in all its beauty, take the place of former chaos? Will the

*changes we are about to experience be the bitter fruit of a civil
war, disastrous in all respects for the three orders and profitable
only to ministerial power; or will they be the natural, anticipated and well-controlled consequence of a simple and just
outlook, of a happy co-operation favoured by the weight of
circumstances, and sincerely promoted by all the classes
concerned?*[136]

History's answer was not the one for which he hoped, though not
until Napoleon seized power did the profits in any sense accrue to
those who currently wielded executive power.

From the opening months of 1789 France entered a state of barely
suppressed civil war, setting the monarchy and its agents ever more
intractably at odds with the people at large, and aligning it ever more
fatally with the residues of the long night of feudal barbarism. The
result was a cauldron of fears, threats and counter-threats in which
any prospect of the simplest and justest of political conceptions
achieving clearly intended and well-controlled consequences
vanished without trace. When democracy re-emerged from those
years of blood and confusion it had gained nothing in plausibility as
a practical model of how France could hope to govern itself in peace,
prosperity and good order. What it lost definitively was its reassuring
air of practical irrelevance. As it won fresh friends across a Europe
ravaged by decades of war, even those most troubled by its new
prominence came to see in it a potently destructive ghost that must
be laid to rest, not a simple phantasm which could safely be ignored.

In most settings beyond France itself (in Belgium, Holland, Italy,
even Germany or Poland), *'Democracy'* served simply to label
contending political factions.[137] Even in France it was seldom employed
to define the terms of political struggle with much precision, let alone
clarify the goals of competing parties or the strategy of key political
actors. But three figures of some importance did, at one point or
another, do their best to show just why the momentum of the

Revolution carried it insistently towards democracy, and why some version of democracy was an appropriate destination, and not an inevitable disaster or a clear disgrace. Two of them are familiar heroes of the Democratic Revolution: the flamboyant English artisan (and former staymaker) Tom Paine, whose pamphlet *Common Sense* had come close to launching America's open struggle for independence, and Maximilien Robespierre, the formidably self-righteous Arras lawyer who became the Svengali of the Jacobin Terror. The third was more surprising: the central Italian Bishop of Imola, Cardinal Barnaba Chiaramonti, in his Christmas Eve homily in 1797, a mere two years before his elevation to the Papacy as Pius VII. The Bishop's message was far from a call to arms. What it affirmed, in effect, was an historically somewhat premature version of Christian Democracy. Democratic government 'among us' was in no way inconsistent with the Gospel. It required all the sublime virtues which only the school of Jesus could teach: 'The moral virtues, which are nothing other than the love of order, will make us democrats, partisans of a democracy in the true sense.' It would preserve 'equality in its rightful meaning', equality before the law, with all due recognition for the marked differences between the roles of different individuals in a society. Its goal was to join hearts together in gracious fraternity. No devout Catholic need fear a tension between democracy and their religious duties: 'Yes, my dear brethren, be good Christians, and you will be the best of democrats.'[138]

Paine's position was more forensic. It appeared in the second part of his very widely circulated defence of the Revolution's goals against the criticisms of Edmund Burke, *The Rights of Man*. Paine presented the Revolution's political outcome as a triumph, not for simple democracy, but for 'the representative system'. That system retained 'Democracy as the ground' and rejected the corrupt systems of Monarchy and Aristocracy.

Simple Democracy was society governing itself without the aid of secondary means. By ingrafting representation upon

Democracy, we arrive at a system of Government capable of embracing and confederating all the various interests and every extent of territory and population; and that also with advantages as much superior to hereditary Government, as the Republic of Letters is to hereditary literature.

For Paine, America's new government was best seen as 'representation ingrafted upon Democracy'. This novel creation united all the advantages of a simple democracy; but it also avoided most, if not all, of its notorious disadvantages. 'What Athens was in miniature, America will be in magnitude. The one was the wonder of the ancient world; the other is becoming the admiration, the model of the present.' It was the simplest, most intelligible and most practically attractive form of government, avoiding Monarchy's ineliminable exposure to the risks of ignorance and insecurity in every heir to the throne, and simple Democracy's all too obvious inconvenience. It could be applied over any scale of territory, and across the most profound divisions of interest; and it can be applied at once. 'France, great and populous as it is, is but a spot in the capaciousness of the system. It is preferable to simple Democracy even in small territories.'[139]

The Rights of Man was Paine's attempt to defend France's Revolution, not only through its own informing political values, the *Droits de l'Homme*, but also through the reassuring precedent of America's relative domestic peace as an independent state. It saw in representation, as Sieyes and Madison had each done before it, an effective system for designing and organizing a form of government accountable over time to the governed and dependably committed to serving their interests. It firmly refused to see in the representative system the slightest element of regrettable concession to political, economic or geographical realities at democracy's expense.

In the Bishop of Imola's homily, democracy scarcely features as a load-bearing element in any serious attempt to understand politics.

Even in Paine's writings or speeches its appearance signals more a relaxation than a tautening in intellectual attention. But with Maximilien Robespierre, for the first time in modern history, democracy at last appears not merely as a passing expression of political taste but as an organizing conception of an entire vision of politics. In due course Robespierre was to become an unnerving figure even to the man who did most to launch the Revolution. ('If M. Robespierre asks for me',' Sieyes warned his Brussels housekeeper forty years later from the depths of flu, in muddled geriatric reminiscence of the year of Terror, 'tell him, I'm out.')[140] By that time Robespierre himself had been dead for well over three decades; but in the five short years between 1789 and 1794 he set his intensely personal stamp permanently upon the entire Revolution, defining its main goals with unique authority, and identifying himself ineffaceably with some of its greatest achievements and many of its most odious political techniques.

At the core of Robespierre's conception of politics lay a fiercely egalitarian and activist understanding of the rights of man, which set him at odds from the outset with even the remarkably broad franchise (all twenty-five-year-old male inhabitants, native born or naturalized, who appeared on the tax rolls) under which the Third Estate deputies were elected to the Estates General.[141] In October 1789, after the Third Estate deputies had transformed themselves boldly into the National Assembly and passed the Declaration of the Rights of Man and the Citizen, the Assembly turned to consider the September recommendations of its Constitutional Committee on the future bounds of the franchise. The Committee, largely on Sieyes's prompting, had already distinguished sharply between two types of citizen: active citizens who pay taxes and 'are the only real stakeholders in the great social enterprise', and the sole full members of the association, and passive citizens ('women, at least under current circumstances, children, foreigners, and those who make no fiscal contribution to the state').[142] Passive citizens are fully entitled to the protection of their person, property and freedom. But only active citizens have the right to take

an active part in the election of public officials. The Committee's proposals restricted the franchise to adult male residents of twenty-five or older, duly qualified by birth or naturalization, who paid taxes of at least three days' local wages.[143] The resulting restriction was criticized by one or two speakers in the Assembly itself (the Abbé Grégoire and the Physiocrat Dupont de Nemours), and assailed in Camille Desmoulins's crusading newspaper *Les Révolutions de France et de Brabant*. But it was left to Robespierre to mount a full-scale attack upon it in the Assembly. The proposal to confine the franchise in this way, he claimed in his opening speech on the matter, clashed directly with three separate Articles in the Declaration of the Rights of Man.

All citizens, no matter who they are, have the right to aspire to every degree of representation. Anything less would be out of keeping with your declaration of rights, to which every privilege, every distinction and every exception must yield. The constitution has established that sovereignty resides in the People, in every member of the populace. Each individual therefore has the right to a say in the laws by which he is governed and in the choice of the administration which belongs to him. Otherwise it is not true to say that all men are equal in rights, that all men are citizens.[144]

'A man is by definition a citizen,' he went on the next day. 'No one can take away this right which is inseparable from his existence here on earth.'[145] Two years later, in the final debate on the Constitution, he rejected the very idea of passive citizenship, 'an insidious and barbarous expression, which defiles both our laws and our language'.[146]

In February 1794, a few months before his death and at the height of the Terror, he linked this view finally with democracy itself, in the Report which he drafted to the Convention on behalf of the

Committee of Public Safety on the 'Principles of Political Morality which must guide the National Convention in the Internal Administration of the Republic'. His ambitions were characteristically lofty, and expressed with more than a touch of bombast.

'We wish in a word, to fulfil the will [*les voeux*] of nature, to accomplish the destiny of humanity, to keep the promises of philosophy, to absolve providence of the long reign of crime and tyranny.' Let France, for so long a country of slaves, eclipse 'the glory of all previous free peoples, and become a model for all nations, the terror of oppressors, the consolation for the oppressed, the ornament of the universe, and, sealing our work with our blood, may we see at least the dawn of universal felicity.'[147]

The sole form of government which could realize these prodigies was

democratic or republican: these two words are synonymous, despite the vulgar abuse of language, for aristocracy is no more the republic than monarchy is. Democracy is not a state in which the people, continuously assembled, regulates by itself all public affairs, still less one in which a hundred thousand fractions of the people, by isolated, precipitate and contradictory measures, would decide the destiny of the entire society. Such a government has never existed and if it ever did, all it could do would be to return the people to despotism.

Democracy is a state in which the sovereign people, guided by laws which are its own work, does by itself all it can do well, and by delegates all that it could not.

It is therefore in the principle of democratic government that you must look for the rules of your political conduct.

To found and consolidate democracy amongst us, to reach the peaceful reign of constitutional laws, we must end the war of liberty against tyranny and pass happily through the storms of the Revolution.

This is the goal of the revolutionary system.

The fundamental principle of democratic or popular govern-
ment, the essential ressort *which sustains it and makes it move,*
is virtue, the public virtue which worked such miracles in Greece
and Rome and which would produce even more startling ones in
republican France – the love of country and its laws.

Since the essence of the Republic or democracy is equality,
the love of country necessarily embraces the love of equality.[148]
It therefore presupposes or produces all virtues, [NB Two possibilities with sharply diverging practical implications] *since all*
are simply expressions of the force of soul which enables a
person to prefer the public interest to all particular interests.

Not only is virtue the soul of democracy, it can only exist inside
this form of government. In a monarchy the sole individual who can
truly love his country (*patrie*), and hence has no need for virtue, is the
monarch himself, since only he truly has a country or is the sovereign,
at least in fact. In effect he occupies the place of the people, and so
supplants it. To have a country one must be a citizen, and share in its
sovereignty. Only in a democracy is the state truly the country of all who
form it, and can it rely on as many interested defenders of its cause as it
numbers citizens. This is what makes free peoples superior to others.[149]

The French are the first people in the world who have established
true democracy, summoning all men to equality and the full rights of
citizenship. This is the real reason why all the tyrants leagued against
the Republic will be conquered in the end.

'Republican virtue is as necessary in the government as in the
people at large. If it fails in the government alone, there is still the
people to appeal to. Only when the latter is corrupted, is liberty truly
lost. Happily the people is naturally virtuous. A nation becomes truly
corrupt only when it passes from democracy to aristocracy or
monarchy.'[150]

In peacetime, popular government relies upon virtue. In revolution, it must 'rely simultaneously on virtue and terror: virtue, without which terror is deadly, terror without which virtue is impotent'.[151] Terror 'is merely prompt, severe and inflexible justice. Hence it is itself an emanation of justice, less a particular principle than a consequence of the general principle of democracy applied to the country's most pressing need.'[152]

The revolutionary government (Robespierre and his associates) was the 'despotism of liberty against tyranny': a grim indivisible war,[153] in which any faltering or holding back must simply increase the strength of the Republic's enemies and divide and weaken its friends.[154]

In this nightmarish struggle, the sole remedy was the *ressort général* (the panacea) of the Republic, virtue.

'Democracy perishes by two excesses, the aristocracy of those who govern, or the contempt of the people for the authorities which it has itself established, a contempt in which each faction or individual reaches out for the public power, and reduces the people, through the resulting chaos, to nullity, or the power of a single man.'[155]

In this great and terrible address the Revolution comes into clear view, rending itself to pieces. But already, mere months before it completed the task of self-destruction, it had inscribed this old, battle-scarred, but for so long also oddly scholastic, term ineffaceably upon its standard, handing it on without apology to fellow humans across the world and far into the future. It was Robespierre above all who brought democracy back to life as a focus of political allegiance: no longer merely an elusive or blatantly implausible form of government, but a glowing and perhaps in the long run all but irresistible pole of attraction and source of power.

Chapter Three

THE LONG SHADOW
OF THERMIDOR

Robespierre is still a figure of reptilian fascination. But what matters for us is not the man himself, nor the role he played within the Revolution's lurid political intrigues. It is the words and ideas which blew through him. In that awesome speech, he saw something which has proved overwhelmingly important, and he expressed a judgement which most of us now in some form confidently presume to be valid. Just as certainly, however, he failed utterly throughout his life to bring whatever he did see into sharp and steady focus, let alone communicate it dependably to anyone else; and we, in our turn, are still straining to capture just where the valid element in the judgement that democracy is the mandatory form for legitimate rule really lies. It is quite possible that we are still at such a loss because there simply is no clear form in which the judgement is valid,[1] just a hurricane of abusive or seductive verbiage, and a blind shapeless human struggle which those words serve to shroud more than illuminate.

We do not need to decide whether in democracy Robespierre himself saw clearly something which was and remains genuinely politically

compelling (how a state must be to fully earn the devotion of its citizens, the Form of the Modern Political Good), or whether what he saw, through a haze of blood, was no better than a shimmering mirage. You can read his speech even now as a conscious projection of Jean-Jacques Rousseau's answer to the central question of the *Contrat Social*: what can render legitimate the bonds of political authority (those bonds which everywhere bind humans each of whom was born free)?[2] You can also hear it, every bit as plausibly, as a desperate plea to his fellow citizens, in face of all the evidence, to feel and act as though the demands of their temporary and shaky rulers were fully legitimate – less a claim to truth than a bid for loyalty very much in extremis.

The democracy which Robespierre affirms is synonymous with the republic as a form of state. By 1794 it made some sense to insist that a republic, the reluctant political product of France's turmoil, could no more be an aristocracy than it could a monarchy. That was a lesson which no one could have drawn solely from the record of history, in which very many republics, from the grandest of all (ancient Rome) to the longest lived and most politically effective of its modern successors (Venice) had been ostentatiously aristocratic. France had begun its Revolution by declaring war on aristocracy; and its efforts to re-educate its monarch into dependable enmity towards its own aristocracy had been a conspicuous failure. The quest to combine democracy with monarchy in varying proportions persisted in France itself at intervals for almost a century, with at least one notable triumph along the way in the person of Napoleon. It was emulated widely elsewhere for quite some time, and is still not wholly discredited in some settings (Morocco, Thailand, Holland, Sweden, Britain, and in future perhaps even Saudi Arabia). But even today the very term republic (*respublica* – the public thing in contrast to the private thing)[3] is more a claim to enjoy the quality of legitimacy than an explanation of what that legitimacy might consist in, or an account of what could validly confer it. Heard clearly, it is far closer to a flat,

indistinct, ideological boast, than an effective structure of ideological justification. By 1794 a republic claiming legitimacy could hope to vindicate its claim by setting itself against aristocracy, and could use democracy, without further explanation, to express and authenticate its categorical opposition to aristocracy.

What it could not do was to use the same category to settle the questions of how exactly its own rule should be organized, what if anything should limit its powers in practice, or who should acquire the opportunity to exercise that rule for how long and by just what means. Ancient democracy was the name of a set of relatively definite political arrangements, worked out to preclude the continuing rule of aristocrats, or self-appointed and permanent monarchs (tyrants, as the Greeks called them). It was also, however, the name of the goal of avoiding either type of subjection, a goal which could be, and was, adopted as a shared purpose by a very active community of citizens. Robespierre was clearly appealing to this aspect of the term's history when he invoked it on behalf of himself and his political collabora-tors. In doing so, he faced the immediate political inconvenience that the practical arrangements to which it had referred in the ancient world differed so starkly from the unnerving routines of the Committee of Public Safety.

When he assured the Convention, in that Committee's name, that 'democracy was not a state in which the people continuously assem-bled regulates by itself all public affairs',[4] he was underlining some-thing salient and evidently important about the term's history. A 'state in which the people continuously assembled regulates by itself all public affairs' was an excellent, if selective, description of what ancient democracy had aimed at with some determination and at times largely achieved.[5] It was a wholly implausible description of France's Revolution at any point along its turbulent way. Even the people of Paris, the *menu peuple* who formed the angry crowds which drove the Revolution forwards, storming the Bastille or the Tuileries Palace, or even surging into the Assembly itself, were in no position to

assemble continuously, and never entertained the fantasy that they might truly be ruling France.[6] They intervened, in the great revolutionary *journées*, not as rulers themselves, but as citizens deeply affronted by the actions or inaction of those who genuinely were ruling France (or at least should have been), to force them into bolder courses, sharply restrict their future freedom of action, or change the cast drastically. To acknowledge that, even in Revolution, France was no democracy in that clear and serviceable sense was merely to acknowledge, as Sieyes and Madison had done before him, that a territorial state on the scale of France, if it was to be democratic at all, would have to be made and kept so by a system of representation. It would have to be, in a phrase casually coined over a decade earlier by Alexander Hamilton, a *representative democracy*.[7]

A representative democracy was no system of direct citizen self-rule. Instead, what it offered was a system of highly indirect rule by representatives chosen for the purpose by the people. To acknowledge this indirection was merely to recognize the obvious. In insisting on applying the category of democracy to France's revolutionary state in this way, Robespierre was not arguing against committed enemies so much as deploying the term in a mildly eccentric manner of his own. What was less obvious was the basis of his urgent repudiation of the second possible interpretation of what democracy might still now mean: 'one in which a hundred thousand fractions of the people, by isolated, precipitate and contradictory measures, would decide the destiny of the entire society'.[8] In this guise, democracy was no unreal dream of political community somewhere else very long ago. It was an all too real nightmare of the chaos into which France had often threatened to descend in the course of the previous five years. The hundred thousand fractions, although a numerical exaggeration, were the local sites and units of revolutionary agitation, the *Section* meetings of Paris itself, the political clubs across the nation, the *Sans-culottes* gatherings which endlessly frustrated every attempt to cool the Revolution down and bring it to a steady and reassuring close. In the

opening years of the Revolution, while Robespierre was establishing his reputation and forging the structures of identification and political support which for a time gave him such power, these sites and their occupants formed his main political resource. With the Terror, the strains of war and the worsening challenge of provisioning Paris with food which most of its inhabitants could afford to eat, his erstwhile friends turned increasingly against him. Their multiplicity, disorganization and practical indiscretion no longer afforded an endless array of opportunities to disrupt the governmental strategies of his ruling enemies. Instead, they became an increasingly perturbing and infuriating obstacle to his own attempts to rule France coherently and effectively in face of its deadly peril.

In February 1794, if ever, France desperately needed a government. The alternative of dissolving into anarchy had no open champions. But at each setting throughout France, the 'hundred thousand' fractions of the people naturally viewed their own purposes very differently; and, even in retrospect, they and their self-conscious descendants saw the closing down of this seething disorder less as a belated recognition of the requirements of political reality than as a crushing defeat in conditions of overwhelming external menace. Two years after Robespierre's death a handful of these former friends plotted clumsily to overthrow the new rulers who had taken power from Robespierre on the Ninth of Thermidor and unleash the second and greater Revolution, which was also to be the last of all Revolutions.[9] The plot itself may have been largely a confused and defiant dream; and most of its participants (real or supposed) were picked up effortlessly by the police.[10] But one of the few who certainly did belong to it, a spoiled and intemperate Tuscan aristocrat, Filippo Michele Buonarroti,[11] lived long enough to immortalize them over thirty years later by publishing in Brussels exile his own stirring account of the Conspiracy, a text from which Karl Marx later drew much of his sense of the Revolution's political and social dynamics.[12]

It was the leading figure in the Conspiracy of the Equals, Gracchus Babeuf, who provided it in retrospect with its name. In his defence before the tribunal of Vendôme he gave it an outline far sharper than the muddled reality of the conspiracy itself, and led promptly to his own execution. The main motif in Buonarroti's account was his insistence on equality as the Revolution's deepest and most transformative goal, and on the profound gulf between the true defenders of equality and their sly and all too politically effective adversaries, the partisans of the order of egoism, or 'the english doctrine of the economists',[13] who had struggled against them throughout its course, and ended by triumphing over them. The Revolution had marked an ever-growing discord between the partisans of opulence and distinctions, and those of equality or of the numerous class of workers.[14] The partisans of egoism saw national prosperity as lying in the multiplicity of needs, the ever-growing diversity of material enjoyments, in an immense industry, a limitless commerce, a rapid circulation of coined money, and, in the last instance, in the anxious and insatiable cupidity of the citizens.[15] Once the happiness and strength of a society is placed in riches, the exercise of political rights must necessarily be denied to those whose fortune provides no guarantee of their attachment to the creation and defence of wealth. In any such social system, the great majority of citizens is constantly subjected to painful labour, and condemned in practice to languish in poverty, ignorance and slavery.[16]

The fundamental struggle on which the Revolution had turned, in the eyes of both Babeuf and Buonarroti, was the struggle between the order of egoism and the order of equality. In the order of egoism, the sole *ressort* of the feelings and actions of the citizens was purely personal interest, independent of any relation to the general good.[17] For its partisans, Rousseau's party, equality formed the basis of sociability and furnished the consolation of the wretched. For their opponents, depraved by the love of wealth and power, it was merely a chimera.

The order of egoism was aristocratic in substance because it inevitably generated inequality, and because it both required and ensured the exercise of sovereign power by one part of the nation over the rest. The freedom of a nation is the product of two elements: the equality which its laws create in the conditions and enjoyments of the citizens, and the fullest extension of their political rights.[18] The second is no substitute for the first; and the friends of equality clearly recognized the destructiveness of concentrating on constitutional reconstruction at the expense of real equality of condition. They saw their more constitutionally preoccupied opponents, the Girondins, as a branch of the vast conspiracy against the natural rights of man.

Throughout Buonarroti's story, '*Democrat*' appears as a party label, the political form of the partisans of the order of equality. It was the expression of *democratic* ideas which shows the partisans of the order of equality re-entering politics after the crushing blow of Robespierre's fall, *democrats* who carried their campaign forward over the next year, *democrats* whom the conspiracy's Secret Directory must ensure were elected to the new national government by the people of Paris, one for each *département*, once tyranny was overthrown.[19] What had lost France both democracy and liberty even before Thermidor was the diversity of views, the conflict of interests, the lack of virtue, unity and perseverance in the National Convention.[20] The new, and carefully vetted, National Assembly at which the conspirators aimed, *democrats* to a man, would display none of these vices and weaknesses. The point of the vetting, and the grounds for operating not merely in secret but as a tightly organized body bound together in shared conviction, was precisely to eliminate them.

One reason why democracy remained such a fiercely divisive political category in Europe for the next fifty years was that Buonarroti's conception of what it meant continued to strike a deeper chord than the very different view worked out in practice at the same time in the United States. In America, once the Constitution was firmly in place,

democracy soon became the undisputed political framework and expression of the order of egoism. It also developed, in retrospect quite rapidly, a rich understanding of its own character, centring, as Tocqueville in due course showed,[21] on the idea of equality, interpreted in terms fundamentally different from those of Babeuf or Buonarroti. American equality was above all an equality of standing, and a comprehensive rejection of all overt forms of political condescension. It arose from and endorsed a society both self-consciously and actually in rapid motion, expanding in territory, growing in wealth, and looking forward to a future of permanent and all but limitless change. Even aside from the long and ineffectively repressed trauma of slavery, it was sometimes a society ill at ease with many aspects of itself; and throughout the nineteenth and twentieth centuries it continued to harbour its own partisans of the order of equality, understood in much the *Babouviste* manner. But no American partisan of equality who wished to deny its compatibility with the order of egoism could afford to offer their followers or potential supporters a political access less open than the rowdy rituals of electoral competition already provided. They might fight long and hard on other terrain, for a time win many battles, and accumulate, as at points with the labour unions, a considerable amount of local defensive power. But in the long run, and on the terrain where they must secure their victory in the end, in elections to Congress and to the Presidency, they were always to find themselves heavily out-spent and out-voted.

In America, therefore, the story of democracy has blended indistinguishably into the political history of the country as a whole. It has remained a potent political counter within the ideological struggles which defined that history, as a goal and as an instrument for hastening (or impeding) movement towards that goal. At points too, often courtesy of the most purposefully anti-democratic element of the Constitution, the well-protected autonomy of the Supreme Court, it helped to break through dense barriers to equality: slavery,

segregation, dismally effective political exclusion. In the long run it has ensured that the great majority of America's adult citizens now enjoy political rights which they can exercise, if they choose to.[22] (A growing number in practice, no doubt for their own good reasons, now often choose not to.)

You can see that outcome at least two ways, as a comprehensive practical refutation of Babeuf's and Buonarroti's somewhat rudimentary understanding of political and economic possibilities, or a crushing historical defeat for the ideals to which they clung. But it is still far from evident that there is anything wrong or confused in seeing the same outcome both ways at once. The order of egoism always had ample reason to rely upon the adequacy of its motivational support.[23] In democracy in America it discovered how to combine the abandonment of distinction as an organizing principle in politics or social form with its uninhibited efflorescence in economic and social reality. America today remains a society uncomfortable with every surviving vestige of explicit privilege, but remarkably blithe in face of the most vertiginous of economic gulfs, and comprehensively reconciled to the most obtrusive privileges of wealth as such. Behind this outcome lies the continuing vitality of its economy, the real source of the victory of the partisans of 'distinction, or the english doctrine of the economists'. Not all the economists, of course, did promise America or anywhere else permanent prosperity, let alone ever-growing prosperity. But the context in which American democracy has developed as it has was given, above all, by the extent to which those who assured their readers that long-term growth in the wealth of nations was to be expected have so far proved to be right, at least in the case of America itself. It has also been shored up quite effectively by the extent to which other economists, who cast varying degrees of doubt on that prospect, and insisted instead that equal or greater prosperity, and on more prepossessing terms, could be provided there or elsewhere on some wholly different basis, have proved more or less catastrophically wrong.

James Madison, as we have seen, provides no explanation of why the form of state which now dominates the world should have come to call itself a *democracy*. For him, as for most of his American contemporaries who were even acquainted with the word, democracy was something altogether different and distinctly unenticing. What his brilliant analysis in the *Federalist* papers does offer, alongside Alexander Hamilton, is a sound explanation of why a state of broadly this form should have proved so successful. It is above all that this form of state alone can hope to represent its own people effectively over time. It, and perhaps in the very long run, only it, can unite immediate practical viability with a convincing claim to act on behalf of and by courtesy of the body of its own citizens. To delegate government to relatively small numbers of citizens but also insist that they be chosen by most, if not all, of their fellows was a cunning mixture of equality and inequality. It could not guarantee sustained victory in practice to the partisans of opulence and distinction. But it could and did open up an arena in which that victory could be sought and won time and time again, and won through the judgements and by the choices of the citizens themselves. By doing so, and by leaving their victory apparently permanently at the mercy of reconsideration, in the long run, it also won them the war.

Unsurprisingly, this has proved a very considerable service to the patrons of opulence and distinctions. But it has done so over time, of course, only because opulence and distinctions (the combination offered) have struck more citizens on balance as collectively beneficial than as simply malign.[24] What gives the formula such strength over time is its elasticity in settings where opulence has duly grown. It could scarcely work for long anywhere where distinction must be sustained through stagnant or diminishing wealth, and has been widely and understandably abandoned, often with very little hesitation, in circumstances of this kind: in Europe of the 1920s and 1930s, in Latin America sometimes for decade after decade, in East or South East Asia, in Sub-Saharan Africa, sooner or later, almost

everywhere but in the post-Apartheid Republic of South Africa itself.

The elasticity never provides a perfect shield. The balance of benefit and revulsion shifts everywhere all the time. But it is hard to exaggerate the political advantage of the protection it does provide. You can see why that advantage is so huge by setting Madison's misgivings about democracy side by side with Babeuf's and Buonarroti's picture of what democracy requires. For Madison what made democracy clearly impracticable was above all its scale. The United States simply could not be governed as a democracy. But its blatant impracticality did not render democracy any less alarming as a political idea. In that guise even Madison had no difficulty in recognizing its disruptive appeal. It was the appeal, above all, of immediacy and directness, with its deliberate openness to the most erratic of judgement, to unrestricted factional passion and to swirling intrigue. At the limit, he noted, it suggested irresistibly to its admirers a remaking of society and a reconstitution of property relations, to render the citizens as equal in other aspects of their lives as they strove to be in the activity of governing themselves.

For Babeuf and Buonarroti the point of democracy was to attain just such a comprehensive equality, the only undelusive and uncorrupting condition in which human beings could live together with one another on any substantial scale. The appeal of that goal has naturally varied dramatically across time and space, at its most acute whenever, as in the aftermath of Thermidor, the partisans of distinction and opulence are unmistakably in the saddle, and very many must live alongside them in misery. What in the long run has blunted equality's appeal as a goal is the unpromising instruments for realizing it and the rigidities inherent in its pursuit. (Had it been reached, the goal would no doubt have proved to harbour further repulsions of its very own; but these, thus far, remain a matter of theoretical speculation, not a truth of experience.) These rigidities come in effect from the goal itself. Conspiracy, of course, was not an instantly plausible political form for democrats to adopt. Still less so was its successor form,

fine-tuned for the next three decades by Buonarroti himself, the closed conspiratorial secret society, of which in some cases he appears to have been the sole member.[25] But anyone in political adversity may have to choose between stealth and surrender; and Babeuf and Buonarroti hoped to conspire briefly, in order to live and act freely and more or less openly, into an indefinite future. The outcome of the conspiracy, such as it was,[26] certainly showed they had every reason for stealth. Under less dangerous and flustered conditions, the goal of equality proved less alluring to most citizens than either had hoped, easily set aside in favour of modest material gains and a quieter life. Wherever the opportunity to vote freely has been extended across an entire adult population, the majority has found it unattractive to vote explicitly for the establishment of equality. (The closest to a counter-example has been the remarkable governmental dominance of Swedish Social Democracy, which has made Sweden a very different country to live in from any of its European counterparts, but even today is clearly widening the room for distinctions as well as opulence.) What Babeuf and Buonarroti hoped for in democracy's triumph has been as far from coming true as what Madison feared from the same outcome. Democracy's real triumph has been a triumph for their word, as much as for Pericles's; but its practical political and economic consequences have proved far more a triumph for Madison's idea.

As soon as it became a word, democracy very clearly implied a form of government. For us it has come to name not merely a form of government, but also, and every bit as much, a political value. In retrospect this extension of meaning must have been quite rapid. By the time that the Old Oligarch set himself to diagnose its political appeals, or Pericles spoke so glowingly in praise of it, it had come to be just as much a political value for the Greeks themselves, as admired or even loved by some, as it was despised and detested by others. For most of its history as a word, as we have seen, far more of those to

whom it meant anything at all viewed it with scorn or suspicion than felt any trace of admiration for it. Today, things could scarcely be more different. In practice, such scorn and hatred are still often every bit as intense as they ever were. But in most settings at most times they now find it prudent to express themselves considerably more surreptitiously. Democracy does still retain principled opponents in some quarters. Iran's Guardianship Council, for example, seldom hesitates to express its contempt for the liberal reformers voted in with President Khatami, and still does all it can to place them beyond reach of popular election in the future. But even in Iran, the advantages of staging elections are implicitly accepted by those who most fear to lose them; and the principled rejection of elections has become very much a minority taste.

The historical momentum of the term *democracy* from 1796 up to today leaves us two very different elements which we plainly need to understand. One is a matter of the fate of political institutions: the diffusion of a variety of forms of state increasingly eager to describe themselves as democracies, and the relatively sudden and widespread victory of one type of claimant to the title over all its extant competitors. The second may at first sight seem simply verbal, the ever more pervasive diffusion of the term *democracy* as a ground of political commendation, a way of capturing the supposed or real merits not just of one set of political institutions against another, but of almost any features in the organization of our lives together, organized as we would like them to be, and not as we would emphatically wish they were not.

If we keep these two targets for potential understanding firmly apart, we would expect to find very different ingredients to their explanations. The fate of forms of government must turn on the capacity to create and defend wealth and enforce compliance, all of which can be assessed with some confidence, at least in retrospect. But it also turns on the sustained capacity to persuade, which is far harder to judge with any accuracy, before, during or after its exercise.

The creation and defence of wealth, too, and even the capacity to enforce compliance, under scrutiny, turn out to require a sustained capacity to persuade (what David Hume called 'opinion').[27] Over the last century and more, the commendatory force of the idea of democracy has proved a key element within the intensely competitive process of sustained persuasion which makes up so much of the political life of every human community. If we try to follow the historical vicissitudes of the state forms and verbal commendations which have implicated the term *democracy* from 1796 to the present day, we shall certainly find the two stories merging inextricably with one another over much of the time and distance which we need to cover. We shall also find, whenever we can keep them apart for a moment or two, each affecting the other quite brusquely and almost at once.

The distinction between being persuaded and being coerced, as every child, spouse or colleague knows, is not necessarily a sharp one within human experience. But there is scarcely another contrast to which most human beings attach greater importance. Undisguised coercion is frequently dismaying; and coercion ineffectually disguised as persuasion can be acutely offensive. A large part of the story which leads from 1796 up to today (the story of modern politics),[28] has been the record of a continuing rise in the practical importance of persuasion in shaping the terms on which human beings live with one another, and the forms within which they seek to do so. As a modern political term, *democracy* is above all the name for political authority exercised solely through the persuasion of the greater number, or for other sorts of authority in other spheres supposedly exercised solely on a basis acceptable to those subjected to it.

Persuasion, of course, had been central to the practice of democracy in Athens itself.[29] It was by the direct force of persuasion, exercised on innumerable and overwhelmingly public occasions, that the political leaders of Athens held or lost control over the city's political decisions. It was by persuasion, exercised in the last instance in the Assembly itself and against all comers, that Pericles for a time, in

Thucydides's eyes, turned Athens effectively into a monarchy, the rule of a single man by continuing consent of the people.[30] *Democracy* is a far more insinuating name than *republic* for a politics openly centred on persuasion. It recognizes the people not merely as notional bearers of ultimate authority, but also as a site of power in themselves, with a capacity to act and exert force on their own behalf. There may be a large element of unreality in that recognition, a stilted and insincere courtesy which veils a sometimes all too authentic contempt. If democracy today, as the Austrian expatriate Joseph Schumpeter bluntly assured his Harvard audiences and in due course the world, is 'the rule of the politician',[31] it is at least the rule of politicians under real pressure to address their subjects politely and solicit their endorsement, and refrain from reconstituting their rule as an informal aristocracy or monarchy of their own. Even in the hands of the shiftiest of career politicians, democracy has not proved a compelling name for styles of government which are openly autocratic, authoritarian or tyrannical. The Big Lie can succeed remarkably as a short-term political tactic; but it has failed to show itself in the long run a potent formula for securing political authority.

As the title of a form of government, in the key ideological outcome of the last two centuries of an ever more global politics, the partisans of the order of egoism have captured the word of the Equals. The Equals, in the meantime, have largely been driven from the political field. But neither their scattered remnants, nor even their more sophisticated intellectual admirers,[32] have felt inclined to surrender a word they still find irresistibly compelling. To them, the capture, even now, seems not a conquest in a just war, but an unabashed theft, secured by expedients they still do not really understand. Even fifty years ago the outcome of that war was very far from obvious to anyone; and the failure to anticipate it no more surprising in the case of those who loathed it than it was in the case of those who longed for little else. By now, however, the incomprehension of the losers is no testimony to

their political intelligence. Once a war is well and truly lost, it is seldom hard to see quite why it has come out as it has.

What is far harder to understand is why the partisans of the order of egoism should have bothered to capture the Equals' word. It was not a word commended to them by their wisest intellectual advisers, by Madison, or Sieyes, or even Adam Smith. It was not a word which appealed to the ruling authorities or military commanders who, for more than the next century, ensured across Europe that the partisans of equality were defeated time and time again: in the revolutions of 1848, in 1871, in 1918. Today, by contrast, no serious partisan of the order of egoism would deny themselves the political advantages of democratic authorization, as anything more than a temporary expedient, an enforced and mildly humiliating departure from the demands of political decorum. In embracing the term democracy so steadily and so purposefully, the political leaders of capitalism's overwhelming advance have not been juggling idly with empty symbols. They have recognized, and done their best to appropriate and tap, a deep reservoir of political power.

This is the vital judgement. If it was wrong, then politics would have no special place in the story of democracy's triumph, and that triumph might well have no real political significance. The sources and mechanisms of the triumph would have had to come from somewhere quite different, above all, no doubt, from the laws of economics and the crushing weight of weapons of ever more massive destruction. The real stories which we needed to follow would be stories of economic organization and technical change, and of armaments and their deployment. Those stories would be insulated and self-contained. They would carry within them the prerequisites for their own passage through time and space, and owe nothing of consequence to the efforts, whether on their behalf or against them, of rulers or politicians. Or, if they owed anything at all, they would owe it solely to the decisions which rulers or politicians make, for better or worse, over the shaping of economies and the acquisition or use of the tools of war.

There have been striking attempts to see human history in these terms, of which Karl Marx's was much the most inspiring, and for a time had by far the greatest historical impact: not least on the development of economies and the deployment of weapons systems. But in the end these pictures are not merely misleading; they are simply incoherent. The ideas which give them their shape and their air of force, seen clearly, do not even make sense. Economies are permanently at the mercy of rulers. Private property, the foundation on which a capitalist economy operates, is sustained or cancelled at political will. Money, the medium through which it operates, must be nurtured by political prudence, and can be jeopardized or even dissolved by the clumsiness or dishonesty of rulers or public officials. Currencies rise and fall, and economies thrive or disintegrate, through the good sense and scruple, or the cynicism and folly, of those who govern. No government can make a country prosper; but any government can ruin one; and most today are in a position to do so very rapidly and extremely thoroughly.[33] Democracy's real triumph, its victory over the last three-quarters of a century, has come in an epoch where the powers of rulers to damage an economy and harm the lives of entire populations have shown themselves greater than they have ever proved before.

Once we recognize democracy's triumph as a political outcome, many things fall into place. We can grasp that it was not, and could never have been, an automatic concomitant of something quite different, beneath, above or beyond politics. We can see at once both how recent and how extraordinary that triumph really is, everywhere beyond the United States itself. We can see that what has triumphed is not merely an exceedingly vague word, and a form of state associated, perhaps somewhat speciously, with that word, but above and beyond both, a pressing and engaging political agenda. An agenda is a summary listing of what is to be done; and every government requires such a list sooner or later. What is special to democracy's agenda is its assertion that in the end it must be the people that

decides what is to be done. This is never a good description of what determines what is done, still less of who takes the decision. What it is is a permanent reminder of the terms in which governmental decisions must now be vindicated, and the breadth of the audience that is entitled to assess whether or not they have been vindicated. Until democracy's triumph, the rightful scale of that audience was always seen as pretty narrow. It was defined by a layering of exclusions: those without the standing, those without the knowledge or ability, those without a stake in the country, the dependent, foreigners, the unfree or even enslaved, the blatantly untrustworthy or menacing, the criminal, the insane, women, children. Democracy's triumph has been the collapse of one exclusion after another, in ever-greater indignity, with the collapse of the exclusion of women, the most recent, hastiest and most abashed of all. Today only the child remains excluded everywhere, openly and without much embarrassment; and even for them, the age at which childhood ends is creeping steadily down.

For most of human history it has been above all dependence and exclusion which have given structure to human societies. With the coming of literacy, and the formalization of many aspects of the relations between human beings over most of the world's inhabited surface,[34] both dependence and exclusion were converted increasingly into self-conscious principles of social order. Democracy's triumph has been above all the backwash from this great movement of subordination. It signals and reinforces the steadily rising pressure to break the sway of these two principles and refashion the relations between human beings on softer and less offensive lines. Democratization is the working through of their prospective successors, the imposition of the apparent requirements of equality on the endlessly resistant material of human lives. No one today could mistake it, as Babeuf and Buonarroti each plainly did, for movement towards a known and clearly defined destination. But for all its open-endedness and untransparency, it shows unmistakably the continuing force of the

Equals' word, even buried deep inside the order of egoism itself.

The market economy is the most powerful mechanism for dismantling equality that humans have ever fashioned. But it is not simply equality's enemy, as Babeuf and Buonarroti confidently supposed. Instead, two centuries later and after much considered thought and many confused struggles, that economy has settled with growing resolution on a single political form and a particular image of society. Each grounds itself directly on the claim to recognize the ways in which humans are equal and to protect them equally in living as they choose. You do not need to accept the validity of that claim (or even its sincerity) to see what a momentous shift the claim represents.

This great choice has been a single story. In all its complexity and opacity, it has also been very much democracy's story. As stories go, it lacks a clear narrative line and conspicuously fails to carry its own meaning clearly on the surface. Its massive silences weigh just as heavily as its loudest choruses. Most prominent on its surface has been the spectacular diffusion of a word, but a word which, on examination, carries no clear or fixed meaning. Almost as obtrusive has been the staccato passage of several competing forms of government, each claiming to embody that word, from one geographical setting to another. The story of the word's diffusion has also been the story of an endless enquiry into what it does or should mean (how it may or may not justifiably be employed). The passage of forms of government has been at the same time an uninterrupted struggle over who exactly is entitled to act in the people's name, and on what grounds, over which forms of inequality, dependence or exclusion are to survive, be suppressed or re-created, and over who is to be subject to whom over what.

If we view the story fastidiously and from a great distance, we can see it above all as the quest for a secular grail: a clear sight of the Form of Equality, which must also be the Form of the Good and the Just[35] In this guise it is as unclear as ever whether what has made the quest so forlorn has been the overwhelming imaginative inroads of the

order of egoism,[36] or the deeper blindness of gender, reaching back far further in the past, or whether the quest itself has been throughout a hunt for a chimera: a treasure which was never there to find, the Form of something which from the outset simply never had a form.

If we view it more companionably, however, it must surely look very different, and in many settings altogether more encouraging. Not a quest for anything at all, but a stumbling, myopic blend of quarrelling and shared exploration of the inescapable issue of how to sustain everyday lives together as agreeably as possible. This is an eminently democratic perspective on the story, a view not from above, before or after, but simply from within. You could see it as a democratic practical enquiry into what democracy as a political value turns out to mean, as one people after another explores it together in the space that history and their enemies leave open to them.

We have followed the story of democracy as word over the two thousand years and more that separates its departure from the country of its birth from the point when it comes back to life in the fashioning and defence of political arrangements at the centre of a great state. There is no clear reason why it should have survived that lengthy passage. All we know is that, sometimes by the narrowest of margins, it somehow just did. No one knows what, if anything, will come after democracy. What we can hope to grasp, if we concentrate our minds on the issue, is four things about democracy as it now is. We can see why the word has changed so sharply in meaning between the days of Babeuf and those of Tony Blair or George W. Bush. We can see why the form of government to which it now principally applies should be so different both from its distant Greek originals and from any political practices which Robespierre or Babeuf can have had in mind. We can also see why the form of government which now comes so close to monopolising its application should have won such astonishing power across the world so rapidly and so recently. More intriguingly, if perhaps a shade less clearly, we can see, too, why this victorious regime should have picked this old Greek word of all

words for its political banner. The contours of the history of a word, the fashioning of a novel form of state, the outcome of a global struggle for power, are all well-defined targets for understanding. Only the last question – the choice of a label by a type of state – may seem at first sight both elusive and relatively trivial.

This is a reasonable intellectual suspicion; but it is also deeply undemocratic. If we see these two hundred years and more as a single sequence of political choice, taking in an ever-widening cast list, the adoption of democracy as preferred label for the winning form of state must emerge as anything but an arbitrary quirk of taste. The history of the word will simply express that political choice as legibly as the clarity of the choice permitted in the first place. The state form can be seen to have won, not through its exquisite adjustment to something altogether different (the requirements for the competitive flourishing across the world of vast corporations of dubious local allegiance), but principally through the changing balance of preference, and in many settings and more directly, the allegiance through the harshest of ordeals, of that ever-widening cast list.

The history of democracy's triumph since Babeuf's head fell from the guillotine has been above all a history of political choice. That one vast overarching choice has been composed in turn of myriads and myriads of other choices, swelling in number, surging out across the continents of the world, but each in the end made by a single partially self-aware living human actor. To make sense out of that story, we need to grasp the contexts in which those myriads of choices were made and register the fierce external pressures which drove huge numbers of persons in one direction rather than another – in the great stampedes into and out of communist rule, or the vast convulsions of the two World Wars. To grasp those contexts and recognize those pressures will to some degree safeguard us against the temptation to romanticize our sense of what has been in play, or draw it too ingenuously from our own parochial horizon of experience. It will not exempt us from the responsibility to take a political attitude of our

own to what the story means. Here democracy imposes an odd and austere requirement. On a democratic view, everywhere's political history must be equally valuable and equally significant (also, equally likely to prove silly, ludicrous or disgraceful). Its ordinary everyday squabbles and bemusements must carry just the same weight whenever and wherever they occur. None of it has any claim to privileged attention; and none can justifiably be discounted or ignored. There can be no elect nations, or continents, or even civilizations.

With democracy's triumph, this is a most disconcerting demand. It dissolves the pretensions of intellectuals and corrodes the claims to authority of all who happen at the time to exercise political authority anywhere in particular. It also decisively undermines any assumption that historical priority in the story could give privileged insight into its meaning (as though the Greeks, or the French, or the Americans, or for that matter the Belgians or the Swiss, might have understood democracy better than those who came later and so be in a position to determine whether or not their successors, or even imitators, have met or fallen short of standards already set once and for all).[37]

When America's President, George W. Bush, assured the world that 'The global expansion of democracy is the ultimate force in rolling back terrorism and tyranny',[38] he was drawing on deep convictions as well as expressing a devout hope for his own short-term political prospects. He was also expressing a political judgement on the record of America's role in the world over the last three-quarters of a century, in which its victories over Germany and Japan, and its triumph with the fall of the Soviet empire and the disintegration of the USSR, were alike testimony to its own political excellence, and the ever more irresistible recognition of that excellence across the world. More edgily, he was announcing too, the shape, if not the timing, of a local political strategy for the use of American military and economic power inside a still imperfectly subdued Iraq. The core of the strategy was to install in due course new institutions of govern-

ment in Iraq, with at least some family resemblance to those of countries which the United States views as democracies, manned with dependable enemies of terrorism and tyranny as the United States elects to define them. This is not a process, rather evidently, which has ever been under firm control. Perhaps more importantly, it is also one which could remain under firm control for any length of time only by continuing miracle, or careful repudiation of its own core pretensions. Under democracy, it must be the people of Iraq who decide whom or what they wish to befriend or oppose. They prove to differ bitterly with one another over the question; and very few of them seem drawn to American views on the matter. If democracy does in the end triumph in Iraq, even in the limited sense of establishing a continuing electoral basis for acquiring new governments, it will do so by a sequence of Iraqi choices, and with abundant mutual odium. It will also do so less by spontaneous imitation of the admired practices of an exemplary model, graciously offered by the present occupying powers, than through grudging acceptance of imposed terms of peace. Terrorism and tyranny lie in the eye of the beholder; and under democracy each beholder not only will perceive them for themselves, but is explicitly entitled to do so.

In its own terms, and by its own standards, the story of democracy's triumph is a story that cannot be told. To tell it as a single story, you must stand outside it, and claim to stand above it, define terms and apply standards to it, which can be vindicated in their own right, and independently of its bemusing struggles. This is a very bold claim; and there is no reason whatever for anyone else to accept its validity. But if none of us can hope to tell the story itself with any adequacy, we can readily recognize that it has occurred, and try to answer some of the more salient questions which it raises.

Democracy's triumph, in the first place, has been the triumph of a word. What triumphs along with that word is a particular way of thinking (and refusing to think) about the authority to govern, and a range of institutions for selecting and restraining governments which

claim to fit with that way of thinking. The way of thinking is never wholly convincing, since it equates ruler with ruled, while everywhere, as Joseph de Maistre noted, ruler and ruled remain stubbornly apart: 'the people who command are different from the people who obey.'[39] But for all its insubstantiality (and often its gross implausibility), it serves admirably to define the central challenge to rulers in the world which capitalism has refashioned. That challenge is to show the ruled that the authority which confronts them simply is their own: that it is their will which stands behind it, and their interests which it is compelled in the end to serve. To close that gap is a forlorn task, in logic, in psychology, in politics. But the acknowledgement that the gap should not be there, that no government has the right to rule anyone simply against their own will, is a vast concession. It marks a whole new world from the days when King Charles I of England on the scaffold, with stubborn confidence, assured his people in his dying address that 'a subject and a sovereign are clear different things'.[40] Only two months earlier Charles himself had picked out a term for that world, accusing his parliamentary enemies and the armies which they had unleashed of labouring 'to bring in democracy'.[41] It was not a word which attracted most of his enemies; and it made remarkably little political headway for at least the next century and a half. But, in the long run, it is the word which has stuck.

What makes it so adhesive is the posture of involuntary self-abasement which it imposes on any ruler who uses it. Self-abasement is neither a natural nor an agreeable posture for most rulers. Many, inevitably, continue to refuse it with some asperity. But it has proved a far more insinuating ground from which to claim authority than every other less dutiful expression of humility (let alone all the open expressions of arrogance or contempt).

For much of the time between 1796 and today there was little agreement over what sorts of institutions of government best met the term's demands. The task of differentiating true democracy from the many impostors which competed with it proved difficult as

well as contentious. Today, the outcome of that competition looks suspiciously clear cut: more natural, or even inevitable, than it very probably should. It is not that the losers did not richly deserve to lose: just that it is still far from clear how far or why the present winner deserved to win and, if it did, quite what enabled it to do so. The Democratic and Popular Republic of Korea, the regime of Kim Jong Il, now seems as exotic as the world of Kubla Khan.[42] As almost the last surviving relic of a lengthy and potent challenger for the term's monopoly, it dramatizes in a particularly extreme way both the arbitrariness with which it can be invoked, and the implausibility of using it at all to describe the institutions of any modern state. Here the people rules twice over for good measure, and is ruled in response with as little apology or recourse as anywhere else on earth.

On a grim but plausible view, the Democratic and Popular Republic of Korea is the *terminus ad quem* of the Conspiracy of the Equals: not what Babeuf and Buonarroti wanted, but what in the end they were always going to get. It is not, of course, the sole candidate for that destination. Others with equally little enduring appeal have been the period of War Communism, which succeeded the Bolshevik Revolution, Mao's Cultural Revolution and the killing fields of the Khmer Rouge.[43] In these later episodes, in all their desolation, the rage for equality becomes for a time something very close to a rage against the reality of other human beings or the very idea of a society. Each made a certain kind of sense for a small group of overweeningly ambitious politicians, and a very different kind of sense for varying numbers of other groups to whom these politicians could appeal, and on whose support they relied. Each was made possible at all by extreme and mercifully unusual circumstances. No one is less equal, at the point of death, than murderer and victim. But what these episodes show is how far the principle of equality can carry, if left without impediment from any other principles, left to structure the lives of human beings all on its own. By equality's

own standard, they may seem no more than a brutal caricature. But they show something far more instructive than the openness to abuse of a beguiling idea. They show that that idea is bound to prove self-contradictory if it ever comes to be treated as the unique structuring principle for the relations between human beings. Elevated to this lonely eminence, it both foments and licenses a deep impatience with the tastes, loyalties and commitments of the existing inhabitants of every real society. Between 1789 and 1796 a great many of the French population were made to ask themselves, sooner or later, whether they were in the end friend or enemy to the *ancien régime*. By 1796, a more select handful had come to recognize that they must side for or against the order of egoism, the global commercial civilization, founded on an ever-deepening division of labour and an endless proliferation of novel tastes. Some of this far smaller number were very clear that the answer to the second question followed from the answer to the first: that any enemy of the *ancien régime* must be an enemy, too, to the order of egoism. But in the long run this handful turned out to be wrong, if not indisputably in taste, at least unmistakably in expectation. Since 1789, throughout the world, the great majority of those who have had the chance have turned against the *ancien régime* in their own habitats. In ever more such habitats, sooner or later, it has proved impossible for their rulers to prevent them from doing so. Rule itself has certainly gone on virtually everywhere more or less throughout, very often on a far more intrusive basis, and sometimes with vastly greater brutality. But in ever more settings also, sooner or later, it has had to make terms with the principle of equality. What it has stalwartly refused to do is to make at all the kinds of terms which the Equals expected. It has chosen their word (perhaps even stolen it). But the subjects over whom it rules, and who permit it to rule them, have insisted for their own part, ever more pervasively, on embracing alongside it, and with at least equal passion and conviction, the order of egoism.

Placed within the order of egoism, equality faces more impediments, with greater powers of resistance, than it could have faced in any earlier form of human association. To Babeuf or Buonarroti, in this deeply inhospitable setting, equality would seem not so much confined, as tamed, or even neutered. But they may not be the best judges. Equality has not simply struck its colours, or abandoned its appeals to the passion and intelligence of its human audience. What permits the rulers to rule, in ever more settings and in the long run, is the response of that audience: the terms which it will accept. The key element in those terms has come to be the offer of a certain degree of equality, extended, as Plato long ago complained, to equals and unequals alike.[44]

This may sound a trifle fanciful. If inequality persists, and still more if it is regenerated ceaselessly by the central dynamic of the order of egoism, why should the proffered equality matter at all? Why should anyone even think it worth insisting on? There are three elements to the answer. In the first place, it matters because some recognition is better than none. Other things being equal, more recognition would plainly be better than less. But other things are far from equal. The Conspirators of 1796, in so far as they assumed anything definite, assumed that only full recognition could be either just or worth having. Only untrammelled and complete equality could bring the last Revolution, and reconcile human beings finally to one another over time. But untrammelled and complete equality is not even coherent as an idea; and the route towards it has always proved savagely divisive. It appeals to too few human emotions, for much too little of the time, and is swamped, rapidly and fatally, by the immediacy and impact of its incessant collisions with far too many other emotions. As a goal for rule it requires of any ruler who tries to implement it extreme and permanent coercion; and it guarantees to their subjects nothing but recognition (if indeed that). Certainly neither ease, nor comfort, nor amusement, and for the recalcitrant amongst them (those with opinions, tastes and wills of their own) not even

much in the way of security. As Benjamin Constant saw it, early in the nineteenth century, it offers ancient liberty, the delusory rewards of a notional share in rule, in exchange for the surrender of modern liberty, the real rewards of living as they please, within the bounds of the criminal law and their own incomes.[45] It then turns this offer into a doctrinaire programme which suppresses the order of egoism en bloc.

In the long run, this last suppression proves simply unsustainable. Ease, comfort, amusement, and most of all security, attract too many too strongly for far too much of the time. Highly coercive rule seldom proves a plausible form of recognition. The order of egoism has no difficulty in generating overwhelming coercive power, and little difficulty in protecting itself, if not everywhere always, at least in more and more settings for more and more of the time, against the many enemies it ceaselessly evokes. The winning offer from rulers to ruled is not a fixed sum, but a highly plastic, and always partially opaque, formula. It blends minimal recognition with quite extensive protection of the institutional requirements of the order of egoism. It ensures property law, commercial regulation, and a due balance between taxing enough to provide the protection and protecting enough against all forms of expropriation (very much including taxation itself) for the order of egoism to proceed buoyantly on its way. The scope of recognition offered and the degree of protection provided are each renegotiated endlessly.

The offer matters in the first place because some degree of recognition (recognition as an equal, if necessary in the teeth of the evidence) carries a very deep appeal, enough appeal for huge masses of human beings to be prepared to fight for it long and hard, and fight with particular bitterness to retain or recapture it, when they are threatened with its withdrawal. It matters too, in the second place, just because the content of that recognition is always open to reinterpretation; and anyone can therefore hope at any point to deepen or consolidate what it has already given them. It offers a field of aspira-

tion and an arena for struggle. It matters, lastly, because the recognition offered, while it may always threaten in practice the fluent operation of the order of egoism, is at least not openly contemptuous of, or hostile to, that order and its requirements. The equal citizens of a modern democracy may not listen very attentively or prove especially practically wise. But any of them can be importuned at any time, through their equal citizenship, to pay some heed to the requirements of the way of economic life on which they depend, and from which they draw the modern liberties they most prize. In this setting, it offers those who volunteer to rule them (and whom they then select for the purpose) at least a set of terms on which to address them on the requirements of collective prudence over time: above all, the need not to starve the goose that lays their golden eggs.

Chapter Four

WHY DEMOCRACY?

It is tempting to believe that democracy has won its present eminence for either or both of two reasons. Some prefer to attribute its victory to its evident political justice, its being plainly the best, and perhaps the sole clearly justifiable basis on which human beings can accept the apparent indignity of being ruled at all. Others find it easier to believe that it owes this eminence to the fact that it and it alone can ensure the well-protected and fluent operation of a modern capitalist economy. Neither cheery view, unfortunately, can possibly be right. Democracy in itself, as we have seen, does not specify any clear and definite structure of rule. Even as an idea (let alone as a practical expedient) it wholly fails to ensure any regular and reassuring relation to just outcomes over any issue at all. As a structure of rule, within any actual society at any time, it makes it overwhelmingly probable that many particular outcomes will turn out flagrantly unjust. The idea of justice and the idea of democracy fit very precariously together. They clash constantly in application. Any actual structure of rule will face incentives quite distinct from, and often sharply at odds with, the requirements for the fluent operation of a capitalist economy. But democracy, quite explicitly, thrusts upon its sovereign

and notionally equal electors the right, and in some measure the opportunity, to insert their own preferences directly into the operating conditions of the economy, in the attempt to do themselves a favour. As a bargain, this has many great advantages. But no one could reasonably see it as a safe recipe for ensuring the dynamic efficiency of the economy at the receiving end.

If we want to understand how democracy has won this eminence, we must set aside these presumptions and think again and less ingenuously.

Let us take again the four questions which must have reasonably accessible answers. Why, in the first place, has the word democracy changed so sharply in meaning from the days of Babeuf to those of Tony Blair? Why, in the second place, is the form of government to which it now predominantly applies, through all its striking variation over time, culture and political economy, always so different, both from its Greek originals, and from Robespierre's or Babeuf's dreams? Why, in the third place, has that drastically different form of government won such extraordinary power across the world, so rapidly and so recently? Why, in the fourth place and somewhat more elusively, should this highly distinctive regime have picked this word of all words for its political banner? The first two questions are quite easy to answer, once you recognize that their answer depends on the answers to the last two. The third question today (now that the victory is in) is also relatively easy to answer, at least in outline. Once it has been answered, it also gives us the vital clue to the fourth question's answer. What is not possible is to answer that fourth question on its own, and solely through its own terms.

In retrospect Babeuf's Conspiracy was always a less than plausible embodiment of democracy. Free and open choice by all the citizens deliberating together can scarcely be mistaken in good faith for a secret conspiracy intent on seizing power and passing it promptly on to a government hand picked to exercise it acceptably.[1] But it was certainly important for Babeuf himself that this new government was

to be only a temporary expedient, in face of the repressive power and will of the existing Thermidorian incumbents, with their shameless dedication to serving the interests of the wealthy. Babeuf himself did not accept the legitimacy of the Thermidorian regime. What he hoped would supplant it was less a clearly defined political structure (like the Assembly and Council of Athens) than a continuing practice of rule, not merely on behalf of the poorer majority of France's population, but with their active co-operation. This was still extremely close to Aristotle's or even Plato's conceptions of the least edifying variant of democracy (the rule of all by the poor majority for the poor majority), with the allegiance simply inverted. Babeuf's democrats might find themselves for a time forced to convert themselves, however nebulously, into a clandestine party. But there was nothing furtive about their political objectives. They saw no occasion for apology in a new regime in which most of the (adult male) population, in the modest circumstances in which they found themselves, would rule on their own behalf, or at least actively monitor and promptly correct any of those whom they chose to rule for them. By 1796 this was not a prospect which attracted the rich anywhere in the world. Today, by a long and winding route, in all the wealthiest countries in the world, the rich have learned to think better of the proposal and become quite thoroughly inured to it.

Democracy has changed its meaning so sharply between the days of Babeuf and those of Tony Blair, above all, because of and through a vast shift in political expectations. It is natural for us to see this shift predominantly as a movement from ingenuousness to sophistication, from the simple-minded delusions of Babeuf to the cool acuity of those who staff the re-election campaigns of George W. Bush (or even Tony Blair). But it is more illuminating to see it instead as a passage from one horizon of political experience to another, very different horizon. On the matter of democracy as each understood it, there was very little difference in expectation between Babeuf and his Thermidorian enemies. What each meant by democracy and

imagined it would imply in practice was virtually the same. Where they differed intractably was in their evaluation of it and in the practical implications which they drew from that evaluation: in what they felt moved to try to bring about or avert.

A blithe view of the history of modern democracy would see this change in expectations as following docilely in the wake of a prior shift in moral and political conviction. It would see democracy's triumph as the victory of a compelling formula for just and legitimate rule, aptly rewarded after a discreet interval by the happy discovery that such rule holds few terrors for the rich, and promises at least some benefits to practically everyone. But with the partial but weighty exception of the United States, that was scarcely the history which in fact occurred.

Babeuf's own political venture was too ineffectual to shed any light on the realism of his political expectations. In the hands of more effective successors, most notably Lenin,[2] political expectations had already been recast purposefully before the bid for power was launched; and the tensions between egalitarian and democratic goals and authoritarian means and structures became and remained acute. It was not hard for those who detested the goals to highlight the gap between pretension and consequence, and present the continuing project of equality, through that yawning gap, as a deliberate fraud or a hideous and murderous confusion. After 1917 this ceased to be a simple debating point and became an extremely potent political accusation. The world of which Babeuf dreamed, a rich-free world at last made safe for the poor, never won widespread credibility. But the grander and far more intellectually self-congratulatory project of Communism, Equality on Stilts,[3] in due course secured very large numbers of overt adherents. For as long as it retained at least their titular allegiance, it clung on tight to Babeuf's political nostrum, interpreted with all the flexibility which he found natural himself. Democracy became in effect the regime name of the route towards equality, gracing whatever political institutions volunteered to

shoulder the responsibility of pressing on towards that elusive goal. It was not until the change in expectations had run its course, and the defenders of equality had formally surrendered, that the claim to a special tie to democracy was surrendered along with it. This was not an internally generated change in belief or taste. It was a capitulation to the crushing weight of a wholly unwelcome experience.

The main battleground on which the struggle for democracy's mantle was initially fought out was the continent of Europe, and more particularly the western parts of Europe which Napoleon's armies controlled for longest and with least effort. The one key setting which those armies barely touched was the largest of the British Isles. (The record of Ireland was somewhat different.) But even in Britain, as throughout the European continent, until almost the end of the nineteenth century, democracy, under that name, remained the political goal of small groups of extreme dissidents, or movements which sought to challenge the existing order frontally and fundamentally.[4] Viewed from today, the practices which make up democracy, legislative elections based on widening franchises, greater freedom or even full secrecy at the ballot itself, executives at least partially accountable to those whom they ruled, were extended dramatically, sooner or later, across most of the continent. But their main forward movements, especially when these proved relatively durable, came not from the revolutionary collapse of the old order, or under the banner of democracy itself, but from deft defensive gambits by audacious conservative politicians, Count Cavour in Piedmont and in due course Italy, Otto von Bismarck in Prussia and later Germany, Benjamin Disraeli in Britain.[5] Even in France itself, under the revolutionary Second Republic, the new electors promptly ushered in the Second Empire of Bonaparte's unexhilarating descendant Louis Napoleon. Universal suffrage, as the anarchist Proudhon noted morosely at very considerable length, was a most uncertain political good and could readily in practice be hard to distinguish from counter-revolution.[6]

The extension of legislative representation and the widening of the franchise aroused bitter conflict sooner or later almost everywhere, often threatening the survival of the regime. With the Great Reform Bill, even Britain seemed for a time to many contemporaries, and at least some subsequent historians, very close to revolution. At least in peacetime, however, the cumulative experience of electoral representation proved remarkably reassuring. The prerogatives of ownership, and even the flourishing of commerce and industry, survived the extension of the franchise more or less intact, and with surprisingly little strain. By the early twentieth century the idea that even women might safely be permitted to vote no longer seemed an extravagance; and mass socialist parties with democracy on their banners could be left to compete with their rivals, if not in most settings yet on equal terms, at least without constant harassment. Madison's early-nineteenth-century discovery that universal male suffrage was no real threat to property was made independently, if appreciably later, in well over half the countries in Europe, not always by direct experience, but by ever more obvious inference. But virtually none of this, as yet, not even the first stirrings of the enfranchisement of women, had happened under the rubric of democracy itself. (The inclusion of women within the electorate was always an excellent proxy for the literal-mindedness of democracy as an idea. If everyone has to rule (or at least have a hand in rule) for rule to be legitimate or safe, what clearer evidence could there be for the idea being treated with reserve than the spontaneous and almost wholly unreflective omission of over half the adult population from the ranks of the rulers?)

What came out with ever greater clarity was the stark political logic of ever-widening representation: that it was obviously in practice quite unnecessary to confine electoral representation, and equally obviously on balance advantageous, both to ruling politicians and to those they ruled, to extend it more or less as far as it would go. This plainly is what we now call democracy, incomplete no doubt, and far

from fully self-convinced, but unmistakably the thing itself. But why should we have come to call it democracy? Why indeed is it even distantly appropriate to describe this form of government as a democracy? Why is the term not an obvious and brazen misnomer?

It is still not clear how to answer this last question. Perhaps democracy simply is a misnomer for any of the regimes to which we now apply it, a flagrant, and at some level deliberate, misdescription. But misnomer or not, the term has clearly come to stay. It is no use wringing our hands at the semantic anomaly or moral effrontery. What we need to grasp is why it has come to stay. The key to this is to register when the term arrived. It made its entry in this essentially new guise, beyond the North American continent, as the christening of a new formula for civilized rule (rule of the civilized by the civilized), offered by the victors of two successive World Wars to a world in dire need of civilization. The first offer was made by Woodrow Wilson, an academic political scientist and former President of Princeton University, who became President of the United States and would-be architect of a new world order.[7] At this point, the offer was not a practical success. Wilson's recipe for world order foundered in the vindictive intrigues of the Versailles conference and was essentially repudiated back home in America (a repudiation which did little to give democracy a good name anywhere else). The Europe it left behind it remained in acute economic peril, riven by bitter social conflict and intense ideological and national rivalries, biding its time none too patiently to unleash world war all over again. Democracy was challenged savagely from the right by those who volunteered to defend Europe's populations against the continuing menace of equality, pressed home by an equally authoritarian political movement with its own primary allegiance to a very foreign power. It was defended principally, and with far greater conviction, by those who still hoped to press far closer to equality themselves. It was neither a natural name nor a compelling practical formula for the unruffled hegemony of the order of egoism.

For it to become so, a second vast war had to be fought and won, and another and far lengthier struggle, which at times menaced even greater destruction,[8] had to be endured and survived. It was in that second struggle, and in face of the horrors of the Third Reich and the brutalities of Japan's Asian conquests, that Europe's threatened and largely conquered peoples joined ranks with America beneath the banner of democracy. At first they did so very much alongside the Soviet ally whose immense sacrifices and sustained military heroism did so much more to check Germany's advance, break its huge tank armies and drive it relentlessly back home.[9] After Operation Barbarossa, the *blitzkrieg* in which Hitler destroyed more than a third of its airforce on the ground and broke through its forward defences for many hundred miles, it also had no residual difficulty in identifying the Third Reich as its primary enemy. On the matter of democracy the Soviet Union learned nothing and forgot nothing from the bitter ordeal of the Second World War. But further west the political leaders of the order of egoism did learn one great and enduring lesson from this overwhelming trauma. They learned that there could be circumstances in which that order, the basic operating principle of their economies and societies, needed this word and the ideas for which it stood very urgently indeed. In the last instance, and in face of intense suffering, they needed it above all to focus their citizens' allegiance, and to define a cause worth fighting to the death for in a way that the order of egoism could never hope to provide for a good many.

Neither the Third Reich or Italy's Fascists, nor imperial Japan in its own phase of fascist militarism, set any store by democracy. So the term served comfortably enough to define their enemies without further need to resolve its ambiguities. Only once the war was over, and the grip of the Soviet Union tightened over eastern Europe, did it become necessary to define democracy more resolutely, to explain the proper bases for political alliance or enmity both domestically and across the world. At that point a quarrel which had mattered intensely for Socialists ever since Lenin seized power became of far wider

interest.[10] Before October 1917 virtually all twentieth-century western Socialists were democrats in their own eyes, however much they might differ in goals, political temperament or preferred institutional expedients. Within three years, socialists across the world were divided bitterly by the new Russian regime, rejecting it categorically for its tyranny and oppression, or insisting that it and it alone was the true bearer of the torch of the Equals.[11] For those who adopted the second point of view, anyone who disputed its title to democracy or censured its governmental style simply showed themselves partisans of the order of egoism: abject lackeys of the rich. The charge that they were lackeys of the rich stung Social Democrats everywhere. But for electoral politicians with other allegiances it carried no special stigma; and they found it relatively effortless to adopt the democratic element in the Social Democrats' denunciation, shorn of any associated egalitarian encumbrances. The ensuing quarrel was never a well-shaped political argument; and it is far from clear that in the end either side can be accurately said to have won it. What was quite unmistakable by 1991, however, was that one side had emphatically lost it.

It was not that the victors' pretension to embody democracy was vindicated by the collapse of the Soviet Union: simply that the claims of the vanquished Communist Party of the Soviet Union to rule as the people, along with their claims to deliver equality in any shape or form, dissolved into absurdity once they no longer retained the power to rule at all. By 1991, too, that absurdity was already a very open secret. The four decades of the Cold War provided something less than transparent collective self-education; but they did establish beyond reasonable doubt that it is a simple and ludicrous abuse of language to describe a wholly unaccountable ruling body, which denies its subjects the opportunity either to express themselves freely, or organize to defend their interests, or seek their own representation within government on their own terms, as a democracy (or indeed, for that matter, a People's Republic).

What made the term democracy so salient across the world was the long post-war struggle against the Soviet Union and its allies. From its outset, that quarrel was certainly between defenders of the order of egoism and those who openly wished it ill. But it came increasingly to be a quarrel, too, over the political ownership of the term democracy. Because of its intensity, scope and duration, the lines of battle within it were often confused and disconcerting. For decades at a time, in Indonesia, in South Korea, in Taiwan, in South Vietnam, in Chile, quite open and unabashed dictatorships were enrolled with little apology in the ranks of the western democrats. (The enemy of my enemy is my friend.) But this lack of fastidiousness attracted unfavourable comment at the time; and as the decades went by, it became increasingly clear that it was not merely politically unprepossessing but also costly to spread the democratic mantle quite so widely. American statecraft became, very slowly, a little more fastidious; and wealthier and better-educated populations in many different countries took sharper exception to authoritarian rule, whenever the latter faltered for a time, or the economic cycle turned sharply against it. Under this American provenance democracy was presented and welcomed as a well-established recipe both for nurturing the order of egoism and combining its flourishing with some real protection for the civil rights of most of the population. It threatened relatively few and held out modest hopes to a great many. Economic prudence (a due regard for the requirements for nurturing the order of egoism) was incorporated, sometimes with some pain,[12] into the professed political repertoires of most contending political parties within democratic regimes.

After 11 September 2001, abruptly and with strikingly little embarrassment, the spread of democracy across the globe shifted in meaning all over again, and acquired a wholly new urgency. From being the heraldic sign on America's banners, it became as well, at least for a time, a key political weapon. As President Bush himself acknowledged in November the following year, 'The global expansion

of democracy is the ultimate force in rolling back terrorism and tyranny.'[13] The United States had found little difficulty in reconciling itself to tyranny in foreign countries for decades at a time, if the tyrants in question proved serviceable in other ways. It had viewed with studied indifference (or even limited sympathy) the practice of terrorism itself, sometimes over equally lengthy time-spans, in a variety of foreign countries, from the State of Kashmir to the Russian Republic, and perhaps even at some points Northern Ireland. What made it suddenly imperative to roll back tyranny was its presumed link to terrorism, and more pressingly to terrorism within the United States itself.

Tyranny, it now appeared, bred terrorism. To stamp out terrorism (or at least prevent it reaching as far as North America) it was now necessary to stamp out tyranny too. The modern name, and the uniquely efficacious modern practical recipe, for eliminating tyranny was now democracy. Only a globe united under the sway of democracy could be a world in which the United States felt wholly safe from terror. This particular strategic appraisal may not last very long. The globalization of democracy, even in this limited sense, is a costly political agenda with many immediate enemies. It is far from clear that achieving it would yield the desired outcome. There is no obvious reason why those who feel bitterly enough to sympathize with terrorism or succour its practitioners should feel more inhibited in acting on their feelings merely because they acquire somewhat more control over their own rulers. Democratizing the West Bank and Gaza would do little by itself to endear the citizens of the state of Israel to most of the existing inhabitants of either. In its present form this looks less like a reliable political talisman than a glaring instance of ideological overstretch.[14] But temporary though it will surely prove, it does represent the culmination of one particular ideological sequence. We may change our mind quite drastically (and even the American government may change its mind somewhat) over whether this is a good way in which to understand what democracy is or

means. Succeeding American leaders will almost certainly modify their assessments of what it is reasonable to hope (or cease to fear) from democracy so understood. What can scarcely happen is that anyone raises substantially this estimate of the benefits which democracy, so understood, is likely to prove able to supply.

We can now see how to answer three of our four questions. Democracy has altered its meaning so sharply since Babeuf because it has passed definitively from the hands of the Equals to those of the political leaders of the order of egoism. These leaders apply it (with the active consent of most of us) to the form of government which selects them and enables them to rule. It is a form of government at least minimally adapted to the current requirements of the order of egoism, shaped within, and adjusted to, the continuing demands to keep that order in working condition. The Greek originals of democracy could scarcely have provided that service, either organizationally or politically; and the service itself cannot plausibly be claimed to have figured in the dreams of either Robespierre or Babeuf. The conjunction of representative democracy with the increasingly self-conscious and attentive service of the order of egoism has faced pressing challenges throughout these two centuries. But within the last fifteen years it has surmounted all these challenges and settled with unprecedented resolution on the conclusion that democracy, in this representative form, is both the source and to a large degree also the justification for the scale of its triumph. What has enabled it to surmount the challenges is still open to question. But much of the answer unmistakably lies in the sheer potency of the order of egoism.

Early in the last century, a determined Russian statesman, Pyotr Stolypin, made a last desperate effort to rescue the Tsarist regime by breaking up the egalitarian torpor of Russia's peasant communities and subjecting them to the stern demands of the order of egoism.[15] His name for this strategy was 'The Wager on the Strong'. It is a good general name for the political strategy of serving the requirements of the order of egoism, whether in one country or across the globe. In

contrast with Babeuf's or Buonarroti's disapproving vision of a political regime centred on defending the privileges of those who were already rich (and always potentially somewhat effete), it captures admirably the momentum of a strategy which aims at constant change, and at harnessing the power to realize that change in whoever proves to possess it. Robespierre's unnerving associate on the Committee of Public Safety, Louis Antoine de Saint-Just, proclaimed thrillingly at one point at the height of the Terror that it was the poor (the *malheureux*) who were the real powers of the earth.[16] But he has proved a most inferior prophet. The Wager on the Strong is a wager on the rich, to some degree perforce on those with the good fortune to be rich already, but above all on those with the skill, nerve and luck to make themselves so. In the long run the Wager on the Strong has paid off stunningly. But what of the fourth question? Why did the Strong select this of all words to name the form of government which has served them best of all in their titanic struggle to mould the world to their purposes?

Even now I do not think we quite know the answer to that question. But what is clear is that the key phase in their selection of it occurred in the United States of America, and did so before the young Alexis de Tocqueville took ship to appraise its implications. From then on it is relatively easy to follow this word as it moves onwards with the stream of history, sometimes hurtling through rapids, sometimes drifting out in great slow eddies, or disappearing for lengthy intervals into stagnant pools. It is easy too to see why it attracts or repels so many different users, summoning up allegiances or fomenting enmities. It is even easier to see why it constantly loses definition along the way, stretched in one direction then another, and largely at the mercy of anyone who chooses to take it up. What still remains harder to see is just how it aids or impedes those who do choose to use it, augmenting their political strength, exposing their deceit or blurring their comprehension of their own goals. (Whatever its other merits, it is hard to believe that this is a term which has greatly

assisted anyone to clarify their own political goals for any length of time.)

At this point democracy's ideological triumph seems bewilderingly complete. There is little immediate danger, of course, of its running out of enemies, or ceasing to be an object of real hate. But it no longer faces compelling rivals as a view of how political authority should be structured, or of who is entitled to assess whether or not that authority now rests in the right hands. Its practical sway, naturally, is very considerably narrower, crimped or disrupted almost everywhere. But the surviving doctrines which still contend with it at the same level, and without benefit of special supra-human validation, and which have also kept the nerve bluntly to deny its hegemony, are all faltering badly. None of them any longer dares to try to face it down in free and open encounter.

This odd outcome leaves many questions open. Is it still right, at this late stage, to think of democracy primarily as a form of government? If so, just what form of government, and quite why? Or is it equally or more appropriate to think of it instead as a political value, very imperfectly embodied in any actual form of government, and perhaps flatly incompatible with many obvious aspects of the form of government to which most of us now habitually apply it? If we see it primarily as a political value, a standard of public conduct or political choice to which forms of government should ideally measure up, should we also go on to recognize in it, as Tocqueville in effect did,[17] an entire way of life, social, cultural and even economic, just as much as narrowly political? Can there be truly democratic politics (for better or worse), without democratizing every other aspect of social, cultural and economic life?

No one, after the last century, can sanely doubt that forms of government matter greatly. It may be true that even the grandest of states are in some respects less powerful today than their predecessors of half a century ago.[18] But it is certainly also true that most states are vastly more powerful in a great many other readily specifiable respects

than they have ever been before. Government may shift elusively between levels, moving upwards and downwards from the individual nation state; and governmental aspirations can shrink as well as expand. But the world in which we all now live is governed more extensively and more intimately than it has ever been before;[19] and few things matter more in practice to most of its inhabitants over time than what form that government takes.

The form of government to which most of us do now apply the term democracy is more than a little blurred in outline. What causes it to operate as it does in any particular setting and at any particular time remains exceedingly obscure.[20] But some aspects of it are more settled and less contentious than they have ever been before. Very few countries which entertain the idea of democratic rule at all any longer dispute that the sovereign ruling body, the citizens, should consist of virtually all the adults duly qualified by birth. There is more continuing dissension even today over the terms on which citizenship can be acquired from the outside, or non-citizens admitted equally to the vote. There is also continuing strife over the terms of personal exclusion, of derogating from the privileges of citizenship by sufficiently egregious breach of its responsibilities, or through crippling mental incapacity (crime, insanity, even the purposeful withholding of tax). But virtually nowhere on earth which stages voting at all as a means for forming a government still excludes women from the opportunity to participate in it on formally equal terms. (Saudi Arabia, which apparently at present still does, emphatically does not envisage democracy as a way of forming its government.) This vast change has come everywhere within less than a century. In most places it can scarcely yet be said to have had the effect of democratizing every other aspect of social, cultural or economic life. But the most jaundiced observer now can hardly miss its impact anywhere where it has obtained for any length of time.

The variations within this form of government, Presidential or Parliamentary rule, judicial review, contrasting party or electoral

systems, even republics or monarchies, matter greatly for the politics of any individual country. In some cases, in practice, they leave little room for doubt that their main purpose is to insulate the rulers as radically as possible from the erratic sympathies and judgements of the citizens at large. What unites them is their common acceptance of a single compelling point, the expediency of deriving the authority to rule, in a minimally credible way, from the entire citizen body over whom it must apply. The claims made by these rulers on their own behalf, and in some measure endorsed by less partial champions of the form of government itself, naturally reach much further. They claim that the election of representative legislatures and executives, however structured, not only confers upon them the authority of the citizen electors, but also provides those electors with an effective control over the laws to which they are subject, and the persons who make, interpret or enforce those laws upon them. In itself this is an extremely far-fetched claim. It is also one which loses plausibility fairly steadily with experience. But it is not absurd. The predicament of being governed by those whom a clear majority can eventually dismiss is far less dire than the corresponding predicament of being governed indefinitely by those of whom you can hope to rid yourself only by rising up and overthrowing them by force of arms.

Is democracy a good name for a system of rule in which, in the end, a steady and substantial majority can be confident that it holds the power to dismiss rulers it has come to loathe? That is not what the term *democracy* originally meant; but it is also not a plainly illegitimate extension of that original meaning. The case against the extension of meaning, nevertheless, remains simple and weighty. In Athens it may have been the Laws, rather than the *demos* itself, who held final authority over the Athenians.[21] But the Laws could exercise that ultimate ascendancy only through the continuing interpretation and the active choice of the citizen Assembly and the Law Courts. Athenian democracy had very serious reservations about the division of political labour. Except under the special conditions of open

warfare, where Generals were elected and often left to fend for themselves for as long as the annual campaign lasted, it simply refused to pick individuals to exercise power in its name, and without further recourse to it. It organized the daily tasks of government, quite largely, by rotating them across the citizen body; and it made every great decision of state, legislative, executive, or even judicial, by the majority choice of very large numbers, whether in the Assembly or the Courts. Under democracy the citizens of Athens, quite reasonably and accurately, supposed that they were ruling themselves. But the vastly less exclusive citizen bodies of modern democracies very obviously do nothing of the kind. Instead, they select from a menu which they can do little individually to modify, whichever they find least dismaying amongst the options on offer. Benjamin Constant, who wished to commend this arrangement, saw the goal of their choice as stewardship, the full management of their interests by suitable persons chosen for the purpose.[22] This, he underlined, was how the rich approached the allocation of their own time. There was nothing humiliating or necessarily alarming in having your interests managed for you. The rich at least were never in serious doubt that they could find many more rewarding things to do with their time.

But even for those who approved of it, this was never the only way in which to view the bargain. Constant was writing well before the professionalization of politics. By the time, over a century later, that the Austrian émigré economist Joseph Schumpeter[23] set out his own more elaborate picture of what democracy really is and means, the practical implications of governing on the basis of electoral representation had become far clearer. To Schumpeter, democracy was essentially a competition between teams of politicians for the people's vote and the power to govern which would follow from it. The victors in that competition won the opportunity to govern for a limited period. As a system, therefore, electoral democracy was 'the rule of the politician'.[24] What the electors picked their politicians for was still the prospective quality of their stewardship. But once the politicians in

question had been picked, the terms of the relationship changed abruptly. For most citizens most of the time there was little room for doubt that they were still being ruled. The rich might find themselves cheated or even tormented by individual stewards whom they had been injudicious enough to select. But it was not a credible picture of the relationship between the two to describe the rich as being ruled by their stewards. The amalgam of rule with stewardship is a far more rigid and committing transfer of power and responsibility than any the citizens of democratic Athens were ever asked to make (except on those rare occasions when they were asked, or compelled, to abolish the democracy itself). It is easy for electors not merely to regret individual past choices (bargains that have gone seriously astray), but also to lose heart more generally in face of the options presented to them. It is not simply because modern liberty can take so many other forms (because it offers so many more amusing ways of spending one's time) that the percentage of those who bother to exercise their vote has fallen so relentlessly across the democratic world. Some of the fall in voting rates is best attributed less to a preference for private enjoyments[25] than to dismay at what electors have got for their votes. At its most dismaying, this can result in the desertion of the electoral forum by very large sections of the population. Career politicians can come to be seen as systematically corrupt manipulators, reliably intent on nothing but furthering their own interests[26] by using public authority ruthlessly in the service of the evidently sinister interests of small groups of independently powerful miscreants. 'Democracy', the French syndicalist Georges Sorel sneered almost a century ago, 'is the paradise of which unscrupulous financiers dream.'[27]

The ethos of democratic Athens evoked in Pericles's great speech could scarcely have been more different. But it is wrong to see the contrast between Periclean glory and the squalid financial scandals of the Third Republic as one which mirrors an essentially valid application of a clear term over against an obvious abuse of the same term. Some of the contrasts between the two unmistakably come out in the

wrong direction. Even in Sorel's day, the franchise of the Third Republic was very considerably less exclusive than the citizenship of ancient Athens.[28] Even those contrasts which do clearly come out in the right direction often turn on something quite other than democracy itself. The citizen pride celebrated by Pericles certainly encompassed the freedom (for the citizens themselves) embodied in the political organization of the *polis*. But it turned more in the end on the splendour and dynamism of the life of the *polis* community, the former funded largely by resources drawn from other communities, and the latter also often exerted very much at other peoples' expense. Democracy probably meant more to some contemporaries of Pericles than it can have meant to any of France's population in the opening decade of the twentieth century. But it did not mean more because the Athenians understood democracy, and the French did not, but because the Athenians saw their city as being at the zenith of its greatness, and associated that greatness with the form of its rule, while the French, in the lengthy shadow cast by the Franco-Prussian War, were in no position to do so, and had correspondingly little occasion to congratulate themselves on the distinctiveness of their political arrangements.

If democracy is simply a way of organizing the relationships between communities and their governments, it can scarcely in itself be an occasion for intense pride. Where communities are self-confident and proud, some of that pride will rub off on their political institutions, however the latter are structured (a point familiar to tyrants across the ages). Under less ebullient circumstances, the attitudes of communities to their governments are likely to be moulded largely by how groups or individuals within them see their own interests as served or damaged by their government, a matter of skill and luck as much as good or ill will, sense of duty or culpable neglect. Political scientists and advertising agencies have each studied these shifts of sentiment and sympathy in great detail, and developed enough insight into what determines them to earn, at least in the latter case, consid-

erable sums of money for passing their conclusions on to the competing teams of politicians. The formidable scale, cost and elaboration of a modern American Presidential campaign, already certain to be larger than ever in 2004, could rouse a sense of personal freedom in most individual citizens only through sheer delusion. But neither the remorselessness of the manipulation attempted, nor the lavishness of the resources squandered, are enough in themselves to invalidate its claims to embody democracy. To run against it, any coherent complaint must in the end once again be made on behalf of the order of equality, and against the order of egoism. However else we understand democracy today, we cannot safely or honourably brush aside the recognition that it has been the clear verdict of democracy that the struggle between these two orders is one which the order of egoism must win. It is above all democracy, in this thin but momentous sense, which has handed the order of egoism its ever more conclusive victory.

The big question raised by that victory is how much of the distant agenda of the order of equality can still be rescued from the ruins of its overwhelming defeat. That question can be seen in two very different ways, as one of institutional architecture and the meanings to ascribe to it, or as one of distributive outcomes (with the ascription of meanings left severely to the individual winners or losers). The first way of seeing the issue is bound to attach special weight to the sense that democracy can only be adequately seen not as a form in which individual states are or are not governed, but as a political value, or a standard for justifiable political choice, against which not merely state structures, but every other setting or milieu in which human beings live, can and should be measured.

Democracy, so viewed, promises (or threatens) the democratization of everything (work, sex, the family, dress, food, demeanour, choice by everyone over anything which affects any number of others). What it entails is the elimination of every vestige of privilege from the ordering of human life. It is a vision of how humans could live with one another, if they did so in a context from which injustice

had been eradicated. Even thought through with limitless energy,[29] this remains quite an elusive idea. What is not elusive about it, however, is that it requires the systematic elimination of power (the capacity to make others act against their own firm inclinations) from human relations. At the very least it demands the removal of any form of power stable enough to disclose itself to others, and resistant enough to survive for any length of time once it has done so. The removal of all power (what thus far causes much of human life to go as it does) from the relations between human beings is most unlikely to prove coherent even as an idea. It is also spectacularly unlikely to occur, since it forswears in the first instance the principal medium through which human beings bring about consequences which they intend.[30] But incoherent and implausible though it almost certainly is, it is also unmistakably the full programme of the Equals, and in a clearer and more trenchant form than Babeuf ever took the trouble to elaborate it. What it is not, however, is a programme ever widely adopted by any groups in the real world, still less one even weakly reminiscent of a form of government. It is a value that might perhaps inspire a form of government, and which, at least in negative forms, often has inspired groups of men and women, sometimes on a very large scale. But it is not a coherent description of how power can be organized, or institutions constructed: not a causal model of anything at all.

The democratization of everything human is not a real possibility: as illusory as a promise as it is idle as a threat. But as a political programme it carries very considerable allure. In many places it has already made far greater progress than the Abbé Sieyes could have imagined. Within the richer countries of the world the back-breaking toil and casual brutality which dominated the lives of huge numbers of people even a century ago have been lifted from the shoulders of all but relatively small minorities. When the conditions of those minorities emerge sporadically into public view they cause as much shock as they arouse shame. Entire dimensions of social, cultural

and economic life have been challenged irreversibly: most dramatically of all the relations between men and women. Usually slowly, often bemusedly, and almost always grudgingly, those relations have begun to recompose themselves comprehensively to fit the requirements of equality. The surrender of the vote was the merest beginning. None of us yet knows how far that transformation can go, or quite where it will end. If you view democracy solely as a value, you can be very sanguine about the extent of this progress. Gender may seem not merely a privileged and uniquely urgent domain for equality to conquer. It can serve as a proxy, too, for every other domain in which equality is still effectively obstructed: race, ethnicity, literacy, even class. The sole boundaries to its progress are the limits to human capacities to think clearly and imagine coherently.

But that gives far too little weight to democracy as a form of government. It misses entirely the significance of its diffusion across the world, as one very particular form of government, over the last two centuries. It simply suspends political causality (what causes politics to work the way it does). Almost certainly, on careful analysis, it must suspend along with it most forms of social, economic and even cultural causality too. If in this guise democracy has spread across the world, especially over the last half-century, by backing the order of egoism to the hilt, the order of egoism reciprocally has built itself ever more drastically at the same time by adopting and refashioning democracy in this particular sense. The world in which we all live is a world principally structured by the radicalization and intensification of inequalities. Between the inhabitants of much richer countries, these inequalities need not result in wider gaps in wealth, status or personal power than those which existed many centuries earlier, or still exist in far poorer countries today. But, by the principle of economic competition and its cumulative consequences, they work through, and have to work through, the sharpening and systematization of inequality in the lives of virtually everyone.

It is by its pervasiveness and its peremptory practical priority that the order of egoism precludes equality. It tolerates, and even welcomes, many particular impulses towards equalization. But what drives it, and in the end organizes the entire human world, is a relentless and all-conquering principle of division and contrast. That was what Babeuf saw and hated. It is still there to see (and, if we care to, to hate) to this day. What there can be, today and as far as we can see into the future, is not the democratization of human life in its entirety, either in one institution, or in one country, or in the globe as a whole. What there can be is the democratization of human life anywhere, as far as the order of egoism proves to permit. This is not a struggle which equality is going to win. The precise limits which the order of egoism sets to equality do not form a clear fixed structure which can be specified in advance of political experience. They are an endless and ever-shifting battleground. What is clear and fixed, however, is the strategic outcome of that long war, and the identity of its victor.

The outcome itself is not one which any of us cares to see very clearly, and perhaps not one which anyone who did see it clearly could unequivocally welcome. It makes no direct appeal to the moral sentiments,[31] let alone the moral sense.[32] To put the point less archaically, it is an outcome which must offend anyone with the nerve to recognize what it means.

The role of democracy as a political value within this remarkable form of life (the World Order of Egoism) is to probe constantly the tolerable limits of injustice, a permanent and sometimes very intense blend of cultural enquiry with social and political struggle. The key to the form of life as a whole is thus an endless tug of war between two instructive but very different senses of democracy. In that struggle, the second sense, democracy as a political value, constantly subverts the legitimacy of democracy as an already existing form of government. But the first, too, almost as constantly on its own behalf, explores, but then insists on and in the end imposes, its own priority over the second. The explorations of democracy as a value vary in

pace, urgency and audacity across time and space. At times, as in the work of the American philosopher and educator John Dewey,[33] the imagery of a democratic way of life bites very deep and summons up intense imaginative energies. More often, the mobilizing force of the value is negative and far more specific – the demolition of spectacular and long-entrenched injustice in one domain after another of collective life. Everyone will have their own favourites among these stirring stories. Many, too, no doubt, their own especial aversions. What adult men or women may or may not do with their own or one another's bodies or their own embryonic fellows. How one (self- or other-defined) racial grouping may or may not treat another. How money may or may not be exchanged directly for office, power or honour, or office, power or honour in their turn be exchanged directly instead for money. The terms of trade, overt or covert, on which we live our lives together.

Most of modern politics is taken up by quarrels over what to revere or repudiate within these struggles. The true definition of democracy is merely one prize at stake in those quarrels. None of the stories ends in unalloyed triumph. What sets the limits to their triumph is often hard to ascertain; but almost always, sooner or later, it turns on definite decisions by powerful agents within the formal apparatus of democratic rule, career politicians or those whom they in the end license. The balance between cultural exploration, social struggle and public decision by ruling institutions of representative democracy is never fixed firmly or clearly. But there are denser barriers to how far it can go in one direction than in the other. The periods when, for a brief time, these barriers seem lifted, like the youth uprisings of 1968, can be times of fervent collective hope, as well as transitory personal transformation. But they offer no rival instruments with which to leave behind them solid institutional guarantees for any ground they may win. Grand victories are often largely undone by long strings of petty defeats.[34] Where they fail to carry through to the laws passed by representative legislatures, and to the political decisions to ensure that

those laws are enforced, they can vanish as easily and rapidly as they came.

One important fact about this strange form of life we now share is that almost no one within it tries to take in the fate of democracy in both of these two key senses anywhere at all. This is neither surprising nor simply inappropriate. Only someone of great arrogance, and probably also someone in considerable intellectual confusion, would dream of attempting to grasp the fate of both across the entire globe. But the sharp bifurcation of attention for the vast majority of us between these two domains, however natural its sources or individually prudent its grounds, has extraordinarily malign consequences. It prompts us to split a preoccupation with the ethical and the desirable from any sustained attempt to grasp what is happening in the world and why it is happening. It sanctions the cultivation of normative fastidiousness, a connoisseurship of the prepossessing and the edifying. It also recognizes and applauds a cumulative knowledge and mastery of the practicalities of political competition. But it makes virtually no demand that these two should meet, and at least confront one another. Except opportunistically and by individual contingency, they therefore virtually never do.

The clearest setting of this disjunction in our social and political understanding is the organization of academic life, the modern intellectual division of labour at its most aspiring and self-regarding. What no competent modern student of politics can sanely attempt is to master both with equal resolution. Even to try to do so betokens either intellectual confusion or personal frivolity. But if the synthesis is beyond any possible professional, how are the huge amateur majorities of modern citizens to undertake it, as the sovereign choosers they presume themselves to be? (And what, if they prove to have neither the time, the nerve nor the inclination to do so, can they honourably do instead?)

There is something deep about the structure of this outcome. The condition of involuntary collective befuddlement which it unrelentingly

guarantees is not what Plato held against democracy. But it is hard not to see it as a blemish within our own form of life. It is hard to see, too, how in the end it can fail to corrupt each sense of democracy pretty thoroughly, abandoning the form of government to the tender mercies of the professionals, and abandoning too the conduct of refined cultural and intellectual enquiry to ever more scholastic and narcissistic introspection.

The strongest pressures behind democratization are resentment at condescension, and the will of individuals or groups to find better ways to defend their own interests. The power of the first is admirably captured by Tocqueville.[35] It focuses essentially on form and appearance, and rightly presupposes that democracy, however obstructed it may prove in practice, must at least surrender privilege at the level of form. It must recognize all citizens as equals and give each at least some opportunity to insist on being treated equally in ways which especially concern them. What it cannot in practice give them is equal power to defend their own interests. What prevents it from doing so above all is the scale and pervasiveness of inequality dictated by the order of egoism. In the Assembly at Athens any fully adult male with the good fortune to have been born a citizen, if they happened also to be present on the occasion and wished to do so,[36] had an equal right to address the people on what was to be done. They could, if only they had the courage, defend their own interests in person with their own judgement and in their own voice. In the law-making (and still more the war-making) decisions of a modern democracy, nothing vaguely similar is ever now true. Ordinary citizens are never present in their personal capacity within a legislative assembly. Still less do they ever hold executive authority as ordinary citizens within a modern state. In most modern democracies, most of the time and on most issues, ordinary citizens are almost certainly freer to speak or think than the Athenians ever were. The penalties they face for voicing views which most of their contemporaries dislike or find scandalous are far less harsh and altogether less public. But most also have

little chance to make themselves at all widely audible; and no one at all, except by resolute, strenuous and extremely successful competitive effort, has an effective right of direct access to legislative deliberation. The newspaper press, which John Stuart Mill offered to mid-nineteenth-century Britain as an effective substitute for the political immediacy of the Athens Assembly,[37] still does something to offset the lobbying power of great economic interests. But most of it, in many different parts of the world, belongs to a relatively small number of private individuals; and the ways in which it operates cannot be said seriously to modify the evident political impotence of the great majority of citizens at most times and over almost all issues. This effect is even more pronounced in the cases of television and radio, the most insistent of contemporary media of public communication. In Italy, in a scandalous but deeply symbolic conjunction, a single man at present owns several of the national television channels (as well as the biggest publishing company), controls most of the other television channels in his capacity as Prime Minister and heads the government as leader of a party which is effectively a personal fief.[38] What furnishes most of us with almost all the effective representation we receive for most of our interests is not our own access to any public forum or site of binding political choice. It is an enormously elaborate structure of divided labour, most of which operates wholly outside public view, and can be dragged into the light of day only sporadically, with great exertion, and as a result of some wholly undeniable political disaster. It is not, of course, part of the meaning of the term *democracy* that the political institutions which govern our lives should be so far beyond the reach of most of us almost all the time. But it remains clearly true that this is what democracy as a form of government now amounts to. How far could it still really amount to anything fundamentally different?

Because this complex of institutions and practices was never designed or chosen by anyone, it must be true that every aspect of it could perfectly well be quite different. Because it has spread so widely

now, however, and spread principally by imitation and competition, it can scarcely also be true that the complex as a whole could readily or rapidly alter into something drastically different. Still less could it hope to do so in ways which relied on winning general applause or even on gratifying most of those who were consciously aware of them. The key issue for this modern variant of democracy is how far it necessitates a level of alienation of will, judgement and choice which any ancient partisan of democracy could only see as its complete negation: at most a partially elective aristocracy,[39] and at worst a corrupt and heavily mystified oligarchy.

If ancient democracy was the citizens choosing freely and immediately for themselves, modern democracy, it seems, is principally the citizens very intermittently, choosing under highly constrained circumstances, the relatively small number of their fellows who will from then on choose for them. There are many obvious ways in which modern citizens have no need whatever to accept this bargain. They could insist on taking particular state decisions personally for themselves: putting them out to referenda, in which every adult citizen is just as eligible to vote as they are in a legislative election. Referenda do indeed play a role in the national politics of some states, both over key issues of inclusion or exclusion, and over especially contentious decisions, sometimes including constitutional amendments.[40] In the case of Taiwan, for example, early in 2004, an incumbent President even used the threat of a referendum asserting the right of the citizens to choose for themselves whether or not to reunite with China, to strengthen his hand against local opponents who favoured a more diplomatic approach to the People's Republic. (This came very close to putting the central issue of state security out to direct popular decision.) What referenda today have in common is that the terms of the choices offered are always decided by a ruling group of career politicians. It is more reasonable to see them as manoeuvres open to career politicians who expect them to work to their own advantage than as real surrenders of power back to the citizens from whom it

supposedly came. Where their expectation is disappointed, or the sway of the ruling group is successfully disrupted by their opponents, the consequences of adopting the expedient may dismay its initial sponsors. But the role of the electors who vote in the referendum will still be principally to hand the victory to one team of career politicians at the expense of another.

A more substantial democratic opportunity would go beyond the right to vote on issues which it suits the incumbent government to put to a referendum (on terms they can largely control for themselves). It would demand as well the opportunity to put to a referendum whatever issues the citizens themselves happen to wish, and permit them to define the terms of the resulting referendum on their own behalf. The first element in this opportunity is quite substantial, and not hard to supply. A right of citizen initiative in placing issues on the ballot has existed for some time, both in the State of California and in the Swiss Cantons.[41] In each setting it has naturally had many critics; and some of its consequences have proved extremely damaging. The right to take such decisions can readily extend as wide as the citizen body, or the openness of the Athenian Assembly to any citizen who wished to speak in it. What cannot be distributed so widely is the opportunity to focus the terms of the choice offered. There the division of labour which rationalizes, and in some degree causes, the professionalization of modern politics enforces an effective alienation of the task of formulation from a constituency as wide as the citizen body to a relatively small group entrusted to think, choose and write on its behalf. To draft a coherent text of any length requires in the end a single process of consecutive thought: if not the mind and pen of a single person, at least a conversation between modest numbers of people, who can hear one another and respond to the pressure of each other's thoughts.

In recent years academic political philosophers have devoted considerable attention to outlining the qualities which deserve most weight in taking public decisions of any consequence.[42] They have

taken their cue from Aristotle's acknowledgement of the principal merit of democratic choice: its capacity to reach out to, and bring into play, the full breadth of knowledge and awareness of the entire citizen body.[43] The assemblage and sifting of this range of experience, as Aristotle saw it, was a process of deliberation. For a group of human beings who can communicate with one another, deliberation might hope ideally to become a common enquiry, and an exercise in public reasoning, which could bring into play every element of wisdom present in the citizen body. It could also hope to subject the less wise and more grossly partial elements within the judgement of each citizen to disciplined public scrutiny and mutually accountable criticism.

Deliberative democracy, democracy which embodies and realizes democracy at its best, attempts to prescribe how a community of human beings should wish for its public decisions to be taken. Many themes have naturally suggested themselves. It should take these decisions reflectively, attentively and in good faith. It should take them as decisions about what would be publicly good, and not as calculations of what would be personally most advantageous. It should take them non-exclusively: ensuring that all those whom they affect, and all who are sufficiently mature and rational to identify their own interests,[44] can play an active part in determining their outcome. More exactingly still, it should take them in a way in which all can enter, and all who wish to in fact do enter, the deliberation as equals, and hold equal weight within it.[45]

The order of egoism clashes more drastically with some of these requirements than it does with others. But both as a form of life and a milieu within which to live, it is at best neutral, and at worst blankly indifferent, towards any of them. Towards some it is, and will always remain, quite openly hostile. Within the order of egoism a large part of the point of power is always money, and a large part of the point of money is always power.[46] Individuals can, and conspicuously do, shape their own lives in very different terms. But it

is difficult (and possibly flatly impossible) for them to override the main structuring principle of the form within which they live. Democracy as a form of government and democratization as a social, cultural, economic and political process have very different rhythms. They are also subject to quite different sorts of causal pressures. Democratization is open-ended, indeterminate and exploratory. It sets out from, and responds to, the conception of democracy as a political value, a way in which whatever matters deeply for a body of human beings should in the end be decided. Democracy as a form of government is rather less open-ended, considerably more determinate and far less audacious in its explorations. Because in government some human beings always extensively control very many others in numerous ways this fundamental contrast between value and form of government has some obvious merits. It is better for there to be clear limits to how far you can be controlled by others. Democratization today can be both more exploratory and braver than democratic government because, unlike the latter, it is neither licensed by, nor responsible to or for, the order of egoism. It sits much lighter within our form of life, always searching out the limits of licence, but leaving the task of securing that form of life, with varying degrees of gratitude, firmly to others.

Representative democracy, the form in which democracy has spread so widely over the last six decades, has equipped itself for the journey by making its peace ever more explicitly with the order of egoism. It offers a framework within which that order can flourish, but also one in which the citizens at large can set some bounds both to its pretensions and to its consequences. Wealth by permission of the people may or may not present less of a practical hazard to any of them than wealth secured in open defiance of their will. At least it is less obnoxious. The battle lines between the two orders which Babeuf and his fellow conspirators saw run very differently in any actual representative democracy, losing all their starkness and most of their political plausibility. You can track the progress of representative democracy as

a form of government from the 1780s until today, sticking pins into the map to record its advance, and noting not merely the growing homogenization of its institutional formats as the decades go by, but also the cumulative discrediting of the rich variety of other state forms which have competed against it throughout, often with very considerable initial assurance. The state form which advances across this time-span was pioneered by Europeans; and it has spread in a world in which first Europe and then the United States wielded quite disproportionate military and economic power.

For much of this time that state form was taken up by others for its promise to withstand or offset the power wielded by its inventors, or spurned instead in favour of rivals (above all communism or fascism) which promised more credibly to provide the same service. For most of the twentieth century, it was spurned with particular contempt in the great wounded former empires of Russia and China. But for much of the first half of the century it was spurned too in temporarily more potent and menacing states like Germany and Japan, with better immediate prospects of turning the tables on their overweening enemies. Its most decisive advances, the largest number of fresh pins moving across the map, came with three great defeats. The first was the breaking of German and Japanese military power in the Second World War. The second, which followed closely, and also required much violent struggle if of a more dispersed kind, was the collapse of western colonial empire across the world, most of it within two decades of the close of the Second World War. Representative democracy was the model imposed on their defeated enemies by that war's western victors.[47] It was also the model which, after much preliminary foot-dragging, they chose to bequeath to most of their former colonies, from the stunning precedent of imperial India,[48] to the most parlous of Caribbean or Pacific island dependencies. Only with the return of Hong Kong to the People's Republic of China was the choice firmly repudiated from the outset by the new sovereign (if scarcely by the inhabitants themselves). With the third great defeat, the end of the

Soviet Union and the collapse of the bloc of states which it had built so painstakingly around it on its own model, representative democracy shook off all remaining exemplary rivals, and became virtually an index of global normality. It was still firmly rejected in China, site of the lengthiest and proudest tradition of political autonomy of any human society, and very little dented in its rulers' sense of self-sufficiency by more than half a century of rule under the aegis of a local variant of an openly western political doctrine. It was excluded tenaciously and brutally in many other parts of the world, in most cases by the rulers of societies visibly faltering in the struggle for wealth and power. But none of its numerous and sometimes well-armed enemies could any longer confront it with a countervailing model of their own, with the power to reach out to and convince populations with different cultures and any real opportunity to decide their political arrangements for themselves. On a global scale nothing like this had ever occurred before, although there were more local precedents scattered throughout history, in the Asian states encircling the Central Kingdom of China,[49] or the long shadows cast by Rome across the continent of Europe.

In the course of this last advance, a number of plausible and widely credited assumptions have been refuted. It is clearly not true, for example, that the western provenance of this political model makes it somehow ineligible for other parts of the world or for populations with sharply contrasted cultural traditions. It can be (and has been) adopted with some success in every continent, in societies with long and cruel experiences of arbitrary rule, cultures of great historical depth, and religious traditions which insist on the profound inequality of human beings and the duty of most of them to view their superiors with the utmost deference, in East and South and South East Asia, in Latin America, and more sporadically and precariously, in Sub-Saharan Africa and even the Middle East. In itself this is scarcely surprising. Every element in these supposed disqualifications had prominent counterparts over most of the history of the

European continent. Behind the resistance to its advance there lies sometimes antipathy towards the western societies from which it originated, and sometimes a more urgent hatred of the immediate power and arrogance of the United States itself. But accompanying both there is also always an understandable reluctance on the part of those who hold power within them on other bases and by different means at the prospect of being subverted openly and from within.

This advance has occurred in a world of intensifying trade and ever-accelerating communication, in which people, goods and information traverse the globe incessantly. It is a world in which human populations are drawn more tightly together, and depend more abjectly for their security and prosperity on the skills and good intentions of those who rule them than they have ever done before. That world certainly needs many facilities which it has yet to acquire, and not a few which it has yet even to invent or imagine. But one facility which it clearly needs all the time, and with the utmost urgency, is a basis on which its human denizens can address the task of ensuring the skill and good intentions of their rulers for themselves. This task has many different components. It requires the searching out and assemblage of a vast range of information, the strenuous exercise of critical judgement, the permanent monitoring of the performance of those who devote most of their lives to competitive politics or public administration. There are no cheap or reliable recipes for guaranteeing a successful outcome, and little evidence that institutional design on its own can hope to shoulder most of the burden. There are also a great many sites, including numerous formally independent nation states, in which the rulers show little sign of recognizing any such responsibility, and the great majority of the population has little, if any, effective power to protect themselves against the fecklessness or malignity of those who do for the moment rule them.

In the midst of impotence and despair, representative democracy is scarcely an impressive recipe for building order, peace, security, pros-

perity or justice. No one could readily mistake it for a solution to the Riddle of History. But, in its simple unpretentious way, it has by now established a clear claim to meet a global need better than any of its competitors. The fact that the need itself is still so urgent, and now so evidently confronts every human population of any scale, make the question of how to meet it genuinely global. They also make it a question to which, for the first time, there might be a truly global answer. The fact that none of representative democracy's surviving rivals acknowledges the need as clearly, and none at all volunteers to provide the question with a global answer, lend it a unique status, fusing timeliness and well-considered modesty with a claim for the present to something very close to indispensability.

It is hard to judge how long this claim will hold up. There are many ineliminable limitations to the form of government, and much that it cannot in principle ensure for any human population. It cannot hope to render professional politics ingratiating to most of us anywhere for any length of time; and it duly fails to do so. It guarantees a disconcerting combination of shabbiness of motive and pretence to public spirit throughout most of the cohorts of practising politicians. That shabbiness might be veiled in more closed and less audibly competitive conditions; but it is bound to be highlighted mercilessly throughout the political arena by the vigorous efforts of competitors, inside and outside their own political groupings. All of this was seen from democracy's outset in Athens itself; and its key elements were described with unsurpassed panache and scorn by Plato himself.

It fashions a world in which political leaders call incessantly for the rest of us to trust them, and rely implicitly on their competence, integrity and good intentions. But within that world they must press their appeal permanently in the teeth of their rivals' indefatigable explanations of just how misplaced such trust would be, and how naïve it must be to confer it. For many decades, in many settings, the mass political party served to some degree to generate and sustain this kind of trust, at least between particular groups of the citizens and

the party itself as an organization. It lent a political shape to communities of residence or occupation, helped to define a sense of shared interest across them, and established salient outlines for political conflict over the exercise of governmental power.[50] But in the long run many different influences have dissipated most of the plausibility of party structures. The struggle to sustain a trust in political leadership has been submerged increasingly by the rising waters of popular disbelief. Schumpeter's electoral entrepreneurs[51] must trade now on a market where trust is more elusive and expensive than ever, and the grounds for distrust easier and cheaper than ever to disseminate effectively. Even the more insistent of their newer weapons, the skills of the advertising profession and the ever-extending facilities of the media of communication, are far better suited to dispelling trust than to nurturing it or creating it in the first place. Whatever you should learn from advertisements, it can scarcely be a generalized credulity.

Seen as a whole, this is a disenchanted and demoralized world, all too well adjusted to lives organized around the struggle to maximize personal income. But it is also a world permanently in quest of opportunities for re-enchantment, and often ready to identify and respond to the most fugitive and unreliable of cues: not just the youth, energy and determination of Tony Blair, but the cinematic vigour of Arnold Schwarzenegger, or the entrepreneurial momentum of Silvio Berlusconi.[52] Viewed with charity the modern democratic politician's world is a strenuous ordeal, scanned intermittently by most citizens, often querulously and always with some suspicion. It is a world from which faith, deference and even loyalty have largely passed away, and the keenest of personal admiration seldom lasts for very long.

If this is the triumph of democracy, it is a triumph which very many will always find disappointing. It carries none of the glamour which Pericles invoked for its Athenian namesake. Over the two centuries in which it has come to triumph, some have seen it simply as an impostor, bearer of a name which it has stolen, and instrument for the rule of the people by something unmistakably different. No one

anywhere nowadays can plausibly see it as rule by the people. In itself, this is no occasion for regret. Had it really been rule by the people, as Madison and Sieyes, Robespierre and even Buonarroti, all warned, it would assuredly not have triumphed, but dissolved instead, immediately and irreversibly, into chaos. The least ambitious case which can be made for it is that it is so very far from the worst that we have to fear: that it offers the inhabitants of the world in which we find ourselves the safest and least personally offensive basis on which to live together with our fellow citizens within our own states. That service is not one which we have yet learned to provide at all reliably by any other means; and no one could reasonably deny its fundamental importance. But that is a case essentially for the practical merits of representative democracy as a form of government. It shows no evident appropriateness in our selection of the word *democracy* as the name for this form of government.

For that name to be appropriate, it must mean more than this. More stirringly perhaps, it must also imply that representative democracy as it now is cannot be all for which we can reasonably hope. There must be some link between the historical fact that the word itself means so much more (or means something so different) and the possibility that the way in which we are now governed can be altered to fit that word better, or at least recover some imaginative contact with it. This may or may not prove to be so. (It will depend, amongst other things, on how we act politically in the future.) There are at least two drastic ways in which the democracy of today might perhaps be altered in this direction. One is in the flow and structuring of information amongst citizens, and the degree to which all governments restrict and withhold information from the governed. Governmental seclusion is the most direct and also the deepest subversion of the democratic claim,[53] sometimes prudent, but never fully compatible with the literal meaning of the form of rule. The more governments control what their fellow citizens know the less they can claim the authority of those citizens for how they rule. The more governments

withhold information from their fellow citizens the less accountable they are to those who give them their authority. Even to fit its own name, modern representative democracy would have to transform itself very radically in this respect. The struggle for that transformation will certainly be arduous because the interests in obstructing it are both so huge and so well positioned to impede it. But the case against transforming it has now become merely one of discretion. No powerful imaginative pressures still survive to challenge the judgement that this is how it plainly should be altered.

The second drastic way in which our existing practice of rule might converge more with its democratic title finds itself for the present in very different circumstances. But it is just as simple, and not obviously any less compelling. As a word, *democracy* has won this global competition to designate legitimate rule largely by courtesy of Buonarroti's order of egoism, the thought-through self-understanding and endorsement of a capitalist economy. For Buonarroti himself its victory in this guise would have been a single vast act of theft. But since he had so little comprehension of the basis on which that economy had grown in his own day, and no foreknowledge of the utterly different world which it has since constructed, his assessment carries very little weight. What still retains most of its original force is the simple perception that a ruling people cannot confront one another in conditions of acute inequality, where a few control many before, during and after every governmental choice or action. For well over a century capitalist economies faced fierce political pressure from well-organized mass political parties, representing many millions of citizens, to compress these inequalities and place all citizens on something closer to an equal political footing. At least for the moment those pressures have largely disappeared. But their disappearance does nothing to lessen the anomaly of the chasm between the meaning of democracy as a word and the substance of contemporary representative democracy in action. At present that chasm seems unbridgeable even in principle. It could be spanned at all only

if we came to understand economies well enough to establish some real control over them, an idea which may not even make sense, and an achievement which certainly seems practically quite beyond our reach.

For the moment, therefore, democracy has won its global near-monopoly as basis for legitimate rule in a setting which largely contradicts its own pretensions. It remains blatantly at odds with many of the most obtrusive features of existing practices of rule. It still clashes systematically and fundamentally with the defining logic of economic organization. But its victory is no mere illusion. It clashes with each as an independent power in its own right, and with an appeal altogether warmer than either. It may for the present have less power than either (certainly far less than the logic of economic organization). But it still mounts a permanent challenge to each. Melodramatically but not essentially misleadingly, you can see the relations between the three as a long drawn-out war of position, in which the fronts are always under pressure, and no one can foresee quite where they will run even a few years ahead.[54]

Beyond (or beneath) this war of position runs another and older struggle, to which democracy as yet barely applies even in the breach. The main elements of rule amongst human beings still occur within the individual politically sovereign units of the nation state. Democracy has won its global near-monopoly as an answer to the question of how a nation state should be governed. Much else is adjusted, co-operatively or quarrelsomely, among groups of nation states in the endless variety of arenas constructed for the purpose. But the scope of the adjustment is still determined by (and its enforcement still overwhelmingly left to) individual states.

Many hope (and a few even believe)[55] that in the long run democracy can and will provide a good name for a quite different basis both for adjustment and for enforcement. It will keep its global title to define the conditions for legitimate rule, but it will also itself enforce those conditions, unitarily and comprehensively, across the entire

globe. In this vision democracy would become global not just in pretension or aspiration but in simple fact. One *demos*, the human population of the whole globe, would not merely claim a shared political authority across that globe, but literally rule it together. This is a natural yearning (with a lengthy Christian and pre-Christian past).[56] It reflects powerful and wholly creditable sentiments. But it is an extremely strained line of thought.

It ignores the direct link between adjudication and coercion in defining what a state is. It thinks away (or temporarily forgets) the vast chasm of power and wealth between different populations across the world. It sets aside not merely the victory of the order of egoism, but also the factors which have caused it to win. It grossly sentimentalizes the sense in which democracy ever does rule even in an individual nation state. As an expectation about the human future it is little better than absurd. But it gets one key judgement exactly right. Democracy may or may not provide either a compelling or a reliable recipe for organizing political choice and its enforcement within one country. It certainly cannot hope, just by doing so, to provide at the same time a compelling or realistic recipe for organizing the political or economic relations between that country and others. Unless we can make more impressive headway in identifying and installing such a recipe within our own country and for our own country, there is little danger of hitting on a remedy for the brutal historical gap between the world's different populations. Perhaps, given world enough and time, there could be such a remedy, and not merely in moral philosophy or welfare economics, but even in economic organization and political practice. If there really could be, what is quite clear is that we are not for the present moving towards it. Until we do, we should at least expect to go on paying the price for the scale of our failure to do so.

NOTES

NOTES TO THE PREFACE

1. This movement of transliteration and translation across the languages and societies of the world is a piece of genuinely global intellectual and political history which has yet to be traced with any care. Until we know why and how it has happened, we cannot hope to understand one of the central features of modern politics (or perhaps simply to understand modern politics?). For a stimulating comparative study centring on concepts and practices of freedom see Robert H. Taylor (ed), *The Idea of Freedom in Asia and Africa* (Stanford: Stanford University Press, 2002), especially Sudipta Kaviraj's superb analysis of India's experience. The most ambitious attempt to assess the significance of its impact in the key case of China (oldest, densest, most defiantly autonomous of the world's cultures, and globalizer in its own right and in its own terms very long ago) has been made over the last thirty years by Thomas A. Metzger. (See conveniently his 'The Western Concept of Civil Society in the Context of Chinese History', Sudipta Kaviraj & Sunil Khilnani (eds), *Civil Society: History and*

Possibilities (Cambridge: Cambridge University Press, 2001), 204–31.) For classic studies of parts of the journey, see Hao Chang, *Liang Ch'I-Chao and Intellectual Transition in China 1890–1907* (Cambridge, Mass.: Harvard University Press, 1971) and Benjamin Schwartz, *In Search of Wealth and Power: Yen Fu and the West* (New York: Harper, 1964). For Japan see chapters by Kenneth B. Pyle (on 'Meiji Conservatism'), Peter Duus & Irwin Scheiner (on 'Socialism, Liberalism, Marxism'), and by Andrew E. Barshay (on 'Postwar Social and Political Thought 1945–1990') in Bob Tadashi Wakabayashi (ed), *Modern Japanese Thought* (Cambridge: Cambridge University Press, 1998), esp 122–25, 297–98 and 326–27; Andrew Barshay, 'Imagining Democracy in Postwar Japan: Reflections on Maruyama Masao and Modernism', *Journal of Japanese Studies*, 18, 1992; Nobutaka Ike, *The Beginnings of Political Democracy in Japan* (Baltimore: Johns Hopkins University Press, 1950). For transliteration into Arabic see, for example, James L. Gelvin, 'Developmentalism, Revolution and Freedom in the Arab East', in Taylor (ed), *Idea of Freedom*, especially (for Gamal Abdul Nasser) 85–86; or into Wolof, in Senegal, Frederick Schaffer's exemplary *Democracy in Translation: Understanding Politics in an Unfamiliar Culture* (Ithaca: Cornell University Press, 1998).

2. It is important to underline how recently this has become a well-secured judgement. Even now, the relative scale of China's population means that only the countervailing weight of India's numbers makes it obviously true. Even twenty-five years ago the presumption that India was as likely to remain democratic as Holland would have seemed (and perhaps been) quixotic.

NOTES TO CHAPTER 1

1. Since we have come by now to mean so many different things by it, and since there is so much about the past of which we are blankly ignorant, you cannot really say when democracy in that sense began, or even, in any interesting sense, when it might have done so.

2. Someone who earned their living from composing speeches or teaching others how to do so. For all three of these roles Athens, at the time and later, offered pre-eminent examples, figures who still tower over the entire history of western culture: Aeschylus, Sophocles, Euripides, Plato, Aristotle, Demosthenes. Some were more friend than enemy of the democracy. But even these did not take the trouble, or see the occasion, to praise Athens's political regime and way of life with the same zest and amplitude in any text which has come down to us. One, at least, went out of his way to do exactly the opposite.

3. Thucydides, *History of the Peloponnesian War Books I & II*, tr Charles Forster Smith (Cambridge, Mass.: Harvard University Press, 1928), Bk I, xxii, 1, pp 38–39. For the novelty and self-consciousness of Thucydides's method at this point see Simon Hornblower, *A Commentary on Thucydides, Vol 1* (Clarendon Press: Oxford, 1997), 59–61.

4. Thucydides, *History*, I, xxii, 4, pp 40–41. Thucydides's claim was to have composed it as a possession for all time, rather than a prize essay to be heard for the moment (Hornblower, *Commentary*, 61–62).

5. Josiah Ober, *Mass and Elite in Democratic Athens* (Princeton: Princeton University Press, 1989); Harvey Yunis, *Taming*

Democracy: Models of Rhetoric in Classical Athens (Ithaca: Cornell University Press, 1996). He did not, of course, hold power solely by making speeches (cf M.I. Finley, *Politics in the Ancient World* (Cambridge: Cambridge University Press, 1983); Finley, 'Athenian Demagogues', *Past and Present*, 21, 1962, 3–24), but the speeches were essential to his capacity to hold it. The principal sources for the career of Pericles are Thucydides's *History* and Plutarch's *Life*. For an excellent brief summary see the article by David Lewis, *Encyclopedia Britannica*, 15th ed, 1974.

6. Thucydides, *History*, II, lxv, 9, pp 376–77: Athens 'became something that was a democracy by name, but actually a rule by the first man'. (See Hornblower, *Commentary*, 346, and for critical assessment of the claim, 344–47.)

7. Buried where they fell, on the battlefield where Athens, standing virtually alone, saved Greece from the massive land forces of the first great Persian invasion in 490BC.

8. For Pericles's speech, see Thucydides, *History*, II, xxxv–xlvi, pp 318–41. For the significance of the funeral oration as a public ceremony, and its determined use in defining Athens as a political community, both to itself and to others, see Nicole Loraux's impressive *The Invention of Athens*, tr Alan Sheridan (Cambridge, Mass.: Harvard University Press, 1986).

9. Thucydides, *History*, II, xxxviii, 1, pp 322–23

10. Thucydides, *History*, II, xxxvii, 1–2, pp 322–23. The translation is disputed, see Hornblower, *Commentary*, 298–99.

11. Thucydides, *History*, II, xli, 1, pp 330–31: 'In a word, then, I say that our city as a whole is the school (*paideusin*) of Hellas.' Hornblower (*Commentary*, 307–8) has a thoughtful discussion of what Thucydides intended Pericles to convey, and commends the translation 'a living lesson'.

12. Thucydides, *History*, II, xl, 2, pp 328–29. Hornblower, *Commentary*, 305–6 & 77–78, citing L.B. Carter, *The Quiet Athenian* (Oxford: Clarendon Press, 1985), 45. Note the balance between committed public concern and the levels of mutual respect and civility which Pericles emphasizes alongside it.

13. As Loraux's work shows excellently.

14. *Metics (metoikoi)* were resident aliens.

15. For the range of intellectual criticism prompted by Athens's democratic experience, see especially Josiah Ober, *Political Dissent in Democratic Athens: Intellectual Critics of Popular Rule* (Princeton: Princeton University Press, 1998).

16. Pseudo-Xenophon, *The Constitution of Athens*, tr G. Bowersock (Cambridge, Mass.: Harvard University Press, 1968). No doubt the main reason for continuing so to call him is, as Mogens Hansen says (Mogens H. Hansen, *The Athenian Democracy in the Age of Demosthenes* (Oxford: Blackwell, 1991), 5), because that is what he sounds like. See too: A.W. Gomme, 'The Old Oligarch', in *More Essays in Greek History and Literature* (Oxford: Basil Blackwell, 1962), 38–69.

17. Cf his repeated formula: 'I do not praise (*ouk epaino*)...' (Pseudo-Xenophon, I, 1, pp 474–75; III, 1, pp 498–99 etc).

18. Pseudo-Xenophon, I, 4 , pp 476–77

19. Pseudo-Xenophon, I, 2, pp 474–75

20. Pseudo-Xenophon, I, 4, pp 476–77

21. Pseudo-Xenophon, I, 1, pp 474–75; 'in making their choice they have chosen to let the worst people be better off than the good (*chrestous*). Therefore on this account I do not think well of their constitution. But since they have decided to have it so, I intend to point out how well they preserve their constitution and accomplish those things for which the rest of the Greeks criticize them.'

22. Pseudo-Xenophon, I, 2, pp 474–75

23. Pseudo-Xenophon, I, 5, pp 476–77: *to beltiston* – literally, the best bit.

24. Pseudo-Xenophon, I, 5, pp 476–77

25. Pseudo-Xenophon, I, 6–8, pp 478–79

26. Pseudo-Xenophon, I, 3, pp 476–77

27. Pseudo-Xenophon, I, 7, pp 478–79

28. Cf John Dunn, *The Cunning of Unreason: Making Sense of Politics* (London: HarperCollins/New York: Basic Books, 2000).

29. Compare the status of 'spin' in assessments of the political merits and limitations of the Blair government.

30. Compare, to take distasteful recent examples, the task of capturing the political realities of Taliban Afghanistan, Kim Jong Il's North Korea, or Saddam Hussein's Iraq.

31. Cf A.H.M. Jones, *Athenian Democracy* (Oxford: Basil Blackwell, 1957); M.I. Finley, *Democracy Ancient and Modern*, 2nd ed (London: The Hogarth Press, 1985) & *Politics in the Ancient World* (Cambridge: Cambridge University Press, 1983); Hansen, *The Athenian Democracy*; Robin Osborne, 'Athenian Democracy: something to celebrate?', *Dialogos*, 1, 1994, 48–58; 'The Demos and its Divisions in classical Athens', Oswyn Murray & S.R.F. Price (eds), *The Greek City* (Oxford: Clarendon Press, 1990), 265–93; 'Ritual, finance, politics: an account of Athenian democracy', R. Osborne & S. Hornblower (eds), *Ritual, Finance, Politics: Athenian Democratic Accounts presented to David Lewis* (Oxford: Clarendon Press, 1994),1–21.

32. They do not make those realities unreal (somehow cancel them), still less render them inconsequential. They merely make them, in many respects and for many purposes, inaccessible to us.

33. Compare three classic pictures: H.L.A. Hart, *The Concept of Law* (Oxford: Clarendon Press, 1961); Ronald Dworkin, *Law's Empire* (London: Fontana, 1986); Michel Foucault, *Power* (London: Allen Lane Penguin Press, 2001).

34. Josiah Ober, *Political Dissent in Democratic Athens*

35. Compare the reactions of Western Europe and North America to the military suspension of elections in Algeria in 1991, and the hideous consequences which followed from that suspension.

36. Hansen, *Athenian Democracy*, 29–32; Simon Hornblower, 'Creation and Development of Democratic Institutions in Ancient Greece', J. Dunn (ed), *Democracy: The Unfinished Journey* (Oxford: Oxford University Press, 1992), 1–16.

37. Only wealthier (and invariably male) Athenians continued, for almost a century, to be eligible to hold such office.

38. Hansen, *Athenian Democracy*, 29–32. G.E.M. de Sainte Croix, *The Class Struggle in the Ancient Greek World* (London: Duckworth, 1981) is the most ambitious modern attempt to place the Athenian experience in the perspective of the history of the Greek world as a whole; but he does not offer a systematic assessment of Solon's purposes or achievements.

39. Plato, Machiavelli, James Harrington, Rousseau, James Madison, Sieyes, Robespierre, Jeremy Bentham, even, as it turned out, somewhat self-contradictorily, Lenin.

40. All Lawgivers/Legislators were men. Contrast, according to Plato (who blandly credited Pericles's to his mistress Aspasia), the real authors of funeral orations (Plato, *Menexenus*, tr R.G. Bury (Cambridge, Mass.: Harvard University Press, 1929), 329–81, 336–39, 380–81).

41. As far as we now know. But compare the argument of Hansen, *Athenian Democracy*, 69–70.

42. Herodotus, *History*, tr A.D. Godley (Cambridge, Mass.: Harvard University Press, 1922), V, 66, 2, pp 72–73; Hansen, 33–34

43. Thucydides, *History*, II, xxxvi, 1–2, pp 320–21; Loraux, *Invention of Athens*

44. Thucydides, *History*, I, ii, 3–6, pp 4–7

45. Hansen, *Athenian Democracy*, 92–93. Hansen's outstanding book provides the best contemporary account of the institutions of the democracy at work.

46. Hansen, *Athenian Democracy*, 90–94

47. Hansen, *Athenian Democracy*, 94

48. In the fourth century BC this may have ceased to be so, at least for some, because of the institution of the *misthos*, a daily rate of pay not merely for acting as a juror on the popular courts but also for attending the Assembly itself. The members of the Council, serving in effect throughout an entire year, had always needed to have their own meals provided for them at public expense. The *misthos* was loathed by critics of the democracy for coarsening the social composition of its principal institutions, supplementing the motives for political participation by grossly material incentives, and altering the democracy's natural political balance by so doing: precisely the consequences which appealed to the citizen majority who opted for it.

49. Hansen, *Athenian Democracy*, chapter 6

50. Hansen, *Athenian Democracy*, chapter 10

51. With some of the smaller units there may have been an element of duress in the volunteering (Hansen, *Athenian Democracy*, 249), as there often still is in small political units to this day.

52. This was not a position which could be held twice by the same person in any given year (Hansen, *Athenian Democracy*, 250), perhaps ever.

53. Plutarch, *Lives*, Vol 2, tr Bernadotte Perrin (Cambridge, Mass.: Harvard University Press, 1916); *Pericles*, 32, pp 92–95; 35, p 103; Thucydides, *History*, II. lxv, 3–5, pp 374–75

54. Although modern historians have sometimes employed the term to analyse aspects of Athenian politics, the Athenians had nothing which distantly resembled a modern political party.

55. See, especially, Finley, *Politics in the Ancient World* & W. Robert Connor, *The New Politicians of Fifth-Century Athens* (Princeton: Princeton University Press, 1971). We can certainly assume, as all the finest historians of Athens always have, that this hard political labour of co-ordination, persuasion, reward, and threat must have gone on all the time.

56. Slave-dependent, women-excluding, unabashedly ethnocentric. No one any longer would care to defend these confines openly.

57. In the case of Plato this remains a partisan judgement. He certainly had personal and family links with men who did try to subvert it; and no one could fail to recognize that he viewed many aspects of it with visceral revulsion. But the reason we still read him today is that he understood some features of it all too well, and can still help us to understand them too, should we happen to wish to.

58. Aristotle, *Politics*, tr H. Rackham (Cambridge, Mass.: Harvard University Press, 1932); *The Athenian Constitution*, tr H. Rackham (Cambridge, Mass.: Harvard University Press, 1935)

59. George Grote, *A History of Greece from the Earliest Period to the Generation Contemporary with Alexander the Great* (London, 1846–56): and for the longer-term historical context see Jennifer Tolbert Roberts, *Athens on Trial: The Antidemocratic Tradition in Western Thought* (Princeton: Princeton University Press, 1994).

60. Which are the words we reach for when we try hardest to steady ourselves intellectually and politically in face of the greatest trauma of modern history? Cf the volume subtitles chosen by Ian

Kershaw for his magisterial study of Hitler's impact: *Hitler: A Life*, Vol 1 *Hubris*; Vol 2 *Nemesis* (London: Allen Lane, 1998 & 2000).

61. Cf Cynthia Farrar, *The Origins of Democratic Thinking* (Cambridge: Cambridge University Press, 1988)

62. Thomas Hobbes, *Hobbes's Thucydides*, ed Richard Schlatter (New Brunswick, N.J.: Rutgers University Press, 1975)

63. Pseudo-Xenophon, I, 5, pp 476–77

64. It would be more accurate to say jury murder. But this is too odd a phrase in modern English to introduce, without explaining it at the same time. The mass juries of the Athenian courts were one of the most potent instruments of its democracy in action. When they voted for Socrates's death, they were making as definite a political choice as when they voted in the Assembly to savage Mitylene, or voted again, a few hours later, to reprieve it (Thucydides, *History*, III, xxxvi, i–xlix, 4, pp 54–87).

65. Plato, *Crito*, tr H.N. Fowler (Cambridge, Mass.: Harvard University Press, 1914), 150–91

66. Plato, *Apology*, tr H.N. Fowler (Cambridge, Mass.: Harvard University Press, 1914), 68–145

67. Whatever his own personal flirtations with incumbents of that role (cf Plato, *Epistles*, tr R.G. Bury (Cambridge, Mass.: Harvard University Press, 1929), Seventh Letter, 476–565)

68. Just what practical conclusions to draw from this (or even what practical conclusions Plato himself went on to draw from it) remains far from obvious – far enough from obvious to provide the main intellectual stock in trade for an entire school of political thought, the extended *clientela* of Leo Strauss, an important element in American (and hence in world) politics over the last three decades: Ann Norton, *Leo Strauss and the Politics of American Empire* (New Haven: Yale University Press, 2004).

69. Thomas Hobbes, *De Cive* (1642) & *Leviathan* (1651).

70. Plato, *The Republic*, tr Paul Shorey, 2 vols (Cambridge, Mass.: Harvard University Press, 1930–35), 559D–562, Vol 2, 295–303

71. *Republic*, 561D, 302–03

72. *Republic*, 561D, 302–03

73. *Republic*, 561C–E, 300–03

74. *Republic*, 562B–C, 304–05

75. *Republic*, 562C, 304–05

76. *Republic*, 562D–563 D, 304–11

77. *Republic*, 563D, 310–11

78. *Republic*, 564A, 312–13

79. *Republic*, 564A, 312–13, 566D–580C, 322–69

80. Plato's later political writings, *The Laws* and *The Politicus* (or *Statesman*), have less to say about democracy and left far less imprint on subsequent political perception or judgement.

81. Aristotle, *Politics*, 1279b, II 19–20, pp 208–09

82. Aristotle, *Politics*, 1279a, II 37–39, pp 206–07

83. Aristotle, *Politics*, 1279a, I 18, 1279b, I 10, 204–07

84. Cf, helpfully, Martha C. Nussbaum, *The Fragility of Goodness* (Cambridge: Cambridge University Press, 1986), Pt 3, 235–394

85. Cf David Bostock, *Aristotle's Ethical Theory* (Oxford: Oxford University Press, 2001)

86. Compare Hegel's dazzling portrait, 'The Political Work of Art', in *The Philosophy of History*, Pt II, chapter 3, tr J. Sibree (New York: Dover, 1956), 250–76. E.M. Butler, *The Tyranny of Greece over Germany* (Cambridge: Cambridge University Press, 1935).

Contrast the findings on the classical Greek *polis* itself of Mogens Hansen's massive collaborative study of the city state form across time and space: '95 Theses about the Greek Polis in the Archaic and Classical Periods', *Historia*, 52 (2003), 257–82.

87. Cf Finley, *Politics in the Ancient World* with Farrar, *Origins of Democratic Thinking*.

88. Cf e.g. Quentin Skinner, *Visions of Politics* (Cambridge: Cambridge University Press, 2002), Vol 1, chapters 8–10

89. Cf Dunn, *The Cunning of Unreason*

90. Cf John Dunn, *Western Political Theory in the Face of the Future* 2nd ed (Cambridge: Cambridge University Press, 1993), chapter 1

91. Cf Neil Harding, 'The Marxist-Leninist Detour', in Dunn (ed), *Democracy: The Unfinished Journey* (Oxford: Oxford University Press, 1992), 155–87

92. For the fate of the San Bushmen (a periphery of the periphery) see Leonard Thompson, *Survival in Two Worlds: Moshoeshoe of Lesotho* (Oxford: Clarendon Press, 1975), chapter 1, esp 13 & 19, or C.W. de Kiewiet, *A History of South Africa: Social and Economic* (Oxford: Oxford University Press, 1957), chapter 1, 19–20; for the Nuer as British anthropologists liked to think of them see E.E. Evans-Pritchard, *The Nuer* (Oxford: Clarendon Press, 1940). For their more recent fate see Douglas H. Johnson, *The Root Causes of Sudan's Civil Wars* (London: James Currey & Bloomington: Indiana University Press, 2004).

93. One of the bravest attempts to do so is Mark Elvin, *The Pattern of the Chinese Past* (Stanford: Stanford University Press, 1972). See also G.E.R. Lloyd & N. Sivin, *The Way and the Word* (New Haven: Yale University Press, 2002), and, in more breathless outline, Jared Diamond, *Guns, Germs and Steel* (London: Jonathan Cape, 1997), chapter 16, 'How China became Chinese', 322–33.

94. Mogens Hansen (*The Athenian Democracy*) claims something close to this for fourth-century Athens, but as a political outcome, and certainly not as a verbal implication of the term *demokratia* itself.

95. See particularly Fergus Millar, *The Crowd in Rome in the Late Republic* (Ann Arbor: University of Michigan Press, 1998) & *The Roman Republic in Political Thought* (Hanover: University Press of New England, 2002), an exceptionally illuminating study of the development of Roman political thought and its historical impact.

96. Though see, still, Ronald Syme, *The Roman Revolution* (Oxford: Clarendon Press, 1939), or Christian Meier, *Caesar*, tr David McLintock (London: Fontana, 1996).

97. Though Vergil's adamantine formula – *Tu regere imperio populos, Romane, memento*: Remember, O Roman, that it is for you to rule peoples with empire (Vergil, *Aeneid*, VI, 851) – scarcely suggests the latter.

98. The great historian of this endless circling back is John Pocock. See, especially, J.G.A. Pocock, *The Machiavellian Moment* (Princeton: Princeton University Press, 1975) and his recent magnum opus on the context of Edward Gibbon's late-eighteenth-century masterpiece, *The Decline and Fall of the Roman Empire*: J.G.A. Pocock, *Barbarism and Religion*, thus far Vols 1–3 (Cambridge: Cambridge University Press, 1999–2003).

99. Millar, *The Roman Republic in Political Thought*

100. Millar, *The Roman Republic*, 48–49

101. Millar, *The Roman Republic*, 23–36; F.W. Walbank, *Polybius* (Berkeley, Calif.: University of California Press, 1972); Kurt von Fritz, *The Mixed Constitution in Antiquity* (New York: Columbia University Press, 1954); Claude Nicolet, 'Polybe et les institutions romaines', E. Gabba (ed), *Polybe* (Geneva, 1973), 209–58. There is an interesting study of Polybius's acutely ambivalent attitude to Roman power and Roman culture by Craige B. Champion, *Cultural*

Politics in Polybius's Histories (Berkeley, Calif.: University of California Press, 2004).

102. Polybius, *The Histories*, tr W.R. Paton, 6 vols (Cambridge, Mass.: Harvard University Press, 1922–27), XXXVIII, 22, Vol 6, 438–9: 'Scipio, when he looked upon the city as it was utterly perishing and in the last throes of its complete destruction, is said to have shed tears and wept openly for his enemies. After being wrapped in thought for long, and realizing that all cities, nations, and authorities must, like men, meet their doom; that this happened to Ilium, once a prosperous city, to the empires of Assyria, Media, and Persia, the greatest of their time, and to Macedonia itself, the brilliance of which was so recent, either deliberately, or the verses escaping him, he said:

> A day will come when sacred Troy shall perish
> And Priam and his people shall be slain.
>   (Homer, *Iliad* VI, 448–9)

And when Polybius speaking with freedom to him, for he was his teacher, asked him what he meant by the words, they say that without any attempt at concealment he named his own country, for which he feared when he reflected on the fate of all things human. Polybius actually heard him and recalls it in his history.'

(This fragment survives only in Appian, *Punica*, 132, though see also *Histories*, XXXVIII, 21, 436–37.) Walbank is sceptical of the significance of this fulsome passage (*Polybius*, 11). There is a careful discussion of the grounds for doubt in A.E. Astin, *Scipio Aemilianus* (Oxford: Clarendon Press, 1967), 282–87.

103. Aristotle, *Politics*, esp 1281b–1284a, 220–24 cf Polybius, *Histories*, VI, 10–18, Vol 3, 292–311. For his central aim see *Histories*, I, 5–6, Vol 1, 2–5: 'For who is so worthless or indolent as not to wish to know by what means and under what system of polity the Romans in less than fifty-three years have succeeded in subjecting the whole inhabited world to their sole government – a thing unique in

history?' A good sense of how far the category of democracy was from suggesting itself as an immediate description of Rome's politics can be derived from Andrew Lintott, *The Constitution of the Roman Republic* (Oxford: Oxford University Press, 1999) and Claude Nicolet, *The World of the Citizen in Republican Rome*, tr P.S. Falla (London: Batsford, 1980).

104. Millar, *Roman Republic*, 170

105. Hansen, *The Athenian Democracy*; compare Millar, *Roman Republic*, 166–67; Polybius, *Histories*, VI, 13, Vol 3, 298–301 (on Senate and diplomacy).

106. Polybius, *Histories*, VI, 57, 396–99: esp 'When this happens, the state will change its name to the finest sounding of all, freedom and democracy *(demokratia)*, but will change its nature to the worst thing of all, mob-rule *(ochlokratia)*.' Millar insists, convincingly, that Polybius at this point can only have had Rome in mind, *Roman Republic*, 30, 35–36.

107. Polybius, *Histories*, VI, 57, 398–99

108. Polybius, *Histories*, VI, 10, 12–14, 292–93

109. Millar, *Roman Republic*, 55–58; Joseph Canning, *A History of Medieval Political Thought* (London: Routledge, 1996), 125–26; Janet Coleman, *A History of Political Thought from the Middle Ages to the Renaissance* (Oxford: Blackwell, 2000), 62; Coleman, 50–80, is excellent on the background of educational practice into which Aristotle's *Politics* was absorbed; Anthony Black, *Political Thought in Europe 1250–1450* (Cambridge: Cambridge University Press, 1992), 20–21.

110. Coleman, *History of Political Thought*, 55. There proved to be effective demand at the apogee of Islamic civilization for many aspects of Aristotle's thinking. But nothing about the political organization of any Islamic society gave pressing occasion for addressing his exploration of the significance of politics. (Dimitri

Gutas, *Greek Thought, Arabic Culture: The Graeco Arabic Translation Movement in Baghdad and Early Abbasid Society* (London: Routledge, 1998); Muhsin Mahdi, *Alfarabi and the Foundation of Islamic Political Philosophy* (Chicago: University of Chicago Press, 2001); Muhsin Mahdi, 'Avicenna', *Encyclopedia Iranica*, Vol 3 (London: Routledge, 1989), 66–110; Richard Walzer, *Greek into Arabic* (Oxford: Bruno Cassirer, 1962), chapter 14, 'Platonism in Islamic Philosophy'.

111. Quentin Skinner, 'The Italian City-Republics', in J. Dunn (ed), *Democracy: The Unfinished Journey*, 57–69; Hans Baron, *The Crisis of the Early Italian Renaissance*, revised ed (Princeton: Princeton University Press, 1966); Philip Jones, *The Italian City State: From Commune to Signoria* (Oxford: Clarendon Press, 1997)

112. Millar, *Roman Republic*, 58–59

113. Millar, *Roman Republic*, 60–61

114. Millar, *Roman Republic*, 62–63

115. Andreu Bosch, *Summari, index o epitome des admirables y nobilissims titols de honor de Cathalunya, Rossello I Cerdanya* (1628), facsimile Barcelona 1974, cited by Xavier Gil, 'Republican Politics in Early Modern Spain: the Castilian and Catalano-Aragonese Traditions', in Martin Van Gelderen & Quentin Skinner (eds), *Republicanism: A Shared European Heritage* (Cambridge: Cambridge University Press), Vol 1, 263–88 at p 280.

116. Wyger R.E. Velema, '"That a Republic is Better than a Monarchy": Anti-Monarchism in Early Modern Dutch Political Thought', in Skinner & Van Gelderen, *Republicanism*, Vol 1, 9–25, esp 13–19; Martin Van Gelderen, 'Aristotelians, Monarchomachs: Sovereignty and *respublica mixta* in Dutch and German Political Thought, 1580–1650', Skinner & Van Gelderen, *Republicanism*, Vol 1, 195–217.

117. *Vrye Politijke Stellingen en Consideratien van Staat*, 172–73, ed Wim Klever, Amsterdam 1974, cited by Martin Van Gelderen, 'Aristotelians, Monarchomachs and Republics', Skinner & Van Gelderen (eds), *Republicanism*, Vol 1, 195–217, at 215–16.

118. Hans Erich Bödeker, 'Debating the *respublica mixta*: German and Dutch Political Discourses around 1700', in Skinner & Van Gelderen (eds), *Republicanism*, Vol 1, 219–46, esp 222–28; Jonathan Scott, 'Classical Republicanism in Seventeenth-Century England and the Netherlands', in Skinner & Van Gelderen, *Republicanism*, Vol 1, 61–81, esp 76–80; Warren Montag, *Bodies, Masses, Power: Spinoza and his Contemporaries* (London: Verso, 1999); Jonathan I. Israel, *Radical Enlightenment: Philosophy and the Making of Modernity, 1650–1750* (Oxford: Oxford University Press, 2001); Hans Blom, *Morality and Causality in Politics: the Rise of Materialism in Seventeenth-Century Dutch Political Thought* (Utrecht: University of Utrecht Press, 1995)

119. The key setting was the Putney debates inside the parliamentary armies: A.S.P. Woodhouse (ed), *Puritanism and Liberty* 2nd ed (London: J.M. Dent & Sons, 1950); David Wootton, 'The Levellers', in Dunn (ed), *Democracy: The Unfinished Journey*, 71–89, & 'Leveller Democracy and the English Revolution', in J.H. Burns & Mark Goldie (eds), *Cambridge History of Seventeenth-Century Political Thought* (Cambridge: Cambridge University Press, 1991), 412–42. The best overall study of the movement remains H.N. Brailsford, *The Levellers and the English Revolution*, 2nd ed (Nottingham: Spokesman Books, 1976).

120. Hobbes, *Behemoth, or the Long Parliament*, 2nd ed, F. Toennies (London: Frank Cass, 1969), 21: 'For after the Bible was translated into English, every man, nay every boy and wench, that could read English, thought they spoke with God Almighty, and understood what he said.'

121. Hobbes, *Behemoth*, 26–44

122. Hobbes, *Behemoth*, 43; *De Cive: the English Version*, ed Howard Warrender (Oxford: Clarendon Press, 1983)

123. Cf Dunn, *Western Political Theory in the Face of the Future*, chapter 1

124. Blair Worden, *Roundhead Reputations* (London: Penguin, 2002), 100. Worden gives a spirited portrait of Toland in action, 95–120, stressing above all his youthful ebullience and manipulative opportunism (p 119). See also Sullivan, *John Toland and the Deist Controversy* (Cambridge, Mass.: Harvard University Press, 1982) and Chiara Giuntini, *Panteismo e ideologia repubblicana: John Toland (1676–1722)* (Bologna: Il Mulino, 1979); Blair Worden, 'Republicanism and the Restoration 1660–1683', in David Wootton (ed), *Republicanism and Commercial Society 1649–1776* (Stanford: Stanford University Press, 1994), 139–93; and Israel, *Radical Enlightenment*.

125. The contemporary translation, Thomas Hobbes, *De Cive: The English Version*, captures the flavour of Hobbes's writing better, despite some inaccuracy. For a more analytically and historically reliable version see Thomas Hobbes, *On the Citizen*, ed Richard Tuck & tr Michael Silverthorne (Cambridge: Cambridge Univesity Press, 1998). For the centrality of Hobbes's engagement with classical rhetoric, see Quentin Skinner, *Reason and Rhetoric in Hobbes's Philosophy* (Cambridge: Cambridge University Press, 1996).

126. Hobbes, *De Cive: The English Version*, X, ix, p 136

127. Benjamin Constant, *Political Writings*, ed Biancamaria Fontana (Cambridge: Cambridge University Press, 1988), 313–28

128. Hobbes, *De Cive: The English Version*, chapter VII, 1, and 5–7: pp 106–07, 109–10; Chapter XII, 8: pp 151–52. Richard Tuck has emphasized the importance of this judgement in shaping Hobbes's vision of politics from the beginning: Richard Tuck, *Philosophy*

and Government 1572–1651 (Cambridge: Cambridge University Press, 1993, 310–11).

129. Hobbes, *De Cive: The English Version*, chapter VII, 1: pp 106–07

130. C.V. Wedgwood, *The Trial of Charles I* (London: Fontana, 1964), 71

131. See particularly *The Correspondence of Thomas Hobbes*, ed Noel Malcolm, 2 vols (Oxford: Clarendon Press, 1994). There is a striking picture of his work fanning out amongst Europe's intelligentsia in Malcolm's *Aspects of Hobbes* (Oxford: Clarendon Press, 2002), chapter 14, 457–545, but as yet no especially illuminating biography. The biography to wait for, once again, is Noel Malcolm's, in preparation for the Clarendon Press.

132. There are two interesting recent biographies of Spinoza by Steven Nadler, *Spinoza: A Life* (Cambridge: Cambridge University Press, 1999) and Margaret Gullan-Whur, *Within Reason: A Life of Spinoza* (London: Pimlico, 2000). Much the most ambitious and learned presentation of his impact on European thought and feeling at large is Israel's remarkable *Radical Enlightenment: Philosophy and the Making of Modernity* (Oxford: Clarendon Press, 2000), always interesting but not invariably convincing in its judgements. Contrast, for example, on the impact of Hobbes, Malcolm's chapter in his *Aspects of Hobbes*.

133. His biographer John Aubrey records Hobbes as saying of Spinoza's *Tractatus Theologico-Politicus* that he had 'cut through him a bar's length, for he durst not write so boldly'. John Aubrey, *Brief Lives*, ed Andrew Clark, 2 vols (Oxford: Clarendon Press, 1898), I, 357.

134. Nadler, *Spinoza*, 44

135. Israel, *Radical Enlightenment*, 166

136. Nadler, *Spinoza*, chapter 6, esp 127–29

137. Nadler, *Spinoza*, 182–83

138. Spinoza, *Political Works*, ed & tr A.G. Wernham (Oxford: Clarendon Press, 1958). For helpful assessments of Spinoza's political thought see especially Malcolm, *Aspects of Hobbes*, 40–52; Wernham's Introduction; and Theo Verbeek, *Spinoza's Theologico-Political Treatise: Exploring 'The Will of God'*, (Aldershot: Ashgate, 2003). For the Dutch background to Spinoza's political thought see, besides Israel's *Radical Enlightenment*, also his The Intellectual Origins of Modern Democratic Republicanism, *European Journal of Political Theory*, 3 (2004), 7–36.

139. Spinoza, *Political Works (Tractatus)*, Chapter XI, 440–43

140. Spinoza, *Political Works (Tractatus)*, 316–17

141. Spinoza, *Political Works (Tractatus Theologico-Politicus)*, 276–78. Compare Hobbes, *De Cive*, VII, 1, 106–7

142. Spinoza, *Political Works (Tractatus Theologico-Politicus)*, 284

143. Spinoza, *Political Works (Tractatus Theologico-Politicus)*, 288

144. Spinoza, *Political Works (Tractatus Politicus)*, 376

145. Spinoza, *Political Works (Tractatus Politicus)*, chapter X, 440: '*tertium et omnino absolutum imperium*'. It is not clear what the intended force of this formula is. For Spinoza all sovereignty is by definition absolute. The sovereign is entitled to (and potentially needs to) judge everything about how human beings should or should not act: *Tractatus Politicus*, IV, 2, pp 300–01. It sometimes appears that he wishes to argue that democracy differs from monarchy and aristocracy in that it will never be (or is incapable of proving) self-frustrating or self-undermining (*Tractatus Politicus*,VIII, 3, 4, 6 & 7, pp 370–73: 'If there is such a thing as absolute sovereignty, it is in reality what is held by the entire multitude'). But in practice democratic sovereigns are every bit as capable of misjudging their own interests or even their future tastes as aristocracies or monarchs. At no point does Spinoza offer any grounds for denying this; nor is there any evidence that he felt the

least inclination to deny it. Under a democracy, there is indeed
nothing but the *demos* itself to stop the state doing whatever it
then chooses. But this gives no guarantee that the *demos* will judge
coherently or accurately, nor that it will appreciate over time the
consequences of its own actions. Did Spinoza not see this? Did he
wish to deny it? I cannot see that we know.

146. Spinoza, *Political Works (Tractatus Politicus)*, 440, 442

147. Spinoza, *Political Works (Tractatus Theologico-Politicus)*, 136

148. *Atque hac ratione omnes manent ut antea in statu naturali
aequales.* (Spinoza, *Political Writings (Tractatus Politicus)*, 135–36)

149. Polybius, *Histories*, VI, 57, 398–99. Nadler, *Spinoza: A Life*,
chapters 10 & 11.

150. Nadler, *Spinoza: A Life*, 306.

151. Spinoza, *Political Works (Tractatus Theologico-Politicus)*, XX, pp
240–243: 'I have thus shown: I. That it is impossible to deprive men
of the freedom to say what they think. II. That this freedom can be
granted to everyone without infringing the right and authority of
the sovereign; and that everyone can keep it without infringing that
right as long as he does not use it as a licence to introduce anything
into the state as a law, or to do anything contrary to the accepted
laws. III. That it is no danger to the peace of the state; and that
all troubles arising from it can easily be checked. IV. That it is no
danger to piety either. V. That laws passed about speculative
matters are utterly useless; and finally, VI. That this freedom not
only can be granted without danger to public peace, piety, and the
right of the sovereign, but actually must be granted if all are to be
preserved.'

152. Compare Hobbes, *De Cive*, X, 8: p 135: 'although the word *liberty*,
may in large, and ample letters be written over the gates of any
City whatsoever, yet it is not meant the *Subjects*, but the *Cities*
liberty, neither can that word with better Right be inscribed on a

City which is governed by the *people*, then that which is ruled by a *Monarch*.' The city which Hobbes had in mind was Lucca: (Hobbes, *Leviathan*, ed Richard Tuck (Cambridge: Cambridge University Press 1991), Chapter 21, 149: 'there is writ on the Turrets of the city of Luca in great Characters at this day, the word *LIBERTAS*; yet no man can thence inferre, that a particular man has more Libertie, or Immunitie from the service of the Commonwealth there, than in *Constantinople*.' The inscription still stands. But contrast Quentin Skinner, *Liberty before Liberalism* (Cambridge: Cambridge University Press, 1998) for the tradition of political understanding which Hobbes sought to overthrow. For the substantial degree of overlap between Spinoza's views and this judgement of Hobbes, see Spinoza, *Political Works (Tractatus Theologico-Politicus)*, XVI, the lengthy penultimate sentence of p 136. As Spinoza himself concludes: '*Nec his plura addere opus est.*' There is no need to say more...

153. Spinoza, *Political Works (Tractatus Politicus)*, VII, 5, p 338–39 insists stoutly that it is stupid to be willing to live as slaves in peace in order to wage war more effectively: '*inscitia sane est, nimirum quod, ut bellum felicius gerant, in pace servire.*' But he does not choose to dispute the common charge against democracy that its virtue is far more effective in peace than it is in war '*ejus virtus multo magis in pace quam in bello valet*'.

154. Algernon Sidney, *Discourses on Government* 2nd ed (London:J. Darby, 1704), 146: 'That is the best Government, which best provides for war'

155. Spinoza, *Political Works (Tractatus Politicus)*, VII, 338–39. This was a judgement in itself which would have astounded any Athenian.

156. Spinoza, *Political Works (Tractatus Politicus)*, chapter XI, 440–41: '*Reliqua desiderantur*'. The rest is missing...

157. The diary of the Leiden scholar Gronovius records that Spinoza
     requested an audience with Johan de Witt to discuss the latter's
     (rumoured) negative reactions to the *Tractatus Theologico-
     Politicus*, and that de Witt responded, unambiguously enough, that
     he 'did not want to see him pass his threshold' (W.N.A. Klever, 'A
     New Document on De Witt's Attitude to Spinoza', *Studia
     Spinoziana*, 9 (1993), 379–88; Nadler, *Spinoza*, 256.)

158. See especially Hansen, *Athenian Democracy*; 71–2, 228–29, 266–68
     (on *ho boulomenos*), 81–85 (on *isonomia* and *isegoria*); Finley,
     Politics in the Ancient World; and cf Martin Ostwald, *From
     Popular Sovereignty to Sovereignty of Law: Law, Sovereignty and
     Politics in Fifth-Century Athens* (Berkeley, Calif.: University of
     California Press, 1986).

159. The political significance of this is well captured by Quentin
     Skinner in 'From the State of Princes to the Person of the State',
     Visions of Politics, Vol 2, 368–413. For its longer-term implications
     see especially Istvan Hont, 'The Permanent Crisis of a Divided
     Mankind', in J. Dunn (ed), *Contemporary Crisis of the Nation
     State?* (Oxford: Blackwell, 1994), 166–231.

160. This great phrase comes from the dying speech (a more
     individualist genre than the funeral oration) of an unreconstructed
     Leveller leader, Colonel Richard Rumbold, decades after the
     movement itself had been crushed by Oliver Cromwell. He
     delivered the speech (as much of it as he was permitted to, and in
     face of considerable resistance from his captors) at the Market
     Cross in Edinburgh in June 1685, shortly before he was hung,
     drawn and quartered for designing the death of the King in the Rye
     House Plot against Charles II. (*The Dying Speeches of Several
     Excellent Persons who Suffered for their Zeal against Popery and
     Arbitrary Government*, London, 1689 (Wing 2957), 24): 'I am sure
     there was no Man born marked of God above another; for none
     comes into the World with a Saddle on his Back, neither any
     Booted and Spurred to ride to him.'

The plot itself drew its name from its intended setting, Rumbold's own house in the Kentish town of Rye, with its conveniently high garden wall, ideal for an ambush: Richard Ashcraft, *Revolutionary Politics and Locke's 'Two Treatises of Government'* (Princeton: Princeton University Press, 1986), 352–71, esp 364.

NOTES TO CHAPTER 2

1. Franco Venturi, *Saggi sull'Europa Illuminista*, Vol 1, *Alberto Radicati di Passerano* (Turin: Einaudi, 1954), 'Deismo, cristianesimo e democrazia perfetta', 248–69; Jonathan I. Israel, *Radical Enlightenment* (Oxford: Clarendon Press, 2001). For a notable example earlier in the seventeenth century (expressed in Latin, as far as we know in strict seclusion, and not yet reliably dated) see the resolute rejection of Hobbes's critique of democracy by William Petty, as a young man a close acquaintance and admirer of Hobbes: Frank Amati & Tony Aspromourgos, 'Petty *contra* Hobbes: a previously untranslated manuscript', *Journal of the History of Ideas*, 46 (1985), 127–32, esp 130 'Whether it is more pleasant to human nature to transfer their power forever into the hands of a single person (that is, for those who hold power to give it away) or whether it is better to serve the very same person but only appointing him to office after a gradual process and for a brief period? I propose that power should be shaped and drawn up by the people themselves; otherwise the monarch will be susceptible to the daily change of affairs and to his temperament.' A cogent line of thought.
2. Gordon S. Wood, *The American Revolution: A History* (London: Weidenfeld & Nicolson, 2003)
3. Alexis de Tocqueville, *Democracy in America*, tr & ed Harvey C. Mansfield & Delba Winthrop (Chicago: University of Chicago Press, 2002)

4. Sheldon Wolin, *Tocqueville Between Two Worlds: The Making of a Political and Theoretical Life* (Princeton: Princeton University Press, 2001)

5. Bernard Bailyn, *The Ideological Origins of the American Revolution* (Cambridge, Mass.: Harvard University Press, 1967). For the variations in political structure and culture from one colony (or State) to another see helpfully Richard Beeman, *The Varieties of Political Experience in Eighteenth-Century America* (Philadelphia: University of Pennsylvania Press, 2003).

6. Bernard Bailyn, *To Begin the World Anew* (New York: Alfred Knopf, 2003), 106

7. Bailyn, *To Begin the World Anew*; Jack N. Rakove, *James Madison and the Founding of the American Republic* 2nd ed (New York & London: Longman, 2002); Gordon S.Wood, *The Creation of the American Republic* (Chapel Hill: University of North Carolina Press, 1969)

8. Bailyn, *To Begin the World Anew*, 106

9. Bailyn, *To Begin the World Anew*, 107

10. Wood, *Creation of the American Republic*; Jackson Turner Main, *The Antifederalists: Critics of the Constitution 1781–1788* (Chicago: Quadrangle Books, 1964)

11. Jacob E. Cooke (ed), *The Federalist* (Alexander Hamilton, John Jay & James Madison) (Cleveland: Meridian Books, 1961) Introduction, xix–xxx

12. Rakove, *James Madison*, 11. Besides Rakove's clear and thoughtful study, and his rich analysis of the intellectual and political background to the Constitution, *Original Meanings* (New York: Vintage, 1997), see especially Lance Banning, *The Sacred Fire of Liberty: James Madison and the Founding of the Federal Republic* (Ithaca: Cornell University Press, 1995). One month earlier, in April 1787, Madison had summarized his conclusions in a striking diagnosis of 'The Vices of the Political System of the United States' (*Papers of James Madison*, ed Robert A. Rutland et al, Chicago: University of Chicago Press (1975), IX, 345–58, esp 354–57)

13. Rakove, *James Madison*, 64–5
14. Rakove, *Madison*, 61–2
15. Rakove, *Madison*, 63
16. Cooke (ed), *Federalist*, 56. Jefferson was Ambassador in Paris at the time. For Madison's letter of 24 October 1787, see *Papers of James Madison*, ed Rutland, University of Chicago Press, 1977, X, 205–220. Like its two predecessors (p 206), it was delayed by the difficulties of finding a reliable transatlantic carrier and the pressing concerns of America's leading naval officer, John Paul Jones (pp 218–19). On the relation of democracy to America's political predicament see especially 212–13:

      'Those who contend for a simple Democracy, or a pure republic, activated by the sense of the majority, and operating within narrow limits, assume or suppose a case which is altogether fictitious. They found their reasoning on the idea, that the people composing the Society, enjoy not only an equality of political rights; but that they have all precisely the same interests, and the same feelings in every respect. Were this in reality the case, their reasoning would be conclusive... The interest of the majority would be that of the minority also; the decision could only turn on mere opinion concerning the good of the whole, of which the major voice would be the safest criterion; and within a small sphere, this voice could be most easily collected, and the public affairs most accurately managed. We know however that no Society ever did or can consist of so homogeneous a mass of Citizens. In the savage State indeed, an approach is made towards it; but in that State little or no Government is necessary. In all civilized Societies, distinctions are various and unavoidable. A distinction of property results from that very protection which a free Government gives to unequal faculties of acquiring it. There will be rich and poor; creditors and debtors; a landed interest, a mercantile interest, a manufacturing interest.' etc.
17. *Federalist*, 59
18. *Federalist*, 60

19. *Federalist*, 60–61

20. *Federalist*, 61

21. *Federalist*, 65

22. *Federalist*, 65

23. *Federalist* (Number 63), p 427

24. *Federalist*, 427

25. *Federalist*, 428

26. *Federalist* (Number 48), p 333

27. *Federalist*, 335–36. Compare Thomas Jefferson, *Notes on the State of Virginia* (New York: Harper, 1964), 113–24: 'An *elective despotism* was not the government we fought for, but one which should not only be founded on free principles, but in which the powers of government should be so divided and balanced among several bodies of magistracy, as that no one could transcend their legal limits, without being effectually checked and restrained by the others...'

28. Wood, *The American Revolution*, 62

29. Wood, *American Revolution*, 67

30. Wood, *American Revolution*, 66

31. Wood, *American Revolution*, 40–41

32. Madison to Edward Everett, 14 November 1831: Drew R. McCoy *The Last of the Fathers: James Madison and the Republican Legacy* (Cambridge: Cambridge University Press, 1989), 133

33. McCoy, *Last of the Fathers*, 116–17. Madison to Thomas Ritchie, 18 December 1825: 'All power in human hands is liable to be abused. In Governments independent of the people, the rights and interests of the whole may be sacrificed to the views of the Government. In Republics, where the people govern themselves, and where, of course, the majority govern, a danger to the minority arises from opportunities tempting a sacrifice of their rights to the interests, real or supposed, of the majority. No form of government, therefore, can be a perfect guard against the abuse of power. The recommendation of the republican form is, that the danger of abuse is less than in any other; and the superior recommendation of the

federo-republican system is, that while it provides more effectually against external danger, it involves a greater security to the minority against the hasty formation of oppressive majorities.' [James Madison, *Letters & Other Writings*, ed William C. Rives & Philip R. Fendall, Philadelphia, 1865, III, 507

34. McCoy *Last of the Fathers*, 193–206: James Madison, *Notes on Suffrage* c 1821

35. Gordon S.Wood, *The Radicalism of the American Revolution* (New York: Vintage, 1993), 270

36. McCoy, *Last of the Fathers*, 195

37. McCoy *Last of the Fathers*, 195

38. Wood, *Radicalism of the American Revolution*, 295–96

39. Wood, *Radicalism*, 296

40. Simon Schama, *Patriots and Liberators* (London: Fontana, 1992); R.R. Palmer, *The Age of the Democratic Revolution* Vol 1 (Oxford: Oxford University Press, 1959). There is an incisive analysis of the trajectory of the Dutch Republic from the Patriot Revolt through to the creation and fall of the Batavian Republic in Jonathan I. Israel, *The Dutch Republic: Its Rise, Greatness and Fall 1477–1806* (Oxford: Oxford University Press, 1995) chapters 42–44. For the very limited Dutch zest for democracy as a regime form earlier in the century see Leonard Leeb, *The Ideological Origins of the Batavian Revolution* (The Hague: Nijhoff, 1973), 114, 132, 144–45 etc.

41. Schama, *Patriots and Liberators*, 80–135

42. Schama, *Patriots and Liberators*, 94

43. Schama, *Patriots and Liberators*, 81

44. Schama, *Patriots and Liberators*, 94

45. Schama, *Patriots and Liberators*, 127

46. Schama, *Patriots and Liberators*, 94–95

47. Schama, *Patriots and Liberators*, 95

48. Schama, *Patriots and Liberators*, 2

49. Palmer, *Age of the Democratic Revolution*, Vol 1, 17; and see further R.R. Palmer, 'Notes on the Use of the Word "Democracy" 1789–1799', *Political Science Quarterly*, LXVIII, 1953, 203–26

50. Palmer, *Democratic Revolution*, I, 15
51. Schama, *Patriots and Liberators*, 127
52. Schama, *Patriots and Liberators*, 630–48
53. Palmer, *Democratic Revolution*, I, 341
54. Palmer, *Democratic Revolution*, I, 342
55. Palmer, *Democratic Revolution*, I, 345–46
56. Palmer, *Democratic Revolution*, I, 346
57. Palmer, *Democratic Revolution*, I, 347
58. Palmer, *Democratic Revolution*, I, 347–57
59. Palmer, *Democratic Revolution*, I, 479–502
60. Palmer, *Democratic Revolution*, I, 349
61. Palmer, *Democratic Revolution*, I, 349–50
62. This is the summary of Suzanne Tassier, the leading Belgian historian of the revolt (*Revue de l'Université de Bruxelles*,1934, 453, cited by Palmer, *Age of the Democratic Revolution*, I, 350)
63. Palmer, *Age of the Democratic Revolution*, I, 351
64. Suzanne Tassier, *Les Démocrates Belges de 1789: étude sur le Vonckisme et la Révolution brabançonne* (Brussels: *Mémoires de l'Academie royale de Belgique*, classe des letters, 2nd ser, XXVIII), 190
65. Arno J.Mayer, *The Furies* (Princeton: Princeton University Press, 2000), 323–70
66. Palmer, *Age of the Democratic Revolution*, I, 355–56. See also Janet Polasky, The Success of a Counter-Revolution in Revolutionary Europe: the Brabant Revolution of 1789, *Tijdschrift fur Geschiednis*, 102, 1989, 413–21; her *Revolution in Brussels* (Brussels: Académie Royale de Belgique, 1985). J. Craeybeckx, 'The Brabant Revolution: a conservative revolt in a backward country?', *Acta Historiae Neerlandica*, 4 (Leiden: E.J. Brill, 1970), 49–83 disputes the emphasis on Belgium's relative economic and social backwardness.
67. Frederic Volpi, *Islam and Democracy: The Failure of Dialogue in Algeria* (London: Pluto Press, 2003)
68. Richard Wrigley, *The Politics of Appearances: Representations of Dress in Revolutionary France* (Oxford: Berg, 2002)

69. René-Louis de Voyer de Paulmy, Marquis d'Argenson, *Considérations sur le gouvernment ancien et présent de la France,* 2nd ed 1784 Amsterdam

70. Nannerl O. Keohane, *Philosophy and the State in France* (Princeton: Princeton University Press, 1980), 376

71. Argenson, *Considérations sur le gouvernement ancien et présent de la France* (Amsterdam: Marc Michel Rey, 1764). Keohane, *Philosophy and the State,* 377

72. *Considérations* 1784, iv–v. The son saw fit to interpolate a considerable amount of material apparently of his own into this (officially) second edition.

73. Franklin L. Ford, *Sword and Robe* (Cambridge, Mass.: Harvard University Press, 1953, chapter 12)

74. Keohane, *Philosophy and the State,* 376

75. Keohane, *Philosophy and the State,* 390

76. Roger Tisserand (ed), *Les Concurrents de J.J. Rousseau à l'Académie de Dijon* (Paris, 1936), 130–31

77. *Considérations,* 1784, chapter 7, 192–297. The first edition, 215–328, is much sparser.

78. *Considérations,* 1784, 195. Cf first edition, 303–4. '*Le Roi ne peut-il régner sur des Citoyens sans dominer sur des esclaves?*' Can the King not reign over Citizens without dominating slaves?

79. *Considérations.* 1784, 272. Cf 1764 ed, 305–10. Compare Montesquieu's classic defence of intermediary powers as devices through which one power can obstruct another throughout *L'Esprit des Loix* (1748) (esp Bk XI, chapter 6), and the defence of the delaying function of the separation of powers in the *Federalist.* Cf Bernard Manin, 'Checks, Balances and Boundaries: the Separation of Powers in the Constitutional Debate of 1787', Biancamaria Fontana (ed), *The Invention of the Modern Republic* (Cambridge: Cambridge University Press, 1994), 27–62.

80. *Considérations,* 1784, 296. Argenson's original formulation (1764 ed, 314) was considerably more tactful towards the monarch's own authority, but just as confident of the indispensability of the people

as a source of information, both to the monarch and to one
another, about the real scope of their interests.

81. Michael Sonenscher, 'The Nation's Debt and the Birth of the
Modern Republic', *History of Political Thought*, 18, 1997, 64–103
& 267–325. For the pressures behind this, see especially John
Brewer, *The Sinews of War: War, Money and the English State
1688–1783* (London: Unwin Hyman, 1989).

82. *Considérations*, 1784, 199. None of these details appears in the
1764 edition.

83. *Considérations*, 1784, 199. This phrase does not appear in the 1764
edition. The galvanizing effects of his Plan on rural productivity
and prosperity figure prominently in the original edition (1764,
274–95).

84. *Considérations*, 1764, 7; the 1784 edition, 12 adds emphasis on the
common interest in the good government of the kingdom.

85. *Considérations*, 1764, 7–8; 1784, 15

86. *Considérations*, 1764, 8; 1784, 15. The original edition (p 12) does
note that Switzerland is a pure Democracy, since, although the
Nobility enjoys a measure of distinction, this furnishes it with no
governmental authority.

There is no compelling synoptic view of the scale, distribution or
quality of Swiss democracy from canton to canton in the
eighteenth century. For an assessment of an individual canton see
Benjamin Barber, *The Death of Communal Liberty: A History of
Freedom in a Swiss Mountain Canton* (Princeton: Princeton
University Press, 1974). For Geneva, a far from democratic
instance, see two chapters by Franco Venturi, *The End of the Old
Regime in Europe: The First Crisis*, tr R.B. Litchfield (Princeton:
Princeton University Press, 1989), 340–50, and *The End of the Old
Regime in Europe: Republican Patriotism and the Empires of the
East* (Princeton: Princeton University Press, 1991), 459–96; Linda
Kirk, 'Genevan Republicanism', David Wootton (ed),
Republicanism, Liberty and Commercial Society 1649–1776
(Stanford: Stanford University Press, 1994), 270–309; and Helena

Rosenblatt, *Rousseau and Geneva: From the 'First Discourse' to the 'Social Contract'* (Cambridge: Cambridge University Press, 1997).

D'Argenson's assumption that Switzerland provided the only protracted modern European experience of democracy in action was still compelling enough a hundred years later for George Grote, the great Victorian historian of Athenian democracy, to make 'an excursion to Switzerland, in order to observe, close at hand, the nearest modern analogue of the Grecian republics', to draw conscious lessons from its experience in interpreting Athenian democracy in action, and to publish his conclusions in *Letters on Switzerland*. (See Alexander Bain, 'The Intellectual Character and Writings of George Grote', *The Minor Works of George Grote* (London: John Murray, 1873), 102–03.)

87. Franklin L. Ford, *Sword and Robe*, chapter 12. Charles-Louis de Secondat, Baron de Montesquieu, hereditary Président à Mortier of the Parlement of Bordeaux and author of the great *L'Esprit des Loix* (1748) is a classic instance.

88. Charles-René D'Argenson (ed), *Mémoires du Marquis d'Argenson* (Paris: P. Jannet, 1857–58), V, 129, Reading note on *Lettres historiques sur le Parlement*. See also the amplification in 1756, pp 349–50 etc. and cf *Considérations*, 1784, 272

89. An exception amongst its foreign admirers should perhaps be made in the case of Tom Paine. Cf *The Rights of Man* Pt II (London: J.M. Dent, 1916), 176–77 etc.

90. For Sieyes see especially his *Political Writings*, ed Michael Sonenscher (Indianopolis: Hackett, 2003); Murray Forsyth, *Reason and Revolution: the Political Thought of the Abbé Sieyes* (Leicester: Leicester University Press, 1987); and Pasquale Pasquino, *Sieyes et l'Invention de la Constitution en France* (Paris: Odile Jacob, 1998)

91. D'Argenson, *Considérations*, 1764, 7; 1784, 15

92. The most vivid and economical synoptic picture of France's movement towards revolution remains Georges Lefebvre's pre-war *The Coming of the French Revolution*, tr R.R. Palmer (New York:

Vintage, 1957). See also Jacques Godechot, *The Taking of the Bastille, July 14th 1789*, tr Jean Stewart (London: Faber, 1970), and more recently Simon Schama's swashbuckling, *Citizens: A Chronicle of the French Revolution* (New York: Alfred Knopf, 1989). There are well-balanced treatments in two books by William Doyle, *The Origins of the French Revolution* (Oxford: Oxford University Press, 1980) and *The Oxford History of the French Revolution* (Oxford: Oxford University Press, 1995), and in Colin Jones, *The Great Nation: France from Louis XV to Napoleon* (London: Allen Lane Penguin Press, 2002), 395–580.

93. On the *cahiers* see the classic analysis by Beatrice Hyslop, *Guide to the General Cahiers of 1789* (New York: Columbia University Press, 1936), and George V. Taylor, 'Revolutionary and Non-revolutionary Content in the *Cahiers*', *French Historical Studies*, 7, 1972, 479–502.

94. Goya's *Disasters of War*. And see Arno J. Mayer, *The Furies* (Princeton: Princeton University Press, 2000)

95. Edmund Burke, *The Writings and Speeches*, Vol VIII *The French Revolution 1790–1794*, ed L.J. Mitchell (Oxford: Clarendon Press, 1989)

96. Despite the fact that he is often credited with just this contribution, for drawing the young General, Napoleon Bonaparte, to the centre of Parisian politics and collaborating with him in killing off the First Republic. For Sieyes's life see Jean-Denis Bredin, *Sieyes: la Clé de la Révolution française* (Paris: Éditions du Fallois, 1988). For his ideas see Murray Forsyth, *Reason and Revolution*. The most accessible English-language version of his political works is now Michael Sonenscher's edition of his *Political Writings* (Indianapolis: Hackett, 2003) which contains all three of the key pamphlets written in 1788, along with a very subtle and suggestive Introduction. For French originals of these see Marcel Dorigny (ed), *Oeuvres de Sieyes* (Paris: Éditions d'Histoire Sociale, 1989), Vol 1.

97. Forsyth, *Reason and Revolution*, 2

98. *Vues sur les moyens d'exécution*, 2 (*Oeuvres*, ed Dorigny, Vol 1) *Political Writings*, ed Sonenscher, 5

99. Plato, *Republic*, tr Paul Shorey (Cambridge, Mass.: Harvard University Press, 1935), 558C, Vol 2, 290–91: 'assigning a kind of equality indiscriminately to equals and unequals alike'

100. Adam Smith, *Lectures on Jurisprudence*, ed R.L. Meek, D.D. Raphael, & P.G. Stein (Oxford: Clarendon Press, 1978), esp 311–30, 401–4, 433–36. John Dunn, *Rethinking Modern Political Theory* (Cambridge: Cambridge University Press, 1985), chapter 3.

101. *Vues*, 127 (*Oeuvres*, ed Dorigny, Vol 1); *Political Writings*, 54

102. *Vues*, 124–29 (*Oeuvres*, Vol 1); *Political Writings*, 53–55. I have modified the translation here, and elsewhere, to make it more literal.

103. *Vues*, 112–13 (*Oeuvres*, Vol 1); *Political Writings*, 48

104. *Vues*, 114 (*Oeuvres*, Vol 1); *Political Writings*, 49

105. *Vues*, 3; 1 (*Oeuvres*, Vol 1); *Political Writings*, 4

106. *Vues*, 3–4 (*Oeuvres*, Vol 1); *Political Writings*, 5

107. *Essai sur les privilèges*, 1–2 (*Oeuvres*, Vol 1); *Political Writings*, 69. The *Essai* was an essay on the idea of privilege; but it was also very much an assault on the highly particular array of privileges which dominated the status system of *ancien régime* France. The definite article, in this case, carries both senses.

108. *Essai*, 2 (*Oeuvres*, Vol 1); *Political Writings*, 70

109. *Essai*, 1–5 (*Oeuvres*, Vol 1); *Political Writings*, 69–71

110. *Essai*, 14 (*Oeuvres*, Vol 1); *Political Writings*, 76. Sieyes cites as evidence the shocked complaint of the Order of Nobility from the last preceding meeting of the Estates General in 1614 that the Third Estate, 'almost all the vassals of the first orders' should have had the temerity to describe themselves as younger siblings of their superiors (*Political Writings*, 90).

111. *Essai*, 53 (*Oeuvres*, Vol 1); *Political Writings*, 74–5

112. *Essai*,18–25 (*Oeuvres*, Vol 1); *Political Writings*, 76–78

113. *Essai*, 29 (*Oeuvres*, Vol 1); *Political Writings*, 80. This is, of course, equally true of the inheritance of wealth in a capitalist economy

and has remained an element of ideological vulnerability (or, at the very least, of implausibility).

114. *Essai*, 37 (*Oeuvres*, Vol 1); *Political Writings*, 84

115. *Essai*, 40 (*Oeuvres*, Vol 1); *Political Writings*, 85

116. *Qu'est-ce que le tiers état?*, 1, 6, 9 (*Oeuvres*, Vol 1); *What is the Third Estate?* (*Political Writings*, 94, 96, 98). See Karl Marx, *Contribution to the Critique of Hegel's Philosophy of Law: Introduction* (Karl Marx & Frederick Engels, *Collected Works*, Vol 3 (London: Lawrence & Wishart, 1975), 184–85).

117. George V. Taylor, 'Non-capitalist Wealth and the Origins of the French Revolution', *American Historical Review*, 62, 1967, 429–96; Colin Lucas, 'Nobles, Bourgeois and the Origins of the French Revolution', *Past and Present*, 60, 1973, 84–126; Patrice Higonnet, *Class, Ideology and the Rights of Nobles during the French Revolution* (Oxford: Clarendon Press, 1981); Guy Chaussinand-Nogaret, *The French Nobility in the Eighteenth Century: From Feudalism to the Enlightenment*, tr William Doyle (Cambridge: Cambridge University Press, 1985). For a powerful presentation of the realities of the First Estate in its eighteenth-century setting see John McManners, *Church and Society in Eighteenth-Century France*, 2 vols (Oxford: Oxford University Press, 1998), summarizing a lifetime's research.

118. Sieyes, *Essai*, 53 (*Oeuvres*, Vol 1); *Political Writings*, 90

119. Sieyes, *Tiers état*, 1 (*Oeuvres*, Vol 1); *Political Writings*, 94

120. Sieyes, *Tiers état*, 1; *Political Writings*, 94

121. Sieyes, *Tiers état*, 2; *Political Writings*, 94

122. Sieyes, *Tiers état*, 2–3; *Political Writings*, 95

123. Sieyes, *Tiers état*, 6; *Political Writings*, 96

124. Sieyes, *Tiers état*, 4; *Political Writings*, 95

125. Sieyes, *Tiers état*, 10; *Political Writings*, 98

126. Sieyes, *Tiers état*, 10; *Political Writings*, 99

127. Sieyes, *Tiers état*, 98; *Political Writings*, 147

128. Sieyes, *Tiers état*, 6–9; *Political Writings*, 97

129. Sieyes, *Tiers état*, 9; *Political Writings*, 98

130. Sieyes, *Tiers état*, 16; *Political Writings*, 102

131. Sieyes, *Tiers état*, 27; *Political Writings*, 107. As the bloodshed of the next twenty-five years placed beyond reasonable doubt, this was not a comparison to take lightly. (Cf R.R. Palmer, *Twelve who Ruled: The Year of Terror in the French Revolution* (New York: Athenaeum, 1965), 218)

132. Sieyes, *Tiers état*, 110; *Political Writings*, 158

133. *What is the Third Estate?*, ed S.E. Finer (London: Pall Mall, 1963), 177. The note does not appear in the Dorigny edition.

134. Sieyes, *Political Writings*, 147n. The note does not appear in the Dorigny edition.

135. Sieyes, *Political Writings*, 147n. Finer, *Third Estate*, 196–97 translates vividly.

136. Sieyes, *Tiers état*, 51; again Finer's translation: *Third Estate*, 96

137. R.R. Palmer, *Political Science Quarterly*, 1953

138. A. Dufourcq, *Le Régime Jacobin en Italie: étude sur la République romaine 1798–99* (Paris: Perrin, 1900), 30; Palmer, *Political Science Quarterly*, 1953, 221 translates more of the relevant text.

139. Thomas Paine, *The Rights of Man*, 176–77

140. Bredin, *Sieyes*, 525

141. M. Crook, *Élections in the French Revolution* (Cambridge: Cambridge University Press), 11. On the development of elections during the Revolution see, in addition to Crook, Patrice Gueniffey, *Le Nombre et la Raison: la révolution française et les elections* (Paris: Gallimard, 1993).

142. Forsyth, 162–65; E.-J. Sieyes, *Écrits politiques*, ed R. Zappéri (Paris: Archives Contemporaines, 1985), 189–206; Crook, 30

143. Crook, *Elections*, 31

144. Crook, *Elections*, 33

145. Crook, *Elections*, 33

146. Crook, *Elections*, 34

147. Maximilien Robespierre, *Discours et rapports à la Convention*, (Paris: Union Générale des Éditions, 1965), 213

148. Robespierre, *Discours*, 214

149. Robespierre, *Discours*, 216

150. Robespierre, *Discours*, 218

151. Robespierre, *Discours*, 221

152. Robespierre, *Discours*, 222

153. Robespierre, *Discours*, 223

154. Robespierre, *Discours*, 227. For a spirited but impressively level-headed analysis of this government in action see Palmer, *Twelve who Ruled*.

155. Robespierre, *Discours*, 236

NOTES TO CHAPTER 3

1. Cf John Dunn, *The Cunning of Unreason* (London: HarperCollins, 2000)

2. Jean-Jacques Rousseau, *The Social Contract*, Bk 1, chapter 1: 'Man is born free; and everywhere he is in chains. One thinks himself the master of others, and still remains a greater slave than they. How did this change come about? I do not know. What can make it legitimate? That question I think I can answer.' (*The Social Contract and Discourses*, tr G.D.H. Cole (London: J.M. Dent), 5; *Political Writings*, ed C.E. Vaughan (Oxford: Blackwell, 1962)

3. Raymond Geuss, *Public Goods, Private Goods* (Princeton: Princeton University Press, 2003), chapter 3 *Res Publica*. For the historical trajectory of the distinction between public and private law see Peter Stein, *Roman Law in European History* (Cambridge: Cambridge University Press, 1999), 21 etc.

4. Maximilien Robespierre, *Discours et rapports à la Convention* (Paris: Union Générale des Éditions, 1965), 213

5. M.I. Finley, *Democracy Ancient and Modern* (London: Hogarth Press, 1985); *Politics in the Ancient World* (Cambridge: Cambridge University Press, 1983); M.H. Hansen, *The Athenian Democracy in the Age of Demosthenes* (Oxford: Blackwell, 1991)

6. George Rudé, *The Crowd in the French Revolution* (Oxford: Clarendon Press, 1959); Albert Soboul, *The Parisian Sans-Culottes and the French Revolution 1793–94*, tr G. Lewis (Oxford: Clarendon Press, 1964)

7. Alexander Hamilton, Letter to Gouverneur Morris, 19 May 1777 (*Papers of Alexander Hamilton*, Vol 1, ed Harold C. Syrett & Jacob E. Cooke (New York: Columbia University Press, 1961), 255): 'When the deliberative or judicial powers are vested wholly or partly in the collective body of the people, you must expect error, confusion and instability. But a representative democracy, where the right of election is well secured and regulated & the exercise of the legislative, executive and judiciary authorities, is vested in select persons chosen *really* and not *nominally* by the people, will in my opinion be most likely to be happy, regular and durable.' Not a bad judgement as prophecies go.

8. Robespierre, *Discours*, 213

9. Sylvain Maréchal, *Manifesto of the Equals* (Filippo Michele Buonarroti, *Conspiration pour l'égalité, dite de Babeuf* (Paris: Éditions Sociales, 1957), Vol 2, 94–95: 'The French Revolution is only the precursor of another revolution, far greater, far more solemn, which will be the last.'

10. Richard Cobb, *The Police and the People: French Popular Protest 1789–1820* (Oxford: Clarendon Press, 1970), 3–81

11. Elizabeth Eisenstein, *The First Professional Revolutionist: Filippo Michele Buonarroti* (Cambridge, Mass.: Harvard University Press, 1959)

12. Jean Bruhat, 'La Révolution Française et la Formation de la Pensée de Marx', *Annales Historiques de la Révolution Française*, 48, 1966, 125–70

13. Buonarroti, *Conspiration*, 26

14. Buonarroti, *Conspiration*, 25

15. Buonarroti, *Conspiration*, 26

16. Buonarroti, *Conspiration*, 26–27

17. Buonarroti, *Conspiration*, 28

18. Buonarroti, *Conspiration*, 33
19. Buonarroti, *Conspiration*, 114
20. Buonarroti, *Conspiration*, 114n
21. Alexis de Tocqueville, *Democracy in America*, tr & ed Harvey C. Mansfield & Delba Winthrop (Chicago: University of Chicago Press, 2000)
22. For the sheer length of the time-span see Alexander Keyssar, *The Right to Vote: The Contested History of Democracy in the United States* (New York: Perseus Books, 2000). For the complexity and ambivalence of the protracted and still severely incomplete process of political reconciliation to the outcome see especially Rogers Smith, *Civic Ideals: Conflicting Visions of Citizenship in US History* (New Haven: Yale University Press, 1997), and James H. Kettner, *The Development of American Citizenship 1608–1870* (Chapel Hill: University of North Carolina Press, 1978).
23. Cf Bernard Williams, 'External and Internal Reasons', in his *Moral Luck* (Cambridge: Cambridge University Press, 1981), 101–13
24. For a classic exposition of this point, see Adam Przeworski, *Capitalism and Social Democracy* (Cambridge: Cambridge University Press, 1985)
25. Elizabeth Eisenstein, *The First Professional Revolutionist*
26. Cobb, *The Police and the People* gives a withering verdict. For the subsequent fate of the Democrats see Isser Woloch, *The Jacobin Legacy: The Democratic Movement under the Directory* (Princeton: Princeton University Press, 1970), esp chapter 6 'The Democratic Persuasion'.
27. David Hume, 'Of the First Principles of Government', *Essays Moral, Political and Literary*, ed Eugene F. Miller (Indianapolis: Liberty Press, 1985), 32: 'Nothing appears more surprising, to those who consider human affairs with a philosophical eye, than the easiness with which the many are governed by the few; and the implicit submission, with which men resign their own sentiments and passions to those of their rulers. When we enquire by what means this wonder is effected, we shall find, that, as FORCE is

always on the side of the governed, the governors have nothing to support them but opinion. It is therefore, on opinion only that government is founded; and this maxim extends to the most despotic and most military governments, as well as to the most free and most popular.' The best picture of the conclusions which Hume drew from this insight is still Duncan Forbes, *Hume's Philosophical Politics* (Cambridge: Cambridge University Press, 1975).

28. François Furet, *Interpreting the French Revolution*, tr Elborg Forster (Cambridge: Cambridge University Press, 1982). The best attempt to tell the story continuously in relation to a single political community has been made (unsurprisingly) in relation to France itself. See Pierre Rosanvallon, *Le Sacre du citoyen: Histoire de la suffrage universel en France* (Paris: Gallimard, 1992), *Le Peuple introuvable: histoire de la représentation démocratique en France* (Paris: Gallimard, 1998); *La Démocratie inachevée: Histoire de la souveraineté du peuple en France* (Paris: Gallimard, 2000); *Le Modèle Politique Français: la société civile contre le jacobinisme de 1789 à nos jours* (Paris: Le Seuil, 2004). For the context of modern politics see John Dunn (ed), *The Economic Limits to Modern Politics* (Cambridge: Cambridge University Press, 1990) (especially the chapter by Istvan Hont).

29. Josiah Ober, *Mass and Elite in Democratic Athens* (Princeton: Princeton University Press, 1989); and Harvey Yunis, *Taming Democracy: Models of Rhetoric in Classical Athens* (Ithaca: Cornell University Press, 1996)

30. Thucydides, *History of the Peloponnesian War*, Bks I & II, tr Charles Forster Smith (Cambridge, Mass.: Harvard University Press, 1928), II, lxv, 9, pp 376–77

31. Joseph Schumpeter, *Capitalism, Socialism and Democracy* 3rd ed (London: George Allen & Unwin, 1950), 285

32. See, for example, Ronald Dworkin, *Sovereign Virtue* (Cambridge, Mass.: Harvard University Press, 2000)

33. The country of which this is least clearly true is still the United States of America; and the obstacles which stand in the way of its

doing so are still a plain legacy from the efforts by Madison and his colleagues to ensure that the United States should not be what they understood as a democracy (cf Manin, 'Checks, Balances and Boundaries', in Biancamaria Fontana (ed), *The Invention of the Modern Republic* (Cambridge: Cambridge University Press, 1994), 27–62).

34. Jack Goody, *The Domestication of the Savage Mind* (Cambridge: Cambridge University Press, 1977)

35. Cf Ronald Dworkin, *Sovereign Virtue*; John Rawls, *A Theory of Justice* (Oxford: Clarendon Press, 1972); *Political Liberalism* (New York: Columbia University Press, 1993)

36. G.A. Cohen, *If You're an Egalitarian, How Come You're So Rich?* (Cambridge, Mass.: Harvard University Press, 2000)

37. The idea of fixed and objective standards enjoyed an intense glamour in the course of the Revolution. The view that measures of time and space can and should be drawn directly from the fabric of the world itself, and not from antique superstitions or habits, led, amongst other things, to the creation of a new calendar and the invention of the metric system: cf Denis Guedj, *Le Mètre du monde* (Paris: Editions du Seuil, 2000); Ken Alder, *The Measure of All Things* (London: Abacus, 2004).

38. 'US Leader appeals to closest friend in the world', *Financial Times*, 20 November 2003, p 4

39. Joseph de Maistre, *Works*, ed & tr Jack Lively (New York: Macmillan, 1964), 93 : 'It is said that the people are sovereign; but over whom? Over themselves, apparently. The people are thus subject. There is surely something equivocal if not erroneous here, for the people which *command* are not the people which *obey*.'

40. C.V. Wedgwood, *The Trial of Charles I* (London: Fontana, 1964), 217

41. Wedgwood, *Trial of Charles I*, 71

42. Bruce Cumings, *North Korea: The Hermit Kingdom* (London: Prospect, 2003)

43. Peter Holquist, *Making War, Forging Revolution* (Cambridge, Mass.: Harvard University Press, 2002); Philip Short, *Pol Pot: The History of a Nightmare* (London: John Murray, 2004)

44. Plato, *The Republic*, 558C, tr Paul Shorey (Cambridge, Mass.: Harvard University Press, 1935), Vol 2, 290–91

45. Benjamin Constant, *Political Writings*, ed Biancamaria Fontana (Cambridge: Cambridge University Press, 1988), 313–28

NOTES TO CHAPTER 4

1. The best picture of Babeuf's political life, the botched conspiracy to which he gave his name, his defiant defence of a lifetime's aims and convictions before the tribunal at Vendôme, failed suicide attempt and prompt execution is R.B. Rose, *Gracchus Babeuf: The First Revolutionary Communist* (London: Edwin Arnold, 1978). There is no good reason to doubt Babeuf's commitment to democracy under less extreme conditions throughout his life: 68, 160–61, 380. On 4 July 1790, from the Conciergerie prison, in the third number of his *Journal de la Confédération*, he gave classic expression to the most drastic vision of what democracy means: 'If the People are the Sovereign, they should exercise as much sovereignty as they absolutely can themselves... to accomplish that which you have to do and can do yourself use representation on the fewest possible occasions and be nearly always your own representative' (p 77). Easier said than done. For the final stage of his life see 325–26.

2. Neil Harding, *Lenin's Political Thought*, 2 vols (London: Macmillan, 1977 & 1981)

3. Cf Jeremy Bentham's verdict on full-fledged natural rights: *Anarchical Fallacies*, in J. Bentham, *Rights, Representation and Reform: Nonsense upon Stilts and Other Writings on the French Revolution*, ed Philip Schofield, Catherine Pease-Watkin & Cyprian Blamires (Oxford: Clarendon Press, 2002), 317–434, esp 330.

4. Dorothy Thompson, *The Chartists: Popular Protest in the Industrial Revolution* (Aldershot: Wildwood House, 1986) ; Gareth Stedman Jones, Rethinking Chartism, *Languages of Class* (Cambridge: Cambridge University Press, 1983), 90–178; Mark Hovell, *The Chartist Movement* (Manchester: Manchester University Press, 1918); Logie Barrow & Ian Bullock, *Democratic Ideas and the British Labour Movement 1880–1914* (Cambridge: Cambridge University Press, 1996)

5. For Cavour see Dennis Mack Smith, *Italy: A Modern History* (New Haven: Yale University Press, 1997), chapters 1–3; Denis Mack Smith, *Cavour and Garibaldi: A Study in Political Conflict* (Cambridge: Cambridge University Press, 1985); Anthony Cardozo, 'Cavour and Piedmont', John A. Davis (ed), *Italy in the Nineteenth Century* (Oxford: Oxford University Press, 2000), 108–31. For Bismarck, A.J.P. Taylor, *Bismarck: The Man and the Statesman* (London: Arrow Books, 1961); Fritz Stern, *Gold and Iron: Bismarck, Bleichroder and the Building of the German Empire* (London: George Allen & Unwin, 1977). For Disraeli, Paul Smith, *Disraeli: A Brief Life* (Cambridge: Cambridge University Press, 1996); Edgar Feuchtwanger, *Disraeli* (London: Arnold, 2000); Maurice Cowling, *1867: Disraeli, Gladstone & Revolution* (Cambridge: Cambridge University Press, 1967).

6. Proudhon thought and wrote about this issue over several decades, usually in a state of some anxiety and dismay. For key episodes see Pierre-Joseph Proudhon, *Idée Générale de la Révolution au xixe siècle*, ed Aimé Berthod (Paris: Marcel Rivière, 1923), 210–14 and 344–45. For characteristic notes see, e.g. p 211: '*Je veux traiter directement, individuellement pour moi-même; le suffrage universel est à mes yeux une vraie loterie*' (a complete lottery); p 208 'Gouvernement démocratique *et* Religion naturelle *sont des contradictions, à moins qu'on ne préfère y voir deux mystifications. Le peuple n'a pas plus voix consultative dans l'État que dans l'Église: son rôle est d'obéir et de croire.*' *La Révolution Sociale démontrée par le coup d'état du deux decembre*, ed Edouard

Dolléans & Georges Duveau (Paris: Marcel Rivière, 1936), chapter 3 & pp 288–97; *De la Capacité Politique des Classes Ouvrières*, ed Maxime Leroy (Paris: Marcel Rivière, 1924), Pt II, chapter 15 & Pt III. For helpful presentations of his thinking as a whole see Robert J. Hoffman, *Revolutionary Justice: The Social and Political Thought of P-J Proudhon* (Urbana: University of Illinois Press, 1972) and K. Steven Vincent, *Pierre-Joseph Proudhon and the Rise of French Republican Socialism* (New York: Oxford University Press, 1984).

7.   Cf Michael Mandlebaum, *The Ideas that Conquered the World: Peace, Democracy and Free Markets in the Twenty-first Century* (Oxford: Public Affairs Press, 2002) Tony Smith, *America's Mission: The United States and the Worldwide Struggle for Democracy* (Princeton: Princeton University Press, 1995); John A. Thompson, *Woodrow Wilson* (London: Longman, 2002) gives a lucid and balanced account. Note the firmness of Wilson in stating America's war aims to Congress, 2 April 1917: 'We shall fight for the things we have always carried closest to our hearts, – for democracy, for the right of those who submit to authority to have a voice in their own governments, for the rights and liberties of small nations, for a universal dominion of right by such a concert of free peoples as shall bring peace and safety to all nations and make the world itself at last free' (149–50). But note also the prudent reservation a year later (remarks to foreign correspondents, 8 April 1918): 'I am not fighting for democracy except for the peoples who want democracy. If they don't want it, that is none of my business' (169, 185). Some Presidents learn slower than others: if at all.

8.   Paul Bracken, *The Command and Control of Nuclear Forces* (New Haven: Yale University Press, 1982)

9.   John Erickson, *The Road to Stalingrad* & *The Road to Berlin* (both London: Panther, 1985)

10.   Tony Judt, *La Réconstruction du parti socialiste 1921–1926* (Paris: Presses de la Fondation Nationale des Sciences Politiques, 1976); *Socialism in Provence 1871–1914: A Study of the Origins of the Modern French Left* (Cambridge: Cambridge University Press,

1979); *Marxism and the French Left: Studies in Labour and Politics in France 1830–1981* (Oxford: Clarendon Press, 1986); George Lichtheim, *Marxism: An Historical and Critical Study* (London: Routledge, 1961); *Europe in the Twentieth Century* (London: Weidenfeld & Nicolson, 1972) Annie Kriegel, *Aux Origines du communisme français*, 2 vols (Paris: Mouton, 1966); Richard Lowenthal, *World Communism: The Disintegration of a Secular Faith* (New York: Oxford University Press, 1964).

Behind this quarrel lay, amongst much else, the thorny question of Marx's own attitude towards democracy, in theory and in practice. This epitomizes the opacity of the story which we need to recover, shrouded in the dense competing smoke screens laid down by well over a century of global struggle. For representative disagreements, see besides the works of Lichtheim and Furet, Shlomo Avineri, *The Social and Political Thought of Karl Marx* (Cambridge: Cambridge University Press, 1968); Oscar J. Hammen, *The Red 48-ers* (New York: Charles Scribner, 1969); Alan Gilbert, *Marx's Politics* (Oxford: Martin Robertson, 1981); Richard N. Hunt, *The Political Ideas of Marx and Engels*, 2 vols (London: Macmillan, 1974); Hal Draper, *Karl Marx's Theory of Revolution*, 2 vols in 4 (New York: Monthly Review Press, 1977–78); Leszek Kolakowski, *Main Currents of Marxism*, tr P.S. Falla (Oxford: Clarendon Press, 1978); Michael Levin, *Marx, Engels and Liberal Democracy* (Basingstoke: Macmillan, 1989) & *The Spectre of Democracy: The Rise of Modern Democracy as Seen by its Critics* (Macmillan: Basingstoke, 1992) and the Introduction by Gareth Stedman Jones to Karl Marx & Friedrich Engels, *The Communist Manifesto* (London: Penguin Books, 2002).

11. François Furet, *The Future of an Illusion*, tr Deborah Furet (Chicago: University of Chicago Press, 1999)

12. Cf J. Dunn, *The Politics of Socialism* (Cambridge: Cambridge University Press, 1984); *The Cunning of Unreason* (London: HarperCollins, 2000)

13. George W. Bush, *Financial Times*, 11 November 2003. Cf Woodrow Wilson, note 7 above.

14. Cf Paul Kennedy, *The Rise and Fall of the Great Powers* (London: Fontana, 1989)

15. Orlando Figes, *A People's Tragedy: The Russian Revolution 1891–1924* (London: Pimlico, 1997), chapter 6, esp 232–41; Teodor Shanin, *The Awkward Class: Political Sociology of Peasantry in a Developing Society: Russia 1910–1925* (Oxford: Clarendon Press, 1972); Geroid T. Robinson, *Rural Russia under the Old Regime* (Berkeley, California: University of California Press, 1967).

16. Louis Antoine de Saint-Just, *Oeuvres Complètes*, ed Charles Vellay (Paris: Charpentier & Fasquelle, 1908), II, 238 Speech of 8 Ventôse An II (26 Feb 1794), a report to the Convention on the contents of its prisons: '*les malheureux sont les puissances de la terre; ils ont le droit de parler en maîtres aux gouvernements qui les négligent.*' [The unfortunate (the poor) are the powers of the earth; they have every right to speak as masters to governments which neglect them.]

17. Alexis de Tocqueville, *Democracy in America*, ed & tr Harvey Mansfield & Delba Winthrop (Chicago: University of Chicago Press, 2000)

18. Cf J. Dunn (ed), *Contemporary Crisis of the Nation State?* (Oxford: Blackwell, 1995)

19. Cf Samuel Finer, *The History of Government* 3 vols (Oxford: Clarendon Press, 1997)

20. J. Dunn, *The Cunning of Unreason* (London: HarperCollins, 2000)

21. Mogens H. Hansen, *The Athenian Democracy in the Age of Demosthenes* (Oxford: Blackwell, 1991)

22. Benjamin Constant, *Political Writings*, ed Biancamaria Fontana, (Cambridge: Cambridge University Press, 1988), 313–28

23. Joseph Schumpeter, *Capitalism, Socialism and Democracy* 3rd ed (London: George Allen & Unwin, 1950), chapters 20–23; esp chapter 23, 'The Inference'. For the life from which these judgements emerged see Richard Swedberg, *Schumpeter: A Biography* (Princeton: Princeton University Press, 1991).

24. Schumpeter, *Capitalism*, 285. And see p 247: 'the people never really rule but they can always be made to do so by definition.' Compare the force of two aphorisms gleaned from his private diary: aphorism 3: 'Democracy is government by lying' (Swedberg, 200); and aphorism 18: 'To lie – what distinguishes man from animals' (Swedberg, 201).

25. Cf Robert Putnam, *Bowling Alone* (New York: Simon & Schuster, 2001). For what may be some of the consequences see Thomas Patterson, *The Vanishing Voter* (New York: Vintage, 2003) & Russell J Dalton, *Democratic Challenges, Democratic Choice: The Erosion of Political Support in Advanced Industrial Societies* (Oxford: Oxford University Press, 2004). For the ecological context within which this seepage of interest is occurring see Harold L. Wilensky, *Rich Democracies: Political Economy, Public Policy & Performance* (Berkeley, California: University of California Press, 2002).

26. For a particularly vivid example see Paul Ginsborg, *Italy and its Discontents 1980–2001* (London: Penguin, 2001)

27. Georges Sorel, *Reflexions on Violence*, tr T.E. Hulme & J. Roth (New York: Collier Books, 1961), 222. The whole of chapter 7, 'The Ethics of the Producers', remains a powerful indictment.

28. Pierre Rosanvallon, *Le Sacre du Citoyen: histoire du suffrage universel en France* (Paris: Gallimard, 1992). Cf M.H. Hansen, *The Athenian Democracy in the Age of Demosthenes* (Oxford: Blackwell, 1991).

29. Ronald Dworkin, *Sovereign Virtue* (Cambridge, Mass.: Harvard University Press, 2000)

30. Cf Thomas Hobbes, *The Elements of Law*, chapters 8 & 9 (Hobbes, *Human Nature and De Corpore Politico*, ed J.C.A. Gaskin (Oxford: Oxford University Press, 1994), 48–60, 138–39), and for the strategic judgement which issues from this vision Thomas Hobbes, *Leviathan*, ed Richard Tuck (Cambridge: Cambridge University Press, 1991), chapter 11, p 70.

31. Cf Adam Smith, *The Theory of Moral Sentiments*, ed D.D. Raphael & A.L. Macfie (Oxford: Clarendon Press, 1976). To the cool eye of the order of egoism in its heyday, the moral sentiments have no privileged place amongst other sentiments; and their causal power, or motivational pressure, falls plainly short of sundry other sentiments.

32. Francis Hutcheson, *An Essay on the Nature and Conduct of the Passions and Affections with Ilustrations on the Moral Sense* 3rd ed (London: A. Ward etc, 1742). First ed 1728. The more sophisticated diagnosticians of the order of egoism are disinclined to believe that there is a moral sense. There is good reason to believe that they are right. Bernard Williams, *Ethics and the Limits of Philosophy* (London: Fontana, 1985); *Shame and Necessity* (Berkeley: University of California Press, 1993).

33. Robert B. Westbrook, *John Dewey and American Democracy* (Ithaca: Cornell University Press, 1991). Alan Ryan, *John Dewey and the High Tide of American Liberalism* (London & New York: W.W. Norton, 1995).

34. Cf Geoff Eley, *Forging Democracy: The History of the Left in Europe 1850–2000* (New York: Oxford University Press, 2002)

35. Tocqueville, *Democracy in America*

36. Hansen, *The Athenian Democracy in the Age of Demosthenes* (Oxford: Blackwell, 1991); Marcel Detienne, *Qui veut prendre la parole?* (Paris: Seuil, 2003)

37. John Stuart Mill, *Considerations on Representative Government* (London: J.M. Dent, 1910), 180

38. Paul Ginsborg, *Silvio Berlusconi: Television, Power and Patrimony* (London: Verso, 2004)

39. Bernard Manin, *The Principles of Representative Government* (Cambridge: Cambridge University Press, 1997)

40. David Butler & Austin Ranney (eds), *Referendums: A Comparative Study of Practice and Theory* (Washington, DC: American Enterprise Institute, 1980) and *Referendums around the World: The Growing Use of Direct Democracy* (Basingstoke: Macmillan, 1994)

41. Yannis Papadopoulos, *Démocratie Directe* (Paris: Economica, 1998)

42. Amy Gutmann & Denis Thompson, *Why Deliberative Democracy?* (Princeton: Princeton University Press, 2004); James S. Fishkin, *Democracy and Deliberation* (New Haven: Yale University Press, 1991), accessible samples from a very large body of recent academic writing.

43. Aristotle, *Politics*, tr H. Rackham (Cambridge, Mass.: Harvard University Press, 1932), 1281b–1284a, pp 220–41 (esp III, vi, 4–10 & III, vii, 12)

44. These remain intensely controversial criteria; and it is hard to see how they could ever cease to be so.

45. Far the most elaborate and pertinacious attempt to think this idea through has come in the massive oeuvre of Jürgen Habermas. For an impressively clear and sceptical assessment of the limits to its coherence see Raymond Geuss, *The Idea of a Critical Theory* (Cambridge: Cambridge University Press, 1980).

46. Thomas Hobbes, *Elements of Law*, chapter 8 (*Human Nature*, 48–49)

47. John Dower, *Empire and Aftermath: Yoshida Shigeru and the Japanese Empire 1878–1954* (Cambridge, Mass.: Harvard University Press, 1979) & *Embracing Defeat: Japan in the Aftermath of World War II* (Harmondsworth: Penguin, 2000); Alan S. Milward, *The Reconstruction of Western Europe 1945–51* (London: Methuen, 1984)

48. Sunil Khilnani, *The Idea of India* (London: Hamish Hamilton, 1997); Sarvepalli Gopal, *Jawaharlal Nehru: A Biography* 3 vols (London: Jonathan Cape, 1975–84); Granville Austin, *The Indian Constitution: Cornerstone of a Nation* (Oxford: Clarendon Press, 1966)

49. John K Fairbank (ed), *The Chinese World Order: Traditional China's Foreign Relations* (Cambridge, Mass.: Harvard University Press, 1968)

50. For a particularly illuminating discussion see Adam Przeworski, *Capitalism and Social Democracy* (Cambridge: Cambridge

University Press, 1985). For a vivid sketch of a great political leader deeply dedicated to this world and to the party as its central form of agency see Tony Judt, *The Burden of Responsibility* (Chicago: University of Chicago Press, 1998), 29–85 on Léon Blum.

51. Schumpeter, *Capitalism, Socialism and Democracy*
52. Paul Ginsborg, *Silvio Berlusconi: Television, Power and Patrimony* (London: Verso, 2004)
53. J. Dunn, 'Situating Democratic Accountability', in Adam Przeworski, Susan C. Stokes & Bernard Manin (eds), *Democracy, Accountability and Representation* (Cambridge: Cambridge University Press, 1999), 329–44
54. J. Dunn (ed), *The Economic Limits to Modern Politics* (Cambridge: Cambridge University Press, 1990); Dunn, *Cunning of Unreason*
55. David Held, *Global Covenant* (Cambridge: Polity, 2004); *Democracy and the Global Order* (Cambridge: Polity, 1995)
56. It asks in effect for the re-creation of the Garden of Eden, to harbour the great and natural community of mankind (John Locke, *Two Treatises of Government*, II, para 128, ed Mark Goldie (London: J.M. Dent, 1993), 179; 'he and all the rest of mankind are one community... this great and natural community') in punctilious shared observance of the Law of Nature itself. Or, if that for some reason proves unavailable, for equally punctilious and spontaneous observance of 'known standing laws' which raise no contentious issues of judgement in their interpretation and provoke no quarrels in their enforcement. Compare J. Dunn, 'The Contemporary Political Significance of John Locke's Conception of Civil Society', Sunil Khilnani & Sudipta Kaviraj (eds), *Civil Society: History and Possibilities* (Cambridge: Cambridge University Press, 2001), 39–57.

INDEX